I0614675

The Cost of LOVING

Wade Kelly

Dreamspinner Press

Published by
Dreamspinner Press
5032 Capital Circle SW
Ste 2, PMB# 279
Tallahassee, FL 32305-7886
USA
http://www.dreamspinnerpress.com/

The Cost of Loving

Cover art by Enny Kraft
http://ennykraft.weebly.com/

ISBN: 978-1-62380-963-8
Digital ISBN: 978-1-62380-964-5

Printed in the United States of America
First Edition
August 2013

ACKNOWLEDGMENTS

First, to my family: Thanks Dad for being proud of me. I wish you were here. RIP. I hope you're looking down and cheering every time another book gets published.

Second: This book is for all the fans who have patiently waited for this sequel for two years. Thank you for your support, dedication, and encouragement. As an author I could not have survived without you!

Thank you: Vio, Deeze, R.B., Lena, Tom, Ijeoma, Candice, Cody K., Mika, Ken M., Enny, Monika, Frances, Meike, Macky, Kayla, L-D, Tina, Darci, Manuela, Dee, Shirley, Barb, Keri, Kat, Kaje, Pam, Kim, Kade, Anna, Alli, Laura, Ken, Summer, Mrs. Condit, Don, Susan, Mark, Bev, Paul, Hans, Jen, Jan, Cory, Melissa, Bev, Connie, Karen C., Darla, Chris, Absynthe, Laura M., Meghan, Dave, Kerry, Karen H., Carole-Ann, West, Debbie, Kazy, Teri, Cassandra, Tue Pol, Jeff, Gary, Simon, Kendra, Kelly, Allie, and last, but certainly not least, Lynn S.... There are many more "fans" and encouragers, but these are the top seventy from comments, ratings, e-mails, PMs, etc.... I thank you all from the bottom of my heart.

Prologue

I FEEL him enter my body and everything else drains away. I'm no longer me. I become the pliable embodiment of orgasmic rapture when he sinks impossibly deep inside and touches those spots that never knew pleasure before. His titillating touch transforms me into a wanton beast of insatiable lust, and I've never felt as ravenous as I do in his arms.

It frightens me—this unquenchable desire. What will I become when the thunderous throes of gratification end and I'm simply left with a hollow heart?

I have no answer.

September 2010

1

September 28, 2010

TEETERING on the verge of an anxiety attack, Matthias Dixon drove to work with his brain on autopilot. His nerves were shot—not because his best friend, Jimmy, affectionately known as "Jamie," died last week; not because he came out to his entire church congregation and faced possible excommunication; not because he feared confrontation from his family; and certainly not because he didn't want to be gay. Matt drove to the fire station Tuesday morning practically hyperventilating and shaking in his skin because he had to step back into his everyday routine and leave one very important piece of himself at home in his bed: Darian Weston.

Inexplicably, Matt could not function without holding Darian.

What the fuck is wrong with me? Matt thought for the thousandth time.

He'd only just met Darian last Wednesday. Any *sane* person would not become attached to another person so quickly… *would they?* Maybe that was the reason. Matt was insane! He could believe it. It had been an extremely difficult week, full of high emotion and stress. Watching as Jamie's casket was lowered into the ground almost did him in. That is, until he saw Darian completely break down.

Matt had been standing there drowning in his own sorrow as the pastor spoke a few last words, but when Darian crumpled to the earth sobbing, Matt felt his inner Legolas—his champion—take over. He couldn't let Darian suffer alone. He *had* to go to him and comfort him—protect him. Darian's heart was broken. Jamie would want Matt to take care of him.

Matt could easily rationalize his actions with the facts: (1) Darian had been Jamie's fiancé; (2) Jamie had loved Darian; (3) Matt had been Jamie's best friend; and (4) Darian was Matt's last physical link to Jamie. Conclusion: Matt needed to care for Darian.

The only complication was *sex*.

Matt had had sex with Darian. Lots of sex! Darian was like a drug, and Matt's senses craved more with every touch. Matt knew it was wrong to swoop in on Jamie's territory so soon after his death, but it had happened accidentally. At least he kept telling himself that. The first few times could be attributed to bad judgment, but the last few… several… *several* several… times could not be blown off as "accidental." Even after Matt knew who Darian was, he still went back for more and unabashedly fucked him without restraint.

As he drove to work, Matt tried to clear his mind. Who was he kidding? He was intoxicated by a living opiate, and there was no twelve-step program to cure him.

Staind came on the radio, and Matt sang along. When the chorus played, he got the eerie impression the song was written for him. "I can't live without, all I think about, all I want is you…."

It was all so true.

For the second time in his life, Matt's hands shook. He turned the corner onto Main Street and thought back to the day he had heard of Jamie's death, and his hands quaked uncontrollably for several minutes. He wasn't able to control his nerves then, and now it was happening again, only for different reasons. At the red light, he groped under the seat for the crumpled brown bag he remembered from three weeks ago. He inhaled the stench of greasy burgers in a desperate attempt to control his breathing. When the light turned green, he flung the useless bag to the floor. *He didn't need a fucking bag!* He couldn't *breathe* because he missed Darian's scent. He couldn't *think* because he missed Darian's voice. Even the steering wheel felt unbearably ridged because his fingers craved Darian's smooth skin.

Matt always brushed his teeth after he ate, but he purposely did not after he and Darian made love before he left. *Made love?* Matt never thought he'd use that phrase in a million years! Except with

Darian, it was way more than fucking. Matt wanted to savor Darian like a French delicacy or a fine wine. He wanted to nibble at his skin and devour his essence. Matt needed to taste Darian as long as he could throughout the morning, which was why he hadn't brushed his teeth.

He moved his tongue around in his mouth. The taste was still there—Darian's salty and tangy, yet slightly sweet, flavor lingered. Matt smiled thinking about the cum he'd resisted swallowing because he wanted to share the ambrosia with his lover.

Darian liked it. He actually *liked* it when Matt gathered Darian's cum in his mouth and then kissed him deep and long, allowing the thick fluid to coat their kiss and saturate it until they could no longer breathe and were forced apart. He'd done it twice now, and Darian didn't mind. Matt was ecstatic.

This was why the sex complicated matters. Matt knew he needed to comfort Darian. They should be focused on helping one another get over the loss of Jamie. They'd even talked about it. Being together wasn't supposed to be about sex, but rather about mutual need and their link to Jamie. Only… Matt's body conflicted with his sensibilities and wouldn't accept that stipulation. Every time he got near Darian's exquisite, lithe form, Matt yearned to do things to it. Kinky things.

In his experience, some guys liked kinky sex—snowballing, chocolate and vanilla, champagne enemas, bondage, toys, and the like. Matt had even participated in such behaviors before, but never had he enjoyed anything as much as being with Darian. He enjoyed sharing cum-filled kisses after breakfast, so he hoped Darian would be willing to try some other things with him in the future. Just the thought of kink was making Matt hard—Darian strapped in a sling, Matt fucking his mouth, stretching his lips wide, his throat swallowing Matt's erection. Matt imagined feeling the ball of Darian's tongue piercing sliding along the length of his hard cock.

"Shit!" Matt exclaimed as he rounded the curve in the road and almost ran over a groundhog. He swerved to avoid the rodent and left tire marks over the double yellow line.

He panted and refocused his attention on the road instead of his heated groin.

"Note to self," he mused aloud, "do not think of Darian's tongue while driving."

Matt shook his head and grinned. There was no way he could go a few minutes and *not* think of Darian's tongue. Or his hands, his lips, his ass…. Fuck, Matt couldn't even keep Darian's toes out of his mind! This morning he'd sucked them. Sucked his fucking toes! That was a first for sure. Never in his life had Matt imagined sucking on a guy's toes and finding it erotic. But it was. Everything about Darian was erotic.

Matt's mouth watered. He yearned to taste all of Darian's skin, toes included. Matt wanted nothing more than to take a week off and lick Darian until his saliva glands stopped working. Except… Matt could not take more time off work. He had taken too much time off already.

Jamie was not immediate family. No matter how close they were, it was still against company policy to request time off due to the death of a close friend. Matt was obligated to work his shifts at the station, and his friends could only switch shifts so many times.

Mr. Walsh, the boss at his second job, understood, but even he could only accommodate Matt so long or business would suffer. Matt wasn't a kid any more. Work was work, and he had responsibilities.

Matt turned the corner of the next street and pulled into the parking lot of the fire station. He turned the engine off and sat for a few minutes. Tuesday. This was his first day back to work since he openly admitted his sexual preference in church on Sunday, two days ago. Matt ran his shaking hand over his buzzed hair. This was the moment of truth. Did gossip travel faster than smoke and fire? He was about to find out.

"Hey, man," Jason greeted him with a smile as he entered the side door.

At least Jason seems to be acting normal. Maybe he hasn't heard yet?

"Listen, I'm sorry I didn't make it to your church on Sunday like I promised," Jason explained. He'd always been a thoughtful friend, and Matt appreciated his sincerity. "My wife wanted to see our friends' baby get baptized. We went to their church and then their house afterward."

"That's cool. You didn't miss much." *Except the part where I came out.* Matt shrugged casually, masking the fact that his insides were squirming as if he'd eaten ten frozen burritos and then jogged all the way to work. "I'm just glad you could make it to the funeral. It means a lot." Matt could fake nonchalance—he had years of practice. Besides, Jason's presence really did mean a lot, so it wasn't like Matt was lying.

"Yeah, me too." Jason nodded as he and Matt walked over to the cubbies where their gear was stowed. Jason shuffled things around as they talked. "Again, I'm sorry about Jimmy. He was a great guy. Well, I mean, he seemed to be a great guy from the few times he hung out with us. He didn't talk about himself much. He was funny, but private. Ya know? I don't think he ever mentioned a girlfriend, either. Did he have one? I don't remember seeing a girlfriend at the funeral."

"No, no girlfriend." Matt felt a cold streak shoot up his spine. He took a brand-new flashlight out of the box and put the batteries in. He wished they had lockers. Lots of fire stations had lockers for the men. Things wouldn't walk off so easily that way! But the chief was not in a hurry to replace "the system," as he referred to it. He liked everything open and quickly accessible. Plus, there wasn't any money in the budget to revamp the place right now. In February, part of the rec hall had caught fire, and their building had to undergo major repairs. Luckily, all the damage was in the rear of the building, and business could go on as usual from the front. Matt's other flashlight "magically" disappeared two weeks ago, but it gave him the excuse to order a better one. This Pelican StealthLite was pretty sweet!

As Jason tinkered with his own things, he continued the conversation. "And who was that guy who started bawling at the grave site? I couldn't hear what he was saying. Me and Anna were standing in the back. She thought maybe he was a brother or something?"

Matt's stomach flipped. Suddenly, he wished he *had* eaten burritos for breakfast because then he would have an incontestable excuse if he ran to the toilet. He knew he could lie to Jason, but what was the point? *I'm the one who came out to my fucking congregation!* If he was nervous about the truth, he should have guarded it more closely over the weekend. Matt tried to keep his voice steady as he responded.

"The correct phrasing is 'Anna and I,'" he ragged. Matt knew Jason would roll his eyes—he did every time Matt corrected his grammar. He also used the opportunity to release some of his own tension; correcting Jason was fun. But his fun only lasted a second. "The guy at the funeral was...," he stammered nervously. "He was.... That guy was Jamie's boyfriend." There, he'd said it! "His fiancé, actually."

Jason's eyes went wide. "Shit! No kiddin'? I had no idea Jimmy was gay. Damn."

Matt didn't know what to make of Jason's reaction. The topic of homosexuality had never come up before. Why would it? If you weren't gay, you certainly didn't walk around talking about it with your straight work buddies unless it was to make fun of people who *were*. Matt remembered lots of times when the guys would laugh out loud at the television and mock something in a girly voice, pretending they were one of *the gays*. It aggravated Matt to no end, but he never said a word. No one ever caught on to his discomfort. The guys were absorbed in whatever sport was playing on the television and never noticed Matt walking away.

Things were going to change now. It was only a matter of time before word of Matt's admission got around to the guys at the station. Matt was positive somebody knew somebody who knew a firefighter who knew one of the guys he worked with. Of course, work was a thirty-minute drive south of his church, but one never knew where the parishioners shopped and who their friends were and who they were going to talk to next. Matt knew word would get around sooner or later.

But he couldn't avoid talking about it now. He owed Jason the decency of being honest and not allowing him to find out second hand. They'd been friends for several years. Jason was the guy who had shown him the ropes when he got hired as a rookie out of the academy. Other guys weren't so open, so friendly, especially when at least six people in this fire station were volunteers, not full-time career employees. Matt had to work hard to get past their grudges. It wasn't his fault he was at the top of his class and this station was looking to hire someone young. That was the way it was! Plus, not all these guys had Matt's skill level, even if they were older.

Jason, in contrast, knew what it was like on both sides. He started as a volunteer, learned, and worked his way up. When a paid position became available, he jumped for it. And when Matt got hired right out of cadet school, Jason was there at his side, mentoring him from day one. Matt knew he owed him, but should he tell Jason the truth *now* or wait a few days? He swallowed hard.

"So, um, Jason? Would it have mattered?" *Please say no, please say no.*

"Huh?" Jason looked up from relacing his boots. He had gone from appearing deeply interested in the conversation to complete absorption in his boots. "Ah, I don't know." He shrugged. "I never thought about it before."

At least he's honest, Matt reasoned.

"I never knew someone who… well, who was *gay*."

Matt sat on the bench next to him. The way Jason whispered the last word didn't sit well on Matt's stomach. He felt more nauseous with every passing second. *Shit*, he reconsidered. *I can't have this conversation now. I have to wait. He's gonna reject me. I know it.* "It's not completely unheard of," Matt replied in a calm, steady voice, masking his trepidation and the imminent projectile vomiting that threatened and burned his esophagus.

"It is in this county," answered Jason. "My parents moved here because it's ultraconservative. The state may be Democratic overall, but this county is definitely full of Republicans. I thought you told me one time your parents voted for Bush."

"They did," Matt confirmed. "And they weren't overly joyful when Obama got elected." He quickly held up his hands and added, "But not because he's black or anything. And they fully support him now, since he's our president."

"Chill, Matt. I know your dad's cool with the color of my skin. It was all in the way he shook my hand." He slapped Matt on the back and grinned. "My daddy always told me you could tell the character of a man by the way he shakes your hand."

Matt gave him a skeptical lift of the eyebrows. "My dad wasn't always that way, believe me. I remember a time when he'd curse black people—I mean, people of color—for stealing his parking spot at the grocery store and shit like that."

"Matt. You can say 'black people.'" Jason winked. "It doesn't bother me. I know I'm black."

"I never know who I'm gonna offend."

Jason finished with one boot and started lacing the leather thong through the first eyelet of the second. When on duty, but waiting for a call, every firefighter had to find something to do. "Not me. If anything I get irritated at people callin' us 'African Americans.' I don't know about you, but I was born in America. My parents, my grandparents, heck, even my great-grandparents were born in America. In my mind, I'm American—simple as that. I don't hear anybody calling you an Irish American."

Matt conceded, "I get your point."

"America from the beginning was a melting pot. Wasn't it? America began as a blending of cultures over the commonality of religion. Our founding fathers fled British tyranny and pursued religious freedom. Am I wrong?"

"I guess not," Matt answered tentatively. He'd seen Jason get fired up before and start preaching about one thing or another to the guys, but never had Matt been the recipient of such a lecture. Who knew calling him "black" would trigger a whole speech on what it meant to be American? One thing was sure, Matt was glad the subject had shifted away from Jamie's orientation. He wanted more time to feel out Jason's opinion on the matter before he threw him another curveball.

"Of course, I'm right. So to get back to your original question—I'm not sure how I feel about Jimmy," Jason continued, talking without shifting his concentration from the task at hand.

Matt squirmed. *Leave it to Jason not to stray for long.*

"To be honest, I liked him. He was funny and nice, and I can't remember him comin' on to anybody. He acted just like everybody else." Jason stood and arranged his boots and overalls in front of his locker. They were meant to be set up perpetually so all each firefighter had to do was toe off his or her normal shoes and slip inside the boots and overalls in one seamless movement when the alarm sounded.

Matt's back went rigid. "Of course he was just like everyone else. What did you think? 'Gay' meant humping every guy's leg like a horny dog at a cocktail party?" he snapped and regretted it immediately. He could have kicked himself. If he was trying to be subtle and keep the focus off *him* being gay, this was not the way to go about it. Jason would know for sure!

Jason tilted his head. "Testy, testy. I guess someone's a little defensive of his best friend's honor."

"Sorry," he lamented, feeling guilty for his verbal attack. But he had been keeping his opinions on homosexuality to himself for twenty-three years; he knew he was bound to explode sooner or later, now that he'd spilled the beans at church. Matt had to try to get his point across. "I just…. It's not fair to assume people are going to act a certain way just because they prefer sleeping with someone of the same sex. It's like people assuming you have no money because you're black, or concluding Billy's stupid because he's from West Virginia."

Jason stood there and stared at him. Just stared. A whimsical grin curved his face, yet he continued to stare. It was unnerving.

"What?" Matt asked. "Dude, stop staring at me like that. What'd I say?" Matt honestly did not know what Jason was thinking to make his lips lift unevenly and his eyebrows arch. Although he could guess. Matt's knee started bouncing on its own. "Would you stop!"

Jason shook his head. "Who knew?"

Matt's mouth went dry. "Who knew what?"

"About you."

"About me, what?" *This is it. He's figured it out!* His guts clenched, readying for the burning coals of judgment.

"That you, Matthias Dixon—the ladies' man and all around horndog on the prowl for the past few years—you have an IQ over sixty and you actually believe in something. I don't think I've ever heard you speak your mind about prejudice before. Good for you!"

Matt breathed a sigh of relief and grumbled, "A normal IQ is between ninety and one hundred nine."

Jason casually continued, "See, yet another factor to add to your set of statistics. You never can tell about people. I always say that. You never know how much they earn or where they're from or how smart they are based on what they're wearin'. You have to get to know people. Just like you." He held out his hand toward Matt. "I knew you weren't a true sleazeball, even if you never had a steady girlfriend. You were simply biding your time. You needed to find exactly the right girl to make you happy. How is your little cutie-pie, anyway? What's her name?"

"Darian." Compulsion spilled that one.

"Darian? Well that's an unusual name. She still rock your world? I remember last week you were dying. Something about her 'tight little ass.'"

Matt's stomach was churning again. First it was his fear of judgment and now it was fear of saying the wrong thing to trigger the judgment. He didn't want to talk to Jason right now about Darian, yet he had to admit the sound of Darian's name made him tingle.

Jason teased Matt last week about being in love. Jason was a romantic at heart. Matt refuted it. It wasn't true. Maybe. Probably. Matt was still wavering, but if he admitted his feelings to Jason, the man would gloat. It had only been six days since they met. Who fell in love in six days? It was surely more than lust, but love? The jury was still undecided.

He had to confess, though: he couldn't hear Darian's name enough, just like he couldn't get enough of Darian's smooth, white skin and his voluptuous mouth. Matt shivered all over thinking about Darian. Even after sex, when they snuggled in bed or ate a meal together, Matt found himself smiling more than he ever had. And that was saying a lot! Matt was generally a happy person. Now, with Darian in his life, he was hitting an all-time high. Maybe it was love?

Matt was only marginally aware of his previous anxiety as he gushed, "Darian's amazing." His voice turned all daydreamy. If he were outside himself right now, Matt might have kicked himself for acting so lovesick. "Adorable, gentle, sweet; I can never get enough of those big brown eyes. My world is seriously rocked and flipped on end. And that body…." He sighed, his head tilting back. "Oh God. Darian's body molds to mine like we were made for one another. His lips taste like fresh strawberries. I can hardly—"

Right then the siren sounded long and loud.

Jason screwed up his eyes and leaned closer. "Did you just say 'his'?"

Matt's instinct drove him to grab his gear immediately. He wasn't sure he heard Jason correctly. "Huh? I…," he started to say but then waved Jason off, grabbing his overalls after toeing off his shoes. This wasn't the time to clarify anything.

Men rushed about them, trying to don their gear quickly. Jason followed suit. Each of them fell into the sixty-second routine they were made for. They were firefighters. Somewhere there was a fire, and it was their job to be ready as fast as possible. Matt and Jason pulled on their gear and followed several others to the fire engine.

MATT was exhausted. He hadn't worked that hard in a week. Last Thursday he'd had a shift before the viewing, but there were no emergency calls. In theory he could have had a lot of sleep that night and every night since, but he and Darian stayed up fucking for hours. Matt chuckled. He often functioned well on no sleep when sex was the explanation.

Although probably not tonight.

Matt's body wanted sleep.

As he turned into the parking lot of his apartment complex, he spied Darian's red Nissan. Relief washed over his sore muscles. Darian. Matt parked his Dodge Dakota next to Darian's car and trudged across the asphalt. He was glad Darian decided to stick around. He could not recall if Darian said he had to work or not. Matt would have to get Darian to write down his schedule and where he worked. He remembered reading something about American Eagle Outfitters in Jamie's journals, but he wasn't positive. Matt and Darian barely knew each other, even though Matt had read all Jamie's journals. The journals contained facts based on Jamie's opinions and experiences, but they weren't necessarily based on reality. So even if Matt knew a lot about Jamie's perception of Darian, he still didn't know Darian. Plus, it was a lot to remember all at once. He knew he would be reading the journals again.

There was also brief talk yesterday about moving in together. Matt wanted Darian to stay, but it scared the piss out of him to think of the commitment involved in renting an apartment together. Right now he lived with his Aunt Peggy. She was easy to live with, mostly because she travelled for work and was rarely home. Living with Darian wouldn't be like that. Peggy had her own room. Darian would be in *his* room, sharing *his* space. Not that Matt minded sharing his space, but the whole experience of a relationship was new and freakin' scary! Plus, Darian was getting over the loss of his first love and fiancé. Matt wasn't sure if and when they should move in together, or even if it was a good idea—no matter how good it sounded when he brought it up.

He needed time. Did Darian want time? Matt wasn't completely sure of Darian's feelings. He seemed to care, yet so far he hadn't said one way or another how he felt toward Matt. Darian needed him, and it was very clear he *wanted* him, but that felt superficial. Matt yearned for verbal confirmation.

Fuck!

Matt was too tired to think.

He opened the door, and all was quiet. *Is Darian really still here?* He shed his jacket and set his keys on the breakfast bar. On the way down the hall, he pulled off his shirt. He opened the bedroom door and saw the lump under the covers. Matt smiled. *He's still here.* As terrifying as moving in together had seemed seconds ago, the thought Darian might have left without a word was even worse.

Matt showered and got ready for bed as quickly as he could. He wanted sleep but couldn't imagine finding it without spooning himself around Darian. He lifted the covers and slid in beside him. Darian was asleep on his stomach with his hands curled up by his neck. *Adorable!*

Matt had left the light on in the bathroom and cracked the door so he could see. He'd never kept a light on at night before, but now he had a reason. He loved looking at Darian. The man was beautiful when he slept and even more so when he came. Matt could imagine making love to Darian on a beach or in a sun-drenched meadow, anywhere and everywhere as long as he could look into Darian's eyes and watch pleasure flow over his features.

A sun-drenched meadow? Fuck! Matt shook his head. *There's Jamie's romantic influence again. Or is it Jason's?* Matt wasn't sure which guy put more notions in his head, but he was sure they came from one of his two friends. Matt had not been a romantic person in the past. He was all about the fucking and didn't give a rat's ass about the trick he picked up. It was always about his own orgasm.

He'd done anyone, as long as (1) they did not live within sixty miles of his hometown, (2) they didn't try to kiss him, (3) they were not interested in more than a one-time deal, (4) they didn't ask to go to his place, (5) they agreed ahead of time to group sex or not, (6) no restraints were used without discussing safewords and fetish preferences, and (7)….

Matt stopped midthought. He'd made his set of conditions, or "rules," years ago, but looking at Darian, he realized none of them applied. He'd broken the first several without a second thought the day he met Darian. He *wanted* Darian in his bed, in his hometown. Matt had already fucked—no! *made love* to—him repeatedly and planned to be with him countless more times. And kissing Darian was heavenly. Matt threw out rule number two after the first swipe of Darian's tongue.

Matt didn't need rules. He needed Darian.

After scooting down until his body was aligned next to his alluring lover, Matt moved his pillow out of the way so his head was flat on the mattress beside Darian's. He pulled the sheet back. He could hardly make out Darian's face because his hair was covering most of it. Matt carefully smoothed it back with calloused, yet gentle, fingers.

"You're so beautiful," he whispered. Suddenly, rule number five popped into his mind, and Matt felt a flush of anger. "No! Ain't no way I'm gonna allow anyone else to touch you. I want this body all to myself."

Do I have the right to say that? he wondered. Were they together? Kind of. Matt had talked to Jason about the prospect of dating Darian last week, but the conversation hadn't actually gone anywhere. Jason had even assumed Darian was a girl, and Matt felt guilty about not correcting him—but he couldn't think about that right now. Matt needed to figure out Darian first. Was Darian his? Sex—no matter how good—did not equate to a relationship. Darian was in no position to make a decision until he had time to mourn. His loss was deep and painful, and Matt knew *dating* was the last thing on Darian's mind. Besides, what they shared was supposed to be about comfort. Comfort. He repeated the word, trying to convince himself.

He intended to comfort Darian and desired comfort in return, but every time he got near Darian, his dick did all the talking.

"Did Jamie make love to you every night?" Asking Darian this question would only happen while Darian was asleep. It was inappropriate. Matt gently touched the side of Darian's face, hoping he could touch him and think out loud without waking him up. "Did Jamie watch you in your sleep? Did he touch your hair and talk to you about things he'd never have the nerve to ask when you were awake?"

Matt wasn't sure. The journals were unclear on that point. Jamie wrote mostly about his conflicting emotions. Jamie had feelings for Darian and Matt, and he didn't know how to handle them. That was the reason Jamie instructed Matt to burn the journals. He would… eventually. For now Matt couldn't let them go. They were Jamie's thoughts, no matter how hurtful or confused or damaging. Matt wanted to commit every word to memory before destroying the evidence.

Matt glided his hand over Darian's bare shoulder. Darian stirred. Matt edged closer. He felt Darian's heat on his belly and groin. Matt touched Darian's lower back and watched the man's brown eyes slowly open. Matt grinned. "Sorry," he whispered. "I couldn't resist touching you."

Darian smiled. He blinked his sleepy eyes.

Matt leaned closer and kissed Darian's temple. Darian sighed. Matt moved his hand over Darian's rounded buttocks and traced his crack with his middle finger. Darian snickered.

"I really intended on sleeping," Matt explained. "Honest. Sex was not on my mind when I slipped in bed beside you." He pressed his erection closer. "But then this happened."

Darian's smile widened, and he turned his blushing face onto the sheet. He spread his legs as Matt's finger probed deeper between his cheeks.

Matt loved Darian's eager response. He pressed his body snugly alongside Darian's as he whispered into his ear, "I'll sleep better after I come. I promise." Matt slowly climbed on top of Darian's body and grabbed a prelubed condom off the nightstand. He tore it open and rolled it into place while leaning his weight on one knee. Matt stuck his fingers in his mouth and coated them before reaching down to Darian's rear. He coated Darian with saliva and pressed his fingers inside, whispering to his lover again. "Mmm, baby, I want you so bad." He pumped him with two fingers a few times and then replaced his hand with his cock. They'd been at it so much, Matt hardly needed to prep him at all anymore.

Darian whimpered when Matt sank inside.

Matt lay over Darian's back as he moved in Darian slowly. He repositioned his arms over Darian's and laced his fingers in each of Darian's hands. His mouth found Darian's as he craned his neck. Their tongues slipped and slid around each other, but Darian pulled away, moaning. Matt tucked his face in Darian's hair close to his neck. "You feel so good, Dare." Matt breathed the words heavily as he undulated his lower body. "So good."

"H-harder," Darian groaned.

"No. I want it slow."

Darian pushed his ass backward. "More," he demanded.

Matt responded by pressing his chest down, pinning Darian more securely to the mattress. "No. I want this to last."

"Matt, pleeease."

"No!" Matt asserted, squeezing Darian's fingers tightly between his. Darian's begging was exhilarating, but Matt was determined to hold his ground. He enjoyed feeling all of his skin touching all of Darian's. Flesh on flesh. They spent so many nights already going at it like animals; tonight he simply wanted to envelop Darian entirely. He could feel his nipples rubbing against Darian's back. He could feel his thighs rubbing along the insides of Darian's. He nuzzled his face in Darian's hair and kissed the nape of his neck. "Oh, Dare… I love how you make me feel." He tilted his hips to the side on the next plunge, and Darian's moans went up an octave.

"Is that it, baby? Is that your spot?" He swiveled again in the same manner, and Darian cried out. Matt grinned. "Oh yeah. That's it." He kept hitting the same angle as he moved, and Darian's pleasure cries hit soprano.

Matt was spurred on to new heights of delight. Darian made him feel like a king, like a sexual god. Inside of Darian, he could do no wrong. Inside of Darian, he would be content for days, weeks even. In, out, in, out. Thrusting. Diving. Plunging his manhood farther into Darian's depths. Hearing his wails of libidinous satisfaction echoing in the quiet of the night. Matt let go of Darian's left hand and slid his arm under his chest, pulling Darian's body tightly to him. Matt pushed his knee forward, spreading Darian's legs wider and giving himself better leverage. He picked up his pace as he climaxed.

Darian must have come, too, because he was no longer wailing; he was panting. Matt rested his weight back down and squeezed his lover. "So good, Dare. So good." He kissed his neck and licked the edge of his ear.

Reluctantly, Matt slid out and removed the condom. He dropped it over the side of the bed and made himself comfortable next to Darian.

"Can you scoot over? I'm lying in a wet spot."

"Sure. Sorry." Matt complied, and Darian slid over with him. Matt pulled Darian close and held him. "Is this better?"

Darian nodded. He snuggled his head in the crook of Matt's armpit and curled both arms between his chest and Matt's side. Darian sighed and closed his eyes.

It was the perfect end to an exhausting day. Matt smiled and hugged his sated lover before drifting off to sleep.

October 2010

2

October 2, 2010

THROUGHOUT that first week, their nights were spent in much the same routine. Darian would be asleep when Matt got home. Matt would wake him up; they'd make love, fall asleep, make love in the morning, and Matt would find Darian in bed again when he got home. Matt didn't think all that much about it. It felt comfortable. Natural. He'd slept well for days because of it. He pushed aside his wavering feelings of moving-in-together paranoia and decided it was easier to enjoy each moment for what it was. On some level, it had become almost mechanical. Matt didn't have to think about it; the days simply rolled into each other.

That is, until Matt walked through the apartment door Saturday night, and his easygoing sleep-sex-work-sex routine shattered.

For the first time in days, as he entered the apartment, he flipped open his phone on the way to deposit his keys on the breakfast bar. Without thinking, he pushed speed dial four, and gasped in horror as Jamie's voice sounded on the other end. Dropping his phone as if he had been stung, Matt covered his face and sat on the couch.

"Shit," he gasped.

Jamie was gone! Matt could not believe how quickly the fact had become distanced from his everyday life. He'd dialed Jamie's number by instinct. He'd walked into the apartment and dialed "four," the same as he'd done a thousand times before. Why? Because he was happy. Matt was elated to be coming home to Darian, and he wanted to share the news with Jamie.

Shit! How fucking messed up is that?

Matt felt sick with guilt. Cold sweat broke out along his brow.

He leaned forward and snagged his phone off the floor, and then he sat back again. He opened his pics app and scrolled through the few pictures stored there. Most of them were of Jamie doing something stupid—Jamie doing a lay-up with a basketball, Jamie crossing his eyes, Jamie sticking out his tongue, Jamie mooning Matt.

Jamie's bare ass made him chuckle. Looking at these pictures reminded Matt of the good times they had shared, and yet, seeing Jamie's goofy smile after hearing his voice punched a hole in Matt's stable charade. Jamie's absence was more profound than ever.

The next picture was of Darian sitting on his couch, drawing.

Matt snapped the phone shut. He couldn't take it. Too much change in too little time.

"Why is this happening?" Matt muttered helplessly, holding back his tears. He knew some of the answers but it wasn't enough. Matt wanted to understand where this all fit together in the greater scheme of things, in God's plan. He knew he wasn't the strongest Christian, but he did believe in God's sovereignty, and his faith was precious to him. There had to be a reason for so much pain. "Why, God?" he asked. "Please help me to understand."

Matt had never really thought about it before. Until this week, life had seemed pretty easy—except for that whole part where he hid his sexuality from his family and friends for most of his life—and Matt hadn't had cause for complaint. He had a great family, he loved his job, and he had an awesome best friend. Now, he had the best boyfriend in the world. Only the boyfriend came at the cost of the best friend.

Matt hung his head. He'd been a fool to think he could jump back into life the way it had been. Everything had changed last week. His perfect life dissolved, and somehow he needed to deal with it and accept it, but he didn't know where to start. Matt was afraid.

His solution by default was avoidance.

Matt hadn't talked to his mom in days, something extremely rare. He was paranoid at work like never before because at any moment one of the guys might confront him with something they'd "heard" about him. Even talking to Jason was strained, as if Jason *knew* but wouldn't say.

Matt felt guilty for not coming clean at the beginning of the week, but the moment had passed and he just couldn't bring himself to broach the subject again. And the whole "boyfriend" thing was a joke! They didn't do anything but have sex. Matt couldn't remember the last time Darian said anything outside grunts and moaning. It wasn't a relationship, no matter how much Matt wanted it to be.

Thinking about Jamie was painful. His best friend was gone. The worst part—contemplating the depth of the deception Jamie had carried out for years. It boggled his mind! Jamie excluded Matt from the most meaningful parts of his life, and knowing that made Matt angry and even more lonely.

His life sucked!

Matt needed Jamie more than ever. So much was going on; he desperately needed his best friend's insight, but all he had left were his journals. *Those fucking journals!* Ink on a page, insignificant and hollow. Yet Matt yearned to read Jamie's words, experience his feelings, and hear his voice in that way you do when you read a letter someone wrote. It was how Jamie phrased things and assembled his thoughts. Every time Matt read the journals, he could hear Jamie's voice, as if he were in the room. Matt wanted to read them now, but he couldn't risk it. They were in the back of his closet in an old backpack where he hoped Darian would not be curious enough to venture.

At least I hope he doesn't.

After Darian spent a few nights at his place, Matt knew it would be dangerous to leave the journals in his shirt drawer. He *should* get rid of them, but he couldn't. Besides being a piece of Jamie, they were also his only shred of evidence Joan Smithers was a complete lunatic.

Most of this is her fucking fault!

Matt clenched his fist but stopped his punch inches from connecting with the wall. Punching the wall might wake up Darian. He couldn't do that and avoid explaining *why* he punched the wall to begin with.

"Joan," he hissed in hatred. Matt remembered reading about all the horrible things she did to Jamie, but last Sunday when he had the chance to out her, he kept the truth to himself. Something inside would not let Matt place the full reality of Jamie's suicide solely on his mother's words. It seemed so very unchristian. He wanted his speech to reflect his thoughts clearly: hatred and intolerance were the main cause of Jamie's suicide. Why couldn't he have said Joan was the one who pushed the button?

Matt knew he'd have to tell someone soon. Joan could not be allowed to abuse her other children in the same fashion. He suspected there was something wrong with her. He and Jamie spoke of it several times. Maybe he could go to Jamie's dad, Dan Miller? Maybe he should show Dan the journals?

Matt leaned his forehead against the wall. His mind was overloaded. And Jamie's physical absence was wearing on him. Matt placed his palms against the wall on either side of his face as if he were attempting to hug something.

"Jamie," he said quietly. "What do I do?" Jamie wasn't going to answer. His words of wisdom had vanished. Matt must sift through his feelings on his own, but the idea of dealing with everything by himself left him restless and anxious. He didn't know how.

Soon he would have to talk to people. His mom and dad heard his speech at church. He'd have to confront them and, more than likely, have a religious debate over homosexuality—he wasn't looking forward to that one. He *had* to talk to Jason. And most of all, he needed to discuss his feelings with Darian.

Whatever those feelings might be.

He felt something real for Darian, but where the caring part ended and the pure lustful desire that overtook his senses began was anyone's guess. Having sex with Jamie's ex was not solving anything. They hardly spoke anymore. And although Matt really enjoyed the sex, it was apparent in this moment as he hugged the wall and agonized over the nightmare his life had become that they needed more. Matt's conflicting emotions over losing Jamie and being with Darian twisted his guts into balloon animals from hell—little headless dogs and legless giraffes chasing each other in the confines of his bowels.

Matt closed his eyes and shook his head. "I'm such a retard." He never knew where the random imagery came from, but it happened to him all the time. He turned around and walked over to the kitchen. He placed his keys on the counter and looked into the living room, continuing to reflect on the past week.

"What made me think everything was hunky-dory? I'm not okay. And Darian's not okay—he's sullen and withdrawn. Fuck!" Matt was so frustrated. He grabbed the pack of cigarettes that sat on the counter and took one out. He had the butt between his lips about to light it when he reconsidered. "Darian…," Matt whispered, glancing toward the bedroom. "You quit for Jamie. I can quit for you." Matt tossed the unlit cigarette in the trash. He held the pack in front of him for a few minutes, considering what he was about to do. Jamie had hated his smoking, but he'd continued the habit for years. But for Darian…. It wasn't as tough a decision as he thought it would be. "I'm done." He tossed the cigs into the trash.

Again, he looked toward the bedroom as he thought about Darian. "What is going on with you?"

The apartment looked exactly as it had when he left that morning. Every morning. Matt knew Darian showered because the towel in the bathroom was usually damp. Darian must have gone out because his car was parked in a different spot a few times. Darian had to have gone to work because there were AE tags in the trash and a neatly folded pile of new clothes on one of the bar stools.

Matt stepped over to the pile and touched it.

Darian had worn Matt's shirts a few mornings, and it was funny to see them billowing around his thin frame. Darian undoubtedly wore a small and Matt wore an extra large. "So," Matt said, touching the shirt lying on top. "You bought new clothes in lieu of going home to get yours?" Talking to himself was a trait Matt got from his mom; he couldn't help doing it.

He turned toward the bedroom again. "And you're sleeping a lot." *Sleeping most of the day and having sex half the night.* If Matt knew anything from watching daytime television, it was that sleeping all the time spelled depression. Even more reason to talk to Darian. But when?

Tomorrow was church. Maybe after?

Matt walked down the hall and entered his aunt's room. He knew if he joined Darian in his room they would end up having sex—they always did. After hearing Jamie's voice on his voice mail, Matt couldn't think about sex. It felt like betrayal.

His mind was racing.

This is supposed to be about comfort, not sex!

To Matt, sex was comforting, but to Darian? Matt wasn't so sure. Darian said he wanted Matt to make the pain go away. Perhaps Darian was using sex as a drug? Matt would have to bring that up as well.

For now, he'd sleep and try to have a conversation in the morning.

MORNING came, and so did Matt. He stirred when he felt the bed move, he opened his eyes when he felt a hand on his penis, and he promptly closed them again and groaned when Darian rolled a condom over his cock and started sucking. It was a fantastic way to wake up, but it wasn't helping matters.

After Darian finished, he cleaned Matt off and sat cross-legged on the bed watching him. He somberly asked, "Why didn't you come to bed last night?"

Matt took a breath. Last night he'd had it all figured out in his head, but after a morning blowjob, he was having a hard time focusing. What was he asking? "Um, last night? Ah… yeah… last night I came home and speed dialed Jamie. It freaked me out a little. I just… I needed time to think, I guess. I wanted to be alone."

Darian lowered his face. "Yeah," he whispered. "I've done that a hundred times. And every time I hear his voice, I start crying."

Matt sat up and reached for Darian. He squeezed his knee. "I know it's bad. We can talk about it." He knew he needed to offer, even if he didn't know where to begin.

Darian stiffened and shook his head. "No. Not yet. I can't. I just can't. It's too hard. Please."

Matt was worried by Darian's sudden panic and instinctively moved to soothe him. "Shhh, baby. It's okay. We don't have to talk." Matt scooted across the space between them and began rubbing Darian's back since that action had seemed to work all the other times

Darian broke down. When Matt felt Darian's back muscles relax, he coaxed him into a hug.

Darian leaned his head into Matt's chest and said, "I need more time."

"I know. You have it. No pressure." Matt embraced him before changing the subject. "You want to go with me to church?" he asked lightheartedly, trying ever so carefully not to sound like his overbearing father.

Darian pulled back. His eyes had unshed tears filling the corners. "Today?"

"Yeah, it's Sunday."

"Do I have to?" Darian didn't sound thrilled at the prospect.

"No. Of course not."

"Good. Then I'll pass." He wiped his eyes. "I didn't like it last time." Darian rolled off the bed and grabbed a tissue to blow his nose.

Matt had to admit it wasn't too much fun for him the last time either. "I don't blame you. It's fine. I'll go and see you later. Okay?"

"Okay."

Matt slid to the edge of the bed. "So we're clear? We *do* need to talk about things. Jamie. You and me. What this might be between us."

"I know." Darian didn't look at him, but Matt was glad he responded at all. He looked so alone.

Matt stroked his arm, then left to get ready for church.

CHURCH. Matt knew he had to go. Well, not *had* to go as much as *needed* to go; not showing up would only prove he was a coward. He had to show up today like every other normal Sunday. Normal. Yeah, everything was normal.

Work was normal. His friends were normal. His life was going back to normal.

Normal.... Just the thing he'd wrestled with last night and realized he was fooling himself thinking it could be. Nothing was normal, despite appearing virtually the same as it had before. Maybe he could humor the world around him and pretend it was all normal? Yeah, he could do that.

He drove up the hill of the parking lot and waved as he typically would at the few congregants walking in. They didn't wave back, but it was possible they hadn't seen him. It was sunny. Maybe the glare off his windshield obscured their view. He drove around to his favorite spot in the corner and parked. He walked to the back door as he did every Sunday. He liked the back door. (No pun intended.) It said, "I feel welcome here." The front door was for people who were new or felt the need to be formal and proper. Matt liked *casual* and *comfortable*. Why shouldn't he? He'd been going to this church most of his life.

"Hey, Matt," Suzy greeted him.

"Hey there. How's my favorite little fourth grader?"

"Good," she chirped.

He smiled and kept walking.

"Morning, Matt," Mr. Gregory chimed. He was setting up the coffee pot for after-worship fellowship as he always did.

"Good morning. I haven't seen you here for a few weeks. Is everything all right with Martha?" Matt asked.

"Oh yes. She's doing fine." The old man smiled and nodded. "Her hip is healing well, the doctors say. I just had a cold the last few weeks and didn't feel right bringing my sniffles to the church."

Matt shook his head. Mr. Gregory was one of the nicest men he knew. Always thinking of everyone else. *Like Jamie.* "Mr. Gregory, I'm sure the nursery has more germs and snotty-nosed kids than one little cold from you could bring into the church. You shouldn't worry so much."

"Nevertheless, it's better to be safe than sorry. It's good to see you, Matt. Tell your mom Martha wants to have tea again real soon."

"I will. Or you can tell her yourself. She's probably upstairs right now."

"I'll do that."

Matt smiled and headed up the steps to the main worship hall.

It was a normal, modern church sanctuary. Wooden pews lined both sides of the room, with a center aisle and an aisle on either side next to the walls. The windows were clear, not ornate stained glass like fancier churches. The pastor stood behind a simple wooden podium on an elevated dais where he could easily peer over the entire congregation. The ceiling was vaulted, with hanging chandeliers, but lacked the flying buttresses of old-style churches.

Matt stepped into the room and walked around to the left. He took the side aisle and slipped into the pew where his family normally sat. His mother jumped. "Good morning, Mom." He smiled.

"Matt. I didn't expect you to be here today."

"Why not?" he said. "I'm here every Sunday, aren't I? Except for when I work."

"Yes, but it's not every Sunday you stand up there and tell the congregation what you told them last week."

That I'm gay? Matt read her mind. She seemed shocked and possibly put off by his being here this morning. She didn't hug him or ask why he hadn't called last week. For the very first time in his life, Matt felt tension between them. "Mom, where's Dad?"

"He didn't feel well." She looked down and arranged her skirt over her crossed legs.

"Mom, do you want me to leave?" he asked directly.

His mom looked up sharply. "No! I mean… no, I don't want you to leave. I'm just shocked to see you, that's all."

Matt covered her fidgeting hand with his. "Mom, I didn't confess to murder."

"No, but you…." She paused. The silence spelled out the answer his mother was unwilling to share. Matt got it. It hurt, but he got it.

He tried to shift the tension by changing the subject. "I'm sorry I didn't call this week, or stop by for dinner like I usually do. It's been a tough week."

"I imagine so." She continued looking at everything else but Matt—leafing through the bulletin, marking the page in the hymnal. Matt was about to get up when the music started. His mother handed him a hymnal. "Your father will be disappointed," she whispered. "We haven't sung out of the hymnal in months. I know he'll be upset he missed it."

Matt grinned. "Yeah, I know he will."

As he had for years, Matt followed the order of worship. People sang. Then they listened to the morning announcements and prayer requests for the week. There was another song and then the weekly offering was taken. When the singing was done, Pastor Dennis stood up and delivered the message. Matt was rather surprised he did not preach a whole sermon on homosexuality, or more specifically, the abomination of homosexuality. Today's sermon was on "the love of money being the root of all evil" and not once did he mention homosexuality, nor did he glance in Matt's direction.

First *unusual* item of the week.

Matt recalled many occasions when he and Jamie squirmed listening to the sermon. It was as if Pastor Dennis's entire mission was to subtly exhort the two of them about God's hatred of homosexuals without confronting the subject directly. Matt loathed that. If the pastor wanted to say something, he should say it! He shouldn't pretend to preach about "loving your brother" and then slip in some non sequitur about gay people. It was ridiculous and completely rude.

Matt hadn't liked most of the sermons for the past several months, or more precisely, for the past couple of years. But he had gone to this church for so long it didn't seem right to consider leaving. Where would he go?

After the benediction, as everyone stood up, readying to leave, his mom turned to him and gave him a weak smile. "It was good of you to come."

"Mom, you don't have to treat me like a stranger." Her indifference was painful.

"I'm not."

"Mom, I'm still me. I'm still your firstborn. I can tell when you're upset, and I can see in your eyes something's wrong. Please don't shut me out." He reached out and touched her forearm.

She heaved a sigh. "I've been under a lot of stress lately. Not all of it has to do with you. Your father hasn't been happy here for a long time. Joan hasn't returned my calls, but I'd rather not get into that here. Can you come over one night this week?"

Matt could see the stress in her eyes. "Yeah, sure," he agreed quickly but then grabbed his forehead. "No, wait. I can't. I'm sorry. I have all long shifts this week, plus night work. I've got to make up for lost time, for the funeral and viewings and stuff."

"It's okay. I'm sure we'll get a chance to talk soon. I have to extract Hannah and Steven from their junior church classrooms. They've turned out to be great helpers, but they never want to leave. The little children just adore them."

"Oh yeah, okay. I forgot." He stepped back out of the pew and let his mom pass.

"Linda!" Ms. Nancy greeted Matt's mother with a smile and a hug. "The Octoberfest picnic is next Sunday, and I still need a volunteer to help carve pumpkins with the children. I wasn't going to ask, but could you possibly help with that? And do you think Hannah would organize the games?" She glanced Matt's way but didn't greet him.

Matt inwardly scowled. *She never did like me.* He stood there feeling awkward, but at least Ms. Nancy was acting as rude as she had in the past. If she was disgusted by Matt's sexuality, he could not discern it from her actions at present.

"I can do that," his mother said. "And I'm sure Hannah would love to organize the games."

Matt continued his mental assessment of the church during his mom's little conversation. *"Octoberfest" is such a strange title. They picked it because it's an October picnic. Surely they know the term is normally associated with a beer festival? Oddly, no one's bothered by the name, yet most people who go here don't condone drinking.* Matt couldn't recall too many people at this church talking about beer unless it was to say, "You shouldn't drink." He wondered how many of them *did* drink but never admitted it to anyone else?

Hypocrites.

Matt hadn't noticed whether his church family was or wasn't doing things that would be deemed hypocritical; but after giving a speech about Jamie loving unconditionally, Matt was pressed to consider what the word "unconditional" really meant. It seemed to him people always attached conditions and stipulations to love. It didn't seem freely given at all! It was all about quid pro quo.

How does one go about loving unconditionally?

He walked toward the door as usual, and several people smiled at him as he went. None of them seemed uncomfortable. Everything was fine. All the judgment he had expected was nowhere to be found. His mom was the only one so far who was acting oddly. Maybe coming out was going to be all right.

Matt stepped out onto the front porch of the building and filled his lungs with the autumn air. It felt good. For the first time, he felt as if being gay wasn't just his dirty little secret. It was who he was, and it wasn't a big deal after all.

I should have come out a long time ago.

MATT went home feeling good about church for the first time in a long time. He was happy. He was even happier to find Darian still awake, since he was in the habit of going back to sleep after Matt left. Darian was quiet, but awake. Matt changed into something more comfortable and plopped down on the couch next to him. *Maybe now is a good time to talk?*

"What ya watching?" he asked, hoping to start a conversation.

"Nothing," answered Darian, staring at the television.

He was wearing a tight blue graphic T-shirt with clouds across the front. It was good to see him wearing a brighter color. Many of the shirts he wore were black. Matt liked the lighter shade. Darian was also in his underwear. Matt grinned in appreciation. He liked Darian's legs. He reached over and stroked his thigh, relishing the feel of his coarse leg hairs prickling his fingertips. But Darian's lack of verbal participation was discouraging.

Should I talk? What did people talk about? *I talked cars with Jamie. Does Darian like cars?* "So, Dare, do you have any hobbies?"

Darian cocked his head in Matt's direction and lifted his eyebrow, giving him a look. "I draw," he said in a tone that made Matt feel stupid, and then he turned his attention back to the television.

"Sorry. I knew that." Matt was trying. Making small talk was difficult. "Did you draw anything today?"

"No."

"Are you into anything else? Cars maybe?"

Darian shook his head.

This was going nowhere fast. Matt moved his hand higher on Darian's leg and caressed his inner thigh. He wasn't as bony as Matt thought. He had muscles. His thighs were seriously fine. *Probably from sitting in my lap several times this week.* Matt's penis woke up. *Shit! Focus, Matt, focus! Hobbies, not sex. So, what was I thinking about?* Matt cleared his throat. "Um, do you ever go to the gym and work out?" Matt figured if Darian worked out, he could develop definition easily. A few squats a day would do a lot for his gorgeous legs.

"No." *Again with the look!*

"Dare, I'm trying. How am I supposed to get to know you if you don't say anything?"

"I don't feel like talking." Darian clicked off the television, tossed the remote onto the table, and tried to get off the couch.

Matt stopped him. "Don't leave. We don't have to talk." Darian relaxed back against the cushions. Matt resumed caressing his thigh, but he spotted a piece of paper on the coffee table next to the remote. "What's this?" He picked it up and looked it over. "Your blood test results? It's dated yesterday. How'd you get them so fast?"

Darian breathed out heavily. "The doctor likes me." He didn't act surprised.

"Wow. I think mine are supposed to be in Wednesday." He looked at the paper again. "You're clean. I knew you would be. It's me I'm not 100 percent sure about."

"I know. I used a flavored condom this morning like you asked. Cherry. It was okay, I guess, but I'd rather taste you."

"Thanks. I mean… I know I'd like a blowjob without one, but it's safer."

Darian nodded.

"You wanna do something? Play cards? Or I could make you something to eat." He was really trying to be a good host, as his mom would want him to be, but Darian wasn't giving him much to work with. "Or we could watch a movie?"

"Or we could have sex," said Darian.

Matt froze, thinking about all the things he'd gone over in his mind since last night. Sex was blurring the lines around everything. "Dare… I don't think we should. Sex is interfering with—"

But Matt never finished his thought. Darian moved Matt's hand from his inner thigh to his rigid penis, Matt felt his hard heat, and his brain switched off. It was obvious what Darian wanted. Matt obediently groped him through the fabric as Darian lunged forward, attaching his mouth to Matt's.

No words were spoken the rest of the day.

3

AS SOON as Matt left for church that morning, Darian went into the bathroom and threw up. The cherry flavor of the condom did not cover up the taste of latex. It gagged him. He didn't want to taste anything other than flesh. Flesh and cum and sweat. Darian thought if he could close his eyes and pretend he was sucking Jamie, the guilt would be less. Jamie wasn't as thick as Matt, but the length was close. Jamie would curl his fingers into Darian's hair and moan, much like Matt did. He would breathe hard and arch his back and thrust up into Darian's bobbing strokes. The only difference, the biggest difference, was that Matt cried out *Darian's* name without fail.

From the countless stories Jamie had told, Darian knew Matt'd had lots of sexual partners. Jamie had often said Matt couldn't be bothered to catch a name. But that would imply Matt wouldn't cry out "Darian" unless Darian was all he had on his mind, wouldn't it? Matt even whispered Darian's name in his sleep. Darian grinned weakly. "Matt…," he mused aloud.

Darian wiped his mouth with some toilet tissue and flushed. He stood and leaned on the sink, staring at his own brown eyes. "What are *you* looking at?" he asked defensively of his sallow reflection. "Don't judge me! Jamie did this!" A tear streaked his cheek. "I don't know what else to do."

The reflection in the mirror faded. Darian's black hair turned into brown hair, and his brown eyes to green. Darian was staring at Jamie, who looked every bit as sallow as Darian had seconds before.

"I'm not judging you," Jamie's image said in a deep rumble.

"You are." Darian's breathing accelerated. "I didn't know where to go. You left, and I panicked. He was there."

"But you enjoyed it." Jamie's voice echoed in the tiny bathroom, distorted and haunting. "I'm not even cold, and you gave yourself to him over and over and over and over and over...."

"Shut up!" The words hissed against his eardrums. Darian grabbed his head and covered his ears, trying to block out the unwanted rebuke. "No!"

"Yes," Jamie accused. "You like what he does to you."

The tone of Jamie's blame poured over Darian like blood. The sounds penetrated his attempts to block them out. Each word was a different pitch, elongated and distorted. They tore at the threads of his sanity.

"No!" Darian yelled again as tears flooded his eyes.

"He makes you forget about me," Jamie's voice rasped in a horrid whisper.

"No! I love you! I need you!" Darian argued. He stared at Jamie's pale face and grabbed the mirror on both sides. "Why did you do this?" he screamed. "You never even told him about me! Didn't you love me? Matt was your best friend. Why didn't you tell him about me?"

When Jamie's image stared back silently, Darian covered his face and wept.

"Because I knew you'd go to him, you little tart," the image sneered finally.

Darian uncovered his face. "No!" he shouted. "That's not true. I would never have left you! Why would you think that?"

"Because Matt is so much hotter than I am."

"No!"

"Because Matt is a better lover than I am."

"No!" Darian refuted.

"Because Matt makes you shiver and quake, and you can't get enough of his big, thick cock!"

"No! No! No! You were all I needed. I did everything for you," Darian wailed and shook. "You said you loved me." Darian's voice faded to a tiny squeak. "You promised to be there for me."

Darian leaned forward and rested his head against the mirror.

"You know how to make all this go away," Jamie taunted.

Once Darian's sobbing subsided, he stood up straight again. Jamie's face had vanished.

Cold and empty, Darian changed his shirt and went into the living room to wait for Matt to return from church. He turned the television on. He wasn't watching—it was only a distraction for his brain.

As soon as Matt walked through the door, he felt his penis pulse. He could pretend to watch reruns of *Friends* as a distraction, but nothing would satisfy the hunger he felt every time Matt entered the room. Maybe Jamie's ghost-vision was right.

THEY'D fucked for hours after Matt returned from church. Darian got up in the middle of the night to piss and glimpsed Jamie's reflection in the bathroom mirror as he aimed for the bowl. He jumped, and a shiver of dread ran down his spine. "Are you haunting me?" he asked, as if Jamie's specter were truly in the room with him.

"Is that what you want?" Jamie asked.

Darian finished peeing and flushed the toilet. He looked into the mirror and kept his eyes glued on Jamie as he washed his hands. This time the vision was more complete, almost tangible. Darian's vision depicted Jamie in jeans but no shirt. Jamie was emaciated, his bones showing at every angle. Dried blood trailed down his lips and chin, and his wrist was slit. The word "zombie" would describe his appearance had his flesh been rotting, which it wasn't.

"No. I want you to leave me alone," Darian answered quietly.

"No, you don't. You're the one who brought me here… slut. How does your ass feel after what he did to you tonight? I bet it throbs!"

"Shut up," he choked.

"You liked it up against the wall, didn't you? Like the first time at the funeral home, only better because you faced him? He slammed so hard as he held you off your feet. I heard you scream!"

"Stop!" Darian covered his ears. "I can't hear this."

"You do, and you will. As long as you let him fuck you, I'll be here to remind you how much you like it."

"I pretend it's you!" Darian cried.

"Keep telling yourself that. And when Matt moves on to the next willing body, I'll be sure to remind you how empty these last weeks have been."

Darian unwillingly looked up, and the apparition was gone.

He returned to bed and crawled in beside Matt, thankful he hadn't woken up from all the noise in the bathroom.

Matt reached across Darian's chest, pulling him close. "Mmm, Dare," he whispered sleepily.

Darian rolled over so he was facing Matt. Matt's hand slid down and caressed his lower back, but his eyes remained closed. He was breathing steadily and evenly. Deeply asleep, yet aware of Darian's presence enough to whisper his name and stroke his back. Darian tucked his head under Matt's chin and nestled himself as tightly into Matt's embrace as he could get.

Matt sighed and squeezed him.

Darian felt wetness rolling over his cheeks. *He does care about me. He does care about me. I know he does. Matt's not using me.*

He didn't understand what he was doing here, but it felt too good to step away. Matt felt so wonderful around him. He was safe. But safe from what?

Darian could hear Jamie's maniacal laughter as he drifted off to sleep.

4

October 4, 2010

DARIAN woke Matt up *again* with a blowjob. Not that Matt was complaining, but it seemed as if Darian was becoming more physically demanding as the days went by and less and less personable. Matt hadn't felt so sexually satisfied in all his years of clubbing, yet a nagging sensation shadowed the back of his consciousness with every orgasm. This week was like a trip to paradise, where all his fantasies came true, but it was only external. He had sex at *least* twice a day, and now he was awakened each morning by having his dick sucked. Talk about fantasies! His favorite porn sites didn't compare. The only thing missing on the physical end was a little more kink and some toys, but Matt was sure it would not be long before he could broach the subject. Darian was a wild thing; he was sure of it.

Still, if Matt was honest, what he felt was missing was intimacy.

True intimacy.

The kind of intimacy you get through talking and understanding a person—the kind that comes through a deep connection. *Doggone Jamie and his fucking ideals again!* Sex was only physical; Jamie wrote about that in his journals. Sex was all the connection Matt had wanted in the past. He never needed anything but the physical because he always had Jamie to come home to, Jamie to connect with, Jamie to talk to. With Darian, Matt felt cheated. He wanted more, but so far there was less and less talking and more and more sex.

Sex! Bloody hell. The things this boy can do with his mouth.

"Oh fuck!" Matt moaned, arching his back. After he came, Matt reached for Darian, but he was already heading to the bathroom. Matt jumped up and followed him.

"Hey, don't you want me to reciprocate?"

Darian shrugged. "I'm good. I jerked off while blowing you. See?" He showed Matt his cum-covered hand as he turned the water on in the sink.

"Oh, okay." Something about Darian was changing, but Matt wasn't sure how to go about pointing it out. *Jamie was so good at asking emotional questions. Why can't I?* "Dare, can we talk later? Maybe tonight or tomorrow morning? I start night shift tomorrow, so I'll have more time after breakfast. You've gotta be going through some hard shit. I want you to know you can talk about it. I'll listen. I want to help."

Darian washed up and turned the water off. He paused as he turned but didn't look Matt in the eye. "Thanks," he muttered as he shoved past Matt and went back into the bedroom.

Matt followed.

"Do you work today?" Matt asked. "I know your schedule's on the fridge but I forget."

"I'm supposed to, but I asked for a couple more days. Saturday was too hard." Darian sat down on the bed, head in hands, elbows on his knees.

Matt sat down and rubbed his back. "Oh? What happened?"

Darian sniffled. "Song came on in the store. Reminded me of Jamie."

Matt knew Darian was trying hard to keep from crying. His back muscles were tense. With a small hint from Matt's soothing hand, Darian turned his face into Matt's chest. Matt held him. "Shhh, it's okay. I've got you."

Matt understood how it could be to suddenly hear a song and try without success to contain the grief. He had only gone running a few times this week because listening to his iPod reminded him of Jamie. He kept expecting Jamie to be running next to him when Shinedown came on. He turned to run backward any number of times—singing out loud, and pumping his fists—only to feel like a fool because Jamie wasn't running behind him to notice his antics. He held the tears in and walked home in silence.

He needed a new playlist, perhaps one with songs that reminded him of Darian. He was willing to try anything, or he'd have to give up running.

Several minutes passed. When Darian's sobbing seemed to have stopped, Matt reiterated, "We'll get through this. I promise. We'll talk later."

Darian sat up, his eyes pleading. "Not tonight. I don't want to think; I want you to make love to me. Please?"

"Okay." Matt smirked. What guy didn't like hearing that? "No talking, only sex." He leaned in and kissed Darian's forehead. "For now, I gotta go." Matt walked over to the dresser and took out his socks. "What are your plans today?"

Darian shrugged again. He seemed so apathetic all the time; Matt really wondered about depression. He must bring it up.

"Why don't you call a friend?" Matt suggested. "Invite someone over."

"Maybe."

MATT left wondering what was going to happen next. The beginning of all relationships could not be this difficult. He didn't know what to do, what to say, or who to ask about all of the above. "Fuckin' Jamie!" he screamed and punched the roof of the truck cab. His anger surged. "Shit! Why'd you fuckin' leave us like this?" His hands shook as he balled his fists. Life had to get better. It had to! This fucking uncertainty and strained conversation was driving him mad. He needed to talk to someone. He needed his best friend! As Matt parked his truck at the station, he hoped for an extra hard day so he didn't have time to think about his troubles—Darian being the most distressing of them all.

THE phrase "be careful what you wish for" haunted Matt's thoughts as he drove home. He had wanted a hard day—well, he got one! The fire was hot, and the smell of burning flesh still assaulted his nostrils. Luckily, they only lost three pigs from the barn fire, but those three stank up the entire area most of the day. He didn't think he would be eating pulled pork for quite some time.

Now, all he wanted to do was crawl into bed—with Darian.

He walked up to the apartment door and held out his key. Music was blaring on the other side of the door. "That's weird," he muttered. "Dare wouldn't be throwing a party, would he?"

Matt opened the door and found a young, blonde girl sitting on his couch painting her toenails.

She looked up and smiled. "Oh hey! You must be Matt. I'm Sara." She held out her hand but made no move to rise off the couch.

"Ah, hi. Where's Darian?" Matt was beyond confused. This was not what he expected to come home to.

"Oh, he's in the bathroom with Lori," she chirped happily.

Matt tossed his coat on the floor in the corner of the room. It stank. He didn't want the rest of the closet smelling of burnt pig. On second thought, he should have left the coat in the bed of the truck to air out.

"Eww, what's that smell?" Sara whined, waving her hand in front of her nose.

"That's me," Matt grumbled, crossing to the kitchen and opening the fridge. "Can you please turn down the music?" He was tired and achy and not in the mood to chitchat with Darian's *friend.* And he was definitely not in the mood for Miley Cyrus booming in the tiny apartment. "Party In The U.S.A." wasn't a song to relax to. It was a wonder the neighbors weren't pounding on his door.

Soft acoustic jazz, now that would be nice.

"Hey, why'd you turn down the tunes?" asked Darian as he entered the room, shirtless, another girl dancing around him as if this were some disco joint.

Matt heard Sara reply, "Your boyfriend doesn't like it." He rolled his eyes.

"Matt?" Darian turned his way, smiling. He rushed into the kitchen and hugged Matt. "Hey, you," Darian cooed as he kissed Matt's neck.

Matt's first thought was *Ahhh.* Relief. Especially when his mouth started watering from just a glimpse of Darian's nipple ring. But sliding his hands over Darian's bare back did not feel right with two giggly teenaged girls looking on. Were these the kind of friends Darian had? And why were they here so late? Didn't Darian know Matt worked hard all day and was looking forward to some quiet? Didn't Darian think it inappropriate to parade around half-naked? Although he was normally a fan of public sex, Matt didn't want these girls ogling Darian's beautiful skin. He wanted it all to himself.

"What is that awful smell?" It was Darian's turn to ask.

"Me! It's me, okay?" Matt rudely answered. "I was putting out a burning barn and some pigs got scorched." He pulled away, shutting the fridge door with a thud.

"Shit, what crawled up your butt?" Darian struck back with squared shoulders and a hard glare.

"Nothing. Okay? Nothing." Matt hadn't meant to yell, but the words tumbled out as if of their own accord. He'd left this morning feeling uncertain about Darian's mood and come home to a drastic one-eighty. It threw him. "I'm tired," he huffed. "I stink. All I wanted was to come home, shower, and bury myself in your ass." He heard the girls gasp, but he continued anyway. "When I get here, I find out you're having a slumber party with your teeny-bopper girlfriends, messing around half-naked. This isn't a sorority house, Darian. It's *my* apartment."

"It's your aunt's, actually," Darian retorted matter-of-factly.

"Whatever!" Matt did not appreciate being corrected. He stormed out of the kitchen toward the hall that led to his bedroom. "I'm taking a shower. When I'm done, I expect your guests to be gone."

Matt slammed the bedroom door. He took a deep breath. Tears welled in his eyes, and he angrily wiped them away. *Why did I just act like that? What came over me?* He knew he should go back in and apologize, but his feet wouldn't budge. He hung his head briefly before removing his shirt and walking over to the bathroom.

He heard the music stop. Then he heard the apartment door close.

Matt turned on the shower and stepped into the tub. The water was hot, and he closed his eyes as he felt the tension ebbing away.

This is such a fucked-up day, he thought. *This is not what I wanted.*

Why did he get so angry when he walked in and found Darian had friends over? Darian was entitled to have a life. Matt had suggested Darian call his friends. What was he expecting?

You wanted him waiting for you, naked on the bed, lubed up, legs spread wide. You're an idiot, Matt.

Matt thumped his forehead with the heel of his hand. *Stupid!*

He was so mad at himself, he didn't notice Darian was in the bathroom until the curtain moved aside. Matt tensed up again when Darian stepped in behind him, expecting a fight. He was not going to apologize. This was his house!

Darian didn't say a word.

Darian's hand slid up his back, and Matt suppressed a sigh. As he felt Darian's lips on his clavicle, Matt tried to control his breathing. Darian stepped closer; his penis brushed against Matt's buttocks. Matt gulped. Darian was breaking down his prickly exterior as if he'd done it for years. He didn't say a word about the way Matt had acted; it was as if he hadn't heard him at all moments ago.

Matt felt Darian's hand snake around his side and grasp Matt's growing erection. He couldn't suppress the gasp that escaped his mouth when Darian's fingers encircled him and slowly stroked. "Oh, Darian." No matter how mad Matt was, his body had a mind of its own, and it reacted to Darian like a barn on fire.

Darian wordlessly turned Matt around so their erections touched. He took both penises in his palm and milked them together. Matt gripped Darian's shoulders and groaned as his lover tugged aggressively. It felt so good, so right, just what he needed. And after they came in unison, Darian rinsed his hand and then picked up the soap. He washed Matt from head to toe without a word. He licked and sucked on Matt's nipple as he lathered Matt's balls. He nipped at his shoulder blade as his soapy fingers slipped up and down Matt's ass crack. Darian even washed Matt's hair while giving him a hickey. All the while, Matt kept his eyes closed and melted into Darian's touch.

This was the tension release Matt was looking for when he entered the apartment. This was just what the fireman ordered.

But as soon as Darian was done, he slipped quietly from the tub.

Matt caught his breath and turned off the water. "I'm sorry, Darian." Silence answered. He opened the curtain to an empty bathroom. He grabbed a towel and hastened after Darian, but the apartment was empty. "Where the heck did he go?" Matt wondered aloud. "He's soaking wet." Guilt carved a gigantic hole in his gut. "Fuck," he whispered. "He'd rather bolt, than stay long enough to get dressed." He felt even worse for his outburst earlier.

Matt pulled on a pair of pajama pants and crawled listlessly into bed. *I am such an asshole.* He touched the pillow next to his. He could smell Darian in the room. *Why did I have to yell at him?* He hated this. Everything was so mixed up.

He rubbed his face.

Not knowing what else he could do, Matt leaned over and picked the picture off the nightstand, a picture of him and Jamie from a few years back. Matt fingered the glass. Jamie was his rock, his safehold. Without him Matt felt like a balloon accidentally let loose in a gust of wind. He didn't know what was going to happen to him. He felt like he was drifting on an unseen breeze, going higher and higher until he'd finally burst. Getting angry about it didn't help.

Talking. Talking about it was the only thing Matt could think of, but who could he talk to? Darian? Maybe. But he said he wasn't ready. Jason? Probably. But he'd have to come out to him first to fully disclose everything that was going on. Hannah? His sister used to talk to him about her boyfriend troubles; maybe she would be willing to return the favor?

The person his heart truly wanted to talk to was Jamie.

Fuckin' Jamie. The phrase was losing its bitterness. Matt was mad at Jamie, but the anger grew from his own anguish over not being the friend Jamie had needed to avoid his terrible end.

Matt's mind wandered back to the times he and Jamie spent together…

"WHAT'RE your plans for Saturday?" Matt asked as he soaped up the bumper on the Jeep. His dad said he could take it out all weekend as long as he washed it before and after.

"Fishing with my dad," Jamie answered.

"Really? Seems like you do that a lot lately. I don't remember you ever fishing so much before. What do you catch?" Matt was genuinely curious. In all the years he'd known Jamie Miller, they'd never been fishing together. Generally, they played basketball, went running, or went to the gym. He took Jamie hunting a couple of times and that was a blast! Matt wondered why Jamie never asked Matt to go fishing.

"Bass."

"You eat 'em?"

"Yeah. My dad's a great cook. He's teaching me all kinds of ways to cook fish—and chicken and steak. I think he cooks better than Mom."

Matt smirked. "Are you turning into a little housewife, or what?"

Jamie flipped him off.

"What'd I say?" Matt batted his eyes innocently at Jamie and put his hand over his heart.

"Stop." Jamie rolled his eyes. After he scrubbed his side of the hood, he grabbed the hose and rinsed. "So, Matt, is that what you're looking for—a housewife?"

Matt wasn't sure he'd heard him correctly. He popped up from rubbing the wheel well and said, "Huh?"

Jamie cleared his throat. "I said… is that what you want—a housewife?"

Matt was baffled. "What? Looking for? Dude, I told you before, I'm not looking for anybody."

Jamie shrugged. "Not even a little bit? Aren't you curious if your dream guy is out there?"

"Dream guy? What teen magazine are you reading?"

Jamie huffed and walked around to his side of the Jeep while Matt carried on a monologue of his own—making fun of Jamie mostly, but playing along with the idea of his perfect match. He flexed his muscles and talked to himself while Jamie fumed.

Jamie was always irritated at Matt for one reason or another, and Matt had learned to ignore it over the years. When Jamie came back around to his side of the Jeep, Matt looked up. "What?" Jamie had a weird look in his eyes.

Jamie laughed deviously and then proceeded to spray him with the hose.

Matt fell back on his ass and flung his soap-sodden sponge at Jamie. Jamie dodged the poorly thrown object and continued to spray Matt from head to toe. Matt reached for the soap bucket, and Jamie turned tail and sprinted for the house.

Matt anticipated this move and ran around the other way. Just as Jamie neared the garage door, Matt hauled back and flung the bucket of water at his exposed back. Jamie froze and turned around slowly. Matt held his hands out to the side. "You asked for it, dude."

Jamie stood there a few seconds in silence, and little by little, a smile made its way to his face. "Yeah, I guess I did."

Matt waved him back. "Come on, let's finish this and go play some basketball."

"All right." He followed Matt back to the Jeep and retrieved the sponge. "Here."

"Thanks." Matt took it and resumed washing the rims….

MATT took his eyes off the bedroom ceiling, got off the bed, and walked over to his closet. In the back were Jamie's journals. He remembered Jamie writing something about that day. Where was it?

Matt flipped the pages until familiar words caught his eye. "Here it is."

Matt read the entry:

I'm not sure why I do the things I do. I just told Darian I had a headache and didn't want sex. I DID! Just not with him. Instead I took a shower and jacked off thinking about Matt. Fuck, am I messed up? Matt will never want me.

He said in his "perfect scenario" the guy he's with isn't strong like he is. His "dream guy" needs protecting and clings to his manly muscles. What a bunch of shit. He even kissed his biceps and flexed them like the Hulk. I know he was just doing all that to mess with me. Manly muscles.... Pft! He said he wants someone vulnerable, who needs protection so he can be his champion or knight in shining armor. Shit! That leaves me out. I am not weak. Sure I'd like to be all over his "manly muscles" but not because I need protecting.

Fuck, come to think of it, Darian fits that profile exactly. One more reason the two of them should NEVER meet! He'd get one hint of Darian's innocent charm and defenselessness and never look at me again.

Matt. Fuck him with his ripped chest and killer thighs. Shit. I can't believe he didn't notice my boner when I hosed him down. He was so hot!

I think I need to come again.

MATT placed the book in his backpack and crawled back in bed. "Fuck, I hate this!" He picked up the picture again and spoke quietly. "Sex with Darian was a bad idea, especially after I knew who he was. I shouldn't have taken advantage of him. No wonder he's not saying anything about how he feels about me. When have I given him a chance to grieve? He lost you, Jamie, just like me. I don't know what I expected. Not this."

Matt rolled over, put the picture back on the table, and turned off the light.

"I guess you were right when you said you thought we should never meet. Darian's the guy I've always wanted to find, but he fell in love with you first. I was so stupid to think this could turn out to be something more than fucking."

Matt fell asleep with Jamie's words echoing in his mind: *One more reason the two of them should never meet! One more reason the two of them should never meet! One more reason the two of them should never meet!*

MATT stirred when the bed moved in the middle of the night. He felt the chill as Darian snuggled his cold body up against Matt's back in silence. Matt wasn't sure what he should do. Should he pretend to sleep and see if Darian made a move to wake him? Or should he reach over and turn the light on so they could hash it out? Darian had to be angry with him.

The answer came to him when he heard Darian crying.

Matt rolled over and took Darian into his arms, instantly apologizing. "I'm so sorry, baby. I am such a jerk. I shouldn't have treated your friends like that. I shouldn't have yelled at you either. I was completely rude. Dare, I'm so sorry." He rubbed Darian's back and pulled his body tight against his chest. Matt whispered, "I didn't want you to leave."

"I tried… to leave." Darian shivered and sniffled. "I pulled my clothes on… o-over my wet body a-after I closed your front d-door. I went to my car and sat in the seat. I t-turned the e-engine on and off four times. I just couldn't… go home. I c-couldn't do it."

"Oh, Darian." Matt felt horrible. "You're freezing." He rubbed Darian's arms and back fervently, trying to warm him with friction.

What Darian said bothered him. Matt knew it had been about two weeks since Darian had gone home to where he and Jamie lived with Jamie's dad, Dan Miller. Dan had even approached Matt at Matt's parents' house after the funeral to check on Darian because he hadn't heard from him in a few days. Matt texted Dan a couple times to say all was fine, even though he had his doubts. Maybe he should call him in the morning and discuss his concerns about Darian.

Matt held him tight and kissed his hair.

"Fuck me, Matt," Darian pleaded. "Please." He pushed at Matt's chest and wormed his hand down between them, inside Matt's pajama bottoms. "I need to feel you inside me," he said, breathing heavily.

Matt knew it was wrong. He knew sex was not the solution, but when Darian took a firm hold of him and stroked the way he did, Matt couldn't think. He moaned and instinctively thrust into that talented fist.

Darian pushed the blankets back, and pulled Matt's pants down his thighs. Matt heard a package tear, and he felt Darian sliding a condom over him in the dark. "I want you from behind, Matt. Be rough with me."

Matt eagerly sat up and moved in behind Darian, exhilarated by his request for roughness (although not surprised, given the other day when Matt had practically fucked him through the wall). The only light in the room was the faint glow from the hallway night-light coming in under the door, but Matt didn't need to see to fuck. He felt for Darian's hips and positioned himself, leading with his more-than-willing cock. He pushed in and felt Darian's groan zing through his nerves. Matt jackhammered his lower body like he was thrusting straight through Darian's chest. Darian thrived on his aggression, and Matt would not disappoint.

He felt Darian move. He was probably reaching for himself. "Don't stroke it," Matt warned, smacking Darian's rear. "You're gonna come when I want you to come." If Darian wanted aggression, then he'd have to learn to take orders. "Pinch the base so it hurts," Matt commanded, smacking him a second time.

When Darian whimpered a cry of pain, Matt knew he was listening. It wasn't pleasant to stem the rush of blood that prompted orgasm, but it did prolong the outcome. Matt was determined to get Darian off with nothing other than his plunging prick. He could tell with every thrust he was striking Darian's prostate because his guttural volume increased. Darian was a vocal lover, and he only hit that pitch when he was at the pinnacle of pleasure.

Darian whimpered again, but this time it was not from sadness, and it was certainly not from pain. Darian whimpered in anticipation. "Grab the headboard to brace yourself."

The headboard creaked and Darian grunted.

Darian had made a lot of noises in the two weeks they'd been together. He moaned, groaned, howled, growled, and whimpered in any number of pitches and degrees and tones. And Matt's ego swelled from it. He could do no wrong as long as he pumped that sweet hole with every bit of zeal he had. Darian ate it up and came back for more. Matt slapped his ass a third time, hard enough to sting, and Darian cried out.

"I know you like it," Matt growled and slapped him again—*thwack*! "Come on, baby, give it to me." Matt slapped his ass cheek repeatedly as he pounded into him. He slapped so hard his palm hurt. "Is this what you want?" Matt gritted his teeth and yanked Darian's body into each thrust. He gripped one hip as he kept smacking the other side. "You want it rough?"

"Yesss. Yesss!" Darian hissed. "I wanna come. Matt, I… please… let me…. Ahhh!"

"Okay, do it," he growled, and then a rumbling "ohhh" escaped his throat between his clenched teeth. He felt the surge in his balls as Darian's body shook and his anus clenched. Matt filled the latex sheath and jerked his hips forward three more times.

They both fell onto the pillows, panting and sweaty.

Matt removed the condom and Darian rolled onto his back. Matt dropped the used condom over the edge of the bed—something he should really stop doing or the carpet would be disgusting—and crawled on top of Darian. He kissed Darian's throat as his legs caressed Darian's thighs. He so loved the feel of their flesh together, sliding against each other, fitting as one. He laced his fingers through Darian's long hair and slid down far enough to capture Darian's nipple ring between his lips. Darian mewled in delight and arched his back, digging his short nails into Matt's shoulders.

Matt tucked his other hand under Darian's ribs and squeezed. "God, you taste so fucking good," Matt commented between licks and nips. He didn't bother asking about Darian's butt cheek. Matt figured if Darian hadn't enjoyed getting spanked, then he wouldn't have come so easily, nor would he coo with such delight afterward.

He made a trail with the flat of his tongue up the center of Darian's chest, sucked fervently on Darian's throat, and then moved in to capture his mouth. Darian's tongue met his in a fiery duel. Darian moaned into his mouth, and Matt widened his lips as if to swallow him whole. He ground his hips. He felt his second erection rub Darian's wood and took the cue. He nudged Darian's leg with his knee without breaking their kiss. Darian opened for him, but as he lined up his cock for reentry, Darian squirmed.

"Con-condom," Darian struggled to say.

Matt sucked on Darian's tongue and bit his bottom lip. "You sure? It would feel so nice to—"

"No," Darian snapped. "Come on, Matt, we already slipped up twice. You haven't got your test results back yet. If I have to use a condom to suck you, you have to use one to fuck me."

Matt knew he was right. They *had* done some risky things. He reached for the nightstand drawer and fumbled around. "I have to turn on the light. I can't find any."

Matt scooted up and reached for the light, still holding onto Darian. He didn't see any loose condom packets in the drawer but found the extra box in the back. *Wow, we used that many? Shit!* He pulled the box out and reluctantly slid off to Darian's side to open it. He took one out and set the box down. He glanced back down at Darian.

Matt's heart sank.

Darian's normally beautiful brown eyes were red-rimmed and swollen.

"Aw, baby, look at you." He tenderly reached out and stroked Darian's cheek. "Did I do that?" He felt a twinge of guilt for fucking him so savagely moments ago. Maybe Darian needed tenderness. "I am so fuckin' sorry I yelled at you. I didn't mean...."

Darian looked away. "No, it wasn't you. I knew you weren't really mad. At least I didn't think so. I figured you were just tired."

"Then what happened?" Matt caressed the side of his face.

Darian looked at him with sad eyes. "Me. Thinking. I sat in my car, but I couldn't do it. I couldn't drive home. I cried so much it gave me a headache. Even having that light on hurts my eyes."

"Oh, Dare, I'm so sorry," Matt said softly, as he reached up and clicked the light off. He leaned in and kissed Darian's puffy lids, one after the other. Then he kissed his cheeks and nose and stroked his hair. Darian's hair was still damp from the shower, reminding Matt his outburst had thrust Darian out into the chilly night air. He needed Darian to know without words how sorry he was.

Their lips met tenderly, softly, entering into a second dance more akin to a waltz than a samba. Darian tugged at Matt's arms, and Matt complied without question. He moved over that supple body and continued to drink in Darian's soft kisses like wine. Matt leisurely opened the condom and dressed himself, making sure not to disturb the languid pace their kissing had set. Darian moved unhurriedly as well, opening his legs wide and wrapping them around Matt's hips. When they joined together, it was gentle and comforting. And when they came, it was a tranquil call to sleep.

October 5, 2010

MATT recognized the scent of Darian's hair before he opened his eyes. He breathed in deeply and hugged the young man in his arms. He loved waking up like this. Maybe moving in together wouldn't be so bad.

Darian sighed.

Matt nuzzled his neck and kissed him. Darian sighed more. He shifted in Matt's arms to lie on his back. Matt playfully nipped his jaw and softly kissed his waiting lips. They made love again and then showered, only this time Darian didn't disappear before Matt stepped out.

DARIAN took a bowl from the cabinet and set it on the counter. "What time do you work today?"

Matt finished pouring his coffee and answered, "I have to leave at four. I work night shift the next few days. I normally have four days on and four days off and rotate day and night shifts and stuff, but I switched some shifts to have off last week, so I'm making them up. I didn't have vacation time left. I mean—this was all so sudden. The guys at work are being very helpful."

"You don't mind working nights?"

"Not really. Half of the time the guys wind up sleeping until we get a call, and it gives me time to work at Walsh's during the day."

"Walsh's?"

"My second job," Matt explained. "I split firewood in the fall, plow snow in the winter, and mow grass anytime of the year it grows.

And as far as working nights, I don't use them the way I used to. I haven't gone clubbing in a long while."

Darian nodded. "Hmm. Jamie mentioned clubbing. He said he went a few times with you. He didn't like it. We only went once."

"Yeah. Jamie hated my lifestyle." Matt observed Darian's sudden glumness. He was eating his cereal at the counter, which was odd; he normally sat at the breakfast bar. His hair hung at the sides of his face so Matt couldn't see his expression. Darian was almost having a conversation with him before he went all quiet. Matt sipped his coffee. He set the mug down and stepped closer. He affectionately tucked Darian's hair behind his ear and stroked his cheek with the back of his fingers. "Are you okay?"

Darian nodded but didn't answer. He ate another bite of cereal.

Matt didn't know what to do. He stood there feeling stupid until the phone on the counter buzzed. He picked it up. "It's a text from Dan Miller. He wants to know if you're with me?" Matt studied Darian's profile. "Dare, why is he asking that? Haven't you talked to him?"

Darian hung his head but didn't reply.

Matt texted: *He's fine. He's here. You want me to bring him home?*

Dan's reply: *No. Don't force him. Just watch him.*

Watch for what? I'm not good with post-traumatic stress syndrome. He looks wasted to me.

Matt may not have known Darian long, but he was getting to know him well. It would only be a matter of time for Matt to take the pieces he read in the journals and fit them together with the real-life individual. He was concerned, but he didn't know what to do with it. Suggest counseling? Darian was already seeing a counselor, or had been at one time.

Matt texted again: *Has he seen his therapist lately?*

I don't think so. He probably should. I think he needs to. Will you ask?

Me? Why not you?

He won't return my texts.

Fine. Matt put his phone down and stepped over to Darian's side.

He touched Darian's spoon hand before he could lift another mouthful. Darian paused, let go of the spoon, and then buried his face in Matt's neck.

"I miss Jamie," he said, choking back a sob.

Matt held him securely. "Me too." He stroked Darian's back. "Me too."

They stood for several minutes without talking, only clinging to one another. Darian cried, but not as noisily as he had before. Matt had never buried anyone as dear to him as Jamie was to Darian, so he didn't know how long the mourning process took. How long would Darian grieve? Would he wordlessly break down every day? Every week? Or would it slowly ebb away into no tears at all? And was it a good thing—not crying at all? Or would that mean he'd forgotten how special their relationship was?

Matt didn't like his inane questions. They disturbed him. He didn't want to think of Jamie ever being forgotten. Except… he'd done that himself last week. The whole situation was sickening. He was about to suggest talking about it for the trillionth time when Darian spoke up.

"I miss Dan too." He sniffled and pulled back. He reached for a napkin and blew his nose.

"Then why are you avoiding him?"

"I'm not." Darian shrugged.

Matt arched an eyebrow. He remembered Jamie writing something about Darian's inability to lie and he was dead on. Darian blushed too easily. "Dare, you can't lie worth shit."

Darian gave in. "Fine. You're right; I'm avoiding him."

"Should I *not* ask why?" Matt was a bit confused. The day of the funeral, Dan confessed to Matt he thought of Darian like a son. Didn't Darian understand that? Darian rubbed his face, and Matt felt the stress emanating from him. Darian shifted his weight back and forth and could not seem to focus on anything in the room. His hands were shaking. He even rocked his upper body slightly, which made Matt wonder if pressing him to open up was a bad idea. Darian probably needed to see a professional as Dan suggested. He looked as though he was on the verge of unraveling. Matt knew the feeling; eventually he would share his experiences with Darian, but not today.

Matt reached out and touched Darian's shoulder. If he didn't want to talk, okay, but Matt had to let him know, if only through a touch, that he was here for him.

"Dan's been so wonderful to me, and here I am avoiding him for two weeks. He probably hates me."

"He doesn't hate you."

"I just shut down, ya know? I heard Jamie died, and my brain just stopped working." He snatched another napkin and blew his nose again.

Matt rubbed his arm. "I know. When my mom got off the phone with Dan, she could barely make a sentence. She told me, but I couldn't believe it. Then I wanted to punch something, but my fingers wouldn't work; I couldn't make a fist. My whole body felt like—"

"Jell-O?"

Matt grinned. It felt unexpectedly nice to have someone finish his sentence other than Jamie. It was a rare closeness he did not enjoy with many people. "I wasn't *exactly* thinking Jell-O, but sure, that's close."

Darian gave him a thin smile in return.

"Come on, let's sit on the couch." Matt took Darian's hand and led him into the living room. He sat facing Darian and brought his legs up on the couch. Darian tucked one leg under the other and clutched a pillow in his lap. Matt took a deep breath. "I'm sorry you have to go through all this."

"You're going through it too."

"I know, but it's not the same. Jamie was your fiancé. You lived with him. You knew him better than I did."

"That's not true. I knew him *differently*, but not better." Darian picked at the fringe on the pillow.

At least Darian wasn't crying. Everything about Darian made Matt feel sorry for him. He was shouldering such sorrow, and Matt was powerless to remove it. "Okay—differently, but I can't imagine how hard it is to wake up every morning without him." Darian didn't answer, and Matt let the silence linger. He was determined to respect Darian's need to open up slowly, or not to talk at all.

After a time, Darian spoke softly. "Waking up here is… surreal." He kept his gaze glued to the pillow, fingering the fringe one strand at a time. "I know it's real, but it doesn't *feel* real. Sometimes I panic until my eyes adjust to the room and I remember where I am. A few times I've looked at your walls and thought I was dreaming. I lie there thinking I'm dreaming and I don't know where I am." Darian looked up, sorrow pouring from his eyes. Matt's heart ached. "And then I hear you mumble my name, and I remember." A single tear streaked his cheek. "You say my name, and I feel safe. Safe… but terrified. I don't know what to do."

Matt tried to put an arm around his shoulders, but Darian stopped him.

"Don't. I can't think when you hold me."

"I thought that's what you wanted? Not to think?" Matt distinctly remembered Darian using the phrase "Fuck me so hard I can't think straight," and he had complied several times.

"I did… I do… I'm so confused." He covered his face and sobbed. "I don't know what to feel. I'm scared. I miss Jamie." Darian dropped his hands. He looked at Matt and pleaded with his eyes. "I don't know what to do. Tell me what to do? I miss him. I miss him so bad, but pain goes away when I'm with you. You touch me and… and it feels like my skin's on fire."

Matt's heart thudded in his chest. This was the closest thing to a declaration of love Matt had heard yet. He yearned to hear how much Darian cared. He reached for him again. "Darian…."

Darian jumped off the couch, holding his arm out, separating them. "No. I can't do this." He brought his arms up to cover the sides of his head and started rocking his upper body. "I can't do this, I can't do this."

Matt instinctively wanted to leap off the couch and grab him, comfort him—anything. He swung his legs down, feet ready to bounce, but he sat very still as he tried reasoning. "Darian, please, I know it's hard, but give it some time. I'll help you. I know I can help. I'll listen; I'll be here for you. Whatever you need. We'll get through this together."

Darian flung his arms down. "No!" he screamed. "I don't think we can. I'm using you!" He gasped and covered his mouth with his hand, clearly shocked by his own sudden admission. Slowly, he lowered his hand. He repeated the terrible truth in a soft, grief-stricken voice. "It feels like I'm using you. I know I said I'd stand by you if you came out and we'd be in this together, but that was only because I didn't want *you* using *me*. I was afraid. I'm sorry."

Matt noticed Darian's body shaking. "I wouldn't do that to you," he said.

"I know… I know that now. You aren't like Jamie described at all. Well, not really. Only partially. He mentioned lots of really nice things you did for your mom. I know you have a big heart." A slight curve touched Darian lips, but it quickly faded.

Darian glanced over Matt's shoulder and fear blanketed his expression. "No! Stop! I can't do this," he said again, covering his ears with his hands as if Matt were yelling at him. Darian closed his eyes and turned away, shouting, "Stop looking at me!"

Matt looked back but saw only the wall. Something wasn't right. Was Darian truly losing his mind? He needed to see his therapist; he had to talk to a professional. Matt's brain took a second to catch up to what Darian had said. "Wait…. What?"

Darian's gaze darted around the room, emphasizing how unfocused he was, before he lowered his hands and continued shakily. "Matt. I need… time. I know I said that before, and then I caved because I'm weak. I didn't want to be alone."

"You're not!" Matt leapt up and Darian backed away. "You don't have to be. I'm here. I *want* to be here for you. I *need* to be here for you."

"I can't be with you, Matt. It's too confusing."

"Darian, please," Matt begged. "Don't do this. Give us a chance."

"I am, Matt. If I don't walk away now, there won't be an 'us' to come back to." Tears flowed freely. "I need Dan."

"Jamie's dad? Don't you think you should see a therapist or a counselor? Somebody professional?"

"Maybe. Yeah. Dr. Loundas might help."

Matt hated watching Darian's hands shake. It was nearly impossible to stand in front of him and *not* hold him. He was breathing so hard his chest heaved in front of Matt's eyes like bellows fanning a flame. Matt had never felt so helpless.

"Matt, I don't know what to do. I've been avoiding Dan when all I want to do is go home to him. I deleted his texts without reading them. I don't answer his calls because I'm afraid he won't want me anymore." Darian sounded so pathetic.

"That's not true. Dan told me he loves you. He wouldn't lie about that."

"I know. I read the text he sent this morning. He said, 'I'm still your dad. I miss you.'"

"See." Matt stepped closer, so close he could feel the heat off Darian's body. It felt nice, given how cold Darian had felt last night. He needed to touch Darian now, but he forced himself to stay far enough from him to not cause Darian to back away.

"That's why I have to go," Darian confessed. It was clear he was fully aware of what he was saying. "I need to work this out with him. Dan and I lived together for three years. I need him. Being with you…." He looked directly at Matt. His eyes held affection this time, not fear. "Being with you is like bungee-jumping on narcotics. I'm free falling and warm air buzzes around my skin, stealing my breath and setting my soul on fire from the inside out. I'm scared if I hold on to you until my pain subsides, what I feel for you will fade too. I don't want it to fade. But at the same time, I don't really know *how* I feel about you. Does that make any sense?"

Matt heard a lot of things in Darian's confession. He liked the part where he set Darian's soul on fire. He also liked that Darian didn't want to use him and wanted there to be an "us." But somewhere between his brain and his mouth the wires short-circuited. "You've been bungee-jumping?" Matt asked.

"Matt!"

Matt cursed his stupidity, realizing his response hadn't gone over well.

Darian threw his hands up in the air and turned to leave the room. It was déjà vu. Matt's mind whirled back to that Wednesday when Darian said he "needed time" the first time. Humor was definitely not called for.

Matt grabbed Darian's arms and pulled him close, not letting him wrench free. "Stop," he commanded. Darian instantly stopped thrashing. "I'm not letting you go." And he meant it. Matt looked directly into Darian's eyes and made every word clear—gentle, yet firm. "I get it that you need time to grieve. I also get that fucking you was the biggest mistake I ever made. Not because I regret one second of it, but because we started out so desperate for one another, now it's hard to know what's real and what's not." Matt released his grip on Darian's arms and pulled him lovingly into his body. "I'll give you time, Darian, I will; but you can't walk out that door wondering if all the things I said to you were just a part of some dream. I love you." Matt needed Darian to know for sure. He looked him in the eyes one more time, and said, "I love you, and I want to be with you." Matt only hesitated long enough to decide whether Darian would resist a kiss, and then he leaned in. Their lips met, and Matt felt the heat roll through his body like it always did when he kissed Darian. Pure heaven.

Darian relaxed and wrapped his arms around Matt's neck, making little cooing sounds.

Matt kissed him softly and then pulled back to ask, "Can I date you?"

Darian scrunched his eyes. "What?"

"Can I date you?" he reiterated. "No sex. I promise. I think we need a break. If you need time and space, you got it. But I want to get to know you. All of you, not just this incredible body." He smirked and caressed Darian's back.

Darian blushed and dipped his head. "Really?"

"Yes, really." Matt tilted his head to peer into Darian's shy face. "So, can I date you? Take you to dinner, a movie, and have a meaningful conversation or two?"

"You're serious?"

"Yes, I'm serious. I know we can't base a relationship on sex; I'm not a Neanderthal. We already know we're great in bed together. I want something more. So I'm asking for the chance to build something stronger… with you… when you think you're ready. Is that okay?"

Darian nodded. "But what about your family? Coworkers? They don't know about you. Not really."

Matt took a deep breath and shrugged. "I don't know. I mean… I came out at church. People know. I don't know how the guys at work will react. My boss might be okay with it. I don't know." Satisfied Darian was not going to dash out the door, Matt released his hold on his waist.

"Are you going to say something? Explain stuff? Or just let them find out one day and say, 'Oh yeah, I've been meaning to tell you….'"

Matt snickered. He liked Darian poking fun at him; it meant he felt comfortable enough to do so. Plus, it was a valid point. "I want to wait. Not long, but I need some time to think. If I get fired, I want to have a backup plan. I might do some research and see if they can fire me legally."

"Even if it's illegal to fire you over sexuality, would you *want* to stay? You're a firefighter. What if, in a fire, they abandon you in a tough situation? I heard that stuff really happens. That would be horrible."

Matt was touched. "Don't worry, baby, I'll be okay. But it is one reason I want to wait. I need to feel them out. Some guys, like the volunteers, I hardly know, but others there have been my coworkers for years. I'm not ready to come out at work yet."

"I can respect that."

Matt caressed Darian's cheek. "Thanks." Matt fidgeted. His body was always in conflict with his good sense. He knew if they stood in the apartment much longer they would end up naked. He needed to break the cycle. "Okay, then…," Matt said, stepping back and rubbing his hands together. "Let's get your stuff, and I'll follow you to Dan's house." He held up his hands. "Just to make sure you'll be fine. I'll leave when you want me to, but I said I'd be there to help you face Jamie's room. I'm not backing out on that."

Darian looked relieved. "Thank you."

Matt followed Darian into the bedroom to change his clothes. For the first time, he felt a glimmer of hope.

5

October 6, 2010

MATT sat in his truck. He'd parked in front of the gym fifteen minutes ago but hadn't managed to move from his seat. He looked over at the passenger side. It was empty. Darian was home with Dan, and Matt was alone.

Of course, mentally, Matt understood Darian needed time to work through his loss and decide what he wanted in the future; Matt needed to do the same thing. Only now, dealing with grief seemed like such a solitary place to be.

He had followed Darian to Dan's house and expected to stay and help him pack up some things—maybe some clothes to bring back to his apartment. Or maybe pack up some of Jamie's things so it wouldn't be as tough for Darian to be in that house. But when they arrived, Darian collapsed into Dan's arms, and Matt knew he wasn't needed. He stood in the living room feeling out of place.

Although he had known Jamie his whole life, he didn't feel at home in Jamie's dad's house. As he looked around the room, nothing looked familiar. There were pictures in frames on the wall of Jamie, some of Jamie and Darian, and some of Dan, Jamie, and Darian. Colored pencils and chalk sat on a side table; there were art books on the coffee table. Dan had an awesome fifty-inch HDTV Matt knew nothing about. How long had they owned it? He and Jamie always talked about watching *Lord of the Rings* in high-def, but Jamie never mentioned getting a cool television. *Why?*

You've only been to this house once, you twat. Jamie mostly came to meet you, but you never came here.

Standing in that house, Matt felt guilty for not being fully involved in his friend's life. Jamie was his best friend, yet Matt never took the time to do things with him. Why hadn't Matt come up to visit or go fishing? Jamie loved fishing. Matt felt comfortable enough to invite himself. Why hadn't he? Why hadn't he shown some interest in what Jamie enjoyed? Matt had been so self-involved for so many years.

He felt awful.

When Dan nodded at him, Matt wordlessly left.

Now he sat in the truck, alone and dejected.

Staring at the empty passenger seat, Matt whispered, "Darian, I'm not going to treat you like that. I am interested in your life, and I'm going to be a part of it."

Matt extracted himself from the front seat and headed inside. The gym was quiet this afternoon. Time check: it was well after lunch but not late enough to get the after-work patrons. Matt had most of the place to himself. He was glad. He could stretch before his workout without feeling eyes on him for using the exercise ball. Not long ago when he stretched over the "big ball," he overheard a couple of guys talking about him. They said something about "never using it because it looked gay." What about using the ball was gay? It was a fucking ball! Who cares?

I do. That's why I never use it if people are around. I don't want them calling me gay.

But he was gay, and the ball had nothing to do with it. Matt was "out" and eventually guys would snicker and talk about him whether he stretched on the ball or not. They would call him gay for valid reasons.

Matt closed his eyes and swallowed hard. "Why'd I have to give that speech in church?"

Matt shut the locker door and headed out to the weight room. He passed all the machines he regularly used and went straight to the mats in the back. He found an exercise ball just right for his height and weight and rolled it over beside the mat. After bending over to stretch his thighs and calves, he sat on the edge of the ball and started some simple crunches.

Crunches.

He remembered watching Jamie do crunches one time. Years ago.

Jamie had been going on and on about kissing for some reason and asking all kinds of questions while Matt was doing dumbbell flys. Until Matt read his journals, he had no idea why he asked all those questions. But now, the memory of Jamie moving over to the crunch machine after grilling him flooded his thoughts. Matt had watched him from across the room that day as Jamie did a record eighty-seven crunches.

Eighty-seven crunches!

Matt couldn't believe it. Jamie was not as dedicated as he was to working out. Matt knew he joined the gym only because Matt joined. Jamie did everything he did.

Matt counted crunches and recalled what Jamie wrote.

What do I want? I want sex... well, eventually. What guy doesn't? But I don't want it to be anonymous. I want to know the guy. I want a connection. I want to be intimate with a person I know inside and out. Matt doesn't want that. Matt thinks I'm straight. Matt with his delicious body thinks I'm straight. Fuck him...! Fuck him? Yeah, I'd like to but that's not happening. If Matt is not an option, then Darian is free to pursue. Darian is incredibly sweet. Yeah... Darian. I really like him. I'm gonna stop being a wuss and go for it. I'll ask Darian to be my boyfriend.

Matt felt the burn in his abs, and he stopped. He absently switched positions on the ball and did push-ups. It was considered "girly" to do them with your lower legs on the ball and hands on the floor, but Matt didn't care. The ball was good for balance. He placed his hands in a triangle in front of his face and started counting.

"Jamie," he whispered. "Fuckin' Jamie. No. Fuckin' *me*! I'm the asshole. I should be mad with my own fuckin' self!"

Matt continued his conversation internally as he did his "girly" push-ups. *Why didn't I see this coming? You always tried to please your mom, Jamie, and it never worked. Why didn't I see how much it meant to you? I always thought of Joan as a bitch, but to you, she was your mom. You did too much to please her. You did everything for everybody, and I never realized how much it drained you. What a shitty friend I was!*

Matt rolled onto his back and stretched. He pushed the ball aside and stretched over his legs, arching over to one side and then the other. Matt stood up and then started lunges.

How did I not *see how much you loved me? You constantly came to my rescue. You were there for me through everything. You covered for me when Pastor Dennis questioned you in counseling. You came with me to firehouse picnics so I wouldn't have to explain about not having a girlfriend. You mowed grass for me when I broke my toe and refused to take more than half the money. I'm so fucking stupid.*

Matt chastised himself for half an hour. Even after he finished stretching and started on the free weights, he could not stop thinking of all the opportunities that had passed by and all the things he *might* have done differently. But would it have changed anything? Would changing moments in his past bring Jamie back? No. Jamie was gone.

Matt started crying on the leg extension machine. He was glad no one could see him blubbering like a fool.

MATT went home to an empty apartment. His aunt wasn't due back from her business trip for another few days, and he was thankful. If he talked now, he'd only sob like a girl. He placed his gym bag on the barstool and collapsed on the couch. The apartment was silent. He heard ticking and glanced around. *Where is that fucking sound coming from?* It sounded like a clock. The sound must be coming through the wall from the neighboring apartment. Talk about nerve-racking? He'd have to turn on some John Pizzarelli to keep his ears from fixating on it.

Matt headed to the bedroom, turned on his iPod, and got in the shower.

Showering didn't help. Darian wasn't washing his back. Darian wasn't touching his dick. Darian wasn't molding his slick, soapy body up against Matt's. Of course, thinking about Darian in the shower gave him a raging hard-on, and Matt had to do his own jerking off. It felt good, but it wasn't the same.

His sleep was restless.

MATT returned to work listless and blah. After that first day back, he and Jason hadn't had time to talk about personal stuff. Nobody seemed to know anything about Matt's "speech," so it was easy to carry on as if it never happened.

"Hey, Matt, will you switch with me for Saturday?" Matt heard Scott's voice from somewhere behind him.

He turned and nodded upon making eye contact.

"You sure?" Scott asked, scratching his scraggly beard. "I know you're on nights until then."

Matt shrugged as Scott walked over to him. "My schedule's screwed up anyway. By the fourteenth, it should be back to normal. I think." He liked Scott. He was nice and easy to talk to. He didn't drink too much.

"Thanks. But it's a Sa-tur-day."

"It's cool, really. I haven't made plans on Saturdays for a while now."

Scott's green eyes almost popped their sockets. "Seriously? I thought you liked your midnight excursions to the bars?"

"I used to. Things are different." To prove the point, he took the unused portion of a carton of cigarettes from his cubby and handed them to Scott. "You want these? I quit."

"Seriously?" Scott grinned and took them. "Sure! Thanks. Are you different because you have a girlfriend? You were up all night having sex, right, that's why you look so wasted?"

"What?" Matt looked at Scott sharply.

"Your girlfriend. Jason said you had one. I was glad to hear it. Thought you might be… you know… *gay*." He snickered behind his hand.

Matt fake-laughed for a second before frowning. "Funny." He grimaced. He was so not in the mood for this. And the gossipy crap around the station didn't sit well with him either.

"I know." Scott punched Matt's shoulder. "Imagine that? A big, muscular guy like you, gay?" Scott laughed some more.

Matt was not going to joke about it any longer. "Dude, it's not funny. Do you have a problem with homosexuals? 'Cause my best friend was gay." *I'm gay too, but I'm sure as fuck not telling you.*

Scott's mirth went out like an extinguished candle. "What? Jimmy? Seriously? Fuck me!" He quickly brought up his hand as if warding off Matt's imaginary advances. "I didn't mean that literally. What I meant was… shit. Jimmy was gay? And I liked him."

Matt was trying to discern the look in Scott's eyes. He looked frightened but also repulsed. And maybe like he'd puke. "Dude, you all right? You look sick."

Scott took a step back, and his eyes widened. "If I liked him, does that mean I'm gay? I was friends with a gay guy; that makes me a *gay lover*." He started shaking. "What if the guys start calling *me* a cock sucker? I never sucked cock."

Panic. The look on Scott's face was definitely the embodiment of pure panic. Matt spoke compassionately, "Scott, don't be ridiculous." He reached out but Scott stepped back more.

"I'm not gay, Matt!" he screeched. "I like women. Lots of women. All women. I don't like guys. I liked Jimmy 'cause he was funny and he didn't pound me when I spilled my beer on him that time at Christmas. But that doesn't make me gay, right?"

Watching Scott have a panic attack reminded him of himself years ago when talking to Jamie. Matt panicked when he thought Jamie might inadvertently "out" him to the pastor. He remembered how he couldn't breathe and nearly fell off his chair texting Jamie that afternoon. If he had a video of himself, would he have looked like Scott? Scott's face reflected the same fear those pigs had trapped in that barn fire. Shocked, frantic, and cornered.

Matt could not allow himself to hold onto that level of fear. He knew right then he needed to come out… and soon. The more he held back the truth, the worse the outcome would be. He didn't want to be like Scott. Moreover, he didn't want to treat Darian the way he had treated Jamie. Matt'd forced Jamie to shoulder his burden and keep his secrets, and his life ended tragically. Darian deserved more.

Dare deserves so much more.

Matt stepped forward and gripped Scott's upper arms. "Scott, look at me. You are not gay." He was assertive even though he wasn't

100 percent sure. Scott *did* give off some sort of vibe, but he didn't need to hear that now. Matt spoke slowly so Scott would be sure to hear every word. "Being friends with Jamie does not make you gay. Desiring men, *that* makes you gay. Sleeping with men, *that* makes you gay. Fantasizing about men, *that* makes you gay." *Like me, thinking about Darian.*

Scott pulled away. "Okay, I get your point. Jeez." He took a few deep breaths, staring at his feet. "Thanks," he said looking back up. "Sorry I panicked. It was stupid."

"We've all been stupid. Shit happens." Matt turned back to his locker when the siren went off. According to the dispatcher, it was a medical emergency.

Just another day.

Somehow, each siren made it easier to slip back into his life. He could go another day without telling the chief. Another month. It would be easy. He didn't want to be like Scott anymore, with his anxiety and paranoia, but was he ready to be "that guy"? The guy they all pointed to when he walked into the station and snickered at behind their hands? That was the real question. Would he willingly take the hits?

THAT night, Matt huffed as he tried in vain to sleep. Normally, if he went to the gym and then worked all night, he was tired enough to crash, but not tonight. His mind kept racing. Darian. Work. Church. Jamie. Too much thinking. He also hated the empty bed. It had never bothered him before. Now it did. He pulled the opposite pillow to his face and breathed deeply. "Darian," he sighed and hugged the pillow.

He wanted to text Darian. *Should I text?* He grabbed the phone off his nightstand and fingered the front. He had promised not to text. He had said he'd wait for Darian, but waiting was driving him batty. "Just one text," he reasoned. "What can one text hurt?" Matt jumped as his phone buzzed in his hand.

A text from Darian: *I'm thinking about you.*

Matt smiled and texted back: *I'm thinking about you too. I miss you.*

I miss you too.

:)

:^]

Matt waited for another text but his phone never buzzed. He shut his eyes tightly before his swirling emotions got the best of him and fell asleep with the phone clutched to his chest.

October 17, 2010

OVER a week went by, and Matt was back at church. He'd worked his ass off trying to forget how much he wanted to be with Darian. It didn't work, but it did make him tired enough not to go crazy waiting for one more text. He barely found the time to sleep, let alone visit his family. He felt guilty for not calling his mom, but what could he do? Work was work, and Matt used it to block everything else out. When he wasn't at the fire station, he was splitting wood for Mr. Walsh at his second job. He was a busy guy!

In the sanctuary, Matt walked around the pews and took a seat next to his mom. She smiled and patted his hand. "You're still coming over after church, right?" she asked. She was not as standoffish as she had been earlier. Matt was grateful.

"Yeah."

"You said that last weekend and didn't show."

"I told you, Aunt Peg's tire blew on the way back from the airport, and she asked me to come get her. And then I worked on Sunday," Matt answered as he opened his bulletin and stood as the choir director prompted. "I'm sorry."

"I understand. I do. I'm glad you could be there for her." The congregation was singing, but the two of them were still talking. "It's just that I haven't seen you in a while and I've missed you." His mom got some stares from two ladies to her right, and she nudged Matt with her elbow.

Matt glanced over and then gave her a grin. "I've missed you too. Where's Dad?" he asked.

"He's taking up the offering this week. He's in the back."

Matt nodded in response. He'd started singing along with "Be Thou My Vision" when his phone buzzed. Adrenaline surged as he retrieved it and read the text.

"Matt, put that away!" his mom scolded.

Matt ignored her. It was from Darian. It read, *"Hi."*

Elated, he typed: *Hi back :) It's been so long. I hope you've been okay. Miss you.* He thought that was good—not too desperate. He would play it casual. Casual was more appropriate than doing a happy dance in church.

"Matt!" his mom hissed. "We're in church for goodness sake. Put that phone away!" She turned the page of her bulletin as the congregation started on the next praise song.

Matt *had* to wait for Darian's reply. Endless days of nothing was seriously driving him insane.

Darian texted: *I miss you too. I think about you all the time.*

Me too. Can I see you soon? Can I call? I miss your voice.

No. Not yet. Please don't call. Dan thinks I need some distance from you.

Oh? :(Matt didn't like hearing that. If Dan wanted him to stay away, then it could be who-knows-how-long until Matt got to see Darian again.

I know. But I think he has good reasons. I went to see my therapist on Saturday.

Good.

"Matt!" His mother's stern gaze told him he had to stop or else.

Matt... I'm touching myself, read the next text.

Matt's balls shifted; it was time to "adjust" things. He could not afford for Darian to say one more word. His mom was standing right there! *Oh fuck... I'm in church, Dare. Please don't say anything else.*

Oh sorry :\ Talk later?

I'll be at my parent's house. I'll text when I can. I love you.

:+]

Matt placed his phone back in his pocket as the congregation sat down for the morning announcements. His mom leaned in. "Make sure that thing stays in your pocket!"

He rolled his eyes at her. "Yeeess, Motheeer."

His mom's glare softened into a smirk all too easily. She patted his knee and all was right with the world.

AFTER church, at the Dixon home, nothing had changed. They sat around the table eating roast beef and mashed potatoes much as they had for years. His brother and sister made faces at each other like normal and stuck out their tongues coated with food (when their father wasn't looking, of course). Steven rolled his eyes at Matt and silently mimicked his sister's every sentence, which made her angry. It was almost as if Matt's "speech" was forgotten. *Wouldn't that be nice?*

"Mom!" Hannah bellyached. "He's doing it again!"

Matt giggled. He loved how close they were. The three years that separated Hannah and Steven seemed a lot less than the four years between Hannah and him. But then, Matt was the oldest and shouldered all the responsibility. Sometimes he envied their ability to simply be kids. If you could call a nineteen- and a sixteen-year-old kids.

"Can you pass me the salt?" his dad asked. Matt handed it over and watched as his father shook copious amounts onto his potatoes while his mom glared. "I take pills for this, Linda. If I want salt, I'm using salt."

Matt's mom huffed. "And when you have a heart attack, don't come whining to me."

Matt snickered. He loved the way his parents jibed and bickered. It was never malicious—only good clean fun. He took a long swallow of sweet tea and felt his phone buzz in his pocket. "Will you excuse me? I need to use the bathroom."

His dad gave him a look. "So? Go. You don't have to announce it."

Matt left the room and swiftly ran upstairs where he could check his message in private. Darian wrote: *Still in church?*

Matt responded: *No. Eating at my parents' house, but I can text for a few minutes.* Matt wiped the sweat from his brow, and texted: *God, I've missed you. Do you know how hard it is to WAIT for a text?*

Darian texted back: *Yeah, I do. I've been trying to find time alone. I'm never alone. Even at night I feel like I'm being watched.*

I'm glad you found time. Matt smiled while his fingers pressed the keys. *I've wanted to talk to you so many times; touch you, so many times.*

There was a pause and then, *What are you wearing today?*

Matt almost laughed out loud and mused, "Oh God, Darian. You're not subtle are you?" He texted back: *Black jeans and a button-down shirt.* Matt took a seat on the closed toilet lid. Darian was texting him, and Matt was jittering with excitement.

Color?

Blue plaid. You?

Nothing.

Matt's groin pulsed. *Nothing?*

Nothing.

Matt closed his eyes and conjured up a mental image of that beautiful white skin stretched out across his bed. God, he loved that skin.

Another text from Darian: *I have a dildo.*

Matt's pulse quickened. He sat up straight and rubbed his genitals through his jeans. *What are you doing with it?*

What do you want me to do?

"Oh fuck!" Matt stood up, unbuttoning his jeans and shoving them down. He palmed his erection through his cotton briefs and then replied: *Tease your hole, baby. Tease your hole and slide it in.*

There was a long pause before Matt got a response. *Done. It's tight. Now what?*

Matt's mouth watered. *Slowly fuck yourself. Are you on your back, or your knees?*

Knees. This is really difficult. I want it to be you pushing it inside of me.

Wow, what a mental image! *You want me to use toys on you?*

Pause. Maybe Darian was reconsidering? Matt was relieved when he texted back: *Yes. Is that okay?*

Oh hell yeah! I was hesitant to ask you, but yeah, I'm into it.

Me too. I can't do this and text. Can I call?

No. I'm in the bathroom. They'll hear me. I'll text. You read.

K.

Matt opened the toilet seat, stepped out of his pants and briefs, and straddled the bowl. He'd had phone sex before with a 1-900 number, but text sex was a new one. And for Darian to want the same things as he did? Matt was turned on even more. *Slide it in and out, baby. Picture me holding it. 69. You have your mouth on my cock and I'm fucking you with the dildo.*

Matt grabbed his erection and stroked. He paused only long enough to send another text, and then continued fondling himself. *I'm picturing you, Darian. I see your mouth around me. Milking me. I feel your tongue piercing gliding up my length. NO CONDOMS!*

Oh Matt. I want that. I want to taste you.

You've got me all the way down your throat. My big, hot cock is thrusting deep while I'm pumping your ass with the dildo. I'm twisting it, Darian. Do you feel it? I'm working it inside your tight hole.

I feel it.

Oh Darian. Baby. I can see us on my bed. On our sides. I lift your leg over my shoulder as I move closer. I remove the dildo and replace it with my fingers.

Yeah?

I slowly work in two fingers... pumping, twisting... then three... four fingers and you're panting. Matt closed his eyes briefly and stopped moving his hand. The image his mind conjured up was moving him along to orgasm too quickly. He swallowed hard. His testicles tingled. It was too late. He couldn't stop from ejaculating. As he felt the pleasure surging he quickly jerked over the toilet, keeping his splattering to a minimum. *Mom wouldn't like to find cum on the wall!*

Matt rinsed his hand and read Darian's next text. *Then what?*

Matt paused before responding. "Then what?" he asked himself. His fantasy was taking him to places he hadn't discussed with Darian before. What would Darian think? According to Jamie, their sexual relationship was pretty bland—strictly vanilla. *What if Dare doesn't like Rocky Road?* He decided to take the chance.

Next, I rotate those four fingers slowly... back and forth... until you relax and open up for me. I work my hand gently into you, Darian. The muscles fight me, but I'm persistent. Slowly.... Carefully.... Tenderly, I twist my hand and squeeze my knuckles together, pressing my thumb into my palm until my hand disappears. Then... I'm inside of you, feeling your warmth, and I hear you gasp my name.

Wait... you're... fisting me?

Matt was nervous. What if that freaked him out? *Yes, Darian. I'm up to my wrist feeling every bit of you. Does that scare you?*

Long pause. *No.*

Relief washed over him. *Really? Would you let me do that?*

I think so. I just came thinking about it.

Wow. Dare... wow! I've never thought about something like that before. But with you... Darian, I want to know you so intimately that the possibilities between us are limitless.

I think I want that too. But what about your comment, "I know we can't base our relationship on sex?"

Darian had a point. Matt was indeed worried about the sexual intensity they shared, but in light of the last ten minutes, what could he say? He wanted it all! He answered: *Well, I guess I need to revise it. What you and I have feels different. You know? The things I want to try with you aren't exactly casual sex types of things. Like fisting. That's serious stuff. I've known guys who got their rectums torn badly. If you go too fast and too hard, you can mess up your colon. That's one reason I never tried it before. It has to be done with someone you trust.*

You trust me that much?

Yes. Do you trust me?

I do, Darian responded.

Yeah? Oh Darian, I never thought I'd feel like this. And to think you aren't scared to try something so kinky. I guess I'm shocked that you're into it. I was hoping you would be. I would never have pictured Jamie doing anything like that.

Matt finished wiping off his genitals and pulled up his jeans. He tucked in his shirt and studied his reflection before he realized Darian had not responded. *Darian? You okay? I didn't mean to imply anything bad about Jamie.*

No. It's okay, I gotta go.

Dare. I'm sorry.

I gotta go.

Matt closed his phone and hung his head. "Stupid. Stupid, stupid, stupid!" he berated himself and then went back downstairs.

6

"DIRTY little fucking whore!" Jamie screamed at him as Darian washed his dildo in the sink. "You just couldn't wait to use your toys and think of him up your ass!" His face was red with anger and spittle flew in white clumps.

Darian closed his eyes.

"Look at me when I talk to you!"

Darian's eyes flew open, but Jamie's apparition was gone.

He panted. Placing the nine-inch silicone penis in the basin, he leaned against the wall and slid to the floor. His nightmares were getting worse. He could almost smell Jamie in the room this time. And when Jamie yelled, Darian's ears hummed. It was harsh and loud and so terrifying Darian was left stunned. He'd seen Jamie four or five times since the first time in Matt's apartment. Each time, Jamie grew angrier and his insults harsher. Darian was stuck between insanity and wondering if ghosts were real.

Should he ask his therapist? He was afraid if he told Dr. Loundas, she might lock him away for being so absurd. Ghosts weren't real. Or were they? He didn't know. All he knew was every time he thought about Matt, Jamie would show up and yell at him for it.

Darian crawled out of the bathroom and staggered back to the couch in the living room. He couldn't go in Jamie's room yet. He was scared. Too much in there to remind him of everything they had shared. Darian pulled the blankets over his head and started crying. It wasn't like he could fight the tears; they were an everyday occurrence for him. Every day, all day, and sometimes all throughout the night.

Dan had comforted him a few times, but really there was nothing to be done. Darian needed to work through it on his own. He was the one who couldn't face their room. He was the one who imagined Jamie haunting him at every turn. He was the one who wanted nothing more than to drive to Eldersburg and fling himself into Matt's waiting arms!

"Little whore!" He heard Jamie's raspy voice.

His eyes popped open, and he saw Jamie under the blankets with him. He was holding a hunting knife in front of Darian's face as he pressed Darian's shoulder against the pillow. Jamie shoved Darian's legs apart with his knees and pressed his groin up against Darian's. "Hard for him? I always knew you were a slut. First chance you got, I knew you'd run to him and beg to be fucked. I was never enough."

"That's not true," Darian whimpered, eyeing the sharp blade. "I never thought about cheating on you."

"I won't give you the chance!" Jamie sneered. He lowered the knife and with a flick of his wrist, sliced open the front of Darian's jeans. "You'll have nothing left to suck!"

Darian watched in frozen horror as Jamie grabbed his exposed manhood and pulled it away from his body, impossibly far, before slipping the knife under his balls.

Sharp pain shot through his groin, and Darian sat upright, gasping for breath. No one was in the room. He heard the ice machine in the refrigerator dump a load of ice. He jumped. Darian pushed the blankets aside and examined his crotch. He rubbed his genitals. Everything was normal.

He flopped back down and stared at the ceiling. "I can't do this."

He needed something. He jumped up and hurried to the kitchen. Darian needed something to stop the pain—something to stop his overactive imagination. He went to the utility drawer and opened it. Inside he found a box of brand-new razor blades.

"No drugs. I promised Jamie no drugs," he rationalized. "No drugs."

He went into the hall bathroom and looked into the mirror. His red eyes and gaunt expression told him how much sleep he wasn't getting.

"Just a few lines. It has to work."

He looked at his wrist. *Too obvious.* He took off his shirt. *This will do.*

He washed the blade off with hot water and soap.

Holding it against his skin, right between two ribs, Darian hesitated, not allowing a cut even though he remembered the sensation from years before. Or maybe it was because of those earlier years that he held still? He knew what cutting did to him. He remembered the sensation of pain and the rush of adrenaline that flooded his chest. To inflict injury on oneself took conviction and fear mixed with desperation and need.

Darian needed to feel something, anything; he wanted desperately to rid his mind of the guilt eating away at him.

It was a new blade with an edge that could slice through paper as easily as a steak knife through butter. Yet merely touching it to the surface of his skin did nothing. He needed to apply pressure. At this point, his heart raced, knowing it took conscious effort to pierce his skin. He felt the corner of the metal tear at his flesh. Pain. A little pain. Not much pain. He needed more.

"I am a dirty little whore, Jamie. I'm sorry. I deserve to be punished."

He pressed the sharp edge down and the flesh gave way, spilling blood down his side. He gasped. The pain was distantly familiar. He remembered how good it felt back then. He pulled the blade away and repositioned it for another line. More blood flowed.

"Ahhh!" He sucked in a quick breath.

After three lines he stopped. His hands were shaking, and his side burned from the pain. He inspected his work in the mirror. Not too deep. He didn't need stitches. No one would know.

Then Jamie was behind him… smiling.

7

MATT hadn't missed anything while he was upstairs sexting. The family still ate. The family still bickered. The family was oblivious to him having text sex with his gay lover. They even overlooked his forlorn expression as he worried over what he'd commented about Jamie. They carried on like normal.

Matt sighed and stabbed a hunk of roast beef.

LATER his mother asked, "Matt, can you help me with the dishes?"

Matt's dad piped in from the other room. "Game starts in a minute, Linda. Don't keep him. Ravens are in New England."

Matt yelled back, "I'll be fast, Dad. I'll grab some beers on the way."

"Good."

Matt jumped aside as Steven ran past with his sister on his heels.

"Give me that back, you little weasel!" she yelled.

"No. You have to catch me first," Steven cackled back.

Matt grinned and joined his mother. "So… what's been on your mind?" He was still down, thinking about Darian; he hoped talking to his mom would get his mind off his troubles.

She set the glass she was washing down. "I don't know how to talk about this, Matt. It is just so disturbing."

"What?" Matt stroked her shoulder, trying to tell her through touch she could say anything.

"Well...," she started hesitantly, "ever since Jimmy... when he... I've been thinking. And then you gave that speech. I don't know what to say about that. But I've been thinking. I never considered how disapproval can be construed as hatred. For a young man to feel so lost with no other options than to take his own life...." She looked at Matt with tears in her eyes. "Oh, Matt."

He pulled her into a hug. "It's okay, Mom. I know how you feel."

She stepped back and wiped her eyes. "No, you don't." She picked up some dishes and put them in the dishwasher. "How could you? You don't have a son. I've lain awake countless nights thinking how it could have been *you*. What if *you* were the one who felt so ostracized you had no other option?"

Matt started to shake his head. "Mom, I—"

"Let me finish." She wiped her eyes with the back of her hand and continued, "I was at the salon last week. Your dad told me to get a pedicure or something; anything to get my mind off the stress I feel. I went. They had the television on, and Ellen DeGeneres was talking about several suicides that happened recently."

Matt was shocked. "Several?" He usually kept up with the news, but he'd been too distracted lately. Time slipped by, and suddenly, it had been weeks since he watched CNN or any local channels. (Because they certainly didn't watch CNN at work!)

"Yes. Apparently Jimmy wasn't the only one who felt bullied and misunderstood."

"That wasn't exactly the reason he did it." Matt couldn't tell her the truth, but he couldn't let her be misled either.

"You said it was over fear of intolerance!"

"Yeah, but there was more to it than that. I just meant he wasn't bullied in school for being gay. Not really." He didn't want to talk about what he read about Jamie's mom in the journals. "You said there were other suicides. Really?"

"You didn't know?" Matt shook his head. She continued; looking out the kitchen window, she expressed her unrest. "Ellen said there were at least six children nationally who took their own lives in the last month. Jimmy would make it seven. All gay youths who thought suicide was the only option to escape the ruthless and unending taunts from their peers." She glanced his way. "I was a youth director for more than seven years."

Matt grinned. "Oh yeah, I remember. The middle schoolers loved you for your wackiness."

His mom did not share his mirth. "I know how hard growing up is for adolescents. So many times one of them would say, 'I'm ugly' or 'I'm stupid' or 'I'm fat,' and I would show them a Bible verse to explain how God loved them just the way they were. Each and every one of those kids was important and loved. But until now, I never thought about the children who struggled with their sexuality. I never considered how hard it might be for them to walk around and feel different, yet have no one to confide in, no one to tell them God loved them. Gay teens don't open up about their fears, do they? They stuff them inside as they try and hide from cutting remarks. Rotting away." His mom gazed at him and cupped his cheeks with both hands. "Was it like that for you? Did you hide away in your room and pray to God I'd never find out?"

"Mom…." Matt choked up from her deep concern.

"Was I that insensitive?"

He was tearing up. "No, Mom. I just…. I was scared. I didn't understand why none of the boys I knew wanted to play dress-up. They wanted to play with trucks. So I played with trucks. It didn't take long to realize I wasn't like them. Jamie was my best friend, and I didn't want to tell him the things that went through my mind. He found out about me by accident."

"What kinds of things?" Her hands eased off his face, to his shoulders, and down his arms. So far she wasn't put off by the conversation, even though Matt was. He'd never imagined talking to her so candidly.

"I don't know…," he forced himself to continue. "Things like kissing Brian Rafferty in the third grade when he was pouting over getting picked last for relays."

"Third grade?" Her voice went up an octave.

Okay, shock slipping into the mix now!

"Yeah. Third grade. I've always been attracted to boys, Mom. And I've also known it wasn't normal, at least not normal like the world thinks of normal. It was only normal for me. I tried fantasizing about girls, but they always ended up having penises."

His mom choked back a laugh and covered her mouth. "Oh dear."

Even Matt giggled. "See. Not normal. But at the same time… normal. I liked boys, so I knew I was gay. Gay at the age of eight."

"Eight." She repeated the age as if trying to convince herself she heard him correctly. "What about Jimmy? When did he know?"

"I'm not sure. I tried talking him out of it in tenth grade. I think it happened because he fell in love with Darian Weston."

"The boy at the funeral?"

"Yes."

"So it's *his* fault?"

Anger surged as it had after the funeral when Joan Smithers talked down about Darian. Matt didn't like it then, and he wasn't going to let anyone talk bad about Darian now—not even his mother! "No! You can't blame this on Darian. None of this is because of Darian. Jamie loved him. He was happy with him. They were going to get married, Mom. Don't you dare blame this on him!"

She gently grabbed hold of both his arms. "Matt, calm down. I didn't mean it was Darian's fault Jimmy killed himself. I only meant he was the boy who turned Jimmy's head. Correct?"

Now he was embarrassed about his outburst. Matt nodded. "Yeah. Jamie didn't know what he wanted for a really long time. He was content just being Jamie. Then one day he met Darian, and I think his world flipped over and not all in a good way."

His mother stared into his eyes, unblinking. Worry passed over her face, and she pulled away from him, taking a seat at the table.

"Mom? Are you all right?" He sat in the chair next to her and took her hand. Her eyes were blank, and Matt knew she was processing something. "Mom?"

"Joan."

With that one-word response, Matt knew she was putting the pieces together. He squeezed her hand.

"Joan hated homosexuals." Her voice was hushed. "She told me years ago she had a bad experience in college—something about a girl in her dorm room. She never got over it." She looked wide-eyed at Matt. "Did Jimmy know?"

"About the college thing? I don't think so. About her hatred of gays? Yeah."

"That must have been so hard for him."

"It was. In fact—"

His mom rose abruptly. "I don't think I want to hear any more right now." She headed toward the door. "You need to go have fun with your father. You still like football, don't you?" She shook her head and answered her own question. "Of course you do. I need to lie down."

No sooner did she leave the room than his father walked in. "Where's your mother?"

"She went to lie down."

His dad looked briefly around the room as if he was searching for something. "Then what are you still doing in here? You said you'd bring me a beer and watch the game. So… get me a beer and get your pansy-ass in the living room. Pronto!"

Matt stood up and went to the fridge. "You're okay with it then?"

"Okay with what? Missing the game? Or yelling at the wide receiver by myself?"

Matt hesitated. He wasn't sure if his dad's gruff behavior was from denial or a genuine irritation over the football game. He snagged a Dogfish Head IPA out of the fridge and handed it to his father. "Here, Dad. I'll grab some Doritos and be right in." He forced a smile.

"Good," he said. He uncapped the beer and took a swig before leaving the room.

Matt took the Doritos out of the cabinet and opened the bag. *I don't know what he thinks about me, but at least he hasn't kicked me out. I guess I'll work on one parent at a time.*

October 22, 2010

"HEY Mom," Matt said as he walked into the kitchen. His mom was on her laptop at the kitchen table. She jumped.

"Oh my! Matt, what are you doing here?"

"Nice greeting." Matt sauntered over to the counter.

"You know what I mean. Why aren't you working or at Aunt Peggy's?"

Matt took a glass out of the cabinet and filled it with juice. "I was. I worked until ten this morning, and then I went home. But Aunt Peggy has a 'friend' over"—he made quote marks in the air—"for the weekend, and I didn't want to chance hearing them having sex."

"Matt! Don't be vulgar."

"I'm not," he squawked. "I didn't describe the sex. I just used the word."

"Well don't. I'm still having a hard time thinking of you as an adult. I don't need to hear you using grown-up terms."

"What—*sex*? Mom, you have to be joking? You know I've had sex before."

She abruptly stood and pushed the chair out of her way. "I can't hear this." She put her fingers in her ears and sang, "La-la-la…."

Matt leaned against the counter, amused. He felt the inexplicable desire to see how far he could go with this. Why was his mom acting so paranoid? Her face was flushed, and she seemed about as nervous as a long-tailed cat in a room full of rocking chairs. "Mom, think about it. I'm a good-looking, twenty-three-year-old, single, gay male; I've had sex. Lots of sex."

She covered her face with her hands. Was she going to vomit? "With men," she whispered.

"Yes, Mom. Men."

When she moved her hands from her face she looked absolutely green. Her eyes were closed. "You've had… anal sex… with men." Her words were slow and deliberate, as if she could not believe she was saying them. Matt saw her throat bob as she swallowed.

"Yes," he answered with the same deliberate tone she used.

"Oh God." She slumped back down into the chair and covered her face again.

Matt rushed over. "Mom, it's no big deal."

"No big deal?" She turned her frantic expression his way. "No big deal? Matt, more than three thousand men your age have AIDS due to having sex with other men."

Matt wondered what she was talking about until he noticed her computer screen. There was a graph showing the number of new HIV infections per year, categorized by age and race. "Mom, what are you looking at?" He reached for her computer.

"Don't—" she tried to warn, but it was too late.

As she reached out her hand to stop him, Matt swiped four fingers down the track pad of her computer. Seven separate screens appeared. He'd told her two years ago to fix it so each click opened a new tab, but she hadn't listened. Now he could see all the Web pages she was browsing in one swipe. She covered her face again—presumably in shame—while he looked them over. Centers for Disease Control and Prevention was the first page he read. After that was aolhealth.com and an article from October the twelfth on "The Surge in Gay Teen Suicide." "Gay Life" on about.com—something about gay men and bareback sex. Matt shook his head. "Oh, Mom." He felt bad for her. This *had* to be a lot to take in all at once. Matt could not tear his eyes away. He clicked on a screen and read out loud, "How to have gay sex by Ramon Johnson. Are you ready for sex? Chances are if you're reading this, your body is ready to seal the deal. But are you ready emotionally? Have you prepared to top, bottom, or looked into other ways to be intimate, like frottage"—*who the fuck uses the word frottage?*—"rimming, or oral sex?" He closed the page and looked at his mom. She was very still and quiet, staring at the table.

Matt's mind whirled. "You don't have to put yourself through this. You can just ask me what you want to know."

"I don't know how, Matt. It makes me ill to think about you having sex with… men."

Matt could hear her anguish. And the way she wouldn't look at him, either, was disheartening. She sat with her hands in her lap, quiet, head bowed. It was obvious she was concerned for his health because of the types of Web sites she was searching, but there had to be more to it than that. "Mom, I assure you I am very careful." She didn't move.

"Mom, please don't shut me out. We've always been able to talk about stuff."

She looked up sharply. "When? When have we talked about anything?"

"Lots of times. We talk about church and how Dad isn't happy with the music. We talk about your friend Rachel and her extracurricular activities." He grinned. "And we talk about your involvement with the school PTA and—"

"But these things are not about *you*," she said. "We gossip. We talk about the weather and the children and my hair appointments and the fire department. But when do I get to hear about you? When do I get to learn about who my son is?" She started crying. "I feel like I don't know who you are."

Guilt gripped him. Guilt. Always guilt. So much guilt one would think he'd been raised Catholic. In all the years he'd kept everything to himself, Matt never thought about what his secrets would do to his mom when they finally came out. "I'm still the same person."

"Are you? I'm not so sure," she cried. "I think I learned more about you over the years from Jimmy than I did from you. I was so foolish to think you were being responsible and wise in your decisions. I'm such a horrible mother." Her body quaked with her sobbing.

Matt felt dreadful. He could not recall his mom ever being so emotional. She was normally strong. Caring—yes, but weepy—no. How could he explain it had nothing to do with her ability as a mother? "Mom, please. I was responsible. I always made good decisions." His "incident" came to mind and he corrected himself saying, "Well, mostly. And Jimmy didn't know everything either. I kept everything inside. Mom…."

"Why?" Her eyes searched his face. "Was I so untrustworthy? Did you think I wouldn't love you?"

He didn't want to say it. Matt looked into her pleading, tear-filled eyes and held back the word as long as he could. "Yes."

"Oh, Matt!" His mom flung her body against his and hugged him tightly. "I'd never stop loving you. You're my son. I love you so much. Don't ever think that."

Matt hugged her back. “I love you too, Mom. I’m sorry.” He held her for a long time. She rubbed his back and kept her face tucked against his neck until she stopped crying. Then she sat back, wiping her eyes and nose. “I really am sorry,” Matt said sincerely. “I never meant to hurt you.”

“I’m sorry too. I never wanted you to think you couldn’t come to me with something like this.”

“It wasn’t that. I knew I could talk to you; I just didn’t. It took me years to accept what I felt. I knew I was gay, but for a long time, I didn’t want to be. I acted like all the guys I saw in school. I became what I thought people wanted me to be: the jock, Mr. Popular. It was easier to keep everything separate. Being gay was the part of me no one saw. I only started freaking about it when Jamie was talking to Pastor Dennis. By then, my life was sweet. I had my cake, and I was eating it too.”

Using such a trite cliché made them both chuckle a bit, relieving some tension.

“I didn’t plan for things to get so mixed up,” he said.

His mom smiled and caressed his cheek. “I know, honey. It’s been hard on all of us. I can’t imagine going through what you’ve been through. But I love you.” She squeezed his neck. “I’m just having a hard time picturing you with a man. *Doing it* with a man.”

“Mom!” Matt screeched, jumping back in his chair. “Don’t picture me at all! That’s gross. You don’t go around picturing your friends ‘doing it’ do you?”

She considered his shock. “Well… no.”

“Then don’t picture me! That’s like… perverted and shit.”

“Matt, language.”

“Whatever…. Mom, if you’re ‘picturing’ me having sex, no wonder you’re getting sick! Don’t! Okay?” He could not stress it enough. “Because if I think you are, I won’t be able to look you in the eyes when I finally muster the nerve to bring a guy home.”

“Oh my.” She put her head in her hands briefly and then looked up again. “Is there a guy? Do you have a steady boyfriend?” She held up her hand. “No. Don’t answer that.” She lowered her hand. “I take it back. I want to know. Is there?”

"Yes. No. Maybe." He exhaled noisily. "That's still up for debate. It's complicated." His mom's face now showed concern, which actually felt pretty good. Then he thought of Darian. *Is there a guy?* If he was honest with himself, he truly wanted there to be one. "Yeah… there's a guy."

"Do you… love him?" He loved how her voice lost its shrillness. It was soft and soothing. Maybe he should have told her how he felt years ago.

"Yes. I do. I love him. I've never felt like this before. He's amazing." Matt had been working through his feelings for weeks now, wondering if it were true. Did he truly love Darian? Confessing it to his mom made everything seem so real and feel so right.

"Then what's so complicated?" she asked.

Now Matt was having yet another unbelievable conversation with his mom. It was so… freeing not to hide and keep everything bottled up. "It's complicated because he was with someone for a really long time; now that someone is gone, and I don't want to be the rebound guy."

"Oh."

"So we're taking things slow for now. I haven't seen him for a few weeks. He texts me, but so far we haven't even spoken on the phone. I really miss his voice."

"His voice," she repeated with a grin.

Matt smiled back. He loved the way her face lit up. He really did love his mother. "Yeah. That sounds so corny, but I do. And I miss his hands. And his smile. And his eyes. I miss the way he kisses my neck and snuggles up really close to me when he's asleep." He looked down at his hands in his lap, gliding his fingers over each other, wishing for Darian's fingers to caress. When he looked up, his mother was smirking at him. "What?"

"I've just never heard you talk about anyone before. It's nice. I like to see that shine in your eyes."

Matt knew his face got red. He knew it! He suddenly felt like a sappy schoolgirl being confronted about her crush on the captain of the football team. "Wait until you meet him, then you'll understand. He just has this 'something' about him. There's an inexplicable magic in the way he melts right into me. It's weird. I think Darian is the sweetest person I've ever met."

Instantly her demeanor changed. "Darian? You don't mean Jimmy's Darian, do you? Oh, Matt...." She shook her head in disapproval.

Matt closed his eyes. He'd said too much. He could have stopped several minutes ago, but he was caught up in the enjoyment of talking about Darian with his mom. How could he explain this one? "Mom. It's not what you think."

"I think you're taking advantage of a hurting young man, that's what I think. I saw him at the funeral. He's adorable. He's also emotionally devastated, as displayed by his actions at the gravesite. Matt, you couldn't possibly think he's simply going to forget everything he had with Jimmy and cleave to you? It will never last."

"But Mom, that's not—"

"Do you think it would be that easy for me if I lost your father? Do you? If I was approached only a few days or weeks after the funeral, I may seek comfort with another man, but it would never last. Relationships born out of grief dissolve quickly. You have to see that?"

Matt hung his head. He knew this. He feared this. He'd met the perfect person but at the wrong time. "I know."

She touched his hair. "I'm sorry."

Matt stood up and headed somberly toward the door. "I'm gonna crash here this weekend. You don't mind, right?"

"We leave your room the way it is because you always have an open invitation to come back."

"If Aunt Peg and her boyfriend go at it for a while, I might just do that."

His mom smiled. "I'd like that."

MATT went to his old room. Sure enough, it was just as he'd left it.

He came to his parents' house practically every Sunday, but he didn't think about going to his room. For the last few years, "his room" meant the one he had at Peggy's. This was his parents' house. He ate here and watched sports with his dad. That was it.

Being back in this room felt like he was in high school again.

His track trophies lined his dresser. Pictures of him and Jamie littered his desk. And one *Lord of the Rings* poster still hung on his wall. Legolas. Matt grinned. He used to be such a dreamer. He was the warrior, and Jamie was his sidekick. Matt picked up a few pictures and took them over to the nightstand as he toed off his shoes.

"I miss you, man. So much has changed. I can't fucking believe it."

Matt crawled into bed thinking about everything.

Would things have been different if he hadn't forced Jamie to keep his secrets? What if he had kissed Jamie that day playing Xbox? What if he had admitted to liking Nick Barrett in tenth grade? What if he had taken dance class in middle school instead of track? How much different would his life have been? Would this thing with Darian fade into nothing? Was he really taking advantage of Jamie's fiancé?

"Yes! You know the answer's yes to that one." He was so angry with himself. "Maybe it would have been easier if I'd come out sooner," he whispered. It was easier to feel guilty in the dark about all those things in the past he wished he'd done differently. "When did life get so complicated?"

If he was honest, it was in middle school. *Middle school.... It could have changed everything.*

8

MATT dropped his skateboard by the front door. School had let out early for some freak teacher conference or something. It didn't matter. What mattered was it only applied to middle school. (That never happened.) Matt was jazzed. He was home alone on a Friday afternoon—no brat siblings to drive him crazy!

Jamie had some chores to do or something. *Leave it to Ms. Joan to give him chores when he has a half day!* But even if Jamie couldn't come over, it was still fun to have time to himself.

Matt wandered into the kitchen and looked around. Hmm, what to get into? He shrugged off his backpack and sweatshirt and walked over to the fridge. Nothing good in there. He closed the fridge and walked to the cabinet. Cookies! At least he'd found them before Steven had. He grabbed the new bag and opened it on his way to the living room. He plopped onto the sofa and hit the remote for the stereo.

Michael Card. It had to be his mom's! His dad listened to Duke Robillard and Lynyrd Skynyrd. Matt's mom liked different styles of music, but lately she listened to a lot of Christian contemporary.

Matt leaped up and promptly exchanged the CD for Third Day. Christian Rock was cool. Matt didn't mind it. They had a great sound and good lyrics. He would have put on Staind, if he had it downstairs, but that CD was under the bed last he saw it, and listening to it now meant going all the way upstairs. He couldn't be bothered; he had cookies to eat.

He turned the sound up and trudged back to the fridge to grab the milk.

AFTER fifteen minutes and half a bag of cookies, Matt was done lounging on the couch. *What else can I do?* He put the lid back on the milk and placed it back in the fridge.

"What do I always want to do and never can because people are home?" Matt tapped his chin. He had one idea that would kill about six minutes! He sprinted up the steps and locked the bathroom door.

With his jeans around his ankles, Matt shook hands with his little buddy. The two of them rarely had a moment's peace. Before that first day, years ago, when Brian Rafferty's pout made things stir, Matt had never dreamed the two of them would enjoy so much private time together. Especially in the past few years! Private time in the bathroom became more than simply marveling at what his body could do.

Matt knew Jamie's penis did things too. They showed each other at camp one year and shared a laugh. But the activities he enjoyed now, Matt kept to himself. He wasn't sure if he *should* show Jamie what happened when you touched it this long. Jamie might freak out! No… Matt thought this private stuff should be just for him.

"Although if Brian Rafferty wanted to watch, I'd let him. Or better yet, maybe I'd ask to touch *his* penis."

Thinking of another boy always made the end come too quickly.

Matt pulled up his pants and washed off his hands.

"Now what?" Matt sighed. "I wish Jamie was here."

He strolled into the hallway and opened his parents' bedroom door. He knew he wasn't supposed to be in there, but for some reason his mother's things always fascinated him. *She's not here. She won't know.*

Matt strolled over to her dressing bureau. He fingered her silver hairbrush. Dad gave it to her for Christmas last year. Matt really liked it. He remembered feeling jealous. He picked it up and ran it over his curly blond hair. The fine teeth of the brush separated each individual shaft from the roots out; the result was a bushy mess. Matt exhaled loudly. He laid the brush back down and tried to flatten his hair with his hands. Which didn't work.

He glanced around in frustration and spied a hair clip. A hair clip? He reached over and snagged it. He remembered his mom twisting her hair and clipping it to the back of her head. Matt mimicked her hand movements and after a couple tries managed to clip his hair in a bun on the back of his head. He smiled at his reflection.

"Mom also puts on makeup," he mused.

He opened her makeup case and pushed the various items around with his index finger. Hmm…. He pulled out the blue eye shadow and brown mascara. The lipstick choices were difficult. Scarlett Harlot was dark and seemed to go well with Matt's complexion, but he also liked the bright shine of her Peach Passion. "What did Mom say? 'Lipstick needs to match the outfit.'"

Matt put the lipstick down and went to her closet. The red dress was too revealing. The pink one was spunky, but he didn't feel like pink today. Matt chose the blue one since he was set on trying the blue eye shadow. He threw it on the bed and yanked his T-shirt over his head. Matt undressed and thought about what he was about to do. *I'm putting on my mom's dress.* "Duh! I can't do that without underwear." Matt opened the dresser drawer and sifted through to find the right ones. "They are way too big!" Even though she wore string bikinis, his waist was several inches narrower, and the bikinis slid right down his thighs. "I can go commando."

He placed them back in the drawer and noticed a plastic compact nestled in her socks. Maybe it was more makeup. Matt picked it up and opened it. Inside was a domed rubber suction cup. (Or maybe it was silicone?) "What the hell?" It was only two or three inches in diameter. Matt could not figure out what it would be used for or why it was in the drawer. He put it back. His parents had weird things.

Matt opened another drawer and picked up a bra. He held it to his chest and looked in the mirror. It was also way too big. He'd have to go without breasts this time. Maybe next time he could stuff the cups and look more womanly, but for now he'd have to use his imagination.

Matt pulled on the dress and found some strappy shoes to match. He sat at her dresser and adjusted the mirror. The eye shadow was easy to apply and so was the blush. It took more skill to coat his lashes with mascara though. Matt poked himself in the eye a couple times and had to wipe the tears and streaked makeup off before he tried again. Ten minutes of aggravation paid off, and Matt soon stared at a very different reflection in the mirror.

He chose the Peach Passion because it complimented the blue dress well. Matt puckered at his reflection.

He grinned. He stood up and walked over to the closet door to stand in front of the full-length mirror. He swooshed the skirt from side to side. "Fuck me! I make a damn fine looking girl." Matt's heart fluttered. He smoothed down the stray hairs around his face and pushed some over his ears. Something was missing. Matt snapped his fingers. He chose a necklace from her jewelry box and returned to admire the complete ensemble. "Perfect."

Just then, the door opened. Matt turned sharply and gasped. It was Jamie.

"Get out!" he shouted.

Jamie stood there staring. "What are you…?"

Matt snatched a pillow off the bed. "I said get out!" He flung the pillow.

Jamie dodged the puffy projectile and walked toward Matt. Matt turned away and sprinted to the closet, thinking he could lock himself in there until Jamie left. When he grabbed the door to slam it behind him, Jamie was right there. His best friend grabbed his arm and held it tight.

"What the hell do you think you're doing?" Jamie squawked.

"I…." Matt didn't want to answer. He didn't like Jamie's stern stare, and he certainly didn't like his harsh tone. Jamie never spoke like that to Matt!

Then Jamie unexpectedly rolled his eyes. "Dude. Peach isn't your color. You should be wearing something dark with this dress. Come here."

Jamie pulled him from the closet to the chair in front of his mom's makeup mirror. He positioned a stupefied Matt and urged him to sit. Matt eyed him curiously as he snatched the tube of red lipstick.

Jamie handed Matt a tissue. "Here, wipe your lips." As Matt did as he was told, Jamie opened the tube of Scarlett Harlot. "Relax your mouth. This is the color you should wear." He proceeded to apply the lipstick to Matt's lips, holding Matt's jaw steady with his other hand. When he was finished, he leaned back to inspect his handiwork. "Much better."

Matt could not believe this was Jamie. He wasn't freaking out at all. He was helping him. Matt looked in the mirror and smiled at his reflection. Jamie was right; this color was so much nicer. "Thanks."

"No prob. You wanna go downstairs and play some Xbox?"

Who was this guy? Wasn't he going to say anything? Matt was too shocked to move.

"What?" Jamie asked, his lips slowly curving up on one side. "You're freaking that I'm not freaking, aren't you?"

"Yeah, sort of."

"It took me a second. I never saw a boy dress up like a girl before. It's a little weird. But the other week I came looking for you and found a woman's bra on your bed. I didn't know what to make of that. And remember, a while ago, I found that lipstick on your floor? Walking in on you now made it all snap together. You like doing this. Right?"

Matt was stunned. "It doesn't bother you?"

Jamie shrugged. "I don't care. But if you dress like this in public other people might."

Matt frantically shook his head. "I'm not dressing like this in public."

"Okay. So… Xbox?"

Matt's body finally decided to relax. His shoulders softened, and he slumped back in the chair. "Sure. But let me change first."

Jamie got up and headed for the door. "Fine. But leave the makeup on for a while?" When Matt's eyebrow shot up, Jamie explained, "I like it. You look pretty."

"Shut the fuck up and go downstairs."

"No, really. You make a very pretty girl."

Matt smiled and batted his eyes.

Matt wasn't sure if Jamie was pulling his leg or being honest. It felt strange sharing this side of his personality with someone else. They were sitting in his living room like always, legs stretched out on the floor, backs against the front of the sofa. Jamie was acting so normal. As he maneuvered his *Nightcaster* character, he laughed and argued with the television screen like he always did. Matt was scared to talk about it. Boys didn't talk—they grunted and punched each other and the subject was dropped. But what if Jamie slipped up and said something to one of his other friends? Matt had to say something.

"Jamie, do you think I'm weird?"

"Huh?" Jamie threw his hands up in the air as he lost his last life. "Oh man!" He handed over the controller. "Here, your turn."

Matt took it but didn't hit play. "Do you think I'm weird?"

"Because you like dressing like a girl? Maybe a little. But you're you, and I like you. So if you like it, I don't care. Just don't ask me to do it."

"Got it." Matt was happy to hear that, but there was one more secret to tell. "Jamie, it's not just that. I also like…." He had to pause and take a breath. His heart was racing. Jamie might reject him and that was the scariest thought of all. "Jamie, truth is—and if I tell you this you have to promise not to tell anyone."

Jamie's expression changed. It was like he finally figured out how serious the conversation was going to be. He turned his attention fully on Matt and *not* the graphics on the TV. "Okay, I promise."

"Jamie… I like boys."

"So? I like boys too. There are some really funny boys in my health class. You should hear—"

"No, Jamie, I mean I *like* like boys. Instead of liking girls. You know? Where I want to *do* things with them."

"What kinds of things?"

Jamie did not look like it was getting through his skull. "Like those things boys do with girls."

"Like what?"

Matt huffed. Jamie was so naive sometimes. "Jamie, are you really asking what boys do with girls? You can't be serious. You've taken health. You got an A. Didn't you learn anything?"

"Not really. I just memorize facts to pass the test. Makes Mom happy. I didn't get why girls get pregnant. How does the sperm get in there? Sexual intercourse doesn't make sense."

This conversation was turning into a biology lesson, and Matt was less and less self-conscious. Jamie was so unaware of life! He needed to educate his friend, or one day he'd find out by accident how girls got pregnant. "Oh, Jamie. Sometimes I forget how sheltered you are. Look, you know how your penis does things when you touch it?"

Jamie looked away and spoke quietly. "I'm not allowed to touch it."

"What? Why?" 'Cause that didn't make any sense. The long pause and Jamie's expression also did not make sense. He'd just seen Matt in a dress! What could be more embarrassing to talk about than that?

"Mom caught me," Jamie said, looking at the carpet.

"Shit. Really?"

"She said it was perverted, and if she caught me again, she'd scald my hand under hot water."

Matt knew Jamie's mom was strict, and often harsh, but this was ridiculous. "How did she catch you? Didn't you lock the door?"

"Mom doesn't allow it. She said if I lock my bedroom door, she'll take it off the hinges."

Matt gaped. "You did it in the bedroom? Dude, always, and I mean always, go in the bathroom. You can lock the door and no one questions why."

"I didn't think of that or I would have. Do you think I'm perverted?" Jamie pleaded with his eyes.

"No." It was a no-brainer. "Jamie, it's normal. God made you with balls hanging between your legs for Pete's sake. Why make you that way if you're not allowed to touch 'em? You of all people are not perverted. Maybe your mom is."

They both chuckled.

Jamie shoved Matt with his shoulder. "Thanks."

Matt grinned. "Any time."

"So… how do you mean you like boys? Have you kissed one?"

Matt's grin grew wider. "Yeah. A couple times."

Jamie's jaw dropped. "What? When? How come you didn't tell me?"

"I'm telling you now. You remember Kenny Litman?"

"That red-haired boy who put worms on the lunch table? I thought he moved away when you guys went into fifth grade?"

"He did. We kissed a couple times behind the tennis court."

"You were in fourth grade!" Jamie screeched and then coughed in his hand like there was something wrong with his throat.

"So? He let me kiss him. And he liked it. I even stuck my tongue in his mouth."

Jamie recoiled. "Eww. That's gross."

Matt sighed. "Oh, Jamie. One day you won't mind. One day you'll find some cute girl and want to try things. When that happens, I'll be here."

"I'm not sure I'll want the same things as you. Kissing is gross."

Matt ruffled his hair. "One day, Padawan."

Then Jamie's eyes grew dark. He inched closer. "Or maybe you could show me now?" he said in a sultry voice. He leaned in and touched Matt's lips with his.

The kiss grew more intense with every passing second. Jamie's hands started exploring Matt's body and Matt froze, unable to comprehend what was going on. His best friend was kissing him. Why was his best friend kissing him?

"I love you, Matt. I love you more than the stars have power to kiss the night sky."

MATT woke with a start. He sat straight up, gasping for breath. The room was dark so he pressed the button on his watch. 3:12 a.m. "Fuckin' hell!" He gradually calmed down from the most disturbing dream he'd ever had.

Matt remembered the events of his dream as if it all happened yesterday: Jamie walking in on him, playing Xbox, and talking about liking boys. Those events really had happened when the two of them were younger. But Matt never—never—remembered kissing Jamie. That had to be the most twisted nightmare his psyche had ever conjured up. "I have to stop reading those journals. Or maybe it's from staying in this room tonight? Fuck. I'm going back to Peggy's."

Matt flopped back on the bed and stared into the darkness. At five, he gave up trying to sleep and went out for a run.

9

October 30, 2010

MATT yanked his painful erection hard and fast. This wasn't about feeling good, it was about having a fucking release! He'd been in the shower so long thinking about Darian he needed to come before the hot water ran out. He wanted it here, in the shower, where Darian magically slid over his skin and washed all his pain away from a hard day's work. He liked imagining Darian's soapy hands working his dick. It made these jerk-off sessions more real.

"Oh," he growled, then quaked and relaxed.

Matt rinsed and turned the water off. Being without Darian for four measly weeks was going to kill him. And technically, it had been less than four, but Matt had never felt the need to relieve himself so often. It was getting ridiculous. He was on edge constantly. He tried working more hours to get his thoughts off Darian, but something always brought him to mind.

Like the other day when they found an electrical fire in the wall of an art supply store. *Art.* Or when Scott came in wearing a new shirt, a shirt from American Eagle. *Hello?* Or when the guys discussed whether they preferred blondes or brunettes? *Brunets... definitely brunets.* Matt went on to have an internal conversation over what body piercings he liked and how much he wanted to lick a certain spider tattoo. When no one was paying attention, he milked his raging hard-on in the firehouse toilet.

By nature, Matt loved sex. Lots of sex—anytime, anywhere, and with practically anyone. He used to club all the time until work got in the way. In high school, it was easier to bounce back after a late night of dancing and fucking, but in the "real world," as his mom called it, late nights before a shift made him unfocused and lethargic. In his line of work, he couldn't chance it. His mother had raised him to be responsible, and he was not going to let her, or anyone else, down. Most firefighters he knew worked two jobs and handled the demands perfectly fine. True, he could blow off his other job—splitting and stacking firewood could wait a day—but his conscience wouldn't let him. Taking off a day because of partying the night before would become too easy. Wouldn't it? He knew better.

He still got his random sex; it was merely less and further between. Which was also fine, until now. He could handle it. Until now. He wasn't picky; anyone would do (as long as they were sixty miles away). Until he met Darian. Now he was constantly thinking of sex. Sex with Darian.

His prick hurt. It was chafed and overhandled, yet Matt couldn't stop. He wondered if Darian was having this much trouble being away from him. He just wanted sex. Was that too much to ask for? Long, sticky, saliva-inducing sex. He wanted to lick Darian and suck Darian and see how many different ways he could bend Darian. Not seeing him blew! And not in a good way. He'd punch a wall, but then his hand would hurt too much to pump his dick. So instead of getting angry, he jacked off… a lot!

AT WORK Matt was fixing the leather strap on his helmet when Scott Turner walked up beside him. "Dude? You all right? You look like shit," he said.

Matt got snarky. "Thanks Scott. Appreciate that."

"No really. You look like you haven't slept."

"I haven't." He could fake cheery, but why bother?

"Girl troubles?" Scott offered.

Matt glared. "Look Scott, I'd rather not talk about it."

"Oh, okay. You always seem to talk just fine with Jason, but you never want to talk to me. That's fine." He slowly backed away, hurt written on his face. "I can go help someone else. I'm not bothered."

But Scott was bothered; Matt wasn't blind. Scott was a good guy, and Matt felt guilty. He stopped fixing his equipment and huffed. "Scott. Come back."

His coworker bounced back over. "So what's wrong?"

Matt shook his head. Scott was way too perky. Something had to be going on with him for him to be asking so much about Matt. "Is there, by chance, something going on at home you want to discuss first? You're not usually this inquisitive."

His shoulders slumped. "Jane thinks I need friends. She says all I do is work here and tinker with my car… alone. Apparently, I'm driving her crazy, which I don't understand. She said she wanted me to live with her after her husband died. So I agreed. It was easier on both of us. Then she discovered how often I'm home, and it bugs her. She says I need to make friends." He heaved a sigh.

Scott looked like a lost puppy. Poor guy. Matt didn't have too many friends either. He used to go clubbing all the time with Darrell, but Darrell lived in DC. He hung out with Jason sometimes, but Jason was married. He used to run all the time with Jamie, but….

Matt smiled at Scott. "Ya know what? I think I need more friends too. Ever since Jamie died, I work more than I should. I barely make time to run in the morning because it just feels weird without him. Do you run?"

Scott's eyes got wide and he shook his head. "Um, no. Running has way too much exercise involved."

"Well, cars then. You said you tinker with your car. I love working on cars. What model is it?"

"Buick."

Matt sat up and leaned forward. "Really? What year?" He'd seen some really sweet Buicks at car shows.

"2001 Buick Century."

He resisted laughing at the absurdity. "A Buick Century? Not a 1942 Buick Super or something, but a 2001 Century. You spend time on it doing what exactly?"

"I grease up the engine. Change the oil. Shine the rims. Detail the interior."

Matt grabbed his shoulder and gave it a squeeze. "Your sister is right, you need to get out. Next time I have a car to work on, I'll call you."

Scott grinned. "Thanks. So now what's on your mind?"

Matt dropped his head and grunted, "Sex."

"Oh. And that's a problem?" Scott said it like sex shouldn't be.

"Yes. Remember how you thought I had someone?" Matt looked at Scott with heavy eyes. "I do. I did. My baby walked out four weeks ago, and the sex we had every morning and evening is gone."

Scott sat slack-jawed. "Twice a day? Dude, you rock!"

"Not anymore. Now I shake hands with my little buddy too often for comfort. I need a good hard fuck, ya know?"

"Tell me about it. I can't remember the last time I got laid. You used to barhop, didn't you? Take your next night off to pick up a hot blonde. It should be easy for a guy like you."

Leave it to a single, sex-starved recluse who lived with his sister to come up with that one! "Thanks, but I'm not sure that's a great idea. I may not officially be with anyone, but we might be back together… soon… possibly."

"Really?" Scott raised his eyebrow. "So… you're what? Going to put off picking up a one-night stand in case you might be with someone… possibly… in the future? That's fucked reasoning, and you know it. I'd respect your rationale more if it was because of religious reasons. Going without sex because your 'possible' girlfriend might come back is just stupid."

Religious reasons. Matt should have thought of that; he was religious. And he did feel guilty having casual sex as often as he did. Deep down he knew it was wrong. Every time he went to church, he was convicted in his heart for fornication. The Bible was clear about sex outside marriage. Matt wanted to change—really he did—but it was easy to skip that part of the Bible and think about the other things in Christianity that were easier to comply with.

However, if he wasn't going to get married, and he didn't have a boyfriend, and he had already committed sins against God for which he was sorry, then what was one more? Maybe Scott was right? He should go out.

"Maybe you're right."

"Of course I'm right," Scott said and walked away satisfied.

Matt watched him leave and felt pretty good himself. He gave Scott a chance, and the conversation was fine. Since Jamie… well, since Jamie was gone, Matt rarely talked to anyone but his mom. He needed more male friends too. This was a good thing.

MATT woke up with a pounding headache. Moreover, he was in a bed that was not his own. He glanced over when he felt the bed move. *Oh fuck!* Matt carefully slipped out of bed and gathered his clothes before the sleeping mystery man stirred. Could his life get any worse? Could he feel any shittier? *Oh God, I hope not!*

October 31, 2010

HE TRUDGED into the station, coffee in hand, and Visine in his pocket. "I shouldn't have listened to Scott," he mumbled, shucking off his jacket by his cubby.

Jason popped his head around the corner, startling Matt. "You took advice from Scott instead of me?"

After recovering from sudden heart palpitations, Matt realized how hurt Jason seemed. Matt couldn't take much more of this touchy-feely girly jealousy. They were men, for fuck's sake. They grunted and sweated, and they didn't squabble over who gave advice to whom—right? If it kept up, Matt would have to rebuild someone's engine to get the testosterone flowing again. He rolled his eyes at Jason. "Yeeess, I followed Scott's advice."

"Well, what happened? You look like death. How come you look like death? Did his advice turn out bad?" Jason's expression changed faster than an adolescent girl's. Now he was all fake-sad and looking to gloat. Matt was irked.

Should he share? Jason would not approve. He didn't like Matt's lifestyle and that was without the whole "gay" part. Whatever. He'd put his head on the chopping block. "Have you ever done something you regret?"

"Sure. I'm human. Stuff happens. What'd you do?"

Before he let it all out, Matt had to make one thing clear. "No judgments, okay? No fire and brimstone from your soapbox?"

"Matt." Jason held his hands out to the side in a gesture that cried "of course".

"Okay. Here it is." He forced himself to relax. It would be fine. Jason always had good advice. "I fucked somebody last night, and I can't remember anything about it. The night's a total blank."

"Damn!" Jason's eyes flew open faster than a faulty mini blind. "I got the impression you held your liquor better than that. What were you drinking?"

Matt hated the quick assumption but understood how he got there so fast. Matt lived in the fast lane; or at least he used to. Assuming drunkenness wasn't irrational. "That's the thing.... I remember doing tequila shots, but normally I stop at eight. I know my limit. Eight ensures I have minimal hangover and maximum memory of the previous night's events. Last night I remember two. That's not enough to get me drunk."

"Then how do you know you were with someone? I mean, if you can't remember anything?"

The moment of truth. "I woke up in a strange bed this morning, and I wasn't alone."

Jason whistled. "I can't believe you'd do that to Darian. I thought you were going to wait for a while and see what happened between you two? What did Scott say that got you barhopping again? I thought he knew about your hottie-on-hold?"

Matt had assumed Jason would get on him for irresponsibility, not cheating on his not-yet boyfriend. Now he felt worse.

"But we're not together. It's not cheating if you're not dating."

Jason cocked his head, crossed his arms over his chest, and glared. "Do you love her?"

"That has nothi—"

"Do you love her?" This time he demanded an answer with a little twist of his neck and an attitude of a black Southern Baptist grandmother. It was a very intimidating voice.

"Yes," Matt said, knowing where this reasoning was headed.

"Does she love you?" More grandma attitude.

"I don't know. Maybe."

"Is the wait to date her idea?"

"Sort of."

"Then Matt, you shouldn't be out fuckin' anybody else. And that's besides the fact that I'm against random sexual hook-ups. It's only been a few weeks. You need to give her more time. And, you need to come clean about last night. Tell Darian the truth."

"But… I can't." Matt was whining and intended to whine some more, but his phone buzzed. He flipped it open.

A text: *Hi. I miss you. I can't stand Dan's rules anymore. I want to feel your arms around me.*

Matt banged his head on the wall next to him. "Fuck!" He thumped it three more times.

"That Darian?" Jason was too intuitive and too omniscient. Matt hated him!

"Yeeess," he bellyached. "What the fuck is wrong with me, Jason? All I wanted was sex; sex with Darian, not some faceless stranger from a club I can't remember. I'm losing it."

Jason inappropriately chuckled. "Dude. You're in love. It never gets any easier."

"Thanks."

"You tell Darian or I will." His threat was real even if he lacked Darian's last name or telephone number. Matt was sure he could find it, or he'd swipe Matt's phone when he wasn't looking.

"Fine. I will. Give me time, okay. Darian's been through a lot lately, and my infidelity isn't going to help. And I promise to keep my dick in my pants."

"Good! Now text back the hottie so we can do inventory."

Jason walked away confidently but without an air of superiority. He was a good man but didn't brag and never said "I told you so" in a way that wasn't jovial. People knew he was right; he never had to lord it over them.

Matt thought about his reply to Darian. *Can we text dirty later? Or talk? I was thinking of new ways to describe what my hand is doing.*

LOL… Dan's home in thirty. I really shouldn't anyway. He heard me moaning your name when I was in the shower. He got mad.

I moan your name all the time in the shower :D

:^] I like that. I'm glad. But when I did it, Dan went on and on about forgetting

The text stopped. Matt thought he was missing the end of the sentence so he waited. A minute went by. Nothing.

Forgetting…. What? he sent.

More time passed. He heard Jason calling for him from the bay. Matt pleaded with his phone, "Come on, Dare. Forgetting what?"

Finally Darian texted the rest: *Forgetting Jamie. Dan thinks I think more about you and I've forgotten about Jamie. How can I forget him? I didn't. I loved him. I still love him. I miss him so much.*

Matt could relate. He missed Jamie too. Perhaps not romantically, but he did love Jamie. They used to do so much together. *I wish I could be there for you. This has to be hard.*

It is. I thought Dan and I could work through this loss together but he's changed. He's possessive and overly protective of me like I'm fifteen.

I'm sorry. I wish I could help. :)

You are, believe me. Just talking to you helps, even if it is only text. :+] I've been going through lots of photos and stuff. It's hard to be surrounded by Jamie all the time. Sometimes I need a break. But when I say things like that, Dan thinks I don't want to remember him, and that's not true.

I understand. I think I feel that way sometimes too. Matt wasn't sure if he should ask, but the thought occurred to him he only had the one photo of Darian he took when he wasn't looking. Was it inappropriate to ask for more?

Another message came through with a pix attachment. *I didn't know if you had any pictures of me so I thought I'd send you one. Hope you don't mind.*

Mind? Are you joking? That's awesome! I was JUST thinking how to ask for a picture and you sent it! Plus, you are sooo HOT! :p

The picture was serious and sensual. Darian's tongue was just poking out of his mouth, touching his upper lip. His long hair was hanging across his face. He sported black eye liner too. Very emo, yet very sultry. That lip ring begged to be tugged on. Matt made it his wallpaper and memorized the look in Darian's eyes.

"Matt!" Jason startled him. His phone flew out of his hand. Jason snatched it off the floor and handed it to Matt. "Sorry. Didn't mean to scare you."

"It's fine. I'm just finishing the conversation. Promise." Matt wasn't sure if Jason saw the picture. Would he mention if he had? Darian had long hair; he could be mistaken for a girl, especially with the eye makeup and the diamond stud on the side of his nose.

"Ah, huh. Sure. Just get out there before the chief finds out I'm doing the work by myself."

"I will." He watched Jason walk away before sneaking one more peak at his wallpaper. His mouth watered thinking about Darian's tongue and pouty lips. His cock swelled. Matt groaned—quietly—and adjusted himself. "Four weeks. Four fucking weeks, and I'm dying for you."

Darian texted: *Matt?*

Oh, sorry. Jason popped around the corner and reminded me I'm at work. I need to go. I miss you so much. I love you.

Don't stop. Promise?

What? Loving you?

Yeah.

Matt pictured running his fingers over Darian's cheek. He wished he was doing it right now. Darian seemed to need some comfort today. *Promise.... I'm gonna call you in a second before Jason gripes again. Okay?*

No. Please don't. I won't pick up. I can't stand hearing your voice if I don't know when I'll see you. I've cried enough today.

Then don't answer. I want to hear your voice mail message. Matt knew it sounded corny but it would be better than nothing. He dialed.

Three rings and it went to the message. "Hey, this is Darian. I can't believe I missed your call! I must not have a signal. Leave a message, and I'll get back to you as soon as I can." *Beeeep.*

No sooner did Matt hang up then the phone buzzed in his hand—a call from Darian. Nervously, he answered, "Hello?" He listened but Darian did not reply. "Darian, I can hear you breathing. Won't you say something? Anything?"

"I've missed your voice so much." Darian's voice was barely above a whisper, but the sound went straight to Matt's heart.

His eyes stung. "Me too. I've wanted to call you, but I wasn't sure I should."

"Me too. Texting is easier. Dan can't hear me text."

"Yeah." The long pauses told Matt this was difficult for Darian. Then he heard him sniffle. "Dare? You okay?"

"No," he squeaked.

He wasn't sure if Darian was crying because of Jamie or because of him, but he gave his advice anyway. "Aw, baby, don't cry. It'll get easier. It will. Give it time." Matt heard him blow his nose and sniffle some more.

"Matt…?"

"Yeah?"

"Do you, sometimes, feel Jamie nearby? Or hear his voice?" Darian sounded so scared.

"Sometimes. It's more like when I go running I look over expecting him to be there." Matt waited, but Darian didn't reply. "Darian? Baby, if I could hold you, I would. You know that." Matt hoped he could convey his love enough to comfort Darian.

"I wish you were here. Dan doesn't understand like you do. I feel so empty."

Matt heaved a sigh. "I know. I'm sorry."

"Matt…. Do you think I betrayed Jamie when I was with you?"

Darian's desperation tore at his heart. Of course he should say no right away. But honestly, if it had been him, he'd be asking the same thing. "Maybe. I don't know. He was gone and you were lonely—hurting."

"Do you think I'm a slut?"

"No! Why would you ask that? You didn't plan it; it just happened."

"But then it happened again. And again. And I wish it was happening now. How horrible am I?" His voice cracked. "Maybe Dan is right. I should be ashamed of myself."

"Darian, please don't beat yourself up like that. I'm as much to blame as you. I took advantage of you. I'm so sorry."

"No. It was me. I'm a horrible person who should be punished. I don't deserve to feel better."

"Darian, don't—" The phone went dead. Matt knew he'd hung up. He texted quickly.

Dare… don't do this. You are not a bad person. You are hurting. Just talk to me.

Matt was relieved to get a text back, even if he didn't like what it said. *I need time.* It was an ongoing theme with Darian. Darian needed time to work through things, and Matt suffered every second waiting until that time was over.

Matt rubbed his blurry eyes and pocketed his phone. There was nothing he could do. His throat tightened, but he wouldn't allow his lovesick self to get emotional at work. He couldn't. He'd be a rock. Yup, a rock! He'd work with Jason like any other day.

He pulled his shoulders back and walked through to the ambulance bay, picked up his clipboard, and opened up the side panel on the vehicle.

Just like any other day, he thought.

But as he went over the inventory and counted boxes of bandages and icepacks and syringes, Matt's guilt bubbled to the surface for whatever it was he did last night. He had to tell Darian he slept with someone else. He should have told him, but he couldn't do it now. Not through a text. And not while Darian was feeling the shame of cheating on Jamie's memory. Matt needed to be face-to-face with Darian so he would see Matt's remorse and hopefully understand.

"I'll do it soon."

MATT slept like the dead. He awoke before his alarm sounded but stayed in his bed, staring up at the ceiling, grinning stupidly. If he had a magic lamp to rub and ask for the best damned dream in the world, he doubted if three wishes would conjure up the wonderful dream he'd just had! This dream was beyond his best imagination. *Darian* was beyond his imagination.

He relived it in the shadows of early morning before the images slipped away. In his dream Jamie was alive, happy, and not with Darian. They were all friends. They were goofing off in Jamie's old room before he moved from Tall Pines Drive. The three of them were on the bed, giggling and rolling around as if nothing could touch their moment. Darian stopped laughing and leaned into Matt. He kissed him tenderly. Jamie watched—unbothered. He looked content.

Matt knew there was more to the dream, but dreams fade as a vapor of smoke.

He heard a faint moaning coming through the wall. He distinctly heard the words "Oh yes, right there, harder," and then more moaning. Matt snatched his other pillow and covered his face, hoping to muffle the sounds. It didn't help. He heard the sounds escalate to a fevered panting gasp for breath. "Oh yes!" his aunt cried out.

Matt felt his lower region take notice. "Oh no!" He flung back the covers and stomped over to his dresser drawer. "That's it! I'm moving out!" He repositioned his semierection before it poked out the front of his boxers. "There is no way I'm going to subject myself to this. It's disgusting. And if I get a hard-on one more time listening to my aunt having sex, I'm going to shoot myself!"

November 2010

10

November 3, 2010

DARIAN lay on the bed, curled in a ball, staring out the window. He hadn't slept; he couldn't close his eyes. Every time he did, he saw images of Jamie. Sometimes they were pleasant images, sometimes they were not. The gray clouds outside only stood to emphasize his gloom.

His phone buzzed.

Darian snatched it up. The text was from his best friend Lori, not Matt. Darian's hope withered. *Hi.*

Hi.

Have you heard from Matt?

No. Not in a few days.

Why haven't you texted him?

Dan thinks I'm too dependent on him.

Screw Dan. Matt makes you feel better, doesn't he?

Darian rolled onto his back and looked at the ceiling. He paused, lacing his fingers across his chest, holding the phone against his body under his palms. "No, Matt makes me forget," he muttered to the empty room.

He closed his eyes, momentarily bringing up an image of the two of them locked intimately together. He remembered the feel of Matt's legs wrapped around him, his arms holding him tight as they kissed. Matt liked rolling around on the bed, exposing their flesh to the room. Matt playfully wrestled with Darian, left teeth marks on him, and passionately twisted the two of them around as his whim dictated. Matt knocked pillows and blankets on the floor, and even tore the sheets a time or two. He wasn't picky about neatness, and he didn't act like he was following a "manual of style" when it came to sex. He dove in hungrily, and Darian gave himself over to the exhilaration without a second's thought.

"Because you're a whore!" hissed Jamie.

Darian's eyes flew open. No one was there. His phone buzzed.

Darian? You still there? Call Matt!

Darian took several deep breaths and answered back. *Do you think I'm a whore?*

Lori's text came back angrily. *What? Where did that come from? You are not a whore, Darian! You are a lonely "widower" who needs to move on with his life.*

But it's only been since September. How can I let go of all the years Jamie and I spent together?

You're not! But you can't mope either. He's not coming back.

I don't know. It feels wrong. I feel wrong. I shouldn't feel like this. If I really loved Jamie, how can I feel like this?

Like what? How do you feel? What does Matt do to you?

He

Darian's fingers stopped. It felt wrong to say anything to Lori about how he felt. It screamed betrayal. He closed his eyes again and conjured up the image of Matt pinning him to the bed. He had his fingers laced through Darian's, crushing him under the weight of his muscular body. The thought of kissing Matt made him warm inside. What did Matt do to him? All kinds of things! Being with Matt promised kinky things Darian dared to dream but never voiced. Until now.

He imagined the feel of Matt's lips pressed to his. A shiver ran through his body. Matt always made him feel so good.

Then a cold streak ran up his spine. The dream image of Matt repositioned their bodies and roughly yanked Darian to the edge of the bed. He grabbed his hair and pulled Darian's face to his cock. "Suck it!" he hissed. "Swallow me whole, bitch!" Matt's face distorted into a sinister grin as he twisted his fist into Darian's long hair, using it as a rope as he forced Darian to comply. "You know you want it. You always want it!" Darian choked on the brutal entry and gagged as he tried to take Matt's cock down his throat.

He couldn't adjust. He couldn't breathe. He tried to pull back, but Matt shoved his hips into his face and tugged his hair on both sides. The pain that enveloped his scalp almost outdid the burn in his throat. He swatted at Matt's thighs, attempting to get his attention. Matt thrust harder.

"Tramp!" he snarled, releasing his hold and shoving Darian away.

Darian coughed and gagged and gasped for breath. He heard quiet laughter and dared to look up at the man he thought he trusted. Matt was gone. Jamie stood there, wearing his green-striped polo shirt and blue jeans. He mockingly laughed at Darian's crumpled form on the bed. "Do you really believe you can *think* about him and I won't know? He doesn't care about you. He only wants to fuck you and use you like everyone else he's had. I'm the only one who can love you. I'm the only one who can look past your sins and accept you for the dirty little harlot you are." Jamie crouched down and whispered, "He doesn't know all your secrets."

A knock sounded at his door.

"Darian? It's time to leave," Dan Miller said from the other side of the door.

Darian frantically looked around the room. He was alone. Lori had sent six more texts, but Darian hadn't felt the phone buzz even though it was in his hand. He rolled off the bed. "Okay," he responded merrily, masking his alarm over the very vivid hallucination. "I'll be right down!"

He went to his drawer and pulled out a long-sleeved shirt. It was cool out. No one would think twice about him wearing it. Before pulling it over his head, he took out a razor blade. He studied the fatter part of his forearm.

"Just one cut. That's all I need," he rationalized.

He held the blade to his arm. It barely touched the surface.

The sharp edge pinched and burned as he pressed down and sliced his skin. A tiny line of red seeped from the wound, but seconds later Darian felt nothing. It continued to seep, but as he dabbed the blood, he could already see where the skin was sticking together, sealing itself up. He hadn't cut deep enough to feel it for more than a second. The rush was in the act. One line was not enough to cleanse his conscience from the guilt inside. A minute later, the blood stopped on its own. He could feel a sting, but it was too faint. He needed more. Darian needed to feel something other than the one word that thundered through his mind.

That one word he dared not voice.

He held the corner of the blade to his arm. It was easier with this angle to slice deeper. His heart raced again. "Just one more pinch," he whispered. He went slower this time, allowing the skin to grab and the edge to sink in. This time more nerves reacted, and he felt a shock go up his arm like electricity. His breath faltered. "That's what I wanted," he confessed as he dabbed the second line of blood. This one bore a burning sting to it as it throbbed and bled.

He took out a bandage to cover it. Nothing unusual, he thought. He could have caught it on a bush or a fence. Or scratched his arm on something at work. It would heal in a day or two, and no one would know.

"Darian?" Dan called from down the steps.

Darian jumped, startled out of his private punishment. He took a few deep breaths and yanked on the shirt before bounding down the steps with a fake smile affixed to his face.

Dan tousled his hair like he normally would and smiled too. "After your visit with Dr. Loundas, maybe we could have lunch or see a movie. Would you like that?"

"Sure," he said, faking a positive attitude. Dan was trying to do things with him, and sometimes he liked it. (When he wasn't pinching himself to make sure he was awake.) "Can we go to a haircut place?"

Dan unlocked the car with his key fob as they exited the house and strolled to the car in the driveway. "Are you sure? I thought you liked your hair long?" Dan asked as he got in and started the engine. "Didn't you bicker with Jamie a few months ago when he asked you to cut it?"

Darian shrugged. "I don't know. I think it's too long."

"Okay, Kiddo. A haircut it is! And then pizza."

Darian nodded.

DARIAN didn't like Dr. Loundas's waiting room. The music was too sterile, and the padded sofa was from the '70s. And he didn't want to review meditation books while he waited. He wanted to get this meeting over with. For some reason, she wanted to speak to Dan first. He hated that. What were they talking about? He was fine. He didn't need help!

Yes, you do!

A voice sounded in his head. Whose voice was it? He didn't know.

You know who can help.

It was Mitch's voice. He hadn't heard it in years, but he knew that's who it was. He took his phone from his pocket. A pause. Did he really want to do this?

Yes, the voice prompted.

He flipped it open and sent a text. *Mitch. It's Dare. I need something.*

Hey buddy, no problem. I got what you need. Meet me at that place tomorrow at 3? Mitch was always quick to reply when a sale was inevitable.

Sure. Thanks.

You got it!

The door opened, and Darian pocketed the phone.

"Thanks, Toni." Dan shook her hand and turned to Darian. "I'll be back in an hour to pick you up."

"Okay."

"Darian," the doctor said, greeting him with a smile. "How are you today?"

"Fine."

"Come on in."

She waved him inside her office and motioned for him to take the ever-familiar seat on the couch. He sat, knowing it was futile to do anything else. Besides, he liked the sofa. It was cozy, and he was allowed to arrange the pillows however he wished. He was even allowed to kick off his shoes and pull his feet up next to him as they spoke. That privilege alone made him feel more comfortable. He liked having his legs tucked underneath him. And sometimes he pulled his knees up to his chest for a sense of security when he felt the conversation diving in too deep.

Darian watched as the doctor leafed through his file. He wondered what else she could be pondering. It wasn't like much had changed since his last appointment. His life was basically the same, except without Jamie. They'd covered his feelings on Jamie's death last time. Jamie was gone, and Darian didn't know how to function without him. What more could he say? She told him it was normal. She told him each day would ease the pain a tiny bit more. She was wrong, but he didn't have anything new to add.

Time ticked as she flipped through documents. How many were in that file anyway?

Darian fidgeted. Her deliberate pause made him nervous. What was she going to ask? Why was it taking so long? What did Dan tell her? Right when he was about to drive himself insane thinking of all the possible conversation scenarios, the doctor of psychology straightened her shoulders and faced him.

"So, Darian," she started cheerfully, "tell me about Matt. When did you start seeing him?"

Darian quivered at the sound of Matt's name and hoped to God she didn't notice. Just to make sure, he stuck to his normal routine of nonverbal communication: he remained perfectly still for another few moments. He wanted to avoid as many questions as possible on the subject and felt that caution and restraint might keep him from blurting out any suspicious answers. Still, he felt a jumble of emotions twisting around inside. What should he say? He and his therapist had only met a few times since the funeral. Before that, it had been more than several months. He actually forgot the last time they got together. He was doing so well living with Jamie and Dan. She told him she was proud of his recovery.

Now, what would she think? He thought of the marks across his abdomen and arm. She wouldn't be proud.

Darian casually lifted his gaze from the floor to her expectant eyes and shrugged.

"Hmm. A shrug? That's all you have to say?" Dr. Loundas asked directly. It wasn't as if the cheeriness left her voice, but frankness mixed in and tightened its grip on Darian's stomach. "Dan told me you spent a great deal of time with him after the funeral, and that you talk about him. Why didn't you mention Matt during our past four visits? Are you trying to hide something?"

Darian unwittingly pulled his knees to his chest and hugged them. It was easier to study the dead stinkbug lying on its back at the base of her desk than to look directly into her piercing eyes. He *knew* she would be able to read him if he looked up. She always could. He'd been seeing her for years, ever since his drug addiction hit rock bottom in 2007. She'd always been patient and understanding, allowing Darian to gather his thoughts before replying to her probing questions. Some topics were easy to respond to, others not so much.

"Darian. You know I can't help you if you won't talk. Dan came in this morning only because he's concerned about you. He mentioned a boy named Matt. Will you tell me about him?"

Darian didn't want to talk about Matt. Why had Dan mentioned him? Was Dan really that concerned over the few times Darian happened to moan his name in the shower? Why was talking to Matt such a big deal? Darian couldn't think of any reason he shouldn't be able to see him if he wanted to. Matt was his friend. Matt was Jamie's friend. They needed each other. Yeah—that was it—they needed one another for comfort!

He pinched his eyes shut momentarily and willed away the hallucination he'd had in his room an hour before. *Talking to Matt is not a big deal! Thinking about Matt is not wrong!*

The stinkbug Darian was keenly observing moved its legs and rolled over. It lifted its flat head as if it were looking at Darian. "If all you want is friendship," it said in a voice disturbingly close to Jamie's, "then why does your cock swell every time you think about him?"

Darian jumped. He sucked in hard and shivered. Hearing Jamie's voice was too much. He was everywhere. *In* everyone and everything. Jamie was always watching and ready to convict him for his darkest thoughts and deepest fears. He wouldn't allow him peace. Jamie's ghost condemned Darian for his adulterous affair. Jamie poured on the guilt until Darian was drowning in it. He had to confess. He needed to repent.

Apprehensively, he spoke. "What do you want me to say?" His eyes darted away from the dead—and again on its back—stinkbug to look around Dr. Loundas's office. The huge tiger-eye poster he normally enjoyed looked angry, and all nine heads of the hydra incense burner appeared to be staring at him—eyes burning into his soul! Darian swallowed, wishing he had a drink. His emotions were churning inside and building like steam in a pressure cooker. He tried to remain silent, but his anxiety was too great. The tension built, and when his trepidation exceeded his good sense Darian verbally exploded. "Do you want me to *admit* I allowed him to fuck me?" he shouted. "Well, I did! More than once, and yes, I enjoyed it. And if that makes me a slut, I don't care!"

He turned his face away from her, impertinently looking at the wall. The pressure he applied to his legs as he hugged them almost cut off his circulation, but he refused to relax his grip.

"I see," she said, softly. "Do you know Dan worries about you? He's concerned that you're transferring your feelings to avoid grieving. Do you think that's true?"

Darian almost wished she would yell at him. Her noncombative, pleasant tones always wormed their way inside his head. He could resist a harsh reprimand, but her sensitivity ate away at his painstakingly built walls. He knew she cared. That's why it was so hard to refuse her. He'd done it before, plenty of times, but as the years went by, Darian began to like Dr. Loundas, and circumventing her wisdom was harder to accomplish.

"I grieve plenty," he replied with an edge to his voice.

"Does Matt know about Jimmy?"

Something innocent in her voice, as well as the question itself, told Darian she knew a whole lot less about Matt than he expected. Dan was in her office a long time; perhaps Matt was not the only topic they'd discussed. Darian moved his gaze from the wall to look her in the eyes. "Yeah…." He might as well have shouted "Duh!" for how belligerent he felt, but he kept his voice calm. He explained, "Matt was Jamie's best friend."

"Oh. I see." She sounded surprised. "Then things between the two of you have been going on since…?" Her question hung in the air between them.

"September twenty-second!" Darian could feel the inappropriate insinuation. "But you know what? I'm done here." Darian jumped up and snatched his shoes off the floor. He was about to bolt for the door when Dr. Loundas grabbed his arm.

"Darian, please. We can talk about something else. Okay?"

Darian stopped. She let go of his arm, and he nodded. After Dr. Loundas returned to her chair, Darian returned to his seat on the couch. He couldn't explain why he stayed. Perhaps it was because going was just as difficult. He couldn't talk to many people about his problems and fears. Lori understood sometimes. And Matt. But Dan wouldn't listen. Maybe Dr. Loundas would give him a chance to explain how he felt. Just not today.

She gently asked, "Tell me how your sister is doing. Did Ariana get another job yet?"

Darian was grateful for the change of subject. He let his shoulders relax into the back of the sofa. "Yeah, she's fine. She got a job in a dentist office or something. She's happy. I think she works nine to four and also does billing from home; that way she can be there when Kyle gets off the bus at four twenty. She doesn't want him to be alone every day. He's got it so much better than I ever did."

The doctor tucked her curly hair behind her ear. "Does that bother you? Are you jealous that your younger brother has someone looking out for him in ways you didn't?"

"No," he answered plainly. "I don't want him growing up like I did."

"Do you spend time with her?"

"No."

"Darian…. Didn't I recommend spending more time with your sister?"

"Yes, but… she works a lot." He knew he was making excuses.

"Your bond with Ariana is stronger than with anyone else in your family. I don't want you to lose the one connection because you couldn't make time to be with her. You said she gets home after four. It wouldn't hurt to have dinner once a week—maybe at Dan's house. Maybe invite Matt to dinner. See what your sister thinks of your new… friend."

As soon as he allowed himself to relax, she hit him with another "Matt" comment like a brick to his head. "Why are you so interested in Matt?" he hissed, rising off the couch for a second time. "This isn't about him. He hasn't done anything wrong." Darian headed directly to the door, and this time she didn't follow. He turned in the open doorway before exiting and added, "I knew you couldn't help me. You just don't understand."

DARIAN was sitting on the curb of the parking lot when Dan returned.

11

November 6, 2010

MATT moved back into his parents' house the following weekend. It wasn't very difficult. He hadn't taken the time originally to move all his stuff; he mainly took his clothes, work boots, and a few personal items. He'd left his trophies, photo albums, tools, and chainsaw in his room and in his dad's garage. Matt was always fixing cars for his family and friends, so it made sense to leave his equipment in the garage where he needed it.

As he considered the reasons he'd left in the first place, he could now see more benefits to moving back home. First, his parents lived way closer to Darian! And second, he spent most of his free time at his parents' house anyway. Matt had moved out to be free from prying eyes with regard to his personal life, but now they knew he was gay. Matt figured they would just have to get used to it. Although, he wasn't sure how it was going to work out once he and Darian started dating. Maybe he'd keep his eyes open for an affordable apartment.

November 7, 2010

AFTER another uneventful and freakishly quiet church service, Matt decided to text Darian. He had to. Darian should know how often Matt thought about him. Shouldn't he? *It's your birthday tomorrow, right? 22 :) Can I see you? Take you out?*

How did you know it was my birthday?

"Shit," he swore quietly. *Um, I think you mentioned it.* If he was going to use the details he'd gotten from the journals, then he'd better make sure Darian shared the information first!

Oh. Um... not sure about a date. Dan's being ultraprotective. He won't let me do anything but work and see Dr. Loundas.

Shit! Why?

I think he's worried. I have a feeling it's because he doesn't want to lose me like Jamie so he's not letting me out of his sight.

But it's your birthday! Matt walked into his bedroom and sat at his newly reorganized desk. Moving back in was a breeze. There was still a bunch of stuff he had shoved into the closet to go through and pitch, but all in all, he was set. He even had Jamie's journals snug under his T-shirts.

Darian responded: *I know. He's taking me to a restaurant. He's been really great lately.*

Oh yeah? How? Matt wanted to know what had been going on in the past few weeks. No news was not good news. In the back of his mind was a nagging feeling his mother would probably disapprove of his text-ersations, but he had no choice. It was killing him not to talk to Darian. His mom would say he was just stringing his heart along to think Darian would feel something real for him. Their last conversation was disheartening. Darian was unquestionably still holding onto feelings for Jamie—as he should be. Maybe Dan was telling Darian the same thing: this would never last. But Matt's heart could not let go. He would gladly set himself up for heartache in exchange for one more kiss from Darian.

Dan, oops—Dad, even allowed me to sleep on the couch since I came back without saying a word.

Matt muttered, "I figured going back to Jamie's bed would be hard." He texted, *Are you still on the couch?*

Yes and no. I tried last week and broke down. Last night I made it most of the way through and woke up screaming. I want to be in your bed, Matt. I feel safe there.

"I want that too." Matt stared at his keys. He wasn't sure what to type back. *In time. Right now you need to get over Jamie.*

I can't. It's too hard. Living here is too hard. Everywhere I look, there he is! It hurts so much.

I know. Do you want me to come by and pack up some of his stuff for you?

No. Dan and I have been doing it little by little. Papers. CDs. Pictures. Dan helped rearrange the room. He was going to paint it, but I like the color. I'm not sure I want everything gone. It feels too weird making everything go away at once.

Can you ask Dan when I can see you? I want to taste your lips.

He said maybe in a couple weeks. I don't know if I can wait that long. My lips miss your lips ;p

Matt groaned. *I can't wait to taste your skin and feel your mouth on me. I have some toys I want to play with and another position in mind.* There was a long pause between messages. So far, Darian was sending them one right after the other. He hoped he hadn't said something wrong. Should he text again?

Then he got an answer: *Sorry. I thought Dan was coming in. He doesn't want me talking to you. I should go.*

Okay. Is everything all right with Mr. Miller? I didn't realize he had a problem with me.

It's not you, it's me. He thinks I'm avoiding my feelings for Jamie by transferring my attachment to you. I keep telling him he's wrong.

Matt wasn't sure how to respond. This was the type of thing he'd thought all along, and the reason why Darian walked out of the apartment in the first place. Matt knew Darian didn't want to simply transfer his emotions but to feel them for real. And now Dan and his mom were both in agreement. Matt did not want to believe their parents were right.

Next he asked: *What does your therapist think?*

She thinks I'm in shock. Maybe I am. She said it would take time to feel strong on my own, but it will happen. I don't want to be on my own, I want to be with you. And being away from you is not as easy as everybody thinks it should be. Jamie has pictures of you everywhere.

Matt felt awkward. He knew Jamie had a thing for him, but he didn't want to let on how strong Jamie's feelings were. He sent another text: *Speaking of photos.... Might you be inclined to send another one?*

Well, I was hoping to surprise you, but I'm not sure when I'll get to see you next. I got it cut. I hope that's okay.

Okay? Why wouldn't it be okay? I think you're beautiful ALL the time. :)

A few seconds later, Darian sent one of himself smiling softly. Nothing provocative like the last one, which was what Matt secretly wanted. Darian's hair was much shorter. His bangs were still long and pushed to the side across his forehead, but the back appeared to be very short or buzzed like Jamie's used to be. Still, it was Darian. And that smile was all for Matt. *Thank you :D*

Do you like it?

Yeah, baby. Of course I do. Makes me want to run my fingers through it. ;)

I'm glad. Dream of me?

Always :)

The texting stopped, and Matt felt lonesome.

November 11, 2010

MATT looked up when the front door opened, and his father unexpectedly walked in, grumbling to himself. This was Thursday, Bible study night; his dad shouldn't be home so early. "Hey, Dad." His gaze followed his father as he walked right out of the room as if Matt hadn't said a word. The door opened again, and his mother came in. "Mom, is Dad feeling all right?"

"Oh, hi, honey. Yes. He's okay. Just a bit upset right now." His mom took off her coat and put her Bible on the shelf.

Matt turned off the television and walked over to her. "Anything I can do?"

"No. There're some things he has to work through himself. He'll come around. He's not thinking straight right now; he even ignored those boys down the street with the firecrackers."

"Was that the noise I heard? I should go yell at them again."

She dismissed it. "Don't bother. I'm sure they'll be blowing up something another day this year. Just leave it."

"Okay." Matt wasn't sure what was going on with her. His mom didn't like the neighbor kids playing with fireworks all year 'round. She knew it was dangerous. Now that he was looking at her closely, he noticed how stressed she looked, and her eyes were pink. "Mom, have you been crying?"

She closed her eyes as if holding back more tears. "Matt. This is just not a good night." She choked on her words. "Things were said at Bible study tonight that hurt your father. I don't understand why people have to be so mean. It was hard enough for me to hear Joan's been very ill and has to go for tests, but to have some of our close friends insinuate her illness is due to stress caused by…." She stopped midsentence, but Matt could see the implication in her eyes.

"Me," he said. "They think it's my fault."

She blinked back some tears. "I'm sorry, Matt. They have no right to say such things."

"Yeah, they do. It's called freedom of speech. I used my right that day in church when I told everyone Jamie was gay, and now they're using theirs to get back at me. It doesn't make it good or even nice, but you can't stop people from voicing their opinions." Matt was no fool. People never accepted blame if they could shift it onto someone else. "I rocked their world, and now they're turning it back on me. Jamie's not here to defend himself, so it makes it easier to say it was all me. And Ms. Joan is a bitch."

"Matt!"

"I'm sorry, Mom, but you know it's true. She's awful. If she's ill, she brought it on herself." He had no sympathy for the woman who pushed his best friend over the edge. "What did they say to Dad that got him mad?"

"They said… they thought…." Matt could feel his mom's hurt through her hesitation. "Someone questioned his authority in the house and suggested he spend less time watching sports and more time… learning how to control his son."

"What?" Matt yelled.

"They said he should use his time more wisely and spend more of it with you. Talking to you."

"This is ridiculous. You mean trying to talk me out of being gay?"

"Essentially. Your dad picked up his Bible and walked out. He was in the car ready to leave by the time I caught up. I thought he was going to leave me there." She leaned against the piano and cradled the side of her face. "He said he's going to write a letter to the church." His mom started crying again.

Matt stepped closer and rubbed her arm. "I'm sorry, Mom. I never meant for it to hurt you."

She took her hand away and looked at him. "You can't help what people say. Your father is… frustrated and confused. They hurt his pride. Kurt McKinley should not have said—"

"Mr. McKinley? I thought he left the church two years ago. His son Mikey used to play soccer with me in the field after church. Remember?"

"I remember. Kurt left when his wife lost her hearing and they needed to find a church that had an interpreter. They were at Bible study tonight because the Bixlers invited them. Kurt and your dad used to be really good friends, but they haven't spoken in over a year. We thought seeing them again was wonderful… at first. Then he jumped in and said… what he said hurt. We never intended on controlling our children when they grew old enough to make their own decisions."

"Which Hannah and I appreciate."

"We raised you up in the way we thought you should go—the way we thought God would want—and for better or worse we allow you all to make your own choices. Your dad needs time to think of the right way to handle the insults endured tonight. You understand, don't you?"

Matt nodded. "I hope he'll be all right. He's been distant lately. Other than Sunday football, he hasn't said a word to me in weeks. I know my choices are not what he would've wished for."

"It's not just you. Your dad hasn't been right since we buried Jimmy. He was very fond of that boy—we all were—and his death's been hard to get over. And then you made that speech… what you said about Jimmy made your dad think… too much. He comes from a very prejudiced family, but I don't think your father ever considered being the recipient of such bigotry."

"Yeah, I remember how he used to call black people some pretty choice things when I was little. He was downright rude."

"It wasn't just black folks. Jewish people. Foreign people. Heck, even old people brought out the worst in him. Your dad is old school. Homosexuals are still detestable to him. I'm sorry."

Matt nodded slowly. Hearing things like this about his father was not shocking, yet it hurt to know it might take a while for things to be okay between them. "What about you? Are gays detestable?" He had to know where he stood with her. "Am I… detestable?"

"Matt, I don't know how I feel right now. I don't want to lie and give you the answer you want to hear, but I don't want to upset you, either. I'm trying. Can that be okay for now?"

"Yeah. I guess it has to be." If he was honest with himself, it was more than he expected. "Do you still want to watch that movie with me when it comes in?"

She stared blankly for a moment and then answered, "You mean *Bareback Mountain*? Yes, I'd like that. We can make popcorn and snuggle on the couch."

Matt chuckled. "It's called *Brokeback Mountain* and I'm not sure I want to watch it snuggled up on the couch with my mom. No. Separate chairs. Please."

"Oh, all right." She didn't look too offended. "I think it should be here next week. There was a wait or something on Netflix."

Matt kissed his mom good night and headed upstairs. The house was quiet. Hannah was staying with a friend from college over the weekend, and Steven had opted to go to bed early. Matt doubted he was sleeping. He probably had his iPod in hand playing game apps.

Matt grinned as he passed Steven's door. He remembered being sixteen. Life was simpler then, even with his "double" life. Jamie had written about being sixteen; he didn't think it was easy.

After he brushed his teeth and undressed, Matt grabbed a journal from his shirt drawer. 2004. Matt could reminisce if he wanted to, and then put the book back in his drawer. Darian had to live in Jamie's room, in that house, surrounded by Jamie all the time. Matt wished so much he could take that burden from him.

Darian.

He opened the cover and read:

August 14, 2004

Happy fucking birthday to me!

I thought turning sixteen would be a big deal for me. Like maybe my mom would view it as some sort of rite-of-passage and she'd treat me different. I guess that only applies to girls, or to moms who give a shit. Obviously my mom couldn't care less; she sent me to my dad's this weekend; no presents, no cake.

I'm just some dumb kid who gets in the way.

MATT knew 2004 was when everything changed. He felt terrible for not noticing. Jamie was going through so much, but Matt refused to see it. He could have helped. He thought he *was* helping. He tried to talk Jamie out of being gay is what he did! He didn't know Jamie was actively gay; he thought he was going through a phase. Like going to the gym with Matt, or working on cars with Matt. He thought Jamie mentioned being gay because he wanted to be like Matt as he had in all other aspects of his life.

"Why did I think that? Because I'm a self-obsessed asshole," Matt berated himself. "Jamie should have said something."

Matt looked over at the picture of him and Jamie that sat on his nightstand—the one he always had there. They were arm in arm, beaming from Matt's last victory in track. Matt held up his trophy, and Jamie looked as proud as proud could be. Matt felt his cheeks get hot. The emotions were flooding in, but he refused to cry. "Fuckin' Jamie," he grumbled at the photo. "Why'd you leave me?"

He knew why, but knowing the truth and accepting the truth don't always coincide. It gnawed at him to think he could have done something to stop Jamie's suicide.

"And poor Dare's probably thinking the same thing—he could have done something." He sighed. "I miss Dare. I should sneak over to see him whether Dan approves or not."

It was easy to have this conversation when no one was in the room to reply. Matt was letting his feelings get the best of him, which made it easier to come up with a plan he'd never carry out. He knew he needed to respect Dan's wishes and Darian's space… for now. If Darian wanted him there, he would have asked. Matt was sure he would.

"Darian. I want to read more about Darian."

Matt hopped out of bed and swapped 2004 for 2005. He flipped though it to the part where Jamie kissed Darian for the first time. Not the time on Dare's bed, although that was sweet; Matt wanted to read the first time Jamie felt his tongue.

"Here we go!" Matt got comfortable, adjusted the pillows, and read:

OMG! Darian is a fucking AMAZING kisser.

"Yeah, he is!" Matt heartily agreed. He reached and moved his cock into a more comfortable position and skimmed the journal to read the better bits.

Maybe I should describe this from the beginning. We met at the pond—the one on the abandoned driveway. He was going to bring a sketchbook and was supposed to draw me or something—I don't know—it was all a part of making excuses to be together in a place that wasn't his bed. Although I loved the bed, I think I was one second from freaking out that day we were IN the bed. It was such a rush, feeling his hands and mouth on me.

Matt skimmed more.

I tried so hard not to give in. I wanted to be in control. I wanted to prove to myself, and Matt, that I was not only into Darian for the sex. He is so sweet. I never really considered sex before I met him. I mean... not literally. It happened so fast. One day I have him looking into my eyes and then next thing I know all I can think about is fucking him. Does that make me a man-slut like Matt? Oh God, I hope not.

Matt went on reading. It was as if he was there with them…

Darian glanced up from his sketchpad and grinned at Jimmy. It was the type of grin that spoke of mischief, like the proverbial Cheshire Cat. His gaze lingered and his cheeks colored. Jimmy swallowed the lump in his throat and watched Darian lower his eyes as he continued drawing. *Why does he keep doing that?* Jimmy thought, as his heart rate increased and his palms started to sweat. *He's trying to kill me with his wordless flirting.*

Jimmy's hands were trembling. They had been going through the motions of chatting for a while, and now they were quietly making eye contact every other second, but Jimmy was sure he knew what Darian had in mind. And it was not sketching his portrait!

"Dare…," Jimmy started, hating how his voice shook. He could not be serious if his voice shook. He started again. "Darian… do you want to…?" He raised his eyebrows, hoping his question would be heard without having to ask it.

"What?" Darian asked as the devil entered his expression and turned his mischievous eyes into brands of fire. He put down the sketchpad and moved next to Jimmy.

Jimmy knew he looked freaked out. He had to! He was breathing like a person who'd just run six miles, and his mouth was as dry as the Sahara. Still, Darian scooted right up next to him and looked him in the eyes.

"Do you want to kiss me?" Darian asked seductively.

Damn that sexy voice. "Uh-huh." Jimmy was embarrassed to sound so mouselike when he knew for a fact he was way manlier than

Darian Weston. He was taller, had bigger muscles, and was pretty sure he could punch out any guy in high school—*if* he had to. Why was he so scared now?

Darian must have seen the fear in his eyes because he changed his expression right away. "Jamie, I'm not going to eat you alive, or—God forbid—make you do anything you don't want to. We don't have to kiss. I'm happy merely sitting here with you."

Jimmy's shoulders eased away from his neck. Darian wasn't pushing—he was waiting. Suddenly, it was not a scary thing but a *right* thing, a *perfect* thing. He reached up and guided Darian's mouth closer to his. Their lips touched. And then touched again. Jimmy shifted his body so they were facing one another. He kissed him again and parted his lips, allowing his tongue to venture out and lick Darian's bottom lip. Darian sighed, and Jimmy did it again. This time there was more than lips to lick. His tongue touched something wet and slippery and tasting of strawberries. Jimmy gasped into Darian's mouth and leaned forward.

He pressed his lips securely to Darian's as he pushed his tongue into unknown territory. The sensation was intense and exhilarating, and it sent shockwaves down his spine and into his groin like his dad warned. Darian's hand was in his hair, and he was moaning. Darian's tongue was doing things to him which went way beyond the tickling feeling vibrating through his gums. Jimmy never imagined what one little appendage could arouse in him. Longings, desires, wants, needs: all Jimmy's thoughts crossed the imaginary line he'd placed in the sand after he had spoken to his father.

Jimmy couldn't take much more. He pulled back, but Darian hung on. He was sliding his tongue around Jimmy's mouth, pulling his body closer. And, oh God, Darian's tongue felt so incredible in his mouth.

Jimmy panicked and shoved against Darian's chest. "Please." He gasped for breath. "Stop. I can't."

Darian reached for him. "But—"

"No." Jimmy scrabbled to his feet. "I need… time. This is… this is too much. Please."

He stumbled his way home and locked the bathroom door. After releasing the pressure in his groin, Jimmy collapsed on his bed and grabbed his journal.

OMG! Darian is a fucking amazing kisser! And I am the world's biggest loser for running out on him. But God, I couldn't take it. Dad told me I'd feel like this, but I wouldn't believe him. As soon as Darian's tongue touched mine I fought the urge to reach into his pants. He made my body burn in ways I never thought it could.

I am officially freaking out now. What do I do now? How can I take it slow if all I think of is getting him naked? I am totally screwed.

Dad was right.

MATT closed the book. He knew where the writing went from there. He looked back at Jamie's picture. "Jamie, I'm on fire. I know how it feels. But I don't want to be the biggest loser. What do I do? Tell me what to do."

He placed the book back where it belonged and curled up in a ball with his pillow. Something would tell him—maybe God would tell him—what to do in this situation. He grabbed the picture off the nightstand and drifted to sleep wondering what Darian was doing and how Darian was coping.

November 13, 2010

MATT picked up the next piece of firewood and stacked it on the pile. He'd been working steadily for hours and went through three tanks of fuel on Walsh's twenty-eight-ton log splitter. Sweat poured down his back even in the cool air. Winter was on its way, and he needed to pick up the pace. Matt was a fireman, true, but most firemen had second jobs. He put in a full week's hours in four days and had the next four off. What do you do with four days off your "day job"?

Work!

Matt had been an employee of Walsh's Wood for the past seven years. He did everything from splitting logs to making deliveries to cutting grass in summer and plowing in the winter. The company kept him hopping all year long, which meant he had two full-time jobs. Mr. Walsh had always given him flexible hours, too, which was a huge perk and gave him time off whenever the need arose. Matt loved working for Mr. Walsh and made sure he always did his best.

As Matt lifted the next piece of wood, he felt his pocket vibrate. A text. Could be his mom—she often texted him with a question or emergency—but Matt swiftly yanked off his glove and fished his phone out of his pocket, hoping it was from Darian. It was!

Hey, what ya doing?

Matt was giddy. He knelt on the cold ground and removed his other glove. *Working. I have another cord to stack before lunch. What are YOU doing? Can I call?*

"Hey, you," Matt answered, happy when the phone buzzed with a call instead of a text.

Darian's quiet voice replied, "Hi. I'm working so I can't talk long. It's dead today for some reason. I guess people are waiting for the 'after Thanksgiving sale' to buy stuff for Christmas."

"How was your birthday? Did you have cake?" It was a stupid question, but Matt could not resist asking. He was still upset he hadn't gotten to see Darian, so he had to make sure it was a good day.

"Yeah. It was your standard yellow cake with white icing and my name written in blue gel. It was fine."

"But you would rather have had chocolate chip cookies, right?"

"Yeah." Darian's voice went up on the other end. "How did you know? I looove chocolate chip cookies."

Matt enjoyed how "normal" Darian's voice sounded. Not all emotional like before. It had pitch and inflection and joy. Matt wanted to hear more. "Speaking of Christmas…," Matt broached. "I want to get you something. And before you refuse the offer and claim I shouldn't because we're not officially together, I want to assure you I *am* giving you space. Lots of space… and time…. I'm giving you space and time—like a continuum. I just want to know if there is something you'd like because I am buying you something regardless."

There was a long pause. Matt worried. Maybe the space/time continuum joke was too corny. Or maybe he was putting undue pressure on Darian. They weren't dating. He hadn't seen him in weeks, but he had to bring it up. He wanted to buy him a gift. Heck, Matt wanted to give him the world!

Finally, a response came in the form of a sigh. "Okay…. If you have to buy me something, I want it to be a surprise. I don't really need anything. I tend to buy myself the things I want when I see them. Jamie never seemed to get the hint that 'I like that' is code for 'I want that.'"

Matt was surprised to hear him speak so casually of Jamie. But instead of saying something stupid, he ignored it. "I do, too, but I don't shop much. I don't have any hobbies. I buy most of my stuff from hardware stores."

"I love shopping," Darian admitted. "Even when I don't have any money, I still love to go. Lori and I haven't been shopping in ages. Should I buy *you* a present?"

Matt moved to a nearby stump so his legs wouldn't go numb from kneeling on the ground. He suddenly felt weird for bringing up the subject of gifts. "Dare, please don't buy something unless you want to. I shouldn't have asked. It was stupid. I didn't want to pressure you, but I think I just did! I know we aren't a couple and—"

"Stop!" Darian interrupted. "You don't have to keep apologizing. Stop making it more complicated than it is. Just let it happen one day at a time."

Matt was surprised to hear him so assertive. He liked it. "Okay. But I can't help wanting to do things for you…. Or to you." Matt mustered his most sultry voice for the last part. He hoped Darian appreciated the humor and didn't think it immature and inappropriate.

He heard him chuckle on the other end. "You are so bad. I guess if you have to buy me something then make it useful. Maybe in leather." Darian chuckled some more.

Matt laughed out loud and threw his head back. He slapped his knee and replied, "Now that's the Darian I'm hard for!" Matt was so intrigued. He was seeing a side of Darian he hadn't experienced. "I'll keep that in mind. Maybe I should shop online at extremerestraints.com?"

"Oh my God! You wouldn't."

"Oh, I would!" Matt let the humor settle, but his intense longing would not go away. "I've missed your voice, baby. I'm so glad you called. It's hard waiting to hear from you."

"I know, but I'm glad you are. Dan doesn't give me much space. It's overwhelming at times."

"I miss you soooo much. I have the last picture you sent set as my wallpaper. I look at it all the time. I just want to hold you."

"Me too."

"And I want to feel your lips on my neck, and I want to feel your chest vibrate against mine when I make you laugh."

"I want that too. How's work?"

"Fine. Fires. Emergencies. Same old stuff."

"Have you told anyone yet?"

Matt could hear Darian's hopeful optimism about the implied topic. He felt horrible when he responded, "No. I think Jason suspects, but it's unclear. He refers to you as my 'little hottie.'"

Darian giggled. "Hottie? Really? I like that."

Matt was only slightly embarrassed. It was a true assessment of Darian's looks, so he shouldn't feel weird being found out for the term he used. "I call it as I see it!"

Darian gushed, "I think you're hot, too. Even if—wait, the manager walked in. I gotta go."

Matt regretted the abrupt ending to their conversation. It was nice talking to Darian and hearing his thoughts. Matt texted his good-byes. *Talk soon? Bye :(*

Yeah. Soon. Bye ;+]

Matt wasn't sure if Darian was making an excuse to get off the phone or not. Perhaps the manager did walk in, but the timing was ironic. No matter the reason, Darian stopped texting. Matt hoped it wasn't because of something he said.

He picked himself up and started back on the woodpile. Loads to be done before "plow season," and the last thing Matt needed was to think about plowing in any other context besides snow!

November 15, 2010

TWENTY-SEVEN dollars and sixty-six cents was all Matt had on him. He shook his head. He'd had two hundred dollars just the other day! Where did all the money go? He knew he didn't buy anything but food—carryout and some groceries for his mom—but had he really spent over one hundred seventy dollars that fast? *Crap.*

Matt contemplated his financial situation in front of his cubby at the station. He was at work early. Two hours early to be precise. He had nothing better to do and staying home would mean dealing with weird looks from his brother after school. So he came here. The guys didn't know. There were no weird looks yet. He wondered how fast things would change if he went to the boss and came clean right now?

Then Scott shouted his name from the bay.

"What? Back here!" he shouted.

Scott popped around the corner with a weird grin on his face.

"What? Why do you look like you've just drawn three aces?" he asked, shoving his cash back into his pocket. Scott was a terrible poker player because he could never contain his mirth over drawing good cards.

"There's a hot chick in the bay waiting to talk to you. Brown hair, brown eyes, very lickable… I mean, likable. Likable."

Matt chuckled at Scott's awkwardness. *No wonder he doesn't have a girlfriend.* "Did you get a name?"

His expression dropped. "Ah, no. Sorry. I just figured she was your little brown-haired babe. You know, the 'hottie' Jason talks about? I didn't think to ask."

Matt gave him a half smile. "That's fine. I'll go talk to her." It wasn't a surprise to Matt that Scott thought the visitor was *his girl*. Darian did have dark hair—albeit black, not brown—and brown eyes. *But Darian's not a girl*, Matt thought. *Am I ever going to get up the nerve to tell the guys my "hottie" is a man?* He walked through the station with Scott in tow.

Before they entered the bay, Scott added, "She also has a kid with her. Could be her brother."

"Okay." Matt was confused, but it didn't matter. In a second, it would all make sense. He stepped through the doorway and saw the very pretty young girl waiting next to the dispatch office. He turned back around. "Scott, I'm not talking to her with you listening in. Go." He pointed in the opposite direction. "Get to work on the new chocks that got delivered yesterday. Okay? I need them inventoried before we can replace the old ones. I won't be long."

Scott hesitated but seemed to get the hint. He backed away. "Okay. Fine." He sulked, turning and leaving Matt alone with the cute, young brunette and what looked indeed like her brother.

"Hi." Matt held out his hand. "I'm Matt. You were looking for me?" He looked from her to the scrawny boy next to her and back again.

Her face lit up as she shook his hand with enthusiasm. "Hello. Yes. Yes, I was."

Matt wasn't sure where to start so he asked, "Do I… know you?" She looked vaguely familiar, but he had no idea why.

"Um, yes. I mean, no. I'm…." The girl stopped her nervous stuttering and took a visible breath. "Let me start again." She held out her hand and shook Matt's once without rattling his spine this time. "I'm Lori, Darian's friend. We met at your apartment in September."

"Oh, right." The revelation was only slightly discomfiting. "You were the one dancing, and the blonde was singing and painting her toes on my couch." He didn't want to come off the wrong way, but that was not a night Matt wanted to revisit. He was harsh to Darian and to his friends, and he regretted it.

"Yes." She laughed uncomfortably. "Her name is Sara." Then she glanced around the room, unfocused.

Her nervousness was making Matt nervous. He looked over at the youth by her side, who also looked nervous and uncomfortable. "Is this your brother?" He hoped asking something simple would calm the tension.

"Yes. This is Ian. He works at Darian's store. I hope you don't mind? I was a little intimidated coming here, and he offered to drive."

Matt didn't think he looked old enough to drive, but whatever. "It's fine. I'm sorry I came off so bad before; I'd had a rough night."

"I know. Dare told me. It's not that; I'm just not good with strangers."

She was trying to smile, but Matt could see her worry. "Did you want to talk about something in particular? Is Darian okay?" he asked, attempting to bring her attention back to him.

It worked. "I, um… Darian needs you."

Matt thought he heard her wrong. "What? What do you mean 'Darian needs me'? Is he in trouble?"

"No. No, he's fine. What I mean is, he needs to know you're here for him." She looked nervous but also sickly. Her face was pale, and her lips were dry. "Darian needs you to be there for him in the way… in a way Jamie wasn't."

"Excuse me?" Matt's anger flared before he had time to think about his response. "I don't know you. So unless you're another 'friend' that Jamie forgot to mention while he was alive, then I'd rather you not talk about him. And his name is Jimmy, by the way. Nobody calls him 'Jamie' but me." Matt lost any and all joy he might have been experiencing talking about Darian—even if they were speaking about him in a weird, uncertain, strained sort of way. Hearing Jamie's name from a total stranger was offensive.

Lori's eyes got huge, and Ian took a step back. "I'm sorry," Lori said hastily. "I didn't mean to…. I didn't know. Darian always referred to him as 'Jamie.' I never meant…." She fidgeted and sniffled and started backing away.

Matt caught her arm instinctively. "Lori, I'm sorry." This was not the way to start a conversation, and he knew it. He could see her panic, and he could see her sadness. She obviously meant no offense and was floundering for a way to save herself before she turned and fled in total embarrassment, crying. "I didn't mean to growl at you. You caught me off guard, and I snapped."

She sniffled. "I'm sorry too. I know this is difficult for you. You don't know me, and yet I know *way* more about you than I should."

"What?" He was feeling defensive again. "What are you talking about? Didn't Darian send you here?"

"No, he didn't. Darian doesn't know I'm here. Darian *can't* know I'm here."

"Why? What is this about? You just said he was okay. You're starting to freak me out; the way you won't focus on my face, and now you're sweating even though it's cold in here. Tell me what's going on."

Lori closed her eyes momentarily, presumably pulling herself together. When she opened her eyes, she was no longer jumpy. "Darian needs you." This time her voice was steady and sure. Matt wasn't sure he liked this serious tone any better than the panicky one. "He is not okay, and he has never been okay since probably the fifth grade. He's insecure, lonely, and afraid. But that isn't the problem I came here about. Right now his problem is you."

"Excuse me?" Matt could only hold back his anger so many times. If she kept saying things like that, he was going to bodily remove her from the premises—mainly because he didn't believe in hitting women.

"Look. I don't know you, but Darian cares more about you than even he realizes."

Now Matt was back to confusion. "Really?"

"Really." Ian spoke for the first time; however, he quickly ducked his face as if he had said something without permission.

Matt looked at the spiky-haired youth and back to his sister. "So… he talks about me?" His fuzzy feelings for Darian started surfacing. He felt giddy at the prospect of being talked about.

"No, he doesn't. Not really. He avoids talking about you."

Fuzzy feeling shriveled up and frustration flared. This was worse than a tennis match. She was really good at getting his emotions all stirred up and swinging in all directions. "Then how do you know…?"

"I just do. Look, I've known Darian since we were three. I was there when his dad walked out, and he cried for weeks. I was there for each of his mom's boyfriends and all the siblings who don't talk to him long enough to know his middle name is Andrew. I'm his best friend, and I'm telling you, Darian cares about you, and he needs to know you're going to be there for him."

"I am. I will be. I told him I love him and I want to be with him, but he said he needed time, so I backed off. What do you expect me to do?"

"You love him?" She looked relieved. "Good. That's good. Okay. We just need to think." Lori rubbed her hands together and looked at the floor for a moment.

"Wait." Some things were not adding up in Matt's head. "He never mentioned that? You said you're his best friend. You also said he doesn't talk about me, so how did you end up here?"

Lori forced a smile. Matt could tell. "I stalked you."

"What?" Not what he expected.

"I stalked you… on the Internet. I'm sorry. When Darian went into the bathroom, I stole his phone to figure out what he's been doing and who he's been texting, if anyone. I found pictures of you on his phone. Naked pictures. Amazingly naked pictures." Her eyes widened as if she heard what she'd just admitted. She threw her hands up in front of her. "Not that I want to think about you naked or anything. That would be totally inappropriate. Not to mention disgusting. So I… I wrote down your number and later Googled your name."

"He's got naked pictures of me?" Matt was not shocked; he felt flattered. And a little irked that he hadn't thought to take any of Darian.

Matt noticed Ian's cheeks flush. Maybe he saw them too.

Lori continued without commentary. Either she was too embarrassed to go back to that subject, or she didn't want to say any more with her brother standing there. "I found where you lived, when you graduated from the academy, your accomplishments in track… too many things, actually. I'm sorry. I'm a really good stalker. I didn't realize it would be that easy, but you've done a lot of things for your community. Your aunt was nice enough to tell me you moved back home and you work here. I just had to talk to you so I took a chance on you working today."

Matt was speechless. He'd never been stalked—that he knew of—and it was disturbing to know someone could find out where he worked and lived, and all that other stuff, from his cell phone number.

"You look mad. Please don't be mad. Darian really likes you. I know he does. I wouldn't be telling you all this if I wasn't trying to help my best friend."

Matt didn't know what to feel. He was angry, somewhat, but also curious. She didn't look like a freak, even though she admitted to researching practically his entire life online. He looked around the station; no one was nearby. Still, he didn't feel comfortable standing there in the bay where anyone could hear. "Maybe you can start by explaining what's going on? Let's sit outside. There's a picnic table around the side of the building. I don't think it's any colder out there than in here."

"All right," Lori agreed. She and her brother followed Matt through the door and around to the picnic table. The sky was overcast—rain likely. No wind. They could sit and talk without being overheard or disturbed.

"So…. What's going on?" Matt gestured for her to continue her explanation.

"Darian… Darian is… confused. He's… he's not in a good place." Her answer was as convoluted as her expression.

Matt wasn't sure what she was trying to say. "You're going to have to be clearer on this."

"Okay. I'm sorry. This is hard for me. I feel like I'm betraying his trust or something. I'm not sure what you *do* or *don't* know about Darian, and I feel bad telling you things. I also get really nervous talking to strangers."

Matt reached over and squeezed her arm. "Lori, it's okay. Just tell me. I promise not to snap again, really. Besides, we're not strangers if you know everything about me, which it sounds like you do. No worries." He grinned. Lori smiled back. "And I promise not to tell Dare you told me. Okay? I want to know what's going on." That was as honest as he could manage to sound.

Matt had a feeling Darian had always had issues. And he also felt for Lori, as he knew what it was like betraying trust and knowing things you shouldn't, etcetera. He knew more about Darian than Darian was aware of because of the journals—journals Darian didn't know he had.

His honesty must have worked because worry fled from her eyes and color returned to her cheeks. "Okay. Here it goes. In a nutshell: Darian started cutting in sixth grade. No one knew except me until eighth grade when the gym teacher noticed. In high school, he started doing drugs, which is way longer a story than I have time for right now, but it was bad. I knew I should tell someone, but his mom never cared about him so I didn't know who I should tell. Then Jamie's dad—I mean Jimmy—Jimmy's dad found out and took him to a clinic to get clean. He cared for him. Really cared. Mr. Dan was the best thing to come along, and I think he influenced Darian in ways he wasn't even aware of. I know Darian loved Jimmy, but I also know it was way more to him than just his first love, or his high school sweetheart. Darian needed Dan to be the father he never had. I know how much that meant to him. So when Darian told me Jimmy still hadn't come out—and that went on for years—and how he was always running off to take care of other things, I let it slide because I understood how much Darian needed the whole package. Darian loved Dan as much as he loved Jimmy. He loved Dan's brother and his wife and Jimmy's cousin Maggie; and even though it hurt when Jimmy would disappear for days to do something for his mother, and—I hate to say this—*you*, Darian hung on because he wanted the whole deal. He said he knew the pain was worth the wait."

When her eyes dropped, Matt knew the next part. "And then Jamie killed himself."

Lori nodded. "Everything's different now. I've never seen Darian act like this, and I'm worried."

"Why? Act like what?" He was curious.

"For one thing, he won't talk to me. We've talked about everything, for years, and suddenly he won't tell me about you. He said he was 'happy in your arms' and that's all I've heard. It's been almost two weeks since he mentioned your name. I ask, but he won't talk. Something isn't right."

"If he doesn't talk, then how do you know he cares about me at all?"

"I saw you at the funeral, when you helped him at the gravesite."

"You were there?" He wondered because he didn't remember seeing her.

"Yeah. Sara and I were in the back. I knew he was with Mr. Dan and my attention would be too much for him. He gets overwhelmed. Then when he collapsed and you stepped in, I wondered who you were. I texted a hundred times, and it took him forever to reply. He's like that sometimes. Always has been. Sometimes he shuts down. But he said he was with you and you were Jimmy's best friend. Which also sounded weird because I remember him being jealous of your connection with Jimmy for years, and then suddenly Darian's spending weeks in your apartment."

Matt exclaimed, "It wasn't planned! It just happened." Why did he always feel so defensive over this? He quickly apologized, "I'm sorry. Go on."

"I know it wasn't planned. Darian e-mailed me and explained some of it. Anyway… Darian has a lifetime of hurt. He was finally happy with Jimmy. Not 'fairytale' happy, but content. Jimmy and his family meant everything to Darian."

"I know how he feels. Jamie was my best friend. I did everything with him, and I have a hard time remembering he's gone."

"So does Darian. That's why he needs you."

"You keep saying that, but what does that mean?"

"I don't know. I'm hoping you can help me figure it out. All I know is when I was with him the other day, and he got a text, his eyes lit up and his hands shook hoping it was from you."

"He said that?"

"No. But why else would he act like that? I asked, but he changed the subject. He won't talk. And then there are other times when he's talking and I feel as if he's talking to someone in the room other than me. He looks past me, and then looks away. I've even turned around a couple of times to see if there was someone behind me. I'm worried. He's changed, and I don't know how to reach him."

He rested his hand on hers across the table. "I'll try. Okay? I'll try to figure out what's going on."

"Thank you. But he can't know I came to you."

"I'll be discreet."

Lori took out her phone. "Here's my number."

Matt wondered what she was doing, but then his phone buzzed and stopped when she snapped her phone shut.

"Are you on Facebook?"

Matt shook his head. "No. Sorry. I did MySpace years ago, but I don't have time for that stuff now. I rarely remember to check e-mail."

"You should. Darian posts a lot of things on there. Pics too. I wish I knew what more to say. Just don't give up on him. Call him. He'd like that."

"He told me not to."

"Don't listen to everything he says. Go with what your heart tells you. He wants you to call. Don't get me wrong, he may not pick up, but if you leave a message, it'll mean the world to him. He likes listening to them over and over again. I know he has at least four from Jimmy. He saves each message when it's about to expire. He has one message, I swear, from two years ago when I called and sang happy birthday to him. He's very sentimental."

Matt grinned. That sounded so like Darian. It was also exactly like him. "Okay. I'll call. I save messages as well. I have six from Jamie, two from my mom, one from my sister nine months ago, and one from a kid in the church youth group—I'm not joking—from three years ago when he called pretending to trek through the Amazon with his friends. I thought it was funny and couldn't bring myself to delete it."

"Oh my God. You two are so right for each other."

"I'm glad you think so, but I wouldn't base your opinion on saved phone messages."

"No, but you're a family guy. Darian loves family because he's always wanted one that cared. You're sentimental. So is he. You're tall, gorgeous, and built like Ryan Reynolds—totally his type. *And* you have the decency to give him space to figure out what he wants. I like that."

"Glad to have your seal of approval." Matt liked her. Really liked her.

Lori beamed. "Thanks. We'll have to do this again soon. I really should go. I have to get back and have dinner ready for Sara when she gets off from work." Lori stood up and adjusted her jacket, zipping up the front.

"You live together?"

"Not yet, but she *is* my girlfriend."

"Oh." Matt voice went up slightly, embarrassing him.

Lori snickered. "See, you're not the only one. But this is new for us. We've been friends for almost ten years. Last year, we decided to make it official, but she's younger than me so we're taking it slow. So far, it's been really awesome. I love her."

"And your family is fine with it?"

"Not really." She shrugged. "They're still adjusting. Not angry, just… adjusting. Her family's cool though. It helps."

"And your brother?" Matt looked at Ian, who'd been almost invisible the entire conversation.

"Um…." Ian cleared his throat. "I'm good. I don't care if she likes girls."

"Well, I wish you luck." Matt held out his hand as he walked around the table. Lori smacked it away and hugged him. "Whoa!" He was taken off guard but hugged her back in seconds.

"Darian is like a brother to me," she confessed. "That makes you family. I'll see you again soon." She started walking away, brother at her side, and turned briefly to add, "Text if you need anything." With another smile, she was gone.

Matt collected his thoughts before venturing back inside. He had a lot to think about. As he was about to walk back in and start his shift, his phone rang. It wasn't Darian. Every time it rang, he hoped it was Darian. Oddly enough it was Dan Miller.

"Hey, Dan. I hope this is a good call and not something to make me worry." He had enough to worry about after talking to Lori.

"No, no. I'd just like to get together and talk with you. Are you free sometime this week for coffee?"

"Yeah. How about Thursday? Eleven thirty. I'm also open Saturday before two."

"Thursday works. I'll see you then," he said, and the line went dead.

Matt could not believe how hastily Mr. Miller had hung up the phone. It seemed so unlike him. Whatever was going on, Matt was sure he would not be sleeping until he found out. Between Lori's bizarre explanation of Darian's emotional needs and Dan's terse exchange, Matt was dumbfounded.

Matt shuffled inside, moaning, "Ah, I need coffee."

Scott popped around the corner. "You need coffee? I can get you coffee!" And off he zipped.

Matt groaned some more. Surely Scott would want more details than Matt was willing to give. Coffee would only satisfy part of his needs—Matt needed a serious emergency. And maybe a strenuous workout after his shift. Something!

12

November 17, 2010

"SOMETHING" came in the form of a four-car collision involving a jackknifed tractor-trailer and a telephone pole. Several ambulances were called to the scene, including the one at his station, and four fire engines.

Matt was the first man off Engine 124, jumping to the ground as soon as it came to a stop. He headed for the officer who seemed to be in charge. "What's the situation?"

The middle-age officer from the county Sheriff's department pointed to one of the overturned vehicles. "We have two people trapped in that car, one bleeding, the other unconscious." He turned his body and pointed to another car. "The car in the median has a man in the backseat; no driver present."

Matt scrunched his eyes, but he held commentary until later. The officer pointed in another direction. "The tractor-trailer driver is stable, but we are going to have to get a tow for the rig."

No doubt, Matt thought. *The thing is on its side, perpendicular to the road!*

The officer kept talking. "There is a woman and a child in that car. She clipped two cars and smashed into the telephone pole."

After the officer gave him the rundown, Matt turned away and shouted at Billy. "Randall! Take Forbes and Shaw and cover the blue Ford on the right side. Woman and child. Head-on collision with that pole."

"Got it, Lieutenant!" Billy nodded.

Matt turned to the next guy, ready to bark out orders. He may have been slow to start, but Matt knew when to kick things into gear. People needed direction, and he was a born leader. Ever since middle school, when gym class started getting ugly and boys would turn on one another, Matt decided he was not about to get picked last for dodge ball. He became assertive then, and he continued that way all the way to his present job. "Captain Riley, check on the overturned vehicle. Have Green fire up the hydraulics. Sounds like those two will need to be pried out of the car."

Jason smirked and nodded. "Yes, sir."

"Turner, I want you to check on the tractor-trailer guy while I search the area for the missing driver of the other car."

"I'm on it!"

Confident in his crew, Matt turned to survey the scene. Glass and metal debris littered the asphalt. There were cars everywhere and police trying to direct traffic around the accident. Several other fire engines had their men on the scene, so things were well under control. Smoke and steam rose from several cars that sat crushed at various spots around the intersection. And the tractor-trailer was blocking half the road.

As he looked around, he spotted one victim standing by an ambulance. He was young, maybe twenty-two years old. He had blood dripping down his arm. It was thick, and the boy looked dazed. Matt stared. He was fixated on the blood. Blood like Jamie's. They said Jamie sliced open his arm. Jamie was twenty-two. Did Jamie look that ghastly?

A dark brown hand appeared in front of his eyes and snapped its fingers. It wasn't a disembodied hand; it belonged to Jason, and he was just about to slap Matt across the face to get his attention. "Matt!" he screamed. "I've been yelling your name for five minutes. What the hell happened?"

"I-I don't know." Matt was disorientated. "I saw a g-guy who was bleeding like Jamie, and…." Matt zoned out again.

"Matt, if you can't deal, then get the hell out of the way."

Matt shook the fog from his mind. *No, he could do it.* "I'm fine. I'm sorry." He knew he'd get an earful later, but for now Jason seemed to understand.

"Fine. I'll take over here. You go check out that car in the median."

"Okay. I'm sorry." Matt hung his head as he hurried over to what had to be the easiest job in the whole accident. He needed to find the driver. He could handle that. He was ashamed of blanking out, but at least he wasn't completely useless. Matt peered inside the car and noticed the man sitting quietly in the backseat. He was elderly and pale, breathing heavily, and staring straight ahead without blinking. Most likely in shock.

"Uh, sir, are you okay?" When the man didn't respond, he asked another question. "Sir, who was driving the vehicle?" Nothing. "Sir, where's the driver?" Matt opened the rear door and peered inside. The man sat perfectly still. He was not buckled, but he appeared to be without injury. "Sir, I need to get you out of the car, and I need for you to tell me who was driving."

As soon as Matt placed a hand on the man's arm, he started screaming, "Don't touch me! Don't touch me!"

Matt jumped back. "Okay. Okay. I won't touch you. Tell me what's going on. Are you in pain? Where is the driver?"

The man slowly turned to face Matt. "I was driving," he said quietly.

Matt was shocked. "You were—"

"Driving."

"Fuckin' hell," he breathed to himself as he looked back into the driver's seat again. Sure enough, the seatbelt was snapped. But how this man ended up in the backseat was a mystery. "Sir," Matt said as he crouched by the door, "I have no idea how that is possible, but I believe you. Right now, I need to get you out of this car and away from this area. It is extremely dangerous for us to sit here too long."

"I can't."

"Sir, I *have* to get you to a hospital."

"I understand all that."

"Then why won't you—"

The man blurted, "I just had hip replacement surgery!"

"You… wait… what?" Matt couldn't believe his ears.

"My hip was replaced, and I was released from the hospital yesterday. I had no one to drive me to Target, so I thought I would get in and drive myself."

"Shit! Sir, that was not a good idea."

"You think I don't know that?" The man looked agitated, which was a good thing because it brought some life back into his eyes. Matt was beginning to think he was in shock because of his former blank stare and his shaking hands.

Matt had to stay focused. "Regardless of that, sir, I need to get you out of this car."

"I know. I'm just in a lot of pain right now, and I'm afraid to move. I don't know how I got here." He put his palms on his thighs and closed his eyes. Matt could hear his deep breaths.

"What if I bring you a stretcher and some morphine, how's that?"

The man grinned and nodded. "Perfect."

AFTER getting his "backseat driver" taken care of, Matt surveyed the progress and was pleased. Jason and Tim, along with some men from other crews, had already opened the overturned car like a sardine can, peeling back the metal with the Jaws of Life. Paramedics were loading up their ambulances with the injured. Everything was rolling along smoothly.

Or so he thought.

"No! Don't touch him!" Matt turned to his left when he heard a woman screaming at one of his fellow firefighters. Billy stood in front of the blue Ford with a woman while Mike helped a paramedic roll a child toward the ambulance. "Let me go!" she screamed, swatting at Billy.

Matt swiftly approached, and as he did, it occurred to him that from behind the woman looked exactly like….

"Ms. Joan?" He voiced his thoughts.

She immediately turned his way. "Matt!" She looked relieved and reached for him. Billy let her go. "Oh thank God! They're taking Jimmy away from me. They don't understand. He hates hospitals. He's afraid of the dark. If they keep him overnight, he'll throw up Jell-O for days. You have to help him!" She clung to the front of his coat and pleaded. Her face was full of terror and pain and desperation.

"Ms. Joan, Jimmy died… two months ago. That's your son Tommy. They're taking him to the hospital for…." Matt paused and shifted his eyes to Billy.

"Laceration to the forehead and a broken collarbone." Billy finished Matt's sentence right on cue. "Ma'am."

"But he…," she started to say, looking at the ambulance as her son was loaded. She looked back at Matt, bleary-eyed. "…and you…." Something in her eyes changed as Matt watched. Her fear faded and rage took its place. She shoved him away. "Filthy sinner!" She hissed. "You're nothing but a disgusting abomination. Get away from me!" She turned to the ambulance and leapt for the doors. "Don't you dare take my son away from me! I'll call the police!" Billy once again grabbed her before she fell off the tailgate trying to crawl inside the ambulance. "Police! Police!" She howled, thrashing in Billy's arms. "Let me go! I'll scream!" She clawed at his hands and writhed in his arms. All she needed was a little grease and this would be almost as bad as when Billy hauled Matt to a pig-catching contest. Matt had no idea Joan Smithers had enough stamina to thrash about so wildly for this long. It was insane!

"Rape!" she hollered.

Billy dropped her cold and backed off, hands in the air. "I didn't do anything."

An officer approached cautiously. He nodded at Billy. "Duly noted. Ma'am, would you please come with me."

"Who are you?" she spat.

He was unaffected by her anger and spoke steadily. "I'm Officer Taglione. I've observed the situation, and I believe I know where they took your son. If you come with me, I can help you get him back."

Immediately, her stance changed. "You do? Oh, thank you, Officer. These men don't understand. I have to get to my Jimmy. He's my baby. He'll be frightened."

The police officer guided the bewildered Mrs. Smithers into the back of his squad car. After closing the door, he motioned for Matt to step into the blind spot where she would be unable to see them talking. "So what is going on here? I take it that boy is not Jimmy?"

Matt shook his head. "No, Officer. The boy in the ambulance is Tommy Smithers. He's about six years old. I was told he has a broken collarbone, and they're taking him to the hospital. That woman is Joan Smithers—his mother. Her son Jimmy was my best friend, and he died two months ago. I don't know if she hit her head in the accident, but she's not thinking clearly."

"Thank you. I'll take her over to the hospital and have her checked out… with restraints, if need be."

"Good idea," said Matt.

"Is there someone to contact? Especially about the boy?"

"Yeah. I'll call his dad. I'll make sure he knows where they both are."

"Good."

After the officer left with Ms. Joan, Matt called Mr. Kevin. He hadn't talked to him in months, and he was not looking forward to telling him now his wife and child were en route to the hospital.

Sometimes being a nice guy sucked.

November 18, 2010

DAN and Matt agreed to meet at one of his favorite restaurants on Main Street. Matt was fifteen minutes early, and he asked for a booth in the corner. He'd always liked the décor and the vaulted ceilings of this place. The restaurant was plain enough to feel comfortable if you were an electrician in for a quick bite at lunchtime—raggedy jeans and calloused, soiled hands—and it was fancy enough for the "suit and tie" crowd. Matt liked the mix. It was reassuring to think people in different walks of life could get along and come together over food. Kind of like the last supper with Jesus….

Matt smiled.

As he waited, he secretly hoped Dan would bring Darian but was not shocked to see Dan come in alone. As soon as the waitress set their coffee in front of them and left, Mr. Miller abruptly spoke his mind.

"I'd like to get straight to the point. I don't want you sleeping with Darian."

Matt almost snorted his coffee out his nose. After he wiped his mouth and composed himself, he said, "He told you?"

"No. His therapist informed me of some details he filled in last week. And later Darian and I had a few discussions on the matter."

Matt eyed him curiously. *So much for doctor/patient confidentiality.* "I see." This was very interesting, considering what Lori had told him about Darian *not* talking lately. Maybe he wasn't talking to her, but he was talking to someone.

"Matt, I'm not sure how to ask this, but… when exactly did you become gay? Or are you bisexual? Because it seems to me that you're jumping at Darian right when he's vulnerable and hurting just to get a piece of his—"

"Whoa, whoa, whoa!" Matt held up his hands to put on the brakes. "What are you talking about, 'become gay'? I've always been gay."

"Matt. I've known you a long time. You've never displayed any interest in—"

"Mr. Miller!" He had to stop this conversation before it started. "I can assure you I've been into boys since the third grade. This thing with Darian isn't some rash decision. It wasn't a one-night stand, and it was completely consensual. Dare and I—"

"He said you fucked him next to a house by the funeral home."

"Shit." Matt tried to remain calm. *Oh, Darian.* There had to be some explanation. Lori said Dare and Mr. Miller were very close—apparently closer than Matt knew. *Unless Dan is threatening him.* Matt would have to remember that. For now, he was completely embarrassed.

"Mr. Miller…," he began, trying to explain and appear unruffled. "I assure you, what happened that first time with Darian was not meant to hurt him in any way. It just happened. And afterward I was trying to be a friend and comfort him, but things just… exploded between us."

"At a very convenient time… for you," Dan countered. "Darian was in love with Jimmy. I saw the two of them all the time, exchanging glances, laughing, and planning their lives together. They were happy. The next thing I know, Darian is at your apartment for weeks. Even the day of the funeral, he had his head in your lap. I didn't say anything because I knew he needed a friend, and he needed time; but when you brought him home, he was different."

Which is exactly what he says about you!

Matt wasn't sure what to say. He'd felt so defensive when Dan started off with such a shocking intro, but now he was listening, and Dan's concerns seemed valid, even worrisome. *I did take advantage.* As time went on, Matt felt more and more remorse over the way things went down. "How is he different?"

"He's quiet. Withdrawn. He won't talk about Jimmy. He doesn't want to put Jimmy's things away, but he seems disturbed they're out. I thought he was having a hard time letting go. Then I caught him staring at pictures of you. I heard him a few times in the shower… moaning your name. And I hear him at night sometimes talking to himself. Having a conversation about you and your… endowments. I began putting the pieces together."

"What pieces?" Matt was suspicious of Dan's deductions.

"Pieces that suggest maybe Darian is okay with Jimmy's death because he was having an affair with you… before Jim died."

Matt reeled. "No! Mr. Miller, we weren't—"

"I think you should back off. I don't want you seeing my son." Dan was cool and stern.

"What? I have backed off," he shrieked. "I haven't seen him in a month and a half."

"I know. But you text often, don't you? And the two of you talk on the phone. Yesterday you left a message, even though he told you not to call."

"He told you that too?"

"No. I check his phone."

"And you don't think that's a little bit over the top? What about his privacy? Does Darian know you monitor his texts?" Matt was shocked. He didn't remember Dan being this scrupulous. Something weird was going on, and Matt felt dangerously exposed. First Lori stalked him online, and now Dan was monitoring his texts to Darian. What was next? A GPS link or a security camera?

Dan held his ground. "No. I'm doing this for his own good. And I'd prefer it if you didn't say anything."

"I guess you would." Matt was uncomfortable and growing more and more agitated. Lori asked the same thing. Matt didn't like what they were asking; he was opposed to lying to Darian. "I'm not going to lie for you. If he asks, I'm not lying."

Mr. Miller tilted his head, and looked at Matt. "Matt, please, I am trying to do what is best for Darian. He needs time to work through his grief. You have to see that jumping into your bed isn't healthy? The relationship won't last, and then he will be alone again and have to face the remorse of rebound sex."

Matt closed his eyes. Dan was right. Disturbingly accurate, and right. He'd been thinking the same thing since he and Darian had hooked up. Even his mom told him it wouldn't last. "You're right. I didn't mean for all this to happen."

"Then you have to back off. No more phone calls. No more texts."

"But what's wrong with texts?"

"Do I really need to spell that out for you?" He began to quote some of Matt's texts. "'I have this fantasy involving a sling…. I can't wait to get my mouth on you…. I'm sliding inside of you and—'"

"Stop! I get your point. No more texts. But I really want to see him, Mr. Miller. This isn't casual sex. It's not an impulsive outcome born from grief. Not anymore. We both want to pursue a real relationship."

"Do you? Both of you? I think you're pressuring him. I think you are exploring new ground and taking advantage of him when you know he's confused."

"Mr. Miller, I'm not! Please. Don't take Dare away from me cold turkey. Let me have one date. Please? Just one date." Matt was seconds from falling to his knees, begging. He had to see Darian one more time.

"Fine," Dan relented. "One date. Against my better judgment. I'll give you four hours in the middle of the day. No bars, no dance clubs, no sex. You take him someplace public where it isn't likely you'll do something unseemly."

Matt did not like his tone of voice. Dan Miller was bartering and doing it with no wiggle room for Matt to counteroffer a different scenario. He knew he had to take what he was offered and be happy with it, or Dan was going to retract it. "I'll take it. I'm off next Saturday. Can I take him to the National Gallery in DC?"

Dan contemplated as he sipped his coffee. Matt hated not having the upper hand. He was subject to Dan's whims and Dan's rules. Darian even said he was having a hard time with the rules. What would Dan do now?

"Fine. Next Saturday. Pick him up at noon. I'll give you until five to bring him home since DC is over an hour away."

"Thank you. Thank you so much. I'll take good care of him, I promise. No sex. Just talking and hanging out, looking at art."

"You will take care of him, and I expect to see pictures from DC. And a brochure from the museum." Dan said it with deadly surety. He tossed some bills on the table and stood up to leave. "You'll follow my rules, or you'll never see him again."

Matt had never been threatened before, but he was pretty sure this was what it felt like. He was trapped. Lori said to text, but Dan said not to. Dan was monitoring his phone. Dan said he'd never see him again. Dan held all the cards. Lori would have to understand.

After Dan was out of sight, Matt took out his phone and started to text Lori his plan. One week without texts to Darian. But what if Darian texted him? Did Dan tell Darian to stop as well? Matt hoped he did. Lori also needed to know Dan would see her texts and she needed to be careful what she said.

Matt was used to deception. He'd kept his sexuality hidden very well over the years. But this was a sticky situation and not exactly the same as slipping out once in a while to have sex with strangers at a gay bar. These were all people he knew. This was about keeping conversations secret and figuring out what was going on inside Darian's head without telling him. Matt wasn't sure he was up to the task, but for Darian, he'd do whatever it took. Plus, in nine days he'd get to see Darian! That was motivation to walk through fire.

"Matt."

Dan's voice startled him into a virtual panic attack. "Mr. Miller!" he exclaimed, bobbling his phone like a hot potato. Once he had a firm grip on it, he snapped it shut and slid the phone over next to the salt and pepper shakers, out of the way.

"Sorry." Dan Miller slid back into the booth; he wore a troubled expression. "When I got to the car...," he said gravely, pausing midthought. "As I got in, I remembered I only brought up half of what I wanted to talk to you about."

"Oh yeah? What else is there?" Matt was afraid to ask, but he gestured Mr. Miller to continue.

"Joan.... Kevin called me the other day to tell me she was admitted into the Greater Baltimore Medical Center for some tests. He said you were at the scene of an accident she had on Monday."

"Um, yeah. I was. I called to let him know Tommy was injured and was being taken to the hospital by ambulance. I also told him something was wrong with Ms. Joan. She wasn't acting right."

"Yes. I'm glad you did." Dan was glum and spent. His expression now bore no resemblance to the accusatory cross-examiner who had been sitting in the booth with Matt moments ago. His finger-pointing was gone. His hostility vanished. Matt now sat with the man he remembered all his life. His best friend's dad. The guy who let them stay up late and camp in the backyard when his wife was visiting her sister in Ohio. This was the gentle Dan Miller.

"Mr. Miller? Is something wrong with her?" Matt could sense it in his expression.

He heaved a sigh. "Kevin told me they found a dark patch on her MRI. It's a tumor. They don't know how long it's been there because this type of tumor only presents itself as mood swings or changes in behavior. Sort of like Tourette's or bipolar disorder, but more intense. It affects personality and eventually memory."

Matt felt awful. True, he'd never liked the woman, but he also would never wish ill on anyone. "Mr. Dan, I'm so sorry." He reached across the table and placed his hand over Dan's.

Dan Miller sobbed quietly. "I never stopped loving her, Matt. Even when she had an affair and got pregnant with Kevin's child, I still forgave her. I still wanted her back."

"I didn't know." Matt had no idea what to do or say next. "Is it cancer?"

Dan shrugged. "They don't know. They want to do a biopsy. And do more tests."

"Tests are good."

"Kevin said she's irrational and explosive. They had to put her in restraints."

"Damn!"

"I had no idea. I always knew she was moody but this…. What if it's my fault?"

"What? No!" Matt didn't want this kind man taking the blame for anything.

"What if it is? Maybe I should have questioned her mood swings more closely. What if they'd found the tumor years ago? Maybe she wouldn't have left me?"

"Mr. Miller… she left you for another man, not because of a tumor. And her treatment of Jamie didn't get violent until well after the fights started and she threatened to leave."

"Violent? Jimmy? What did she do to him?" Dan leaned forward and studied Matt. "How much do you know?"

"I, um…." Matt had gotten himself cornered this time. His big mouth did him in. "Mr. Miller…. All I know is that she hit Jamie sometimes. She'd get mad about his grades, or his laziness, and clock him with a candlestick or something. I never thought it was mental illness." And he knew that was a lie. He and Jamie always spoke of schizophrenia. "Okay, maybe that's not true. Jamie and I joked about her being 'mental,' but we didn't mean it."

"How come he never told me?"

"He was scared to break up another family. He said she might do jail time for abuse, and Mr. Kevin would be stuck raising a baby. He didn't want to cause that."

Dan nodded. "I can understand that. So, this has been going on that long? Since Tommy was a baby?"

"The physical abuse? Sort of. I think it started earlier than that. She's always been… well… a bitch. It's hard to know what's from 'personality changes' and what is pure personality. Ya know?"

Dan half smirked. "Yeah, I know. She's a tough one. I'm going to have to let Kevin know these things. He needs to tell the doctors and give them dates and incidents. Would you be able to write some down? Sort of recount history for me? I'd appreciate it. Anything will help them pinpoint the type of tumor or disease she has and get her treated properly."

"Sure," Matt said. He'd just have to skim over Jamie's journals and jot down shortened details and dates. It would be easy.

Dan stood up again and stuck out his hand. Matt took it. "Thank you, Matt. I'm sure Darian will be in good hands. This is the person I remember you being. I guess I have to factor in the gay part and remember you've always been this way."

"I have. I promise. This is me." He held his hands out to either side. "Apart from keeping my sexuality a secret, what you see is what you get."

"Okay. Thanks. I'll see you next Saturday at noon." Mr. Miller nodded and walked away.

Matt collapsed in the booth. "Forget coffee, I need a fuckin' beer!"

November 27, 2010

MATT rang the doorbell and heard barking. He instinctively took a step back; he didn't remember Darian mentioning a dog before. He didn't want any dog to come flying out and jump on him before he could hand Darian the flowers he had painstakingly picked out. It had been a long time since they had seen each other, and he wanted to make the best impression possible. Plus, if Dan was only going to allow one date, it was going to be a gosh-darn good one!

The door opened, but no dog attacked. Still, Matt was assaulted by a sudden adrenaline burst and loss of breath at the sight of Darian standing in the doorway. He was stunning. His skin was more luminescent than Matt remembered. His hair was short, exposing his neck and ears, but not buzzed as it had appeared in the photo from three weeks ago. His long bangs were swept to one side and contained several streaks of blond. Matt itched to touch it.

He wore a long-sleeved, graphic T-shirt, and his tight black-and-purple zebra-striped skinny jeans. The look was very "Darian" and incredibly hot. Matt absent-mindedly licked his lips. Today would write a new definition of "self-control." He had promised Dan "no sex," and he was going to make good on that promise even if it killed him!

He stepped forward and held out his bouquet. "Hi. I brought these for you." *Fuck, why do I sound so nervous?*

Darian must have detected his edginess because he smirked. Matt loved that smirk. Then Darian blushed as he took the flowers and said, "Thanks." He brought them to his face and smelled the carnations. "I can't remember the last time I got flowers."

Matt stepped closer. "I hope you don't think it's stupid. I wanted to do something nice."

Darian shyly shook his head. Instead of backing up and allowing Matt to step through the door into the house, he stood still and gazed at Matt. Their eyes melted into one another's. Matt's breathing got faster, and his eyes dropped to Darian's glistening lips. He loved that lip ring! He wanted to bite Darian's bottom lip and pull his lip ring into his mouth.

Darian whispered, "You can kiss me if you want."

Matt could envision the outcome if he kissed Darian the way he ached to kiss him. He'd lean in and touch his lips to Darian's, but the contact would quickly heat up his groin, and Matt would be powerless to keep his hands from sliding down Darian's back, squeezing his tight little ass. There would be breathlessness and nakedness in seconds. No, kissing was not a good idea.

"I don't think I should," he replied. Matt tried to slip into the house past Darian, but when he heard Darian practically beg with a barely audible "please," he paused. "Dare, I won't have the strength to stop."

Darian fixed a licentious gaze on him and said, "Yes, you will." He put his hand on Matt's chest and stepped closer. "Please," he whispered again.

Matt could feel the heat of Darian's palm through his shirt. Darian's cologne filled Matt's nostrils, making him breathe more deeply and absorb as much of his scent as he could. Darian was surely *his* narcotic. The little vixen knew how to play him; from his tight jeans to his enticing cologne, he was a walking aphrodisiac and Matt was powerless to resist. *But I have to!* He'd promised Darian, and he'd promised Dan. No sex. *I shouldn't kiss him.*

But those eyes.... And those lips....

Just one kiss. One little kiss. Surely he could keep his dick in check long enough for one kiss?

Matt's face inched closer to Darian's. He could feel Darian's breath on his lips. Their noses touched, and Matt hovered there, savoring the closeness. He reached up and cupped Darian's cheek as he closed the distance between them. Their lips touched, and Matt heard Darian inhale sharply through his nose. His lips were warm and tasted of vanilla-mint toothpaste. He released Darian's mouth after only a few seconds of pressure and felt a wet swipe across his lips. He could have groaned, knowing what Darian wanted, but a clearing-of-the-throat from inside the house reminded Matt one kiss was all they should risk. Matt stepped back and looked at Dan.

"Hello, Mr. Miller."

"Matt," he said, hovering like a mother hen, all-knowing and implying his stern warning with just the utterance of a name. He reached out and shook Matt's hand. "I trust you'll take good care of my son today."

Matt squared his shoulders. "Yes, sir. He'll be safe with me, sir."

Dan turned to Darian. "I trust you'll remember what we talked about?"

Darian looked down. "Yes." He held up the bouquet. "I'll just get these into some water."

Darian hurried out of the room before Matt could offer to help. Matt questioned, "Is he okay? He was really relaxed just a second ago."

"He's fine."

"Mr. Miller, you and I had a really long and unforgettable conversation the other day, and I assure you I'm not going to try anything. We don't have to go over it again and again as if I can't remember what Darian's been through. We're only going to a museum, not a rave party."

"I know. And it's not you I'm worried about. Just be careful."

"What?" *That was vague.* He wanted to know more, but Darian came back into the room and asked to leave. "Yeah, sure, we can go," Matt said.

Darian grabbed his jacket from the closet. "Bye, Dan… er, Dad. Dad. Good-bye, Dad."

"Good-bye, Mr. Miller." Matt waved and headed for the door.

Dan squeezed Darian's shoulder. "It's okay. Stop worrying about calling me Dad. When it happens, it happens."

"Okay."

"Okay?"

Darian smiled. "Yeah, bye."

Matt walked to the passenger side and opened the door of his truck for Darian. It felt good to do the gentlemanly thing. He closed the door and walked around to his side. After a few minutes, Matt worked up the gumption to ask about Dan's comment. "So, what did Dan say to you?"

"About what?" Darian asked, but he clearly knew very well what Matt was asking.

"You know, at the house, when he said to remember what you talked about."

Darian looked out the passenger window. "Oh, that. He's worried about my… my addiction."

"To drugs? I thought you were over that?" Matt glanced over at Darian. Why was Darian looking out the window and not at him? And what about the chasm of space between them across the seat?

"No. Not drugs. My… sexual addiction, but I don't want to talk about it."

Matt practically ran a stop sign as he turned his full attention on Darian. "Shit! Sorry about that."

Darian let go of his newly acquired grip on the dashboard. "It's okay. Jamie wasn't the best driver in the world. We stopped short loads of times."

Matt pulled away from the stop sign and drove for a few minutes in silence. He was about to address this "addiction issue" again when Darian urged him to pull over. Matt was still trying to figure out what was going on. "What?"

"I said pull over—now!"

Darian was staring straight ahead. Maybe he was sick? Matt pulled off the side of the road and put the truck in park. "Are you feeling all right? Are you going to throw up? I can take you back home."

Before Matt had time to figure out what was going on, Darian turned toward him, undid his seat belt, and pressed his mouth to Matt's. Darian practically crawled on top of him while kissing him deeply and making the most wonderful sounds: hungry and needy. Darian pressed against his body as he ran his hands all over Matt's chest and groin.

"I want you, Matt. It's been so long."

Matt knew he should resist, but it was very difficult to adhere to the rules for this date when Darian was coming on so powerfully. "We… can't," he said between Darian's fervent kisses. "Promised… Dan." *But God, his tongue feels so good in my mouth.*

"Please. I need you."

Matt was getting tired of hearing the word "need." Darian's need and want were obvious. Matt desperately wanted to hear "love" instead, but he didn't say anything. He pushed Darian away and said, "No. You can't lie, Darian. Dan will know. I'm not gonna to fuck you in my truck."

Darian sat back, dejected. He was thinking, and Matt was worried. Then a mischievous look crossed his face coupled with a glint in his eyes. "A hand job isn't sex."

Matt shook his head. "That's debatable." He was trying to think of how to protest *any* sort of sexual favors when Darian stripped off his jeans faster than Matt thought possible, given the fact they were painted on. Matt groaned. Darian's rigid cock slapped against his belly as he slipped out of his boxer briefs. He had a beautiful cock, and Matt wanted nothing more than to wrap his lips around it.

Darian turned over on the seat and lay back in Matt's lap, outstretched in the truck cab. "I want to come in someone else's hand; I'm tired of my own. Please, Matt," he begged.

Matt didn't have to think long. He wanted to feel his lover's body again, and if this was the only option, he'd take it. "Okay. Scoot up more." Matt pulled Darian higher in his lap so he was pinned between Matt's chest and the steering wheel. He pulled Darian's shirt up enough to reveal his flat belly and hopefully avoid getting the shirt spunked. Then he reached for his prick.

It felt wonderful to wrap his fingers around it again. Thick and heavy, Darian's cock had a natural curve to the left. Matt ran his thumb along the length and across the tip, smearing the oozing fluid over his sensitive skin. Darian gasped, "Oh, Matt, so good." He lifted his hips and thrust into Matt's fist.

Matt looked back into Darian's eyes and gave himself over to a passionate kiss. Why deny it? He'd restrain himself from fucking, but he'd be damned if he was going to jerk Darian off and not kiss him with all the lust he had building up inside. He slipped his left arm under and around Darian's back, pulling him as close as possible while his right hand tugged and twisted. After a minute, he broke his kiss and liberally licked and coated his palm. "Don't want you to chafe, baby." He winked. Matt wiped his saliva over the top of Darian's shaft and resumed his ministrations.

Darian moaned, "So good. So much better." He rocked his hips in time with Matt's hand. "Oh God. Matt. I'm gonna come. Matt, I'm gonna…." He arched his back slightly and threw his head back. "Oooh." White ropes spurted from his slit.

Matt continued to stroke until Darian shuddered from the intensity. "Too much?" He smirked.

"Yeah. Too much." Darian gasped for air and finally relaxed, resting his head on Matt's chest. "It's so sensitive after I come; it's difficult to let you keep going. I like it, but I almost can't take it 'cause it feels *too* good. Ya know?"

"Yeah, I know." Matt grinned. He knew the feeling. That point when your balls draw up and send wave after wave of ecstasy through your body, and each nerve ending feels like it's on fire, and you want it to go on forever, but then the ecstasy hits a peak, and if you don't break the contact with that "perfect spot" you just know your body will explode. And then, seconds later, you can't help but touch it again anyway. "You feeling better?"

Darian nodded. "Yes. Thank you." Darian climbed out of Matt's lap and snatched some napkins out of the glove box. After wiping off, he pulled his pants back on. "Now we can go to the museum."

Matt chuckled and put the truck in drive. He marveled at how easily sexual release could calm a person down. Darian was so tense before, and now he was completely relaxed.

Darian reached over and held out an open palm.

Matt took his hand and drove the rest of the way to the Metro station grinning like a giddy teenager. It felt good.

When Matt parked the truck, they spent a few minutes languidly kissing before venturing into the Metro. Matt wanted to taste Darian as much as he could, knowing eyes would be on them as soon as they were in public. He hoped his erection would calm down before they got downtown.

After an unspoken agreement to let go of each other and get out of the vehicle, Matt grabbed his backpack and jacket and smiled at Darian. "By the way, I like your hair. It looks even sexier in person than in the picture." Matt winked at him.

Darian walked around to his side of the truck. Smiling, he automatically tried tucking his hair behind one ear, but there wasn't enough to tuck. Matt thought the motion was endearing. "Thanks. I was worried you wouldn't like it. I didn't ask you before I did it."

Matt shut the door and locked the truck. "Darian, I'm not attracted to you for your hair. I mean, I love it, but even if you shaved your head bald, I'd still want to see you."

Darian snorted. "Could you see the look on Dan's face if I did that?" Then he snorted again.

Matt motioned for them to walk, and Darian stepped in beside him.

They stopped at the elevator, and Matt pushed the button.

Darian swung his arms out wide and clasped them behind his back. He also did a little thing where he rocked onto his toes and then back on his heels. He looked nervous.

When they stepped onto the elevator, Matt noticed Darian's eyes grow wider. He was staring at Matt's neck. "What?" Matt grabbed his shirt collar. "Do I have a spider on me or something?"

Darian's face paled. "No. I'm really sorry." Darian reached up and touched Matt's neck. "I gave you a hickey. I didn't know I sucked that hard. I'm so sorry." Darian looked inexplicably remorseful. Matt hated that!

"Baby," Matt said, covering Darian's hand with his, "it's fine." Matt inspected the red spot on his neck in the shiny steel doors. "I must have sensitive skin. I didn't think you sucked that hard either. Oh well." He shrugged it off. "It's not like you haven't given me a hickey before."

Darian was not convinced. Matt looked over and found him studying the floor. "Darian? It's fine. Really. I don't care."

He was blushing when he looked up. "I know you're not out. People will see. Jamie got mad a few times when—"

Matt interrupted, "I'm not Jamie." Darian didn't look satisfied. "And I *am* out! People at church know; my family knows; I'm only dickin' around telling the people at work." Darian's expression softened slowly. As they stepped off the elevator and headed down the pavement to the Metro station, Matt continued, "I know I've been paranoid for years, and I appreciate the fact you're sensitive to my situation, but really—I am out. I can't hide who I am anymore, nor do I want to. See, there's this guy at work who's all paranoid about being gay just because he liked Jamie as a friend." The dark tunnel of an entrance was before them, and they walked up to the closest machine to pay for a fare. Matt put some dollar bills in. "I see a lot of myself in him. And I was thinking—I don't want to be like that."

After Darian had his ticket, Matt reached for his hand and continued proudly, "Take this situation. Here we are, miles from home. Why should I be scared to take your hand if I want to? We're on our first date, and I want to hold your hand. I should be able to act on impulse if I want to."

They stepped on the next train to DC and found a backward-facing seat. "I like being with you. I want other people to know I like being with you. Holding hands is a normal date-like thing to do, isn't it?"

Darian nodded.

Matt stopped rambling. "I'm talking too much, aren't I? I don't know what's gotten into me. Are you okay?"

Darian nodded again. "I'm fine."

"Then what's that look on your face?"

Darian shrugged. "I don't know." Reluctantly, he added, "Jamie hated riding backward. He got nauseous."

Matt started to stand up. "We can move. I don't mind."

Darian sat still and gripped Matt's arm. "No. I like it."

Matt reached his arm over Darian's shoulders and squeezed. "We're gonna have a great time. I promise. It will be fun, and we can stay as long as you like. Well, as long as we have time; I have to get you back by five."

Darian gave Matt a worried look. "I know it'll be fun. I just… sometimes… I feel guilty having fun without Jamie. Like it's somehow wrong."

Matt couldn't fault him for that. He felt that way too sometimes. He pulled Darian closer and hugged his shoulders, kissing the top of his head as the train jerked into motion. All the way downtown, they sat silently, snuggling in the seat. It wasn't awkward at all. Matt always wondered if it would feel foreign—he'd never done this before, but it came so naturally. Matt wanted to act more like a boyfriend than a pal, and he thought it would be hard to do it in public where people were watching. But here with Darian, it wasn't weird at all.

After they exited the train station and found their bearings at the Mall, Matt took Darian's hand again as they headed over to their destination.

"Wait a minute," said Darian, stopping short on the sidewalk next to Constitution Avenue. "We're going to the museum."

Matt tilted his head. "Yes. You knew that."

Darian pointed to the huge building in front of them. He threw his hands in the air. "Museum. As in the National Gallery of Art. I can't believe this."

Matt walked up to him, closer than a guy normally would step up to his pal, and stroked Darian's jawbone. "Can't believe what? What's wrong? I thought you liked art?"

Darian's face lost all expression. "I do. But I haven't been thinking very clearly lately. If I had thought about it, I would have brought my camera or a sketchpad… something. I've been so caught up in following Dan's rules and talking to my therapist and wondering if I'd ever get to see you again that when you said 'museum' I thought, 'Cool. Museum.' I never thought *art* museum. I'm an idiot. A stupid, brainless idiot."

Matt had hoped to get inside before surprising Darian, but the look on his face told Matt he had to fix the mood quick. With Darian kicking himself for being too distracted, it wasn't fair to wait any longer. "Come over here." Matt motioned toward some benches within a circular outdoor garden next to the wide steps of the entrance. He put his backpack down and unzipped it. He grinned at Darian playfully. "What do you think I have in here?"

"I don't know. Lunch?" he answered halfheartedly.

"Nope. We can buy lunch inside." Matt watched Darian's eyes. He seemed to be searching his brain for an answer, but none came so he shrugged at Matt. "Hmm, well, let's see…." Matt reached in and fished around. "We have a… camera," he announced upon pulling it from the bag. Darian's eyes lit up. "And we have—" He reached back in. "—a sketchpad."

"Matt!" Darian cried, grabbing the pad to his chest.

Matt kept right on pulling out items. "And a No. 6 pencil." Darian took it from his fingers. "And…."

"Square chalk!" Darian absolutely glowed. "How did you know? About the No. 6 pencil and all?"

Matt knew the bushes gave them some privacy, so he risked gliding the back of his finger down Darian's cheek. Wanting to get over his paranoia was one thing; acting out on it was another. He was still nervous. "I watch. I pay attention," he admitted to Darian. "And I saw a stack of art stuff in Dan's house I assumed was yours. I wanted this to be the perfect date—something special for you. Besides, I like watching you draw."

Darian hugged his treasures to his chest. "You did all this for me?" he whispered.

Matt nodded. "Of course. I've never really been on a date before, so I had to ask my friend Jason how to do it right. He knows stuff about romance. He said to make it something I knew *you* liked a lot. I know you like drawing, and I know you like art. So… is this good?" He wasn't so sure because Darian wasn't talking. He was staring at the ground. "We could easily go someplace else. Whatever you want."

He saw Darian's inarticulate approval when he looked up with tears in his eyes.

"Oh, baby, don't cry." Matt stepped closer and wiped the tears from Darian's cheeks. Like before, it felt so natural. He took the few items and put them back in his backpack before he wrapped his arms around Darian.

"What about people seeing?" Darian questioned.

Matt squeezed him. "It doesn't matter." Matt nestled his nose in Darian's hair and took a deep breath. He rubbed Darian's back. "At this point, I think you're more paranoid than I am. I haven't been to the National Gallery since a school trip in tenth grade. Who down here would know me anyway? I seriously need to lighten up, and being with you is making it that much easier." Matt relaxed his hold and pulled back to look into Darian's eyes. "It just feels right." He caressed Darian's face and slid his fingers into his hair. He asked again, "Are you sure it's okay to come here? These are happy tears, correct?"

Darian nodded and smiled. "Yes. I can't believe you did this. It's the nicest thing anybody has ever done."

Matt liked hearing that, but it worried him to think Jamie wouldn't have done this. "I love you." It was the most logical response Matt could think of.

With only the slightest bit of paranoia whispering in his ear to be cautious, Matt leaned in and kissed Darian softly and slowly. He threaded his fingers into the back of Darian's short hair. (He sort of missed the long strands, but liked this style too. Plus, it was so soft.) He pressed his chest against Darian and pulled him close.

He knew they were only partially screened by the bushes and architecture. People could see them, but was it really that big a deal? They were in DC. This was just the thing to help Matt lighten up. He was out, gosh darn it! He had to let himself act on impulse. Sometimes that would mean public displays of affection. Perhaps not as lingering a kiss as this, but it wasn't as if he was groping Darian. This wasn't vulgar. It was sweet. He was going to kiss Darian as long as he wanted and then spend the day enjoying his company. This was new. And this was wonderful.

When their lips parted, Matt heard a gasp from behind them. He forced himself not to look. So what if someone was shocked? He would stand his ground, not run and hide. *I can do it. I can do it. I am not afraid!* He psyched himself up. "Guess I have to get used to that," he said, motioning with his eyebrows in the direction of the surprised onlookers. He hoped they had moved on and weren't staring. "Are they still watching?"

Darian glanced to his left. "No. They're up the steps. And yeah, sometimes people act weird. But I figure I can't make everyone happy. I just need to be true to myself."

Matt had to kiss him one more time. "You are amazing. I wish I had that kind of strength." Matt let him go and zipped up the backpack. "You're gonna have to help me be strong in this. I'm not used to people judging me."

Darian fell in beside Matt as they climbed the steps of the National Gallery. "But people always judge other people, don't they? As humans we can't help noticing another person's weight, age, sex, religion, political stands; heck, I've known people who get bent out of shape over others eating meat. There's always something to judge."

"Yeah, I guess you're right. It's funny, I was talking to my friend Jason at work about assumptions based on race."

"Exactly what I'm saying. Neutrality takes effort, and lots of people don't think about it."

Matt showed the security guard his backpack and grabbed a map of the gallery before he continued. "I'm really glad you had off today. I was worried about the after-Thanksgiving sales and stuff you mentioned." He pointed to the "Old Masters" wing.

"I did work. I got off at eleven thirty, rushed home, and changed my shirt."

"You did?" Matt stopped in the first room to open the map, not that they needed it.

Darian nodded. "Yeah. My manager wasn't happy. I was supposed to work until two, but he likes me. All I had to do was beg a little and stick out my lip, and he caved."

"Ha, ha. That's great! You gonna try that stuff with me to get what you want?" Matt asked, knowing he'd probably cave too.

Darian blushed and shook his head. "I don't need to. Somehow you seem to know what I want before I ask."

Matt smiled. "I was beginning to think the same thing about you."

Darian's eyes glinted right before he leaned forward and kissed Matt's lips.

Matt beamed. *And you always know the right moment to kiss me.*

MATT knew he had a stupid grin plastered across his face the rest of the day, but he couldn't help it. He could not get over the fact that Darian made him feel so refreshed. As they wandered through the museum, Matt found out all kinds of things about Darian that Jamie never wrote about. Not only was Darian adorable, sexy, and thoroughly lickable, he was also intelligent, witty, and politically savvy. *Jamie hated politics. No wonder he never wrote about it!* Darian mentioned his view on government healthcare, and Matt practically jumped out of his skin to add his opinion. He did it a little too loudly, and they both got shushed. Apparently loud debates were frowned upon. Matt made a mental note to explore the topic at a later date.

Silence dominated their remaining time together.

Which was fine. Matt amused himself by casually observing the people in the museum as he pretended to study paintings by artists long since passed. Mostly, the day was about Darian: an artist in his element. Matt needed nothing more.

13

November 28, 2010

ALL eyes were on him as Matt walked into church, and Matt wondered what was so different about today from the past several Sundays. Ms. Carrie was acting weird. She gave Matt a look of pity he didn't understand. It was not like his dog died yesterday. And his mom barely said three words to him through the whole service. Still, he sat there contentedly reliving the best date of his life.

Darian. He was head over heels in love with Darian.

Yesterday they talked and walked and laughed, and it all came so easily to Matt. He never knew it could be like that. He'd told Jamie so many times he wouldn't want a relationship, not until he was older, because what more did he need beyond sex? But, oh man, there was so much more to happiness than that. After he got Darian off in the truck, Matt thought for sure he'd go around half the day hard as a rock—but he didn't. He was fine. Relaxed. He didn't think about sex at all in the museum. Matt enjoyed Darian in a totally nonsexual way.

He enjoyed a few kisses here and there, and they walked around holding hands; Matt spent the entire five hours wishing the day would never end.

"WOULD you stop smiling? You look ridiculous!" His mom's harsh whisper jolted Matt.

"What? Sure." Talk about a killjoy.

"Were you even paying attention?" his mother asked as they stood and made their way out of the pew. "I looked over at you a few times, and I swear you never blinked."

"Sorry. I guess I was daydreaming. What was the sermon about?" *Not homosexuality, please.*

"Parenting. He preached on how to train up your children so they will not depart from the Lord."

Matt heard her sarcastic tone. Why would she use her sarcastic tone in church? Mom never did that. Dad did, but Mom never used sarcasm with regard to the sermon. Weird.

The family left church without stopping to chat, which was also weird. Matt drove and his dad sat in the backseat next to his brother. Everyone was quiet on the way home. Matt watched as they each got out of the car and headed off to different areas of the house. His mom went to the kitchen to cook; his dad flopped on the sofa in the family room and clicked on the television; and his brother took the steps two at a time, racing to his room. It was good Hannah was off somewhere with one of her friends, or Matt was sure she would have been just as aloof as everyone else. Without knowing what else he should do, Matt went to his own room and flopped onto the bed.

"Bored now," he huffed.

His phone buzzed with a message from Lori. *Don't you ever read e-mails?*

Matt scratched his head. He texted, *How the heck did you find my e-mail address?* He had three; the only question was which one did she stumble upon? He seriously doubted she found it in the church directory.

On Goodreads.com. I was stalking Darian. I can tell what mood he's in by what he's reading.

But how did you find me *on there? My user name is E124, not Matt Dixon. And the account is private.*

I know Darian's password so I logged on as him. You and Dare are "friends"—didn't you know that? You have eighty-seven books in common, Matt. Don't you talk to people online?

"No shit!" Matt marveled at the revelation. He hadn't been on there in ages, mainly because he had no time to read. He answered her text: *Not really. I don't have time. But how did you know E124 was me?*

Your icon is a pic of a fire hose between a guy's legs! And when I was at your station I saw Engine 124. It wasn't hard to figure out. Plus—youknowyouwantsome@gmail.com? Oh please! I took a shot and got it right. I gave the address to Darian; I hope that's all right.

That was not going to help him downplay his huge ego. True, he always expected guys to want his body, and every time he went out, that expectation was proven correct… but now? He didn't want Darian to know he was full of himself. He was trying to get over his vanity.

Sure. When did you give it to him?

Lori replied, *Around the 20th I think.*

You couldn't have told me last week?

I forgot! I e-mailed. I thought you would respond!

Matt flipped open his laptop and turned it on.

"Importing 1 of 242 e-mails" popped up on the screen. "Crap! I think I need to get on the computer a little more often." When did he have the time? He worked two jobs and helped out family and friends with most of his free time. He rarely thought about the computer unless it was to surf porn.

He had three mailboxes. Each one was filling with spam and notifications from Goodreads and MySpace dating back three months. The first one to come in on his mail server for youknowyouwantsome was from Darian. From a week ago! He clicked that one while the others loaded.

Hey,

I just spoke to Lori and she said you guys talked. Now I see why you haven't texted in a couple days. Sorry if I got you in trouble at work. ☺ But you can e-mail… right? I'd like to hear from you SOMETIMES. I know you're busy. Whenever you can make the time.

Thinking of you,

Darian

Now Matt was curious what she had said. He didn't like lying, but Lori had already said something and he had to know what it was.

His inbox was still loading. He deleted the spam as it popped up. Viagra. Hot singles network. You've WON! All a bunch of crap. Then one from Lori imported from November 20.

Hi Matt,

I wanted to give you a heads-up. I told Dare you haven't texted 'cause you got in trouble at work. I just couldn't tell him it was because of Dan. Darian has a hard enough time already. Just go with it. If he asks or pushes, I understand if you tell him, but can you try to hold out for now? Darian is just really excited to get to see you on the 27th. I don't want to spoil that.

Later,

Lori

At least now Matt knew why, but he still didn't like it. He replied:

Lori,

I don't like lying. Darian already e-mailed saying he's sorry for getting me in trouble. If he brings it up again, I'm claiming ignorance, "Really? I never got that e-mail...." I'm not going along with it if he persists. You should have asked me first before you said something.

I DO understand about Dan. He's acting weird anyway. I'll try to play this as cool as I can.

~M

More mail came in, including another one from Darian. It had a picture attached. His new haircut. The caption read:

Dan asked me to do it. Please don't be mad. I know you liked my long hair. I did too. But it can grow back, right? I just wanted to make him happy. This is my natural color, barring the blond streaks. He didn't like me dying it black when it's naturally black, and he totally didn't get that the dye has a blue shimmer to it. Oh well. I thought you'd like another picture.

Matt had wondered why there was such a drastic change. Now he understood. If he kept up with the rules, Matt figured he'd have to have *another* conversation with Dan!

No worries, baby. I love your hair. Yes, I like it long but as I said before, I didn't fall for you because of your hair. It was all in that first kiss.... ☺BTW, I am super lame and haven't checked e-mail in a while. I'm just reading them now. Brb

He scanned over the long list as it came in; at least six were from Darian and four from Lori. Matt deleted twenty-two spam messages, hitting "delete" repeatedly to weed out the messages he didn't want to read. As he moved the cursor down to the next mailbox to see if anything in the matt.dixon87 box was worth reading, his eye lit upon one from mjmckinley. "That's weird. Why would Mikey e-mail me after all this time?" Curiosity prompted Matt to open it.

Matt,

I used to think you were a Christian. You led Sunday school lessons and helped in youth group, and you always treated people the way I thought Christians should. What happened to you? I heard about your little speech in church. Why are you glorifying homosexuality? That is not what a good Christian does. I just don't understand what prompted you to leave your faith behind? I feel sorry for you.

I heard my dad talking to someone on the phone. He mentioned "going to your father first" and then something about "don't you think telling the pastor is a little drastic?" I don't know exactly what is going on but I thought I'd give you a heads-up. We used to be friends. I may think homosexuality is a sin, but I don't think you should be confronted without warning. It sounded to me like the pastor was going to come to your house.

I just don't want to believe you were kissing some guy on the street!

All I can say is: REPENT.

~Mike

Matt burned with anger. How could this self-righteous hypocrite bash him like that?

After balling his fists and then relaxing his fingers, and balling them up again a few more times, Matt's anger subsided. His beef wasn't against Mikey, or "Mike" as he now went by, as wrong as he thought Mike was. His real anger was aimed at the nameless person Mike said was on the phone with his father who was going to nark Matt out to the pastor. The pastor already knew Matt was gay. *Kissing is not a criminal offense.* And where did they see him? DC? It couldn't have been anywhere else; Matt hadn't been to a club in a while, and if the person was in a gay club then they were just as "guilty" as he was.

Then the thought occurred to him that the pastor was coming to his house. *His house!* When? *Shit!* He had to tell his dad. The pastor would probably want to talk to the family. *Fuck!* What was he going to do? Matt had to say something. When?

Matt stood up and paced the room. He rubbed the back of his neck, thinking of the right way to explain to his father about the e-mail. At least Mike's was dated today. Had the e-mail been from a week ago, the pastor could show up this afternoon or something. The phone rang. Twice. Matt went to the bedroom door and opened it. He couldn't hear what was being said downstairs, but a moment later, his dad yelled up the steps.

"Matt? Are you going to be home Tuesday night?"

Matt swallowed his panic. "Yeah," he called down the hall.

"Pastor Dennis wants to have a chat."

"Okay." His fake-casual voice quivered but was believable. *Tuesday. I have until Tuesday to tell him about Mike's message.* "Although, Dad can probably guess why the pastor is showing up," he mumbled, closing the door.

MATT paced for another hour before his feet were so tired he had to lie down. Worry and dread made it inconceivable to eat. His mom looked shocked but said it was fine if he skipped dinner. Matt rolled from one side to the other but could not get comfortable on his mattress. He couldn't rest, he couldn't pace, and he couldn't even cheer himself up by looking at the pictures of Darian on his phone.

Well, it did make him feel a *little* better.

Matt flipped the phone open. His new wallpaper was one from yesterday. Darian posed in front of a window in the museum, partially covering his coy smile with his fingers. He was such a ham! His eyes looked positively devilish. After Matt took the picture, he kissed him soundly before they moved to the next room. Matt craved the affection between them. He remembered telling Jamie he didn't kiss because it was too intimate. And it was. Kissing Darian pulled him closer and opened his mind to all the ways you could touch a person without thinking about sex. A light stroke across his lower back, a soft caress down his cheek, or a tender squeeze on his shoulder didn't cause Matt to think about tearing his clothes off. Each touch they shared in the museum—even touching fingers across the table when they ate lunch—only convinced Matt of how much he wanted Darian in his life—every moment of every day.

Matt saw his mom and dad touching all the time. They had been married twenty-six years and seemed very affectionate. Seeing his parents kiss over the years was normal. They were a couple. They were intimate without sexual innuendo or explicit contact. (Of course, he did *not* want to think about his parents having sex at all!) Matt had been against close contact for years because it seemed to be intended for the one you chose to spend your life with.

Probably why the Bible speaks against sex before marriage, he thought.

He'd never considered "fucking" in that context before.

How many guys in his past were looking to Matt to fill their idea of a life partner? How many who reached for a kiss afterward were crushed when he denied them? How many guys he'd picked up looked to Matt as "the one"?

Matt groaned. Too many thoughts. He rolled over and buried his head under the pillow.

November 29, 2010

MATT paced on Monday evening. It was his theme of late. He was frustrated and antsy. He hadn't heard from Darian in eleven hours, which made things worse. He had to talk to his dad. But how? He'd tried that morning but chickened out. It had to be tonight. He needed to talk to his dad before the pastor sat in his living room and… what?

Matt didn't know.

Matt greeted his father as soon as he walked through the door. "Hey, Dad. Got a minute?" He tried to play it cool while everything on the inside was jumping.

"Hmghgha…." John Dixon's noncommittal and incoherent grunt was not encouraging.

"Dad? Can we talk? Please?" Matt pleaded.

He hadn't pleaded with his dad in ten years, but what could it hurt? Pleading always worked for Steven. Steven got whatever he wanted, and all it took was a "please" and another "please" followed by a final "pleeease," and their father would say yes to anything. Matt may have been the golden child who received all the best without asking, but Steven and Hannah got what they wanted too. Their mom and dad spoiled all their children, just differently.

His dad stopped in the doorway to the kitchen and answered, "Fine. Let me grab a beer first."

Drinking? On a weeknight? The thought did not sit well with Matt. His father was off in more ways than one. He waited patiently, and after fifteen minutes, his dad reemerged from the kitchen. Matt had about fifteen more minutes until his mom and Steven would return with carryout. He had to talk quick.

"Well?" His dad sounded stiff as he gestured to Matt with a flip of his hand. "What do you want?"

Nothing like a little irritated pressuring to squelch all Matt's gumption. "Um, yeah, I wanted to…."

"Spit it out, Matthias. I don't have all night!" Matt jumped. He hated his angry tone. His dad rarely raised his voice to him in the last twenty years.

Matt ripped off the proverbial bandage by blurting, "I kissed a guy the other day." It all came out in a rush. Matt hoped he wouldn't have to repeat himself to be understood. He rattled off the rest without breathing in between. "I kissed a guy the other day in public, and somebody must have seen us. Maybe from church, I don't know. I got an e-mail from Mike McKinley who said he heard his dad talking to someone. They mentioned the church and the pastor, and Mike said they would probably pay us a visit. And then the phone rang, and you asked if I'd be home. So when the pastor comes over, that's what he wants to talk about—me kissing a guy. I never meant for this to happen. I never meant to involve the family. I'm sorry." He finally took a breath. He'd said all he needed to. Now he waited for his dad's reaction.

His dad groaned and clamped his hand over his eyes. And then he groaned some more. "I knew this was not going to end well." He stumbled over to his favorite chair and sat down. "I knew that speech would hurt us; it was only a matter of time."

"Dad, I had to say those things." Matt followed him and sat on the sofa as close to his dad as he could get. "It wasn't fair what they were saying about Jamie."

"I know, Son." John shook his head and raised his eyes. "Ever since that day I've been trying to understand. I have. I know we haven't talked about it. I don't agree with you, and I don't understand how you could choose the path you're on, but I've been trying to respect your lifestyle choice by not reacting rashly as I wanted to. Now this. Why Matt? Why do you have to flaunt it in public?"

"What?" Matt pulled his shoulders back and sat up straight. "Dad, I wasn't—"

"You couldn't let this all blow over first, could you?" His voice grew louder. "I've been taking hits for two months. Two months! I almost had people convinced this was simply a juvenile phase you needed to get out of your system. Even after Kurt McKinley had the audacity to confront me at Bible study, I held it together. I didn't let the profanities fly like I wanted to." He stood up and paced in front of Matt. "I bit my tongue and rose above the scrutiny. I thought if time passed and people saw you hadn't changed, things would go back to normal. Our family would go back to normal."

"But Dad—"

He glared at Matt and pointed his finger in his face. "Don't! You don't get to interject with your feelings on the matter. You spewed out enough of your *feelings*—and in front of the whole freakin' congregation no less! And I'm the one left to clear up the mess. Me! And what am I supposed to say?" He then faked a pleasant tone. "'I'm sorry, Pastor Dennis. My queer son can't help his perversion. He claims to have been born that way, so when he's slobbering all over another *girly-boy* on the street, please… just look the other way.'" He resumed pacing.

Sarcasm cuts, and Matt felt the wounds. He'd never seen his father so angry. His face was red, and the vein on his neck stood out. It made Matt feel insignificant and ashamed of his decisions. Maybe he *should* have been more careful? Maybe he shouldn't have been so cavalier in revealing his true self in front of all those people at church, especially without talking to his family first. His heart sank.

His dad stopped and glared at him again. "Do you know how hard this has been on your mother? She hardly sleeps at night. And your brother? The school called me at work this morning to say he was in a fight. Steven never fights at school. And *what* was it over? *You*—his faggot brother!"

The word "faggot" hit Matt like a slap across his face. He was glad when his father turned to face the window and rubbed the back of his neck, because it gave Matt a second to wipe the sudden tears from his eyes.

His father continued cruelly, "I can't bear to even look at you, Matt. Get out. I need time to think about what I'm going to say. McKinley! It figures. I knew he wouldn't stop with one argument." He turned abruptly. "I said get out." He pointed to the stairs. "Go to your room or something. Anywhere but in my sight."

Matt bolted from the room and dashed up the stairs. He closed his bedroom door and fought the tears. This wasn't happening. It wasn't real. Right on the heels of the best day of his life came the scolding of a lifetime. Matt was the good son, the perfect son; he never got yelled at. He fought the tears in vain as paroxysms of grief racked his body. He could hardly breathe through the sobs. His eyes burned.

He turned sharply and punched the wall. The drywall dented and pain coursed through his fist. Two knuckles were cracked and bleeding, but his hand wasn't broken. One punch was not enough. Matt had way more rage building up inside. He punched the same spot and broke more skin on his hand. Then he tore the *Lord of the Rings* poster from his wall. Stupid poster was too fucking old anyway! He turned to his desk; rushing over, he swept it clean with one arm. Books and photos and bric-a-brac fell to the floor. The next victim was his trophy shelf. He grabbed track trophy after track trophy and flung them in all directions. One hit his mirror, sending shards of glass to the carpet. He grabbed his Bible off his nightstand and heaved it at his door.

When the leather-bound book connected with a thud and fell to the floor, Matt collapsed. He cried with his head in his hands and his back against the bed frame. Why? Why did everything have to end up this way?

After several minutes, his blubbering died down, and he lifted his tear-stained face. His room was a disaster. His pictures littered the floor. His CDs and his trophies and his books: everything he owned was strewn across the carpet as though it didn't matter. As if his life didn't matter. What meant the most to Matt didn't matter. Among the mess, his eyes lit upon a picture of Jamie.

Jamie.

Jamie trashed his room right before he ended it all. For Jamie, the persecution was more than he could bear. Jamie led two lives, just like Matt. Jamie felt the pressure, just like Matt. For Jamie, hatred and intolerance of his personal choices weighed him down more than his happiness could buoy him. He didn't possess the strength to stand up for what he believed. Was that true of Matt?

What do I believe in? Matt asked himself.

Matt's eyes shifted to his Bible, lying in a heap. He crawled over and picked it up. He thumbed through to Romans 1:27 and read out loud, "In the same way the men also abandoned natural relations with women and were inflamed with lust for one another. Men committed indecent acts with other men, and received in themselves the due penalty for their perversion."

The Bible fell from his grasp. "I don't know what I believe." He looked up at the ceiling, but his mind went past the physical structure to the God beyond. "I don't understand. Help me understand. Why do I feel like this? If it's so wrong, then why does it feel so right when I'm in his arms? Why let me fall in love if it's 'indecent'? I cannot believe you're that cruel. There has to be a reason. Oh God, please. Help me to know what you'll have me do with my life. There has to be a plan. I love Darian!" Matt cried. His head drooped, and he repeated, "I love him."

Matt pulled the comforter off the bed and curled up on the floor. He fell asleep reliving the horror he read in Jamie's journal when Jamie hit the wall and found release only in death.

November 30, 2010

MATT drove home like a zombie on Tuesday. His brain was wasted. He couldn't concentrate at work but somehow managed to direct the crew at a crash site. No one was injured, amazingly, but a boy was trapped in a mangled car. After the truck returned to the station, the chief got a call that a fellow firefighter and friend was in a coma. It was sad news, which brought morale down—the men milled about with long faces. Seems he suffered a stroke and ended up in a coma. Matt didn't know him well, but he remembered working with him his last year before retirement. The man wasn't old, not really, at fifty-three. He'd worked thirty years for the fire department. His days were supposed to be full of gardening and fishing, not lying in a hospital bed.

Matt left work wishing he could go anywhere but home.

He was numb from the neck up and was about to walk into a potential hornet's nest. Life sucked.

He entered the house late. He knew his mom would be angry about making them wait, but fear and dread kept him away. As soon as he entered the house, Matt felt the icy chill of judgment. His mother, father, the pastor, and another man sat in the living room. When he closed the door, conversation fell silent and all eyes bored into his soul like daggers.

“Matt, please, come join us.” Pastor Dennis’s condescension grated.

He removed his jacket and placed it on the chair. His mother’s head was bowed. His father’s eyes were fixed on the pastor’s shoe. Matt felt like a lamb being led to the slaughter. *Is this what Jesus felt? Did he feel exposed and helpless when he carried his cross up that hill?* Matt reluctantly sat on the edge of the cushion next to his mom.

The pastor looked at him directly. “Matt. Let me get straight to the point. As I have already explained to your parents, we are here tonight to address some concerns brought to us by an outside source.”

“An outside source?” he asked timidly, unsure of what the boundaries were.

“Yes. Someone spoke to Bob Bixler, who brought it to my attention that you have been delving into… unseemly practices.”

Unseemly practices? Does he seriously hear himself talking? Matt sat quietly for a moment—processing the information. Bob Bixler? He was his dad’s friend. They watched football sometimes. Why did Mr. Bob go to the pastor and not talk to his dad? Matt broached, “Then, if I may ask, why isn’t Mr. Bob here? If he’s got something against me, I’d like to hear it from him.”

Pastor Dennis smiled that smirky kind of smug smile that makes you want to punch the person wearing it. “I thought of that,” he said. “I suggested he come here himself, but after he told me what was witnessed by a mutual friend, I thought to address this matter myself. It seems someone saw you kissing a boy in front of the National Gallery. Is this true?”

Gulp. Just what Mike warned. “Yes.”

“So, I am forced to conclude you are not only professing to be gay but actively pursuing a homosexual lifestyle? Correct?”

Why does this feel like a trial where I am already convicted without bail? “Yes.”

“I see…. Matt, do you realize the church views this as a sin?”

“Yes.” Matt felt a bubble of courage surfacing and added, “But there are other sins like adultery that—”

“They are not the same. Homosexuality is called an abomination.”

Surprisingly, his father spoke up. "And we have all sinned and fall short of the glory of God, Pastor Dennis. The Book of Romans makes that clear. Jesus died for the sins of the world and counts all those who believe as overcomers. No one is perfect, Pastor, and my son is just another example of why Jesus died in the first place. 'All fall short'—we are no better than he is."

The other man, whom Matt didn't know personally but recognized as a church elder, replied, "No other sin is referred to as an abomination. God is very clear on how much worse this trespass is. Matt cannot be allowed to act out on his sinful desires and infect the church with his practices."

Matt's father came back with another retort. "He kissed one boy, for goodness sakes! I see no reason to conclude it will somehow damage the entire church."

"Enough people are aware of this scandalous act that it should be addressed in front of the congregation," the pastor replied.

"What?" his dad scoffed. "You must be joking? It was one kiss. He wasn't naked on the church doorstep flagrantly groping a member of the church."

"Kissing or groping, the consequence is the same. Matt needs to ask forgiveness and seek repentance, or the church is forced to expose his disobedience." The pastor was adamant. His eyes were hard, and his jaw was squared. Matt knew his dad did not stand a chance.

Matt interjected, "Fine. Repentance. Whatever you want." He could not endure his father's disgrace any longer. People were talking, that much was obvious. Even if Matt hadn't kissed Darian in public, the talks would have gone on about his father's ability to maintain control over his children. *Wasn't that what Kurt McKinley said?* Matt would swallow his pride for now.

The pastor looked shocked. "So you acknowledge your behavior isn't going to be tolerated? And you understand you must flee from the Devil's snare?"

Lying. Matt hated lying. "Yes," he agreed. The lying needed to end soon or it would kill him like Jamie. He was stronger than Jamie, though. Matt would endure this manifest hatred and figure out his next move when Darian was through his trials. They would figure it out together.

Pastor Dennis asked, "No more nonsense about being gay? No more kissing in public and partaking in shameful acts?"

Matt somberly shook his head, staring at the floor, trying to look as convincing as possible. "No. No, sir. I understand I've made bad decisions. I'm sorry."

"Well, good." The pastor slapped his knee in victory. "I am glad we could work this out tonight."

Fuckin' smug arrogance. That man should not be a pastor of a church! Matt boiled on the inside.

"Of course, I will also strongly suggest counseling… and conversion therapy. I can check my schedule for—"

"I think we have a psychologist in the family. Don't we, Linda?" His dad's interruption made both Pastor Dennis and Matt's mom jump. "Isn't your sister's brother-in-law a doctor of psychology?"

"W-what? Y-yes. I think so." Matt's mom stuttered as if she could not believe his father asked her a question in front of them all.

The pastor looked irked, but he replaced his distaste for Matt's father's interruption with a shrewd grin. (Matt hated that grin.) They all stood. The elder shook his father's hand, followed by the pastor. "John, I hope you understand we are here because we care about your family. We want to help you on your road to recovery." They turned to Matt's mom, who looked as scared as a mouse in a hawk's talons, smiled politely, and shook her hand as well. Matt was last. Pastor Dennis piously smirked. "Matt, I know you think we hate you, but we don't. We love you, and we are here to help you overcome your weakness. Remember, turn from darkness and enter the light. God hates gays, and we want to save you from his wrath."

Matt bowed his head and dutifully nodded in agreement. Inside, his gut was seizing and threatening to erupt. He knew what they wanted to see. He knew what they wanted to hear. As much as he wanted to punch the pastor in the face, he could not bring more shame to his father.

After the pastor and elder left, Matt walked up to his dad. He wanted to thank him for defending him as he did. His father didn't like his choices, but he also didn't dive into the argument on their side. He spoke up for Matt, and that was something Matt didn't expect.

"Dad, I…." He stopped when his father turned away, eyes seething.

"Don't. I sat here and defended you because I'm your father and that is what I'm supposed to do, but don't assume everything is fine between us because it's not. I still don't understand you. I know fucking well you didn't mean a damned word you said!"

"But Dad—"

"Matt, I'm not having this conversation. You just lied to the pastor of our church! You know very well you have no plans to repent. Did you hear what he said?" his father asked, gesturing wildly. "God hates gays! That self-righteous son of a bitch!"

"John!" his mom exclaimed, covering her mouth.

"Linda!" his dad yelled, turning his anger on her. His voice shook the walls. "How dare that man come into my house and tell me 'God hates gays' while I have a gay son sitting right here in front of him! I may not understand what the hell's gotten into that boy's head, but I will be damned if I am going to believe God hates him because he kissed some boy. That's not the Jesus I believe in. I'm through with that church, Linda. I'm through!"

Matt stood stock-still, in shocked disbelief because he'd never heard his father speak like this in all his life.

"We've been friends for more than ten years. Ten years, Linda! And that good-for-nothing Bob Bixler has the gall to conspire against me with Kurt McKinley and not even have the decency to talk to me first? After all I've done for him and his family? If being queer is the *unforgivable* sin, then I need to read that for myself! As far as I know, it's blaspheming the Holy Spirit that is *unforgivable*." He turned his burning eyes toward Matt and growled, "Did you blaspheme the Holy Spirit, boy?"

Matt shook his head fervently. He was afraid to even answer. "No, sir!"

"I can't believe this is happening," his mom cried.

"Good! Make sure you keep it that way." Without another word to Matt, he walked out of the room, consoling his wife. "They aren't really our friends, Linda. If they were, tonight wouldn't have felt like a Jerry Springer confrontation. We'll get through it. Together."

"Together."

Matt stood in the silence of their exit, the clock ticking on the living room wall, and his heart thudding as it threatened to break in his chest.

14

DARIAN looked out the window. A squirrel was trying to get into the bird feeder. Its tail twitched as it hopped from one side of the feeder to the other. Normally, Darian enjoyed watching the squirrels on his day off. Not today.

In the background of the room, his iPod played quietly. "Your Call" came on, and Darian heard the soft tones of John Vesely's voice sing, "Waiting for your call, I'm sick, call I'm angry, call I'm desperate for your voice…." *How appropriate*, he thought.

"I miss you," he said, looking at the photograph in his fingers. He'd found it between the mattress and the box springs when he changed the sheets the other day. It was of Matt in high school. His hair was pulled into a ponytail, and he was poised on the track, ready to start a race.

Feeling more numb than normal, Darian left his seat by the window and curled up on the bed. Sleeping was his favorite pastime; only sleeping didn't seem thrilling of late. He dreamed too much. Disturbing dreams of Jamie.

Secondhand Serenade's song continued in the background. Darian reached over and pressed stop; he couldn't bear listening to sappy love songs, especially when the lyrics spoke too many truths to his soul and he wished to avoid his feelings entirely. His feelings betrayed logic. His feelings conflicted with what he *should* want and what he *should* need. His feelings were wrong!

"I'm such an awful person," he whispered to Matt's image. "No wonder Jamie left me. Why would you even want me around?"

"To use you like a whore," Jamie answered.

No longer startled by Jamie's unwelcome intrusions, Darian answered him calmly. "That's all I am, isn't it? He only wants to be with me for sex?"

"Of course, you adulterous bitch. Matt's incapable of commitment."

Darian rolled over, turning his tear-stained face in Jamie's direction. As always, the hallucination or apparition or ghost, whatever it was, stood near him. This ghastly vision of Jamie had red-rimmed eyes surrounded by dark circles. His hair was greasy and stuck out in all directions, as if it had never been washed or combed. His skin was always gray like death, his lips purplish-blue. The vision was so familiar now that Darian spoke to him as if he were really there.

"But he refused sex the other day. Matt was so romantic. I didn't know he could be sweet. It was the best date I've ever had."

Jamie blew it off. "A fluke. He probably spent the day with you and fucked some guy behind Tevco after he kissed you good-bye."

"He wouldn't." Darian challenged Jamie's claim, but deep down he worried about that very thing. Would Matt sleep with someone else? Darian hadn't asked him not to. And now with this "no sex" rule from Dan, could Darian blame Matt if he took care of his needs with someone else?

"You did." Jamie's harsh accusation made Darian flinch.

"Stop. Leave me alone." Darian pulled the pillow over his head.

Jamie's malice lashed out. "I wasn't even cold, and you gave yourself to him. How do you explain that?"

Stomach acid burned Darian's esophagus. "It was an accident," Darian protested from under the pillow. "I was lonely."

"Excuses!" Jamie spat. "Always the same. Excuses. When will you tell the truth?"

Someone knocked on Darian's door.

Darian flipped the pillow up. Jamie was gone. "Yes?" he answered the second knock on his door.

Dan Miller entered. "Hey, Kiddo, why are you in here with the lights out?"

Darian sat up when Dan flipped the switch, bathing the room in harsh fluorescent light. The soft glow of early evening from the window vanished. "I was watching the squirrels for a while. I think they're mad at the new feeder."

Dan walked over to the window and peered out. "Oh yeah. Cheryl was watching them yesterday. She said they chattered up a storm, jumping around it trying to get the seed." Dan sat on the edge of the bed next to Darian. He reached out and touched his leg. "You spend a lot of time alone lately. Do you want me to call Lori and Sara? I'm sure Cheryl would love to fix dinner for them again. And we could play Uno." He smiled and squeezed Darian's knee.

Darian grinned. "Yes, I'd like that. Are you sure your girlfriend doesn't mind?"

"No. She's fond of you, too, Darian. She suggested we do more things together as a family. Listen," Dan carefully broached, "I know you and I don't talk like we used to, before Jimbo died. I miss those days. We used to sing in the kitchen while making dinner. Remember?"

"Yeah." He grinned.

"Everything changed in September, but I'd like to think you and I can pick up where we left off and continue being open with one another. Do you think we can?"

Darian knew what Dan wanted to hear. "Yes."

"Darian, you know why I'm reluctant to let you see Matt Dixon."

Darian abruptly stood and walked across the room. "I don't want to talk about Matt."

"Darian," Dan said, in a reasoning tone. "You know I've spoken to Dr. Loundas on several occasions. She doesn't understand your hesitancy to talk about Jim's death. She says she tries to bring up Matt's involvement in your life, and you won't speak about that either. You need to open up. You need to come to terms with Jim's absence."

"Come to terms?" he asked, fighting hysteria. "How do I come to terms with that? He said he'd be there for me! He promised he'd never leave! He told me he loved me! How can I come to terms with the lies he told?"

Dan rose off the bed and reached out for Darian. Darian swatted at his hands. "Stop." Darian protested. "No. I don't want to…. No!"

But Dan grabbed his shoulders and pulled his struggling bones to his chest. Darian wiggled, but moments later sagged into Dan's embrace.

Dan held him and stroked his back. "There, there. You don't need to fight. I know he hurt you. He hurt all of us. I don't know why, and I can't bring him back. But you can't live your life by avoiding the pain. You need to talk to Dr. Loundas about it. Diverting your feelings from Jim onto Matt won't bring him back."

Darian pulled away. "I'm not. Matt has nothing to do with Jamie. I mean, yeah I know he was his best friend, but the thing between us is different."

"Then what is it?" Dan asked bluntly. "Help me understand. Because from my perspective, Matt's using you to explore his sexuality, and you're using him to bury the pain of Jimmy's death." Dan held out his hands. "What part of that is incorrect?"

Darian stumbled to reply. "I… he… it isn't…." He felt his stomach threatening to revolt again. He hadn't thrown up in a while, but Dan forcing his hand wasn't normal. Dan was patient. Dan let Dr. Loundas do the talking. Dan never confronted him with the truth like this.

"Darian. Sex can be an addiction. We talked about this with Dr. Loundas, and she agrees. You're avoiding reality by burying yourself in sex. That's why I took away your computer for a week after walking in on you staring at the screen, pleasuring yourself."

"But I wasn't—"

"Stop! I know what I saw. It's why we agreed you wouldn't see Matt. He's messing with your head. You can't heal if you let him dominate you."

"He's not!"

"Darian, I've known Matt a while. Albeit, I didn't know he was gay until recently, but I do know he's the kind of guy who fucks around. Mrs. Dixon called on many occasions looking for her son when he was supposed to be spending the night with Jimbo. I'm not stupid. I went along with the lie because I used to be their age, and I, too, snuck out at night to go to parties. Matt and Jim always kept their grades up and never got into one lick of trouble. I'm not saying I was right to keep their secrets from their mothers, but it's wrong for me to hold my tongue now. Matt is nothing but trouble. You don't need that. Forget Matt Dixon and move on. Last week's date was your first and your last."

Dan gave Darian a stern eye to eye and then walked out.

Darian shook and collapsed on the floor. "Last?" he sobbed.

"That's what the man said," Jamie taunted.

"Shut up! What do you know?" Darian looked up at a very pleased dead man.

"I know it hurts. I know you're itching to leave through the window and go to him. You can't wait until he fucks you again. That's why you cut. That's why you pop pills. You'll do anything to substitute for the orgasm you desire from him!"

"That's not true," he cried.

"Yes, it is. You're glad I'm dead. And you're too much of a coward to admit it."

"Nooooo."

Darian wept long after Jamie's image disappeared. He fell asleep curled up on the floor.

December 2010

15

December 3, 2010

"THANKS for meeting me for lunch. I've had a crappy couple of days," Matt greeted Jason as they stood in line at his favorite restaurant and waited for the next available cashier.

"I'm glad you called. We haven't had lunch together outside of work since… when? Before Scott started, or was it Billy?"

"Billy. I remember us all sitting at the restaurant; I was waiting for my chicken wrap, and Scott was griping about the taste of his iced tea. Billy started the very next day. Wow!" He was shocked. "Has it been that long?" Time really did fly.

"Yeah. Long time," Jason agreed. "You know… Anna keeps bugging me about when you're coming over for dinner?" He lifted an accusing eyebrow. "She said you and your significant other need to make an appearance."

Matt jested with a fake-announcer voice, "Noncommitment Man takes a shot to the chest." Matt faked a gunshot sound as he zeroed his finger in on his heart, clutched his chest, and groaned. "Ah! You got me!" He fake died and Jason laughed.

"You're not off the hook with Anna, even if you're dead."

"I'll try to remember that."

It had been a long time since Matt laughed for no good reason. It felt good to let loose and goof around like he used to do with Jamie. But when the cashier called him to the counter, Matt stuffed his immaturity in his back pocket. He didn't want to appear like a complete buffoon.

The two of them got their food and looked for an open table. The place was crowded, as usual, on a Thursday afternoon. Jason pointed to a mom who was just zipping up her child's coat, and they maneuvered their way over. Across from them sat an elder and his wife from Matt's church. Matt greeted them cordially. "Hello, Ms. Betty. Hello, Mr. Pete. How're you two doing this lovely afternoon?"

"Fine. Fine." Mr. Pete smiled and nodded.

Matt noticed he'd forgotten napkins as he put his tray down next to Jason's. "I need to get napkins. You need anything while I'm up? Sauce or a straw maybe? How about salt? Did you get a knife and fork for your salad? Sometimes they forget."

Jason rolled his eyes and poked fun at Matt in a high-pitched voice. "No Mother Hen, but if you want to, I'll let you cut up the lettuce and feed it to me."

Matt chuckled. "Shut up." He shook his head and walked around the island that separated the dining room and the cash registers to find the napkins. As he stepped back, he noticed the table opposite them was empty. "What?" He stopped short. "Where did they go? I was gone for like two seconds."

"Out the door, man. You turned around, and they fled the place like roaches when the light comes on."

"That is a terrible analogy." This restaurant was the cleanest in town; Matt cringed at the slight mention of roaches.

"Sorry. But yeah, they left." He gestured toward the door. "Did you run over their cat recently or something?" Jason took a bite of salad and waited for an answer.

"No. They go to my church."

Matt sat down and took his chicken sandwich out of the foil-lined bag. He stared at it. The tasty-smelling steam wafted up into his nostrils. His stomach growled. Still, he stared but did not take a bite. Now was the time to say something to Jason. It felt right. He'd put it off long enough, and it wasn't fair to prolong it any more. He couldn't eat until he got it off his chest. Either Jason would accept him, or he wouldn't, but not knowing was somehow worse.

With a racing heart, Matt said, “I have something to tell you.”

“Me or the chicken? Because if you’re going to start talking to chicken sandwiches, I think I might need to move to a different table.”

Matt looked up and glared. He tried to glower; he tried to scowl and look angry in every possible way, but it was impossible to remain serious when Jason was one breath away from busting out laughing. Jason pinched his lips together, but Matt could see the smile itching to break free. Jason even had tears welling in the corners of his eyes! Matt couldn’t be mad; instead he started laughing. “Shut up, man. I’m serious. I have something to tell you and I don’t know how.” Matt was laughing so hard at Jason laughing he had tears in his own eyes. “Stop! I’m telling you to stop.”

“You stop.” Jason grabbed his sides and continued cackling.

“I can’t! You’re the one who started it.” Matt’s chuckling slowed. He sighed. “Oh God… I haven’t laughed like that in ages. I don’t even know why we were laughing in the first place.”

“We were laughing about you talking to chickens.”

“No. You were being stupid,” Matt protested.

Jason smiled: not a goofy, laughing smile, but a comfortable smile. The kind of smile you give your brother after having a heart-to-heart talk. It said, “You’re an all right guy. We can get through this.” Matt pondered why he would have that sort of smile. And then he wondered why he was pondering it to begin with. Who was he turning into? Matt was never this touchy-feely. Jamie was. Matt was about the self-gratification and moving on to the next conquest. Jamie was the one who brought emotion into the mix. He was the one asking probing questions about feelings and the future. So much had changed in such a short time. Matt needed to confide in someone. He needed Jason, and he needed him to be okay with what he was about to say.

Nervously, he started again. “I have something I need to tell you.”

“Matt, it’s okay,” Jason interrupted, reached across the table, and patted the back of his hand. “I know what you’re going to say.”

Matt watched Jason’s fingers as they touched his hand and slowly pulled away. *What was that about?* Guys didn’t touch like that. Jason was acting weird. Matt asked, “Is something going on with you? You look odd.”

"I'm just trying to make it easy for you. I know what you have to say, and I don't want you worrying yourself sick over it."

"I doubt you know what I'm about to say. And I'm not sick about it. I'm ready. I need to tell you, and I'm only sorry I didn't tell you sooner." He took a deep breath. "Jason, I'm gay."

Jason stared at him for about three seconds and then took a bite of his salad.

Matt was sure Jason was about to flip, possibly even walk out. But he took another bite, and then another. *Crap! Maybe he's fuming. Maybe he's so mad he can't even talk. Maybe he's sick thinking about it, like my mom. What if he doesn't want to be my friend? Why won't he look at me? Maybe he didn't hear me because it's too loud in here.*

"Did you hear me? I said—"

Jason looked up from the salad. "You're gay. I already know."

"What? How? When?" sputtered Matt.

"September."

Matt's jaw dropped.

Jason chuckled. "And, so you don't ask a bazillion times, it was lots of things. For one, you didn't date or talk about it forever. Then when you do, you refer to your date as 'my honey' or 'my cutie' or 'my baby,' but I can't remember you ever saying 'my girl.' Then in September you distinctly said '*his* lips taste like strawberries' right when the siren went off. I pretended not to hear it. Ever since then, I listened real close every time you talked about your *hottie* and you never once said 'she.' Darian's a 'he.' Correct?"

Matt was shocked. All along he'd thought he was so stealthy. He was so wrong. "So… you're okay with that?"

"No. Not really." Jason shrugged. "I don't agree with your choice of lifestyle, and I'm not exactly okay with you not telling me sooner, but I understand why. At least I think I do. We've known each other for a long time. So, I'm a little pissed you didn't think I could handle the truth. Buuut… we've been friends a long time."

"You just restated the same fact."

Jason gave Matt a half smile. "I know. These past few months, I've had a chance to *know* about your secret without you *knowing* I know, and it gave me time to think. I know you. Your being gay doesn't change that. You and I talk all the time about accepting people the way they are, and here I am, faced with the very same issue. When I heard you say 'he' and not 'she,' I couldn't think all night. One of those pigs died because I wasn't paying attention when the thing was squealing right in front of me. I feel bad, but it was a pig. What if it had been a person?" He took a deep breath as the question settled in the air between them. "I thought all night about letting a pig die because I was freaking out about you dating another man. Eventually I asked myself 'why'? You're still the same guy who saved my ass that time the wall fell over on Bond Street. You're the same guy who put whipped cream in Scott's helmet on New Year's Eve when we were stuck at the station all night. And you, Matt Dixon, are the same guy who brought Jimmy to the firehouse barbeque at my house and whopped my ass playing horseshoes."

Jason chuckled, and Matt could not resist joining in.

"I love you, man, in a totally platonic way. You're like a brother. But I can't pretend it's all okay. I'm Baptist. Historically we don't condone homosexuality. So you're gonna have to accept me for who I am and not hold it against me if I disagree with you from time to time."

"Do the other guys know?"

"No."

"Are you going to tell them?" The thought was scary, but it would make it easier if Jason broke the news instead of him.

"No. I think you need to tell them. It's only right."

Matt nodded. "I know. I will. But could you give me some time to think about how and what to say?"

"Yeah. But only *some* time, not months."

"Agreed."

Matt tried to process everything as he sat in the noisy restaurant. Kids giggling in the background, moms correcting their kids, friends sharing lunch. Matt was dumbfounded by Jason's sincere opinion. He had gone over this moment in his head for weeks, and the outcome never resulted in what boiled down to "let's agree to disagree." Jason didn't walk out. Jason didn't yell. Jason didn't call him a nasty sinner. Jason was still his friend. Matt felt like crying.

(But he wouldn't!)

"Thanks," Matt managed to say as waves of emotion crashed around him.

"Matt, don't go all girly and hug me or nothing. I'm just speaking my mind. You and I always speak our minds. I'm still your friend, but I am still not sure how to handle your boyfriend."

"Darian is great. You'll like him. He's funny and smart. He's a really great artist and—"

"I'm sure he is, but Matt, I'm still getting used to you being gay. I don't know how I'll react seeing you with another guy."

"You mean… you don't want to meet him?" Disappointment sucked the joy out of Jason's acceptance. If Jason wouldn't accept Darian, then Matt wasn't sure how to maintain their friendship. Darian was part of him, like a heart. He couldn't disregard his heart—he'd die.

"No. Sorry. I… I can't, Matt. Not right now."

"But you might want to soon?" A glimmer of hope.

"Yeah, maybe." Jason strained to smile.

Matt could live with that. It was something.

"Do your parents know?"

Matt heaved a sigh. "Yeah. Mom's acting weird but trying. Dad and I had a huge blowup, and he's not talking to me. Steven's fighting at school. I'm not sure about Hannah because she's never around. Pastor Dennis even came to the house. That's why Mr. Pete walked out. Everything's crashing down around me."

"Is it worth it?"

"What? Being who I am without hiding it anymore?"

"Choosing to be gay?"

Matt looked him squarely in the eye. "It wasn't a choice; it's who I am." Matt got up and took his trash to the bin. He went to the counter and ordered a chocolate milkshake and a piece of lemon pie. He returned to the table and watched Jason eating in silence.

He didn't want to argue about choosing to be gay or being born that way. It was still up for debate in many circles, and he wasn't sure what the statistics proved. For him, he'd always been this way; he was born gay. But was it true of everyone? He didn't know. But no sane person would choose homosexuality and willingly face all the shit he was going through.

They ate quietly, but by the end of the meal, Jason was picking on Matt like normal and stealing a forkful of his pie. When they walked out to the parking lot, Matt showed Jason the new rims on his truck, and they stood talking for twenty more minutes, despite the wind and the cold.

When Jason left, Matt sat in his truck thinking. *At least this went smoother than with my dad.* Matt longed to talk to his dad like they used to.

December 6, 2010

MATT sat outside on the picnic bench wishing for lightning to strike. He felt horrible. It was as though he'd experienced his own Gethsemane, relating to the anguish Jesus must have felt the day he died. He wanted to die himself.

"Dude. What are you doing out here? It's freezing!" Jason walked up and punched his shoulder before joining him. "I thought maybe you got back on the smokes."

Matt looked up briefly, shook his head, but turned back down to the table. Taking up smoking again would have been easier to deal with.

Jason leaned forward. "Oh man, what's up with you? I can't remember you looking like this since…. Shit! Did something happen to Darian?"

Matt could hear the genuine concern in his voice. He shook his head. "No. It's me. I'm an ass."

Jason smirked. "I could've told you that."

"Shut up. It's true."

"What happened? What did you do?"

Matt considered avoiding the subject. He'd only *just* told his friend he was gay a few days ago. Why stir up judgment? Why take the chance Jason would truly reject him if he saw Matt for who he really was: a slut! "I…," he reluctantly said. "I've had a hard week."

"Yeah, so? We covered Thursday. Parents still giving you a hard time? Or is it the church? I guess you lucked out working yesterday because you had a good excuse to avoid the service."

"We don't attend that church anymore," Matt answered. "My dad was super clear on that. I think he thinks they're a bunch of hypocrites."

"I've met plenty of Christians who are. You should check out my church sometime. I think they're a pretty fair bunch."

"Maybe," Matt replied with zero enthusiasm. It was hard to get enthused when everything seemed so pointless.

"Then what's with the dour?"

"Me. It's all about me and the fact that I'm an ass… and a slut."

"What?" Jason seemed shocked to hear it, but Matt didn't know why.

"Jason, look, we both know how often I used to go out. You used to think I was picking up girls left and right, and even though you had the gender wrong, your assessment of my character was accurate. I'm a pig. I admit it. I'm a cad, I'm a slut, I'm a man-whore; whatever you want to label me—I'm it!"

Jason touched his wrist. "Matt, I wasn't labeling anything, especially your character. Your character is solid! Your choices—they could stand some reevaluating."

Matt grinned. "You always have a way with words."

Jason tapped his arm affectionately. "Seriously. What did you do?"

"I picked up a guy in a bar."

Jason shook his head and sighed disapprovingly. "Why?"

"I don't know. I've had a hard week. I needed to unwind. I wasn't thinking. I was stressed, and it happened."

"Did you really think that having sex with a stranger would make you feel better?"

"No. Yes. I don't know. It was an impulse. A stupid impulse."

"Damn right!"

"Look, I already feel bad. You don't have to keep going. It doesn't change what I did."

"But Matt, I thought you said you had an awesome date with Darian. Why cheat like that?"

Matt hated Jason's scrutiny, but he was glad to have someone to talk to about his troubles. "It isn't cheating if we aren't a couple."

"Bullshit!"

"And a hand job isn't sex." He tried Darian's logic.

"Like hell it isn't. If you really believed that you wouldn't look like this." He gestured at Matt's expression.

Matt huffed. Jason was right. He needed to come clean on the whole misadventure. "The worst part is that I let him kiss me."

Jason looked confused. "Oh."

Matt rubbed his eyes. "It was stupid." Matt hated filling in the details, yet as he did, it felt freeing. "We were done. He zipped up his pants while I did up mine. And then… and then he leaned in. I wasn't thinking at first. It just happened. One second I felt relieved of all my tension from the week, and then he kissed me. I felt his hand on my chest. It felt nice. I went with it and opened my mouth, but when I felt his tongue sliding over mine, all I could picture in my head was Darian—kissing Darian. I shoved the guy back and ran out of the stall as fast as I could." Matt struggled not to cry as he buried his face in his hands. "I feel awful!"

After a few minutes of silence, he wondered if Jason had up and left. Matt sniffled and wiped his eyes. When he turned, Jason was still there. He looked a little pallid, but he was still there. Silence stretched, and Matt grew concerned. "Jason? Are you okay?"

He gulped. "I'm okay," he replied, although he looked far from it.

"You look like you're gonna chuck, man."

"Nope. I'm good. I just…." He paused and took a breath. "I just got a visual I'm not accustomed to."

"Oh." Matt felt embarrassed.

"Dude. Like I said before…. Over the years, you and I rarely talked about sex. And then the other month you hit me with this visual of eating out your girlfriend's ass. That threw me! But I manned up. I handled it. And I think I gave you some pretty darn good advice," Jason explained with a sickened look on his face. "But then you admitted to the gay thing. I was handling that. Until now, it was separate in my mind from our other discussions. But describing to me what exactly went on with the guy you hooked up with, patched everything else together. If you're gonna fill in details, we can't have these discussions anymore. I'm not ready."

"I'm sorry! I never meant to gross you out. I just… I needed to hear myself say it. I needed to admit to someone I screwed up big time."

"That you did!"

"Jason, I'm sorry."

Jason looked him in the eye and slowly returned a grin. He stuck out his hand. "Truce?"

"But we're not fighting." Matt shook his hand anyway.

"No. But if you describe for me again about having a guy's tongue in your mouth, I'm gonna have to punch you."

Matt grinned. "Fair enough."

"Now listen to me. You're a good guy. And yes, pretty slutty, but you can change. If you love Darian—you'll change. No more sleeping around?"

"No. I promise."

Ten seconds later, the alarm sounded.

IT WASN'T a huge deal. One-alarm grease fire at a local restaurant. It was the same place he and Jason had eaten the other day. Matt knew the layout of the building and quickly directed people to the kitchen. Matt told Billy to go inside while he scanned the crowd outside for injuries. One paramedic was wrapping up a burned wrist on one of the cooks, and another was checking someone for smoke inhalation. Everything was under control.

Then someone in the throng of people caught his eye. Two someones.

At the edge of the crowd of customers who left the building when smoke started filling the place, stood Matt's brother Steven and Jamie's ex-rival from high school, Joey Taylor. Jamie hated Joey. He had made Jamie's life a living hell for years, always bullying him and never letting up. Matt almost rushed over and let him have it for all the problems he'd caused Jamie, but what was the point? Jamie wasn't here. And high school was long over.

Instead, he figured he could ignore Joey and talk to Steven.

Matt approached on Steven's side and asked, "Hey, Steven, are you okay? Were you in the building when it filled with smoke?" He reached out and touched Steven's arm.

Steven flinched. "I'm fine."

"Steven, if you were in the building, you should have someone listen to your lungs."

Steven glared. "I said I'm fine."

Joey chimed in, "Steve, he knows what he's talking about—he's a fireman. You should listen to him. I think you should have an EMT look you over."

It irked Matt that Steven needed prompting from anyone other than himself, but for it to be Joey Taylor…. Matt wanted to scream. He addressed his ex-classmate gruffly. "Thanks, Taylor, but I got this one."

Joey looked at him for a second, and then his eyes sparked. The switch obviously went on, and Joey knew who he was talking to. "Dixon? Is that you? I barely recognized you. You look so much older, and you look like your dad."

Matt rolled his eyes. "Taylor, I've always looked like this. You simply never paid attention long enough to realize it. And you can leave my little brother alone. I'm sure he'll go see a paramedic without any suggestions from you." He was not about to get into the differences between paramedics and EMTs.

Joey held up his hands. "Dixon, seriously, I don't know what I ever did to you, but I'm sorry. Steve and I are friends. I was only trying to tell him it was a good idea to listen to a firefighter. Now that I know it's you, I'll urge him even more to listen." Joey turned to Steven again. "How come you never said Matt was your brother? We went to school together."

Steven's glare intensified as he leveled his eyes on Matt. "I guess it slipped my mind."

Matt didn't know why his brother was acting so hostile, but he was certain he needed to find out. Perhaps tonight at home? Steven hadn't talked to him since the pastor's visit. In fact, Steven had acted differently toward him ever since he came out after Jamie's funeral. Matt knew he'd been beaten up in school. It couldn't be easy for him. Matt felt even worse now than when he was talking to Jason about cheating on Darian. He realized, now, he'd let his brother down in a huge way by neglecting him.

Matt came out and Steven took the hits for it. Isn't that why he was getting beat up at school? Their dad had said something of the sort.

He was going to say something, but Steven shook his head and wandered over to an ambulance. Matt watched as a paramedic nodded and pointed to a spot where Steven could sit as he took out a light to inspect his throat. He felt confident Steven was in good hands.

"Steve's pretty pissed at you, ya know."

Matt turned to Joey. "You're still here?"

"He's really strong about it, but kids at school have been rough on him." Joey kept talking and Matt felt defensive. He should be the one to know what was going on with his own brother!

"I can handle it, okay?" he shot back crossly.

Joey, in contrast, remained calm and rational. "Matt, I know you and I were never friends. I beat on Miller and you beat on me—high school was a big mess. I regret it, I do. I was really sorry to hear about Jimmy. Two years after graduation, I started to realize I had no friends, no real ones. All I ever did was rag on people and act like a screw-up. I always wanted to talk to Jimmy and apologize for being a dick, but I never did. He was your best friend; do you think he would have forgiven me?"

Matt's day was not getting any better. Guilt and shame just kept piling up. Now, the biggest jerk of Jamie's past was asking for forgiveness? *Shit! I'm getting the message, God!* Internally, Matt looked up to the heavens. He knew he needed to talk to Darian. He was the one who needed to ask for forgiveness. Joey's words brought it all into perspective.

Matt reached out his hand. "Yeah, he'd forgive you," he said.

Joey shook his hand and smiled.

"So how do you know my brother?"

"I work here." He gestured to the building. "He comes in all the time. We started talking and found we have loads in common. He's a great guy."

Somehow he felt cheated. Why should Joey Taylor, of all people, have to tell Matt how great his brother was? He should know himself! He needed to talk to him.

"Matt!" someone called from the side entrance to the restaurant.

Matt looked over and waved. To Joey he said, "Sorry, gotta go. Duty calls." He shook his hand again.

"Okay. It was nice talking to you."

"Yeah." Matt nodded and walked away. He felt strange. Joey was not the guy he remembered. He'd matured. Something Matt needed to consider doing before he stumbled his way to twenty-four and alienated everyone in his life.

He needed to be honest, and he needed to talk to Darian… and Steven.

LATER, after a shower and a few minutes with his mom, Matt knocked on Steven's door. "Steven? Are you in there?"

The door burst open. "What do *you* want?" Steven asked none too pleasantly.

"I want to talk to you," Matt said.

"Well, I don't want to talk to you." He tried to slam the door in Matt's face, but Matt placed his hand on the door. Steven's voice grew louder. "I said I don't want to talk to you!"

"Steven, I'm sorry. Whatever I did, I'm sorry!"

"Sorry?" Steven spat. "Are you kidding me? Sorry doesn't take back all the shit I get at school. Sorry doesn't take back being called a 'fag lover.'" Steven stepped closer and got in Matt's face. He continued yelling, "Do you know how many times I've been asked if you bring guys back to the house to fuck, and if I can hear you through the wall?"

Matt stepped back, and Steven moved with him. "Steven, I—"

"I hate you!" Steven snarled and then slugged Matt in the stomach.

Matt wasn't poised for a fight, and he stumbled back against the wall. Steven hit him one more time before Matt could get out of his range. Matt sidestepped, and Steven pivoted. He swung again, but this time Matt caught his fist in his hand. Steven had some power to him—Matt would give him that much—but he was also at least fifty pounds lighter and five inches shorter. Plus, Matt was pretty damn strong!

Matt twisted his wrist and pulled Steven's arm around behind his back, and Steven yelped. "I give!" This was the code phrase they'd always used when Matt was a teenager and wrestled with Steven. Matt released his arm.

Matt tried again. "I'm really sorry," he said, placing his hand on Steven's shoulder.

Steven gave him a hard glare and rubbed his arm. "Whatever," he huffed. "Just keep your queer ass away from me. Okay? I don't want to look at you."

"All right," Matt agreed, although it hurt to do so. "Can you tell me one thing…?" Matt started to ask, but the door slammed shut. "Or not."

"What's going on up here?" his mother asked as she reached his end of the hallway.

"Nothing. Steven hates me 'cause I'm gay." Matt's despair was hitting an all-time low.

"Oh, honey, I'm sure he doesn't. He needs time to adjust, that's all."

Matt appreciated her encouraging tone, but he had serious doubts Steven would ever talk to him again without venom in his voice.

16

December 8, 2010

"THREE weeks!"

Matt held the phone out as his mom shrieked on the other end. When he didn't hear anything else, he returned to the conversation. "Yeah, Mom. I'm sorry. I guess I figured you'd find out right away from someone at church. I didn't think, or else I would've said something sooner."

"But three weeks?" she cried on the other end. "I can't believe Joan's been in the hospital, and no one mentioned it for three weeks. Not one person called me."

Matt felt even worse knowing none of her friends had called to tell her. "I'm really sorry," he said again.

"She must be scared. Is she scared, Matt?"

"I don't know, Mom. Last I heard she was in restraints."

"Restraints!"

Again, Matt yanked the phone away from his ear to ensure he could hear for the rest of the day. "I guess I forgot to mention that too."

"You think? I'm going to call Kevin again and see if he can give me her room number. I want to see her."

"Mom, just be prepared in case she flips out on you."

"Matt, the woman has a cancerous tumor in her brain. She has the right to flip out. I've been her friend for twenty years. I am going to go see her!"

"All right, Mom. Call me later."

"I will. Bye, honey."

Matt hung up the phone and waited a few minutes before pulling back on the road. There was traffic, so he let his truck sit on the shoulder as he mulled over the conversation with his mom. Matt knew his mom was an emotional train wreck. She cried almost all the time lately. And when Dan told him the news about Ms. Joan, he was glad. And then he felt guilty for being glad she was sick. And then his heart shifted over to rage because her sickness wasn't enough to punish her for the things she had done to Jamie.

After the rage settled down, he felt sad—for his mom, not for Joan. Matt knew his mom would take the news hard. Even if he hated Ms. Joan, his mom liked her. They were friends. And if she died, then his mom would feel the same kind of loss he felt when Jamie died. Matt really didn't want that for his mom.

His phone buzzed. It was a text from Bob Shaw at work. *Chief's friend died. (The one in the coma.) Guys are putting together something for his wife. Funeral is Saturday.*

As if Matt needed one more thing to think about. *Shit!* He covered his face with his hands and took a few deep breaths. His life was crumbling around him. He didn't think God would give him more than he could bear, but these burdens felt so substantial that any moment he was sure his back would collapse under the pressure.

Please, God, help me get through one more day. Just one more day.

Matt looked up after praying silently and waited for a tractor-trailer and a smaller car to pass him before pulling back onto the two-lane road heading south. Traffic was pretty light, since it was well after morning rush hour. He almost hadn't gotten out of bed this morning. He wasn't due into the station until seven tonight, so in theory he had about ten hours to kill. He could have been sleeping. But Matt hardly slept anymore. His mind was always on Darian. He checked the computer all the time now for e-mails. Darian hadn't sent one in a while. Lori was no help at all. Matt wondered if Dan was preventing him from e-mailing, or whether he really wanted contact at all. Where they stood in the relationship was still nebulous.

The car in front of him was turning, so Matt slowed down.

He turned on the radio. Nickelback. "I like your pants around your feet…." He could listen to that. He'd left his iPod home this morning when he dashed out. He was only going to look at a muffler for his dad's friend's Mustang. As soon as he picked it up, he'd head back home.

A Mustang. Jamie liked Mustangs.

The tractor-trailer pulled off to the right. Matt slowed down and waited until it was completely over the white line. When it appeared fully at rest, Matt proceeded to drive past it. Three seconds later he saw the blinker on its driver-side fender impossibly close to his hood. The tractor-trailer was turning… into his truck!

He couldn't even react before the fender of the tractor-trailer collided with his passenger-side door and spun his truck out in a semicircle across the road. His tires screeched. Matt gripped the steering wheel as he helplessly rode out a rollercoaster ride from hell. His truck was headed for a telephone pole on the side of the road. No, the angle was too tight. He missed the pole and cruised impossibly fast toward the corner of a brick house.

A house. Holy shit, I'm going to hit the front of that house!

Matt turned as best he could, covering his face and bracing himself for the impact. His Dakota slammed lengthwise into a van parked next to the house. Glass shattered. Matt's body banged against the driver-side door.

Matt lowered his arms. "I hit a van," he said out loud. "I didn't even see a van. I hit the van and not the house." He couldn't believe it!

The white van, which was smaller than his truck, got struck along its side and consequently flipped over from the transferred momentum. This was the best crash he could have possibly gotten into.

"I'm not bleeding." He checked over his arms. He moved his legs. His thigh hurt, but only slightly. "I'm okay. I'm talking to myself, but I'm okay." He grinned. "Oh my God, I'm okay."

The next thought that entered his brain after realizing he was not going to die was, "Shit! My truck! My poor truck."

People approached his truck. "Hey, are you injured?" one man asked.

"No. I don't think so."

"Just sit still. An ambulance is on its way."

Matt undid his seatbelt. "No really, I'm fine." He slid across the seat to the passenger-side door. It was difficult to push open, but someone helped him.

As soon as he got out, he could see why the door was hard to open. The metal was crushed in right where the extended cab started, and the rear tire was blown and angled forty-five degrees out of alignment. Matt repeated, "My poor truck."

He ignored the siren as the police arrived. Walking around the back of the truck, he gasped. The driver's side was completely smashed in from the front fender to the rear. The windows on that side were gone. The doors were crushed and inoperable, and the tires were mangled and twisted. In short, his truck was totaled!

The van that used to be where his truck now sat was on its roof a few feet away, totaled as well. If the van had not been there, Matt would have careened into the side of the brick house. Houses don't flip out of the way. Houses, brick houses especially, stand firm while objects such as trucks fold in on themselves upon impact like accordions. Matt would be dead if that van had not blocked his path.

"Excuse me, sir, are you the driver of this vehicle?"

Matt turned to the questioning police officer. "Um, yes. Sorry. I was pondering how close to death I was." *And mourning the death of my truck.* Matt felt the pangs of sorrow. His beloved truck.

"That's understandable. But I'd like to speak with you and get some details if you don't mind."

"Of course," Matt agreed and followed him over to his cruiser.

After the police took statements from each driver and the witness, Matt was allowed to leave. His truck would be towed later and assessed by the insurance agency. Matt crawled into the cab and retrieved as many of his personal belongings as he could: his phone, the registration to the truck, a pair of pliers Jamie had given him, and some work gloves. Matt thought about who to call.

Not Mom; this would send her over the edge.

Matt called his sister, and fifteen minutes later she picked him up.

"Thanks for coming, Hannah. I really appreciate this." Matt got in her car and shut the door. He leaned over and kissed her cheek like he'd done for years. He was pleasantly surprised when she didn't pull away and make a gagging face at him.

She was talking on the phone and held up a finger, signaling him to wait. "Okay, thanks. Talk later. Bye." She put the phone down and pulled onto the road. "So, totaled your truck? That sucks."

"Yeah, ain't that the truth? Wait… you're still talking to me?" He realized the two of them hadn't been alone in months. He was sure she'd been avoiding him.

She downshifted and slowed for a red light. "Yeah, why wouldn't I be?"

"I don't know. Maybe because I'm gay and suddenly the family treats me like I have bubonic plague?" Sarcasm flowed off the tongue so easily.

"No, they don't."

"Ah yes, yes they do. Mom goes around spewing stats on HIV and AIDS. She thinks I'm gonna die. Dad yelled and said he can't look at me anymore. And Steven gets in fights over being called a 'fag lover' at school. He won't talk to me either."

"Steven got beat up?"

"I guess. I saw a black eye as he dashed up the steps the other week and slammed his door. I didn't want this to happen. Why'd I have to come out… and at church of all places?"

"Maybe because you were tired of living a lie?"

Matt was not prepared for her casual reaction. He cocked his head and watched Hannah drive. Who was this girl? It seemed like just yesterday she had strawberry braids and freckles and giggled at octaves only dogs could hear. She was still as loud and annoying as ever, but also cuddly and cute. She was practically a woman now. Her reddish hair had darkened into a rich auburn. She was still loud at times and could definitely be annoying, especially if you asked Steven, but she was more mature. Hannah had turned into a young woman with hopes and dreams and opinions, and Matt was suddenly yearning to know more about her. She'd always been his sister, but now she was a person.

"How come you aren't ready to disown me?"

"Um, you're my brother. Family sticks together."

"I wish Mom and Dad thought like that. And Steven. I'm fairly certain he may never talk to me again."

"They do. Give them time. Plus, they're old. They don't have progressive thinking. I think there's a lot more gray out there than black and white. And Steven is sixteen. He'll come around. I think it's a lot for them to take in, in a short period of time. So you're gay." She shrugged behind the wheel. "You're not the first person to tell me you like boys. I know two guys on campus who are gay, and my lab partner in physics is a lesbian. You're not a freak, Matt. You're simply part of a minority. More people need to have balls like you to admit who they are. If they did, then I think they'd find they weren't alone. No matter what you are, alone is a horrible place to be." She turned at the light but slowed down significantly. "Matt, where am I going?"

"Oh, uh, what time is it?"

"Almost three."

"Mom's not home until after four, or even later if she goes to see Ms. Joan. Take me home. I want to shower, and then you can take me to the rental car place. I think I have glass bits in my underwear. It's very uncomfortable. I also don't feel like talking Mom off a ledge right now. Please don't tell."

"I won't. She called me this morning to tell me about the news. I feel bad for her. Ms. Joan is like her best friend. So sad." Hannah sighed. "I'm staying with Julie tonight anyway. I won't tell."

"Thanks. Ya know, you've turned into a really neat person, Hannah. I never thought we could just talk like this. I like it."

She smiled at him. "Me too, big brother. So, what's your guy like?"

"My guy?" Matt was shocked.

"Yeah. Don't you have a boyfriend? You have to have a boyfriend. You're *hot*!"

Matt opened his jaw in horror and embarrassment. "What? No. I did not just hear my baby sister refer to me as *hot*."

"Matt, don't be a prude. Come on! You know you're hot. So what's the guy like?"

"I'm not talking to you about him."

"So there is someone. Cool. I'm glad. Will I get to meet him?"

"Eventually."

Matt was glad when they parked in front of the house. He didn't want any more of Hannah's probing questions. It was so embarrassing.

MATT parked his rental car down the street in hopes that if Dan was home, then at least he wouldn't wonder why a strange car was parked in front of his house. Matt hadn't been given the all clear to date Darian or even visit Darian. In theory, Matt could potentially be screwing himself by showing up without permission. On the other hand, Matt had been hit on so many fronts in the last few days, he really needed to see Darian. Between the church, his family, Steven, Ms. Joan, and now his beloved truck, Matt's brain was fried. Pressure and tension pressed in on him from all sides. He needed release and not purely on a sexual level. He needed Darian.

Matt rang the doorbell and waited. The dog barked. The curtain in the front room moved, and Darian peeked out. He smiled instantly and disappeared. The barking-dog sound moved from beyond the front door to what sounded like the back of the house—maybe into the kitchen? Then the dog was in the front window looking out, and Darian reappeared to remove the dog.

Matt waited patiently, and then the door finally opened.

"Matt!" Darian cried, flinging himself into Matt's arms.

The two of them stumbled inside and somehow managed to close the door between kissing and groping and moaning and grinding. The growling dog was the only thing distracting Matt from undoing his fly. "Dare…." He tried speaking between desperate kisses. "Dare… the dog."

Darian hopped into Matt's arms and secured his legs around Matt's waist. "Ignore him." He thrust his tongue into Matt's mouth and mewled so happily it gave the impression he hadn't been kissed in years.

Their sloppy sucking, slurping sounds filled the room. Matt ran his hands down Darian's shirt and rested them on his buttocks, riding out the frenzy. He figured eventually Darian would run out of air or attempt to undress him while they clung to one another; either way, they would soon have to pull apart in order to move to the next step. But oh, did Darian feel good! Having Darian's arms and legs wrapped around him, and that incredibly gifted tongue sliding over his own, was rapturous.

When the kissing slowed, Darian released his lips and asked, "Did Dan…" *Kiss.* "I mean Dad…" *Kiss. Kiss.* "…say you could come by? He didn't mention it before he left." Darian rubbed his cheek against Matt's. "I didn't think he'd call you."

"No. I came over because I needed to see you."

Darian leaned back and opened his eyes. "He doesn't know you're here?" He released Matt and landed back on the floor. He went to the window and looked out. "I don't see your truck. Did you park down the street? He won't like you being here without permission." He closed the curtain and turned around to face Matt. "What if Dan gets home early from his date? He'll think I called you as soon as he left. He'll stop trusting me. I don't want to make him mad. He's just starting to loosen up. What if—"

Matt grabbed Darian's upper arms and pulled him into another kiss. It was a proven method for calming someone's nerves. Or at the very least, shutting them up! Matt hoped he calculated correctly. "It's okay," Matt assured him, kissing him a few more times. "Dan isn't home." He stroked his face. "My truck isn't out there."

"Then where?"

"It got totaled."

"What?"

Darian's wide-eyed panic, as well as his shrill voice, signaled for Matt's comforting nature to kick in. "Shhh, calm down." Matt touched his hair. "I'm fine. A tractor-trailer hit me, and then I hit a parked van. I bruised my leg, that's all." He kissed Darian's eyes as he continued to stroke his hair. "Shhh, baby, I'm fine. I'm right here. I came because I really needed to see you. This has been an awful day, an awful couple of weeks."

Darian's alarm drained from his eyes and his grip on Matt's hips relaxed. "You're fine?"

"Yes." Matt nodded. Then he tilted his head and smirked. "Well, no… not completely. I need *you* in bad way. You think your dad'll be gone long enough to give me one of those 'nonsex' hand jobs?"

"Absolutely!" Darian grabbed Matt's hand and practically dragged him up the steps. "Dad and Ms. Cheryl should be gone for a couple hours. They said they would be. I only got home twenty minutes before you got here. I'm supposed to be doing laundry." He pulled Matt down the hall and into his room.

Matt stopped short in the doorway. "This is Jamie's room." He whispered as if the space were sacred.

Darian watched him. "Yeah. It was Jamie's and mine."

Matt stepped into the room and looked around. He'd never been in this room, but it felt familiar all the same. So many things he recognized as Jamie's: pictures, posters, and a calendar from 2008. He even remembered being with Jamie when he picked out the comforter at Walmart. He walked around the room, and a chill went down his spine. *Should I even be in here?*

"Are you sure you want to do it in here?" Matt asked skeptically.

Darian walked up and laced his fingers through Matt's. "Yes." And then he reconsidered. "Maybe. I'm not sure. Can we sit on the bed and talk for a while? Seeing you weirded out is making me feel weirded out, and I don't think I can get hard right now."

Matt grinned. "Okay." He lifted their joined hands and kissed Darian's knuckles. "To tell you the truth, I'm fine if we do nothing but hold hands. I've missed you so much just being with you is all I really need."

Darian's pleasant smile lit up the room more than the overhead light, and he squeezed Matt's hand.

Matt kept hold of Darian's hand and looked at the pictures on the walls. He spied two chalk drawings similar to the one Darian did of him in September. One was of Jamie from what looked like 2005, judging from the shirt he wore, and the other was a self-portrait of

Darian. Some others were Darian's sketches, but most of the pictures on the wall were photos of Matt. Some of Jamie and one or two of Darian, but the majority were of Matt from when he was fifteen all the way to the present. "No wonder Dan thinks you're obsessed with me."

"But they're not mine. They were all in Jamie's things. Tucked in books and under the bed. I found a whole shoebox full in the closet. I started sticking them on the corkboard as I found them. Dan just doesn't understand that Jamie was obsessed. He loved you."

Matt noticed the drop in his voice and looked at Darian instead of the wall of photos. Darian was staring at the floor. Matt hooked a finger under his chin. "He loved you too."

Darian released Matt's hand and strolled over to the bed and sat down. Matt thought he was going to say something, but he didn't. Darian was disturbingly quiet. He needed to think of something to cheer him up. But what?

Matt glanced around and spotted his iPod. It was hooked up to a set of speakers on his dresser. "Mind if I put on some music?"

Darian shook his head.

Matt went over and scrolled through his music library. He was astounded at the vast selection Darian had. "You have over nine thousand songs. Dude! This is incredible." He caught Darian's grin out of the corner of his eye. "All Time Low, Anberlin, Barenaked Ladies, Breaking Benjamin, Cars, Charlie Musselwhite, wow!" He kept scrolling. "Eagles, ELO, Evanescence, Fall Out Boy, Good Charlotte, Hawk Nelson.... This is amazing. I have almost everything you have. All right, I *don't* have Hannah Montana or the Jonas Brothers, but REO Speedwagon, Rush, Secondhand Serenade, Skillet, Shinedown, Staind! Oh my gosh, Dare, we practically have the same taste in music."

Darian shrugged. "I like a wide variety. I tend to listen based on my mood."

He said it like it was no big deal, but it was a huge deal to Matt. He loved music! Lived for it. With the amount of running he did all the time, he needed music to survive. "Panic! At The Disco, Stone Sour, and The Red Jumpsuit Apparatus. Holy crap, Dare." He put the iPod down and bounced over to Darian's edge of the bed.

Darian's eyebrow shot up. "What?"

"You don't get it, I know, but every time I'm with you I find one more reason to love you. We're going to be perfect together. Seriously. When you're ready." He kissed Darian and went back to the iPod. "The Used? I love The Used." He hit play and "Paralyzed" came on, bass chords thumping against the walls.

"Me too," Darian said. "I can play the opening riff to 'With Me Tonight.'"

Matt eyes bulged. "You play guitar? I play guitar!" Matt clapped his palm against his chest. He didn't remember Jamie mentioning that detail in his journals.

Darian answered nonchalantly. "A little. My mom couldn't afford guitar lessons, so I had to teach myself. I'm a better drummer than guitarist. My friend Ben has drums. He lets me play sometimes."

"You play drums?" Matt plopped back down, causing the bed to bounce.

"Yeah. Not like Neil Peart, but I'm okay."

Matt's heart swelled. He ran his fingers through Darian's hair marveling over every little thing that spelled out love. "You're perfect."

Darian blushed. "No, I'm not."

"You are." Matt kissed him softly. He eased him back on the bed and caressed his chest through the fabric of his shirt. He moved his mouth to explore the soft spot behind Darian's ear while he reached down and slid his fingers along the waistband of his underwear where it stuck out above his jeans. Matt licked and nibbled Darian's neck, mapping out a path with his tongue over to the ridge of his ear, sucking on his earlobe. He slipped his fingers under the hem of Darian's shirt, but as soon as Matt felt the flat of Darian's stomach and his bellybutton piercing, Darian stopped his hand from moving any higher. Matt pulled back. "What's wrong?"

"I just…. It feels weird. I'm afraid Dan will come in any second. I'm still not sure I want to have 'nonsex' with you in Jamie's old bed."

Matt leaned back, one arm supporting his weight on his elbow. "It's okay. I understand." Matt caressed Darian's lower belly as he looked down into his face. He remained right up next to his body with one leg looped over Darian's thigh. "We don't have to do anything. I just wanted to be with you. I've been having a horrible time lately, and *you* are the one good thing I got going on. I need you."

Darian's eyes shifted away from Matt's. He looked troubled. Matt glided his fingers over to Darian's hip and back along his belly. Darian had always responded well to that action before, so Matt was attempting it now to soothe whatever was on his mind. In fact, it seemed no matter where Matt rubbed him (not speaking sexually, of course), Darian always calmed down. Matt said, "I hope you know you can talk to me. Whatever's bothering you. I may not have the answers, but I'll listen. My mom always tells me I'm a great listener."

Darian's eyes darted to different objects in the room, everything but Matt's face. "I'm worried you'll get to know me and find out I'm a complete basket case." Darian sounded so desperately troubled.

"Dare, baby, I won't. I love you."

Darian finally brought his attention back to Matt. "Why? I'm not that special. I can't make complete sentences most of the time because my brain doesn't function clearly. I don't have any condoms in here even if we wanted to have sex. I have a bee phobia, but I like spiders. My mother moved to Seattle in October and didn't even say good-bye. I think Jamie's haunting me. I want to learn French before I die. I'm allergic to coconut. I don't like mint chocolate chip ice cream. The only time I feel safe is when I'm with you. And sometimes I wish I had wings, like that guy on X-Men."

Matt gazed into Darian's eyes, waiting to make sure the list was done before he burst out laughing. He knew it was inappropriate, given Darian's serious expression, but he couldn't help it. "Oh, Darian." Matt flopped over onto his back. "That was the longest list of random thoughts I've ever heard."

Darian sat up on one elbow and leaned over him—still quite melancholy. "If you think I'm perfect, you'll only be disappointed."

Matt knew he should ask about Darian's mom moving, or his disturbing comment about Jamie haunting him, but those topics seemed so serious. Matt didn't do serious. He avoided serious. He'd had enough serious for a while. He shoved "serious" deep inside and kept it there, like he did with his "incident." Plus, what if talking opened up more problems? Darian needed a professional for this stuff. Darian needed his therapist.

Matt took his proven safe route of avoidance. "Dare, it's meant figuratively. No one is *perfect* perfect. I think you're perfect for *me*.

That's all I meant. The only questions I have left are about hunting, jogging, and dancing. Do you like to hunt?"

Darian shrugged. "No. I don't think I could shoot Bambi. But I'm not opposed to eating him."

Matt grinned. "Okay." Not only did he like Darian's simple answer, he also liked how his shoulders relaxed. This conversation was becoming less complicated. "I can live with that. How about running?"

Darian furrowed his forehead and cocked an eyebrow.

Matt laughed. "I take that as a 'no.' So how about dancing?"

"Yeah, I like to dance. Lori said I'm pretty good."

Matt felt his heart swelling again. Everything inside told him Darian was *the one*. If only Darian could see it that way and let go of his doubts. Matt stood up when the songs shuffled and Staind came on. He held out his hand to Darian. "Dance with me?" Darian placed his hand in Matt's, and Matt pulled Darian off the bed and into his arms. The two of them swayed to the music. With their bodies moving together, Matt sang the first line of lyrics to "Tangled Up In You" into Darian's ear. He moved in time with the slow beat, and Darian stepped with him in perfect harmony.

On the second line of the song, Darian chimed in without missing a beat. "You're the pills, that take away my pain."

Matt smiled softly into Darian's eyes as he sang the next line.

Matt waited and allowed Darian to fill in the next phrase of lyrics and he didn't disappoint. And then, without missing a word, they sang the chorus together and Matt could have wept for how happy he felt dancing in Darian's arms while harmonizing one of his favorite songs.

They danced more synchronously than Ginger Rogers and Fred Astaire. Dancing with Darian made Matt acutely aware of how good their bodies felt together. He had *intended* to hold back when he came over, but being around Darian was intoxicating. He always felt giddy and drunk, and his groin behaved as if he was on Viagra. He knew a hand job would not suffice as soon as Staind came on. Hearing Darian sing was breathtaking.

Before the song faded, he lowered Darian onto the bed again. He was going to make love to him; there was no stopping it. A hand job would have been fine for satisfaction and release, but being with Darian was more than a physical need. Matt wanted the closeness, the intimacy, and what Jamie would call the complete connection: mind, body, and soul.

Darian was utterly relaxed this time as Matt licked his neck and massaged the hardness in his jeans. His eyes were closed as Matt kissed his chin and undid his belt, making his way into Darian's boxers. Darian clutched the back of Matt's head and groaned and tilted his hips up.

Avril Lavigne sounded in the room singing "Hey, hey, you, you, I don't like your girlfriend" and jolted Matt out of his captivation with the most amazing man on the planet.

Matt muttered, "Sorry. I can't make love to you with this on." He got up and changed the song. "Classical okay?"

"Yeah."

Matt pulled Darian's jeans off. "No more shuffle. It will play down the list." He reached up to Darian's shirt. "Whoa, what happened?" Matt pointed to the angry red scratches by his ribs.

Darian blurted, "The dog. He jumped and scratched me."

"Wow, wicked nails. They need to be trimmed, man. You should probably put some ointment on that."

"Okay," Darian said. "Listen, can we do this half-undressed? It might make it easier if Dan gets home early. Rushing to get decent and all."

Matt didn't understand his concern; Darian had said Dan would be out for hours, but he went along with it. "Sure. Whatever. But next time I want all your skin exposed. You know I love your body." He winked.

Darian smiled and pulled Matt into his arms.

"Are you okay with this? I know we said no sex," Matt asked, as he got comfortable between Darian's legs.

"Yes," he moaned, pushing onto Matt's fingers. "Oh God, yes."

"I know I promised Dan, I know I should hold back, but I can't seem to do that when I'm with you," Matt explained as he kissed Darian's neck. Matt was a verbal processor, so more times than not, he felt the need to explain his actions while executing them.

"We… oh… we revised that rule. Remember?"

"Oh yeah," Matt gladly recalled. "You're not as tight as I thought you'd be."

Darian smirked as Matt moved his mouth from his lips to assault his throat. "I told you I have a dildo. I use it. Often."

"That is so hot." Matt practically came thinking about it. "Let me watch next time?"

"Yeah." Darian's body jerked when Matt touched his prostate.

Matt grinned.

When the anticipation was just too great, he withdrew his fingers and placed a pillow under Darian's hips. He lined up his cock after rolling a condom down its length. Darian may not have had condoms, but Matt did. He'd never show up unprepared for sex. That was just wrong.

"Do you want another position?" he asked. "Missionary is seriously ordinary."

Darian reached out and Matt sank on top of him. "No. I want to feel you all over me—covering me. I want to wrap myself around you and feel every pulse your body makes."

"Sounds perfect."

Sliding inside Darian was like coming home. It felt warm, comforting, and right. He never wanted to be anywhere else. They moved together as if continuing their dance on the mattress. Synchronous—of one accord. Their cries of passion added to the music and filled the room.

"I love you, Darian." Matt held his beloved tight, affirming his joy by repeatedly saying Darian's name while kissing him all over his face and neck, thrusting deeper and deeper into his body. Darian answered by squeezing Matt's hips with his thighs and crying out Matt's name. They were wrapped around each other, intent on becoming the embodiment of one flesh, both moaning in release when the door to the room opened and the dog barked.

"Holy shit!" Matt heard Dan Miller's voice and froze.

There was nothing like getting caught in the act by your boyfriend's father. Especially if it was in the buff, on top of the covers, with your dick well sunk into his ass. There were no excuses like "we were just kissing" or the ever popular, "we weren't doing anything!" Matt was caught, red handed, balls-deep and with nowhere to run.

Mr. Miller turned his back and left the room, but Matt knew it would only be minutes before he returned. He yelled from the hallway, "Turn that fucking music down!"

Matt gazed into Darian's terror-filled eyes. He held the base of the condom, pulled out, and turned off the music. The utter silence magnified the dread each of them felt. Matt reached for Darian, but Darian sat up and pulled his knees to his chest, further isolating himself. Matt knew this was not going to end well.

"Are you dressed yet?" Mr. Miller growled through the door.

Matt answered when it was obvious Darian couldn't. "Um, almost." Was he frozen in fear? Matt yanked on his jeans and went to Darian's side. "Dare. Dare. You gotta get dressed. Dare. Snap out of it." He snapped his fingers in front of Darian's face.

"He's never going to let me see you," Darian mumbled.

"Dare. You're twenty-two years old. You have every right to see whomever you want. If you want to see me—you can."

Darian shook his head. "No. He's going to tell me to leave. He's going to hate me because I betrayed his son. He's going to punish me for having you in Jamie's bed."

Matt sat back and watched tears stream from Darian's eyes. The poor wretched soul was blankly staring past Matt's shoulder at something in the room. He looked sick. Darian had to be in shock. "What the hell's going on in this house? What did he do to you? Does he hurt you?"

Matt hoped for an answer, but Dan Miller stormed back in. He grabbed Matt's arm and pulled. "Get out!"

"Mr. Miller, I—"

"I said, get out!" He shoved him into the hall and pushed him until he stumbled toward the stairs. "I told you my rules, and you just had to disregard every concern we discussed. Get out! You will not be seeing my son any more. You lost your privilege."

Cheryl met them at the bottom of the steps. "Dan? What are you doing? Dan!" She jumped out of the way as Dan shoved Matt down the last two steps.

Dan threatened Matt all the way to the front door. "Get out. And if I see you around again, I'll take out a restraining order." He slammed the door.

Matt heard Cheryl question Dan. He could hear Dan yelling his way up the steps. He never remembered Mr. Miller acting so volatile. He was a passive aggressor. He kept silent in the face of conflict. At least that was the way he had been for the past seven or eight years. Early on, when Jamie's parents argued, Matt remembered hearing Mr. Miller loud and clear. Then one day, his yelling ended. Maybe that was the point when he discovered yelling solved nothing? Then why was he back to yelling again? And at Darian? Why?

Matt quaked with anger and fear. He should do something. Did he have the right to do something? Darian wasn't Dan's son despite what he called him. He was his legal guardian, if Jamie's journals were correct. Regardless, Darian wasn't a minor. Maybe Matt could do something, but what? He walked to the side of the house where Darian's window was. He couldn't hear all the words and wished the window were open.

"…believe you had the gall to bring him into…." Matt strained to hear what was going on. "…defiled… grounded… trusted you, and you sneak around behind… with him! How could… Jamie's best friend… like an animal…." The words got more garbled. Then the window opened and Matt flattened himself against the siding between the bushes. If he was caught listening there was no telling what would happen. Suddenly it was raining photographs. All the ones of Matt were floating down to the grass. Then Mr. Miller chucked Darian's drawings out the window, even the framed ones. Everything that had any hint of Matt on it was thrown out.

Matt didn't understand what he'd done so wrong. He didn't know why Mr. Miller had turned into a psychopath. He was not himself. Something was way wrong, and it went beyond Matt breaking the rules tonight. He could kind of see why he'd get angry; walking in on Darian in bed with Matt was, of course, the worst activity he could witness. But still, something was wrong and Darian was feeling the force of it head-on.

When the computer came flying out the window, Matt figured he'd seen enough. It was painful to be this helpless. He wanted to go back in and shelter Darian, but that would only make matters worse. He had to talk to Lori and find out if she knew what was going on and if Darian was being abused.

NO SOONER did Matt get home than Lori called him on his cell. "What the hell is going on?" she squawked. "I called Darian to ask if he wanted to watch a movie, and he was bawling. What happened?"

"Didn't you ask Dare?" He closed his bedroom door and sat on the edge of his bed.

Lori answered, "Yeah. He said Dan yelled and chucked his stuff out the window. Then the rest of the conversation was pointless because I couldn't understand a word. What happened?"

"Dan walked in on us."

"Walked in on you? Doing what?" she asked but mentally caught up seconds later. "Oh, you mean…?"

"Yeah. And we were going at it pretty good. No misconceptions possible. Dan freaked. I mean freaked! I haven't heard him yell like that in years. He even threatened me with a restraining order."

"Shit! I'm sorry. This is bad, really bad. I've never heard Darian so upset, well, except at Jamie's funeral. He said he's not allowed to text or e-mail, and Dan was going to take his phone as soon as he hung up. He's restricted to work only."

"I thought you said you couldn't understand him?"

"Smartass. I got some of it."

"Have you noticed Dan acting weird? Asking things of Darian that he shouldn't? Or maybe restricting him without good reason?"

"You mean besides tonight? No. Sara and I went over for dinner a few weeks ago. Dan and Cheryl seemed fine. Darian was fine. We played Monopoly, and he kicked my ass like usual. Nothing weird except he got his hair cut, but you knew that. He said Dan thought it was too long."

"But Darian likes it long. Why would Dan ask him to cut it?"

"I don't know. But how many times have you cut your hair when your mom or dad asked, even though you liked the way it looked?"

"Good point." Matt heard a beep and checked the call waiting. "Hey Lori, work is calling. I gotta go." He checked his watch. "Shit. I'm twenty minutes late. I forgot I worked tonight. Fuck!"

"Sorry. Bye. Call me."

"I will. Bye."

MATT apologized profusely when he finally got to work. This was officially the worst day he'd had in his life, barring September 19. He just needed to take one day at a time. He knew he would think of something. Matt felt like he was at the end of his sanity rope. *Is this what Jamie felt like?* The answer was disturbing to consider.

17

AS SOON as the door opened and Darian heard Dan's voice, his exhilaration drained out of his body like blood from a gaping wound. He was helpless to salvage even his own beating heart as the chaos swirled around him. Just as strong as the mind-numbing orgasm that had rocked his body seconds before, the icy talons of death gripped his throat when he opened his eyes and saw Jamie staring at him from across the room.

"Tsk, tsk," Jamie said, brushing his right forefinger across that of his other hand. "Naughty, naughty." Jamie shook his head from side to side.

"Dare, Dare!" he heard Matt saying. "You gotta get dressed. Dare. Snap out of it." He vaguely registered Matt's fingers snap in front of his eyes.

"I told you you'd get caught," Jamie taunted. "Bad boys with dirty little secrets always get caught." He grinned in satisfaction.

Jamie casually stepped closer. He blinked, and he glared at Matt, then he blinked again and his attention was back on Darian. Darian felt sick. What would Jamie do? Would he lash out? If he was a ghost, could he do something awful to Matt?

Then Dan reentered the room and forcefully removed Matt. "Get out!" he screamed.

Darian could hear Dan yelling all the way downstairs. The door shutting felt like a wall slamming against his chest.

Jamie smirked. "You did this to yourself. It's all your fault. If he hadn't kissed you that day, none of this would have happened."

Dan came back and continued screaming demands and insults at Darian. At least Darian presumed them to be. The man was ranting and flailing his arms. He ripped pictures off the wall and flung photos of Matt out the window. But Darian didn't really hear any of it.

As he sat there on the bed, holding his knees tight against his chest, he felt all the sound seeping from the room like an echo swallowed up in a great chasm. Dan's voice was distorted and fractured. Darian heard words like "defiled" and "whore," but he wasn't convinced they came from Dan's mouth. Jamie had thrown those words at him so often, Darian was convinced it was Jamie who possessed Dan and caused him to say those things. Why else would Dan act this way?

"Maybe because he hates you," Jamie hissed in Darian's ear. Darian turned sharply and found Jamie right next to him, the decaying flesh of his lips close enough to kiss.

"No!"

"Of course. Why else would he forbid you from seeing Matt? He hates you. He's probably glad you broke the rules because now he can kick you out. And with your mom gone, and her house in foreclosure, where will you sleep?"

"With my sister. She found a place."

Jamie wagged his head. "If she wanted you, she would have asked you months ago. She only has time for Kyle. They don't want you. You are nothing—nothing but a worthless whore. And now your blond sex toy just got kicked out. How does it feel to be alone?"

Jamie stepped away from the bed, cackling, clutching his sides, amused with himself to no end.

Darian blinked and realized he was, in fact, alone. Dan was gone, and the room was empty. He was half-naked. He wiped his eyes and crawled off the bed to retrieve his jeans. Once they were zipped, he heard the phone ring.

Dan walked in and handed him the phone. "It's Lori. Tell her you're grounded. No phone, no computer, no nothing except work. You got that?"

"Yes, sir." Darian took the phone, and Dan closed the bedroom door.

The reality of the last twenty minutes came crashing down. He was sobbing before he sank to the floor to say hello.

He could barely make intelligible words to explain there was something wrong with him. He was being haunted, and he thought Jamie was going to win.

18

December 22, 2010

TWO weeks went by, and Matt still hated himself for not being more respectful of Mr. Miller. True, he needed Darian, desperately—he was dying without him—but in that moment of desperation, Matt had ruined his only chance that Dan would come around. He knew he shouldn't have gone to Dan's house without permission. He called Dan several times to apologize, but Dan wouldn't answer. Matt felt sick. He was worried for Darian as much as he hated himself for being weak.

Work was boring, so it didn't distract him as it usually did. It was cold most of the time but hadn't snowed. Snow normally meant fun-filled days of medical emergencies involving automobile accidents because Maryland drivers didn't know how to drive in bad weather. It was absurd. But today, and for several days, work had been slow and boring. Matt ended up sweeping the floor while Scott was inventorying restock. *Whoohoo!* One crew was out in the squad truck because a vehicle reportedly flipped over, but not everyone was needed. Matt wasn't involved with every emergency, although he wished he was. The ambulance was transporting someone to the hospital and was due back soon. When it arrived, Matt would take care of inventorying its supplies. At least it would pass the time.

"Yay!" he sarcastically cheered himself on. "Can't wait."

Sarcasm: Matt depended on it. He had no thrill left in life. He hated getting out of bed in the morning. He had nothing to look forward to because he was banished from seeing the one person he yearned for. And he was not about to go to a bar or club! Although the environment helped him relax, it posed too much temptation for a libido that was severely neglected.

No one even cared he was suffering.

Matt's mom told him to end the relationship. She thought it was a bad idea from the start. His dad still wasn't talking to him. Hannah was no help; she suggested he date her friend from college. Even Lori shot him down. She was angry he went over to Dan's house in the first place because Darian was now grounded and she only got a few minutes of texting a day. She said Darian was fine. Quiet, but fine. Lori said Darian hardly talked at all about Dan except to tell her what he made for dinner and the activities they were doing together. Matt was jealous Lori even got that much.

Matt dumped a dustpan of dirt into the trash and went to the bathroom to wash his hands. He heard Scott's voice bellowing up the steps as he finished and turned out the light. "Hey Matt, some guy named Darian is in the bay asking to see you."

Matt heart leapt from his chest, and he dashed to the top of the steps leading from the sleeping bunks to the main workroom behind the bay. "Dare!" he exclaimed, right before halting on the very top step. *Shit. One look at Darian and they'll know he's gay.* Matt hadn't told anyone yet. He'd meant to, but time got away from him. Jason knew, but he was the only one. Luckily Scott hadn't asked for his "girl's" name. Maybe Matt could pull this off and pretend they were just friends? It would be unfair, but it was also unfair that Darian showed up unannounced. Matt was sick with excitement as much as fear. He would play it cool. "Okay," he called down to Scott. "I'll be right down." Maybe he could feel out the guys and see if they liked Darian first. It would be easier if they liked him.

Matt headed down the stairs, expecting Scott to be with Darian. Instead, he noticed Jason in the ambulance bay talking with someone altogether unexpected. If Matt hadn't known it was Darian, he wouldn't have guessed it. He was dressed in camos, work boots, a Stihl sweatshirt, and a baseball cap turned backward on his adorable little head. *Fuck me.* Matt shivered. *He's so damn sexy.* Matt hoped no one saw the look on his face.

"Yeah, I'm Darian," Matt heard him answer Jason as he walked up beside them. Jason stuck out his hand, and Darian shook it.

"Nice to meet you," Jason replied, turning a glare Matt's way. "I've heard a lot about you. You're Matt's... *boyfriend*, right?"

Matt saw the light spark in Darian's eyes. "Yeah." He smiled.

He agreed he's my boyfriend. Matt was elated. "Hey, Darian." Matt tried to sound cheery and suppress the Snoopy dance he was doing on the inside. He could feel his heart thudding in his chest. If only he could risk a quick kiss. Instead, he clapped Darian on the back as a good manly gesture.

Darian nodded in that way guys do with a tilt of his chin of recognition. "Hey," he greeted Matt calmly. "I hope you don't mind. I know I shouldn't be here, and you're probably busy. I just wanted to see where you worked." Darian was holding back too. Something in those eyes told Matt he was fighting his natural urges.

Matt played casual. He glanced at Jason but would not answer his indignant hairy eyeball. He waved Darian to follow. "No, not at all. Come on, I'll give you the tour." Matt felt Jason's eyes burning into his back. "This is the bay." He swept his arms out wide. "We keep two fire engines in here and an ambulance. On the other side of that wall, there's another area for the squad truck and the ladder truck. Right now the ambulance is finishing a call. In the back, we have a Duty vehicle and a Brush truck." The two of them slowly walked through the building. Matt felt as though he could walk on air; he was simply pleased as punch to have Darian walking next to him. "And over here is where we store our gear. See, this is my cubby."

"Wow." Darian was in awe.

Matt felt a wave of pride flow over him. This was *his* place, *his* work, and he'd often wondered how he'd feel if Darian ever wanted to visit. Answer—he was proud! Proud but slightly nervous about what the guys would say. "What do you think?"

"I think you're like a superhero or something."

Matt chuckled. "No, not super. And most of the time we rescue cats or burning pigs and shit."

"You still save lives, Matt. That makes you pretty darn special."

"So are you," he whispered. Matt was trying to be casual and act like this was any other day showing any given friend around the firehouse. He could stand here and point out different items of clothing and equipment and explain what they were needed for, and any given visitor would be satisfied. But Darian wasn't just another visitor, and Matt longed to stroke his back or touch his hair.

Darian also seemed to be attempting the same casual air. He wasn't making eye contact. Darian looked around at Matt's stuff and touched his helmet and other gear as if he was trying to appear absorbed. Only his voice, low and somber, gave away his true feelings. "Christmas is in a few days. Between missing Jamie and wanting to see you, I'm not much in the spirit of things. Dan's trying too hard. Cheryl made me chocolate chip cookies, and I haven't even eaten one yet. I don't feel like doing anything but sleeping."

Matt spoke quietly, too, hoping no one would overhear. "I know what you mean. I haven't done anything either. All I think about is you." Matt tried to cheer him up. "And here you are. I'm so happy about that… and a little worried. Dan made it real clear I shouldn't be around you."

Darian agreed, "I know." He looked in the cubby and not at Matt while he spoke. Matt wanted to lift his chin and stroke his cheek, but restrained himself. "After Dan threw you out, I was sure I'd never get to see you again. And each day after, this gripping fear kept closing in on me, and I knew I had to see you or I'd die." He looked up, the fear in his face plain as day. "This wasn't a planned trip. I was at work an hour ago and started to panic. I had to see you. It's been horrible. There are so many things I want to tell you. Things I'm scared of."

Matt half reached up yet stopped, squeezing his fist tightly. Darian glanced down at Matt's hand and seemed to understand how much Matt was holding back. He reached out and grazed Matt's fingers with his before pulling them back. Matt took a deep breath. If Darian could get through this, so could he. Matt finally said, "We'll find time to talk, I promise. I'm so glad you're here, but I can't believe it. You could get into huge trouble, Dare."

"It doesn't matter. I couldn't stay away any longer. My fingers burn to touch you." His voice was barely above a whisper.

"I know the feeling." Matt smiled and Darian blushed.

Matt loved those eyes. They glowed. His pupils were also abnormally constricted, which was odd. Perhaps Darian was more nervous than he was giving away in his voice. Matt wanted to ask so many things but couldn't risk being overheard. Why was he wearing these clothes and what happened to his facial piercings? He even had stubble on his chin, which was unlike Darian's normal habit of maintaining a clean-shaven body.

Matt gestured to Darian's clothes and risked one question. "Can I ask, why are you wearing Jamie's clothes?"

"I—"

They both jumped when Tim, a volunteer, appeared out of nowhere and interrupted. "Hey, I heard you had a friend here." He looked at Darian. "Do you play poker?"

Matt answered "no" at the same time Darian answered "yes." They looked at one another. Matt smirked. "You do?"

"Yup." Darian grinned back.

Tim slapped him on the back and almost knocked him over. "Good! We're a few short. Bring your friend, Matt, and help make things more interesting."

Interesting is what I don't *want.* "Sure."

Jason came up behind them as they headed to the table in the back. "I'm in, too, at least for a little while. When the ambulance gets back, I'm scheduled to scrub her down. I wouldn't want to miss the fun." He winked at Matt.

Billy walked up also and said, "Great!"

Great, Matt sarcastically thought, punching Jason's arm.

Jason suppressed his mirth while punching him back.

STEREOTYPICALLY, people thought firefighters played poker most of the time and sat around waiting for a fire. In reality, they studied a lot and kept up-to-date on medical certifications, as well as new regulations on fire and safety. They worked forty-eight hour weeks on the easy end of the spectrum and did everything *but* play poker. Today was a fluke.

With the snow, more guys were hanging around than normal. Not everyone was on salary; there were about fifteen volunteers at this station, and by coincidence, eight showed up around the same time.

They'd decided to play poker. Matt would normally decline, but if Jason was going to relax, then Matt could indulge as well.

When Darian won the first hand, Matt knew this was going to be a very unexpected pleasure.

"Three kings and two sixes, hee-hee." Darian did a little dance in his seat as the guys groaned in defeat. He raked in the small bit of coins and dollar bills as Bob shuffled the cards. Mike scratched his head in bewilderment, and Jason counted the last two dollars of his betting money.

Poker could not have gone better if Matt had scripted it himself. Darian may have been smaller and less scruffy looking than most of the guys, especially Billy, but he fit right in. He had those guys scrambling to win. It started off fun, with jokes and introductory questions, but turned to serious play when the other guys kept losing. In ten minutes, they shut their traps and got down to business. Only when Scott reported the chief pulling into the parking lot did they call it quits.

"DO YOU think I pulled it off?" Darian asked as they walked to the front of the firehouse.

"Pulled what off?"

"Being straight? It's the first time I ever tried."

Matt stopped, and Darian turned to face him. "Wait… you acted straight… for me?"

"Y-yeah." Darian nodded slowly, stuffing his hands into his pockets. "I know you're not out to your friends. I didn't even know you told anybody about me, but Jason Riley mentioned…."

"I've only told him. I'm sorry. I wanted to tell Scott and Billy, but the timing never seemed right."

"But you will tell them soon, won't you?"

"Yes, I promise."

"Matt," Darian said, glancing at his feet briefly, "it took Jamie years to work up the nerve to act normal in public. Everywhere we went, I felt like I had to be on my best behavior so I wouldn't inadvertently give us away. It was hard, but I restrained myself for

Jamie's sake. I don't think I can do it again. Well, I can, but I don't want to. I want to be myself, and I want to be able to touch you if I feel like it."

This was the most direct Darian had ever been. Matt liked it. He knew Darian was right. *He shouldn't have to deny who he is. Not for me. I came out in front of church, for Pete's sake!* "Dare, I want you to be yourself; I want to act that way too. Do you know how bad I wanted to sweep you off your feet and kiss you in the bay when I first saw you talking to Jason? I know how it feels to be trapped by social stigmas. I want to be myself; I'm just scared. You have to help me be strong, okay?" Matt gestured to Darian's body. "And you dressing like this today is really nice, but I hope you know I like you the way you are. If you showed up in pink stilettos, I'd still have been happy to see you."

Darian shrugged. "I don't know. I dress too feminine sometimes. I was going through some of Jamie's things, and I thought it'd be fun to look butch for a day."

Matt could not stop his chuckle; it just came out. "Butch?" He shook his head and reached out to grip Darian's shoulder. "Oh baby, you look more like a redneck skate-punk than anything." He laughed some more before he could be serious. He pointed to the sweatshirt. "Do you even know what Stihl is?"

Darian shook his head.

"They make chainsaws. You should've gone for Jamie's Ford sweatshirt instead."

Darian looked away. "Not that one. He was wearing it the last time we went fishing at the pond."

Matt cupped his chin. "No tears. Right? We're moving on one step at a time?"

Darian took a deep breath and nodded. "No tears. I'm okay."

"Okay." Matt continued stroking his chin. "I also noticed you removed your piercings *and* you didn't shave."

Darian looked worried. "Is that okay? I don't really have enough hair on my chin to pull off a goatee. Does it look stupid?"

"Nope. It looks sexy." He rubbed his thumb over the prickly hairs.

Darian blushed. “People are going to see you touching me.”

“I know.” Matt took a bold step closer. “You’re too fuckin’ sexy, and I want to lick you from your stubbled chin all the way down to your sweaty balls.”

“Matt…,” Darian gasped, his eyes glazing over.

“Baby, what’s really going on?” Matt whispered. His lips were so close he could kiss Darian, but he held back. For the first time, Matt noticed a yellow tint to his eyes.

“Nothing.” Alarm flashed across Darian’s face.

He knew him enough to see it was far from nothing. “Dare, I was outside when Dan threw your stuff out the window. I heard him yelling. Lori said he apologized, but Dan hasn’t yelled like that since before he divorced Ms. Joan. Something isn’t right. Are you dressed like this by choice, or is Dan trying to change you?”

Darian looked down.

“Dare?”

“I don’t want to talk about it.”

“Darian. You need to talk about it. Is Dan hurting you? Is he forcing you to do things against your will?” Matt forced down his growing anger and calmly continued, “Your hair? Did he make you cut it?”

Darian remained silent.

No answer was more of an answer than Matt could take. His suspicions might actually be true, and if so, Darian shouldn’t remain with Dan any longer. “Do you know wearing that hat backward makes you look like Jamie, especially with your hair this short? You’re wearing his clothes, Lori said you were helping Dan remodel the bathroom recently, and every quirky thing that makes you *you*, you aren’t allowed to wear. Don’t you see Mr. Miller is turning you into Jamie?”

“No, he’s not. I wore this for you, I swear. I didn’t want to *out* you when I came to visit. And I thought the piercings would clash with the outfit. And my hair… I don’t want to talk about my hair.” A tear streaked his cheek.

"Okay. We won't talk about it. But I want you to know I'm here to listen if you need it." Matt brushed away the tears.

Darian nodded. "I know. You're always willing to give me whatever I want."

Matt smiled. "That's because I love you." The longer they stood there with Matt caressing his face, the more Darian's worry dissipated. In minutes, Matt saw desire taking fear's place. When Darian took a step closer, Matt asked, "So… what *do* you want?"

"No holds barred. No more restraint. I want to act on desire and passion like we did those first two weeks. You made me feel… insatiable."

"It was amazing." Matt licked his lips. "All righty then, unrestrained it is! Relatively speaking. No ripping our clothes off in the middle of the street or anything."

Darian giggled. "Okay."

Matt *had* to kiss him. If Darian wanted to go with his desires, then Matt was helpless to resist. The closet door was officially off its hinges. He tilted Darian's chin up and guided him to his lips. Matt held the side of Darian's jaw, and Darian slid his hands up Matt's chest. Matt relished how easily Darian melted into him. He knew just how Matt liked to kiss and met each brief swipe of Matt's tongue with a tender lick of his own. It was exciting to find out how gentle they could be one moment when Matt knew just how animalistic they could be in the next.

The public display of affection was short-lived as Matt heard one of the guys swear, "Motherfucker!"

He released Darian's lips but kept his eyes on him. "I'm getting over my fears," he explained. "I'm not backing down. I'm gay, and you're my guy."

"Should I go?" Darian sounded frightened.

"Yes," Jason answered for Matt as he appeared beside them. "And I think Matt should join you for a while. Get lunch or something. Go get your coat, Matt, I'll stay with Darian."

Matt looked his buddy in the eyes but saw no malice there. Only strength. He nodded. To Darian he said, "I'll be right back." He touched his upper arm and walked away.

Jason and Darian walked to the open bay entrance as Matt walked farther into the building. It took less than a minute before the name-calling started.

“Are you queer?” Scott inquired incredulously.

“I always knew you were a faggot,” Billy spat.

“Is it true?” asked Tim.

Matt ignored them all and shoved his way to his cubby. He grabbed his coat and headed back without comment. These were his friends. Or they used to be. He would give them time to think things through and cool down before he knocked their lights out for insulting him. He was set on holding his tongue… that is, until he heard Billy hiss under his breath, “And to think I played cards with him. Awwuck. I should’ve known he was a fag with a name like *Darian*.”

Matt turned on his heel quicker than backdraft, cocked his fist, and let Billy have all his anger in one punch. When his fist connected with Billy’s jaw, Matt roared, “Don’t ever talk about him like that!” He swung again, but this time Billy was ready. He turned his head and pivoted out of Matt’s range.

At once, the guys started yelling. Chants of “Bil-ly, Bil-ly,” erupted all around them as the two men gritted their teeth and threw punches at one another. Matt squared off and snorted in rage. Billy wiped the blood from his lip and spat on the floor. As soon as Billy made a move, Chief Burtrum interrupted the fray.

“That’s enough!” he hollered and separated the men. “I don’t know what this is about, but I am not going to stand here and watch two of my men brawl like adolescents. This is a place of work, not a schoolyard. Take it outside, and do it after your shift! Do I make myself clear?”

Both Matt and Billy glanced at the chief with a blush of embarrassment. They were not used to being reprimanded in such a way. Men fight, but not over things like this.

“Billy, get the mop and bucket and get that blood off my floor. Matt… I’ll speak to you later.”

The chief glared, and Matt felt sick. *He knows. He heard. I should have told him long ago.* Matt nodded and picked his coat up off the floor.

Jason and Darian were still at the entrance talking when Matt entered the bay. Matt wondered how Jason was handling it. *Shit!* He'd wanted Jason to meet Darian when he was ready, not like this.

Just as Matt got within ten feet of his friend, he heard tires squealing, and without warning or visible reason, Jason shoved Darian out the door onto the concrete.

"What the…?"

A split second later, the firehouse ambulance crashed into the brick support arch of the bay's entrance, clipping Jason and hurling him backward. Had the vehicle not hit the archway, it might have driven right over Jason and into Matt and the parked fire engine behind him.

Stunned momentarily, Matt's brain then kicked into overdrive, and he reacted on instinct. He grabbed the walkie-talkie from his belt.

"Dispatch, this is Fire Engine 1-2-4; we have a medical emergency pending inspection at the firehouse entrance on 6680 Sykesville Road. Repeat, a medical emergency. Copy?"

"Copy that, 1-2-4. Awaiting instructions," replied dispatch.

Matt ran to Jason, who was flat on his back moaning. "My leg. Matt, my leg."

Matt saw blood on the back of his head, dripping on the firehouse floor. "Just lie still, Jason. Your head's bleeding." He yelled to anyone who could hear. "I need help over here!" But the men were already converging on the spot, emergency equipment in hand. Matt fed on their presence of mind. He spoke more instructions into his walkie-talkie. "This is Engine 1-2-4. We have several injured parties needing transport to the ER. No ambulance available from this firehouse, you copy? I need transport from another district. Copy?"

"Copy that 1-2-4. Ambulance dispatched and in route."

"Ambulance driver unconscious and unresponsive," Scott called out.

Matt repeated Scott's report to the dispatcher as he left Jason to Billy's capable hands. He stepped around the mangled ambulance carefully, avoiding the debris that littered the floor from the vehicle's impact. The radiator spewed steam.

As Matt neared the ambulance door, he heard the chief from the other side. “Matt. Get over here!”

He rushed around the back of the ambulance to see the chief crouched over Darian. “Dare!” he cried, diving to his side.

“I’m not sure what happened here,” Chief Burtrum said. “I don’t think the ambulance hit him, but he’s out cold. I need help turning him over.”

Matt had a mini flashback. “Jason shoved him out of the way seconds before the crash.”

“Then I guess he saved his life. Otherwise he would have been crushed between the ambulance and the brick archway.”

Matt reached out and carefully touched his back. “Oh, Dare….”

“Look,” Fred Burtrum said bluntly. “I don’t give a fuck what you and your boyfriend do behind closed doors, but I’ll be damned if I’m gonna watch you get gushy right here. He’s injured. Act like the fireman you were trained to be. Emotion is left at the door, Lieutenant!”

Matt took a breath and steeled himself. “Yes, sir!”

The chief nodded. “Good. Spine’s clear. Help me turn him over. We need to clear his airway and make sure he’s breathing.”

Matt got on one side of Darian while Fred stayed on the other. Matt gently turned Darian over, as Fred kept his neck straight. They heard a faint moan. “He’s coming around,” Matt said. They rolled him practically into Matt’s lap, and Matt winced looking at his wrist. “Oooh. Nasty break.”

Darian’s wrist was definitely broken. His hand was cocked to the side and the bone was all but sticking out of his skin.

“Cheek looks bad too,” Fred said. “Not sure if it’s broken. He hit the ground hard, could have a concussion.” He turned on a small flashlight and lifted Darian’s eyelids. “Difficult to tell. Pupils are constricted, but responsive. He’s also got a yellow tinge to the whites. Does he have liver problems?”

“I don’t know. Darian, can you hear me?”

“Y-yeah. Matt, what happened?” He blinked a few times and tried to sit up.

"Don't move, baby. Your wrist is broken. I'm not sure about your cheek, but it's red and bleeding and could be fractured. You probably have a concussion too. The ambulance is on its way."

"Ambulance?"

"You need to go to the hospital and get checked out."

He tried to pull away from Matt. "No hospitals."

"You have to, Dare. Your wrist is broken. You might need surgery if they can't set it. And your cheek could be broken. Don't you feel any of that?"

"I do. But…." Darian hesitated, and Matt dreaded what he might say next. "I… I took Oxycontin before I got here. Tell the doctors."

Matt swallowed his shock. "Okay. How much?"

More hesitation. Matt hated seeing Darian so scared. It was as if he waited for punishment. He looked powerless and vulnerable. No matter what, Matt knew he could not treat him as an evil sinner for doing drugs and hiding it. Darian did not need judgment; he needed love and support.

"Darian. Tell me. How much?"

"A thousand milligrams."

"Shit." He exhaled. "Dare, that's a lot. How many days in a row?" he asked, knowing continual ingestion would not break down fast enough in his system.

"About a week after Dan threw you out, I couldn't take it anymore. I started taking one 500-milligram pill every time I felt anxious."

Matt sighed, "Which is all the time. Oh, Dare, you've taken too much. Your eyes are yellow, which could mean liver failure. Baby… why'd you take so much?" He heard Chief Burtrum groan about his endearment.

"I don't know. I'm sorry. I was scared. I wanted to see you." Tears seeped from his eyes. "I knew Dan would never let me see you after what we did. I got Ian at work to switch with me, and I took a chance you would be here. I took one more pill in the parking lot. I needed it to calm me down. I can't stand being away from you any longer. The pills numb the pain and make my mind foggy, but you're the only one that makes me feel safe. Without you, I didn't know what else to do. I swear. Before Dan threw you out, I was doing really well. I wasn't taking them that often. I was trying to be good. Jamie hated drugs. He told me not to take them. I tried, Matt, I tried." He started crying harder.

"Darian. Calm down. I'm not upset." He made sure his words were soothing, not harsh. He heard the sirens. The ambulance was on its way. "We need to get you taken care of. I'm gonna help the chief cut this sweatshirt off so we can get a better look at the rest of your arm."

"No!" He flinched. "Don't cut it! It was Jamie's. Please."

Matt caught Darian's other hand before it swatted him in the face accidentally. "Fine. No cutting. But we have to slide it off, and it's going to hurt."

"I can't feel much anyway."

"Okay." Matt looked at Fred, who was following the conversation and knew what had to be done. "Help him get that side off and over his head. I'll make sure this arm doesn't move. Be careful of his cheek."

Fred nodded.

"Matt… I'm sorry."

"It's all right."

"No, I mean…. There's more…. I was…. I'm so sorry."

Matt listened to his stumbling apology while he watched the ambulance pull in and the paramedics go right to Jason first. He was loaded while Matt and Fred slid Darian's sweatshirt over his head. It was cumbersome and slow but came off without being sliced apart. Luckily, he was wearing a white T-shirt underneath.

"You doing all right?"

Darian nodded, and leaned his face on Matt's chest. Matt watched as Chief Burtrum carefully assessed his wrist and then noticed the other bloody marks on Darian's arm—marks not made by the accident. Six neat slices lined his forearm a quarter-inch apart, and a jagged *J* was carved right above his extensor digitorum muscle. *Cut* marks. Serious cut marks.

"Oh, Dare…."

Chief Burtrum looked Matt in the eye and nodded. Matt understood his silent consolation. Cutting on top of drug abuse was a sure sign of mental illness. Darian was facing much more when he got to the hospital than surgery for his arm. A psych consultation would most likely send him into a rehab clinic.

Matt stroked Darian's hair, as much to reassure himself that things would be all right as to soothe his lover. He felt eyes on him, and Matt turned his head in time to see Billy crinkle his face in disgust and walk away. His friend's reaction was disappointing, although not completely unexpected. Matt hoped one day Billy would change his mind.

MATT traveled in the ambulance to the hospital. He was even allowed to be with Darian through most of the procedures. (Knowing people in the business really had its perks.) He waited until after Darian was out of surgery to call Dan. He knew he should not have waited, but had Dan gotten there before surgery, Matt would have been told to leave. He wasn't about to leave!

Darian was in recovery for hours before the nurse allowed Matt to visit. Matt took Darian's hand in his. He looked so pale despite the redness around his bandaged cheek.

Darian slowly opened his eyes. "Hey." His greeting was barely audible.

Matt smiled. "Hey back."

"You… didn't… leave."

He shook his head. "Why would I? I'm in this." He winked. Matt affectionately smoothed Darian's bangs over to one side like he normally wore them.

"I… have… *issues.*"

Issues? That's putting it lightly. Matt chuckled. "I know. I don't care. We'll get through them together." He squeezed Darian's fingers.

The doctor walked in and picked up his chart. "Good, you're awake. How do you feel?"

"Tired."

"Are you a family member?" he asked Matt.

"No," he said automatically, but reconsidered. "Er, yes, I'm his boyfriend." He straightened his shoulders and tightened his grip on Darian's hand.

Darian looked up at him with a warm, contented expression. Matt suspected he liked the reference.

"I see." His disapproval could not have been clearer if he spelled it out. "Mr. Weston, I need to discuss your treatment. Do you want your…." His eyes went to Matt and he hesitated to finish his sentence.

"My boyfriend can stay," Darian asserted.

"Fine."

Matt felt Darian squeeze his hand back.

Just as Matt suspected, they suggested a psych consult. Medically, he was not as bad as Matt thought. Darian had a mild concussion, but his cheek wasn't broken. They put a pin in his wrist to hold the bone in place while it healed, and he would have the cast removed in six weeks. His drug abuse had not gotten to where it was when Jamie wrote about it. (They didn't find heroin in his system.) Matt was thankful. But he would have to undergo drug rehabilitation and suffer through withdrawal symptoms. Oxycontin was highly addictive.

When the doctor left, Darian started crying.

Matt leaned against the bed beside him as close as he could get without crawling in. He rested his head on the pillow next to Darian's. "Shhh, baby, I'm here."

He sobbed and tilted his face into Matt's. "I'm sorry."

"It's okay, Dare. I understand. You've been through a lot. We'll do this together."

"I don't know what I'd do without you."

Matt held his hand until he fell asleep. His mind swirled with questions about how he could help and who he could talk to about addiction and self-harm. Matt was worried that Darian was too far over the edge. *What if he's really, really sick? I don't know what I can do.* Then Hannah's words came back to him: "Alone is a horrible place to be." Matt would not leave him alone.

However, his good intentions wouldn't do any good if he was there when Mr. Miller arrived. He knew he needed to leave. "Darian?"

"Hmm?" he groggily sighed.

"I gotta go before Dan gets here. I called about ten minutes ago to let him know you were in the hospital. I know he's pissed I didn't call sooner. I'll come back when I can, or I'll find some way to visit you no matter where you are. I promise." Then Matt sang softly, hoping Darian would get his reference to The Used's song "Smother Me." (Darian seemed savvy that way.) "Surely you can take some comfort, knowing that you're mine." Matt winked and added, "Baby."

Darian smiled weakly.

Matt gently kissed his forehead and left.

BEFORE leaving the hospital, Matt found out where Jason was and risked a visit. Luckily, Jason was in a different wing from Darian. *There's no way Dan is going to know I'm still here*, Matt reasoned. Jason was the closest thing Matt had to a best friend, so he needed to make sure his buddy would be okay. Plus, he needed to thank him for saving Darian.

He knocked on the door and Anna turned her attention his way. "Matt, please, come in."

He smiled at her and entered. Jason was still asleep from surgery. "How is he?" he asked.

Anna sighed, "He'll be fine, I guess. The doctor said he broke his femur. It will take a long time to heal. His head is fine. Apparently his skull is harder than concrete." Matt and Anna both chuckled, and then she continued, "The chief was by. He said the ambulance driver died."

Matt felt a lump form in his throat. "Oh God. Really?"

"He said his name was Ernest. I don't recall an Ernest working with you."

Matt replied, "No. He was only there a week. He transferred. Did the chief say what happened?"

"Heart attack."

"Damn."

"Chief Burtrum also mentioned Jason saving your friend's life."

"Oh?"

Anna grinned knowingly. "Is it the same friend you've been gushing to Jason about?"

Something in her eyes told Matt she knew. "Yeah. He's my… boyfriend."

"You don't need to look so scared. I've known you're gay for a long time."

"What? How?"

She chuckled. "Honey, when Jason brought you to the house that very first time, I caught you checking out his fiiine posterior when he bent over to pick up a biscuit I dropped on the floor. No matter how nice my husband looks, no straight man would ever look at his bum the way you did."

"But you never said anything."

"It's not my business to tell you how to live your life. But now that it's out in the open, you better straighten yourself up and treat your man right!"

"I will." Matt blushed. "I gotta go. Will you tell Jason I was here?"

"Of course I will. You just make sure to keep yourself out of trouble."

Matt nodded and left the room.

He felt slightly frustrated, somewhat anxious, but unexpectedly… free. For the first time, Matt realized, no matter what happened next, he was liberated from all his intricately orchestrated disguises, excuses, and pretense. True, he *could* have found a better way to break it to the guys than kissing Darian at the station, but what was done was done. Matt was officially out to everyone he feared the most. He wasn't sure of the outcome, but it sure felt good to be released from the binding chains of secrecy. If only Jamie had seen his lies as a prison. Perhaps things could have been different.

19

December 27, 2010

CHRISTMAS sucked, although they did have a few interesting emergencies involving chimneys and Santa. New Years was going to suck, unless some unintelligent kids who lived down the street decided to set off fireworks inside the house again. Matt's home life sucked, and there was no real potential for random stupidity there to lighten the tension. And now his job was probably going to suck, because he might be out of a job where saving people from their own mistakes was actually fun—oh yeah, and putting out fires! Matt couldn't foresee things getting any worse, but every week something else cropped up to make his living hell even more hellish. Now he stood in the fire chief's office waiting to find out if he still had a job.

Since Darian's visit, his friends at work avoided him and gave him looks that ranged from seething hatred, to disgust, to absolute confusion. He tried to keep to himself, but it was hard in an environment where teamwork was essential. Jason visited the station in his cast, wife by his side. Matt received at least one warm smile, and a hug from Anna.

His sister Hannah was correct. "Alone is a horrible place to be." Matt felt very alone lately. He was dying to hear about Darian, but Lori wasn't cooperating. She was mad because she wasn't allowed to see Darian, so she refused to speak to Matt. The accident that put Darian in the hospital led to more psychiatric evaluations and the last Lori reported, Darian had been admitted to a rehabilitation clinic or something, for the next eight weeks. Eight weeks!

Matt was driving himself insane thinking about the enormity of it all when the chief finally walked in and sat behind his desk.

“Thank you for coming in, Matt.” The chief smiled warmly.

Fred Burtrum had been chief for fifteen years. He’d lived in Maryland all his life and trained in several fire stations. He was good at his job and well respected. Matt had liked him from the first day he started working at Station No. 12. The chief praised him on his work habits and rarely said anything negative. Until today.

Matt sat as asked and waited, nervously bouncing his knee up and down.

“Matt. I’m not sure what’s been going on around here. I like to think I know everything; but in light of recent events, I think I’ve learned how much I don’t know. There’s a lot of talk going around. Some of the guys have said they will not work with you.” He sighed. Matt could tell this was not an easy thing for him to say any more than it was easy for Matt to hear. “Matt, I’ve known you since the day you started. I’ve seen you work hard and long hours to be the best you could be. I have never seen you bring your personal life to work. And in all these years, I would not have guessed you… that you preferred….”

“Men, sir.” Matt filled in the blank.

Fred looked Matt in the eye and nodded. “Men. Right. The point is there is no reason to believe you would change your habits now. You have always had a good rapport with your coworkers, and just because they know you to be a homosexual, that shouldn’t change things, but it does. Some of them think you may….”

“Sir, with all due respect, stop prancing around the subject like I’m going to cry about it. Some of the guys think I’m gonna come on to them, right? Some of them think I’m going to start watching them when they undress and grab their cock when I get the chance. Is that it?” Men could be so homophobic!

“To put it vulgarly, yes.”

“So what’s the answer? Do you want me to quit?”

“No, not exactly. But working here is not in your best interest either. I can’t fire you legally, but I can suggest you look around at other stations. I’ll write a recommendation letter for you, but you have to see that working here is risky. If the men aren't comfortable with you, then...."

"It could get someone killed. I know."

"Or... it could get you killed. Matt, with Jason out possibly months for physical therapy, I'm down a good man already. I don't want to lose you. I meant what I said the day of the crash; I don't care what you do in the privacy of your own home. My sister has a life partner whom she's been with for twenty years. It is not an easy lifestyle, depending where you live, but I understand that love is love. If you love that young man, and it seems to me you do, you must learn to deal with prejudice and hate, especially if you live in a conservative town. That's just the way it is."

"But it's not fair."

"Fair? Nothing in life is fair. It is what it is. You just have to take what you're given and make it work. You are a good man, Matthias. I have no doubt this trial will make you even stronger in the end. Nothing worth having is acquired easily."

Matt grinned. "My dad told me that when I was six."

"See, there you go! I'm sorry things have to be like this. You have the option to stay. Or... take an extended leave of absence, in which time you can seek other options. I'll pay you for two weeks. Information which should remain between you and I, if you please. Use it to look for another job. Best scenario, the guys will think it over and come back around."

"I hope so. I don't really want to work elsewhere." Matt stood up and said, "Thank you, sir." He shook his hand.

"That's what I'm hoping for, Matt. They've known you a long time. I think this was a shock to the system."

"Yeah. I thought they were my friends." Matt headed to the door but turned back when the chief added one more thing.

"They are your friends, Matt; men can just be stupid sometimes. My wife is always telling me that. I just hope all this is worth it."

Matt grinned. He had his doubts. *Was it worth it?* So far he'd endured more trials than ever before in his life, and over what? Homosexuality. Could he take much more? The church rejected him. Now his coworkers rejected him. He wasn't sure yet about his parents, but they weren't happy with him. Jamie was no longer there to support him. Matt had even lost his truck! There wasn't much left to lose. *Was it worth it?*

His mind conjured up an image of Darian lying naked in his arms. Darian. His smile, his eyes, his voice, his touch. Matt could not let go of his hope yet. He confirmed, "It is, sir, I know it is."

December 28, 2010

AT HOME, in the middle of the day, Matt found he had nothing to do. He played on Steven's Xbox for a while, but it was no fun without someone to play with. He grabbed a bowl of ice cream and curled up on the couch under his favorite blanket; he was watching ESPN when his mom came home.

"Oh, Matt, I didn't expect you home today." His mom hastily wiped her eyes and greeted him with a hug.

This is Tuesday. Was she visiting Ms. Joan? Matt wondered, but he refrained from asking. "Yeah, well, technically I'm on vacation—oooh, no, Chief called it an 'extended leave of absence.'"

"In winter? Aren't there snow emergencies to take care of?"

"I guess they can handle them without me. It's 'extended leave' because the chief couldn't fire me, but basically I'm laid off while the guys at work have their space."

"What?" She dropped her coat and quickly joined him on the couch. "What happened? I thought they loved you there."

"What do you think happened, Mom? They found out I'm gay and no one wants to work with me. Like being gay is a contagious disease." It sounded even more depressing saying it out loud. "But it was my decision to leave, at least for now. The chief couldn't fire me because I'm gay, but it just seemed like it would make everyone's life easier if I left."

"Oh, honey." His mom rubbed his leg through his blanket. "I'm so sorry. Have you ever thought… have you tried… *not* being gay?"

He frowned. "No, Mom. Not really an option. It's not like switching shampoos."

"I'm sorry. I'm still figuring it all out. I just thought if it was easier to—"

"It's who I am." Matt was irritated. How long would it take people to realize he wasn't pretending? "It's not like I suddenly decided to take up skydiving. It's not a rash decision. It's permanent. I'm gay. And all those times I went clubbing, I did it in a gay bar—with men!"

She bowed her head and covered her face. "I didn't need to know that."

"Yes, you did! Until you understand I have always been like this, you'll hold onto the belief that I'll go back to who I was before. I won't. I'm not. This is me." He tossed back the blanket and got up. "And if you can't accept it, then maybe I need to find a new place to live."

"Matt…." Linda reached for her son, but Matt stormed past her and headed up the steps.

"MATT! Get your ass down here!" Matt's dad yelled up the steps.

Matt jumped off the bed. He'd been lying in the dark for hours and had finally drifted off when his dad's bellow jolted him upright. His dad was not belligerent by nature. Matt saw him as a controlled force, influencing people by his intelligent candor more than might. True, Matt had received a few beatings in his youth, and some with a belt, but for the most part, his father's stern discussions did more than his fierce hand. If his dad chose to yell, Matt was not about to dilly-dally. He rushed down the steps in his boxers.

"Yes, sir?" A formal greeting was more acceptable in moments like these. Matt knew when to call him "Dad" and when to say "sir."

"Go apologize to your mother."

"Dad, I'm sorry. I didn't mean to snap at her."

"I said, 'apologize to your mother.' It's bad enough I have a queer son, but I will not have a disrespectful one as well. You will go in there and tell her you're sorry for whatever it is you did."

"Yes, sir." He lowered his face and stepped in the direction his father pointed. His mother must be in the library.

Before Matt walked three feet, his father grumbled some more. "Do you think this is easy? Do you?" Matt stopped and turned slowly around as his father spoke. "You drop all this on the family and expect us to just… what?—suck it up and move on? I get that you think it's for the best. I get that you had to tell us the truth in order to break free from a life of deception and lies. I've read all about it. I understand a closeted life is painful and saturated with shame and fear, but don't you think for one second coming out of that closet made everything sunshine and daisies for everyone else. Your little 'confession' cost the rest of us too. Now we are the ones with the pain and humiliation. Us—your family. And you didn't see fit to give us any warning. You didn't come to me privately or have a 'family chat' over your decision to live a gay life. No! You do it in front of the fucking church!"

Yelling, his father moved closer and closer until he was screaming in Matt's face. The word "church" carried spittle with it as it slammed into Matt's pride. Matt was shaking. He couldn't run, but he was fearful his father would strike him any second. If he did, Matt would take it. He couldn't back down, but he was surely considering it. Hiding would be easier.

"We've been going to that church for ten freakin' years! Ten years, Matt! In all that time, you've been secretly indulging in perverse behavior and laughing at us for not noticing!"

"I wasn't—"

Mr. Dixon lifted his hand and held it in check inches from Matt's face. His eyes bulged, and the vein in his neck throbbed. "You don't get to speak." He lowered his hand and turned away, rubbing the back of his neck with one hand and balling a fist with the other. "I love you, Matt," he declared begrudgingly. "That's what makes this so difficult."

What is he saying? Is he disowning me? Throwing me out?

He turned back to Matt with tears in his eyes. "If I didn't love you, I'd throw you out without another thought. I'd side with the church. I'd confess your sinfulness to the congregation and accept whatever discipline they saw fit for our family for rearing you this way. I would demand you leave and never disgrace our family again. It would be easy. But I love you." He broke down and wept, shoulders bobbing. "Or… I'm trying to. Some days… I don't know if I can."

Matt's compassion swelled. He reached out and touched his father's arm, expecting him to pull away. When he didn't, Matt took a bolder step and pulled him into a hug. He rubbed his back and said, "I'm sorry, Dad. I'm so sorry. I didn't mean to hurt the family."

His father stiffened and pulled back. "Do you know how fast gossip spreads? It's affected me at work and your brother at school. Your mom's so-called friends shake their heads in pity. Everyone says they'll be your friend no matter what; they also go around saying sin is sin, until *you* are the one with a gay son. Then they make excuses about how it's worse than all the other sins, how *you* are worse because you must have done something to create the problem. I never knew people could turn on you after so many years of friendship."

"But it has nothing to do with you or how you raised me."

"You don't think I know that?"

Matt wasn't sure what to say. His father was so unstable, he was scared to say the wrong thing. "I don't know."

"I do. It's you. Not me. I spent weeks thinking it was something *I did.* That's when I started reading books on having a gay son and what it means to be homosexual and lots of other topics. I didn't understand what I did wrong. Then the fucking church turned on me, and I lost faith."

"In God?"

"No. People. People who I thought were my friends. People who I thought I could trust with my life. I discovered how very alone I was in this. Instead of helping me understand my son and how I can best help you, they continually passed judgment and defended their position far beyond my understanding of the Bible. The 'Christians' in my life told me my son needed to repent of his sin. They weren't friends; they were hangmen, and I was the head of a family sentenced to dangle from the noose."

Matt worked up the courage to ask a question. "Do you… think it's a sin? Being gay?"

His dad sighed, "I don't know, Son. I've been looking into passages of scripture that deal with homosexuality, but I think I need to research it more. I don't understand. I believe God makes us who we are, so by that same argument, he made you the way you are. Should I force you to deny who you are because I can't deal with it? Then who's the selfish one?" He cupped Matt's cheek. "I love you, Son. And if being gay is part of the person I love, then I have to work through it, accept it, and move on."

"I love you too, Dad." He started to reach up to touch his dad's shoulder, and his father stepped back.

"I'm not there yet. I'm sorry, Matt. I want to be okay with this, but right now… it makes me ill to be near you. I need more time." He backed away. "I need more…."

Tears rolled down Matt's face. "I understand."

Matt's father stopped before going upstairs and said quietly, "I'm not perfect. I'd be lying if I said I never thought about beating the shit out of you until you changed. But then, I would be no better than them. I would abuse my son and therein commit another sin? It's all a vicious cycle really. The self-righteous would say some sins are necessary evils to correct the wrongs of others. I've come to think it's a bunch of bullshit."

Matt liked this. He hadn't talked so openly about religion in a long time. Mainly because Matt thought differently than he did in his youth and didn't want to hurt his dad's feelings by challenging his beliefs. Perhaps now they were meandering onto the same page. Matt thought open discussion was a healthy way to spiritual growth. Maybe soon he could tell him all the things he'd been pondering about God.

His dad looked him squarely in the eye. "Of course, if you bring your *girlfriend* over to meet me, you may experience a certain amount of cynicism all over again. I'm trying, Matt. I have a long way to go to fully accept your decisions."

"I can live with that. So… you'd let me bring him over?" Matt was scared to ask, yet exceedingly curious.

"Oh, Lord help me," Matt's dad said. He shook his head, but something in his voice told Matt the answer was "yes." His father cleared his throat and changed the subject. "I'm also looking for another church. We've visited six, but nothing feels right. I want reformed theology, but at a church where the average age is below sixty-five. Church shopping isn't fun. It's hard on your mother. Your brother doesn't want to go. I'd give up except it means a lot to me."

"I know. I miss church, too, even though I dreaded going the past few years. I wasn't growing in my faith at all. I really think Mom only went because she had friends there."

"I think that too. Although now, none of her so-called friends talk to her. And Joan won't let your mother in to see her. That's why I want you to apologize. She is having a rough time. Worse than me. Worse than you, even, and that's considering you lost your job."

"You know about that?"

"Your mom told me. I'm sorry. I'll ask around, see if I can find something for you."

"Thanks, Dad."

"And when you're ready, I guess I'm willing to meet this guy you're seeing, despite my apprehension. Your mom says you're in love with him."

"Moooom," he groaned.

"Is he a Christian?"

"No. I don't think so. I don't know. I don't think he's been to church more than once in his life. I'm not sure what he believes."

He nodded as though considering his response. "Whatever happens, I want you to be happy, but more than that, I want you to be committed and content. Don't compromise your beliefs or your dignity in order to feel happy. Feelings come and go. When you know it's right, hold onto it beyond the blissful happiness that comes from falling in love. Relationships always have a downside—they always take work. Nothing easy is worth having."

"Thanks Dad. I'm gonna go talk to Mom."

"Good. She needs you."

As he walked to the library, Matt considered just how hard life became after he met Darian. Sure, he came out at church because he'd needed to defend Jamie, but Matt wasn't convinced he would have come out if he hadn't met Darian first. He felt like Job from the Bible—everything was crashing around him, testing his faith. But just like Job, he would not give up, no matter what happened. He saw

Darian as a gift from God. No matter how hard his life was, Darian was worth every second of hell.

December 31, 2010

OF COURSE, "hell" kept on coming. Matt was bored out of his mind doing nothing for days. Xbox was fun when he was younger, but it just didn't hold his interest for long anymore. He wanted to work. He wanted to feel accomplishment at the end of the day, but nothing was happening. He was glad for the couple of inches of snow that fell. He could zip out to his regular customers and shovel snow at least for half the day. Mr. Walsh had many elderly customers who could not handle sweeping their sidewalks, let alone shoveling their driveways. Matt hopped in his rental Captiva SUV and drove off.

He was thankful the rental-car place allowed him to upgrade to a four-wheel-drive vehicle as long as he paid the difference from what the insurance company paid. He couldn't wait for the settlement so he could shop for a new truck.

He pulled into the first driveway, but it had already been done. He thought that odd, but dismissed it and drove to Mrs. Ruxton's house. Same thing—the job was already done. He tried three more addresses and finally called his boss.

"Hello?"

"Mr. Walsh, it's Matt."

"Hello Matt. You inside enjoying the snow?"

"Um, no." The notion was absurd. "I'm at Mrs. Henderson's and her property has already been done. Do you know anything about that?"

"I sent Josh Pierce out this morning."

"Mr. Walsh, you know I take care of this property, and I've done it for years. And it's not just this one. Mrs. Foxx and the Ruxton place have all been done. Was that Josh too? Because I'm getting a little pissed here."

“Matt, to be honest I was hoping I wouldn’t have to have this conversation over the phone. Can you come in so we can talk?”

Why did he sound as though he was consoling Matt for something? That pissed Matt off further. “No. Just tell me what is going on.”

“Matt…. One of the ladies said she heard something about you at bingo the other week. She called and asked me to have someone else take care of her property. Without your truck, I figured I’d have to get someone else anyway until you could get your plow rigged up. I didn’t want to trouble you until this whole thing blew over.”

“You didn’t want to ‘trouble me’?” That was the most ridiculous thing Matt had ever heard of. “Mr. Walsh, I’m not troubled, I’m out of work!” He didn’t know how to make it clear how upsetting this was without yelling. He knew he shouldn’t be so disrespectful, but then again, Mr. Walsh didn’t exactly show any decency to him by calling him first. “I can’t believe this. Now I have little old ladies at bingo talking about me being gay. Terrific!”

“No. That’s not what she told me. She said she heard you were in a cult. Worshipping Satan or something like that. I figured the absurdity would all blow over in a week or two, and everything would be back to normal. Nobody said you were gay.”

“Oh.” He paused, thinking of how to respond to that.

“Matt? Is that what this is all about? Are you gay?” Mr. Walsh sounded confused but not put off.

“Yeah. That’s what it’s all about. I know Ms. Carrie from my old church runs the bingo hall for St. Joe’s. She knows I’m gay. And all the ladies I plow for in this area go to bingo there. How it got to Satanism or cults, I have no idea. Talk about hyperbole.” It was outlandish where things had escalated.

“Matt, I don’t know what to say. I’m not about to let you go because of what you choose to do behind closed doors, but if these ladies ask not to have you on their property, I can’t change that. Business is business. I’m sorry. Give it time. I’m sure they will forget all about it.”

“Fine,” Matt begrudgingly agreed and hung up. Matt appreciated Mr. Walsh’s honesty even if he didn’t agree with the outcome. Again, he was out of work because he dared to tell the truth. When was this going to end?

DEPRESSED and lonely, Matt wound up at a gay club downtown. He hadn't been there in years. Normally, Matt avoided Baltimore—too close to home. But he was tired of taking hit after hit. He needed a drink and some relaxation, maybe a dance or two. It used to be he'd hit a club every week or two, depending on when his itch coincided with availability. He'd fuck somebody and be done for a while. Until the itch started up again.

Darian cured his itch. Matt hadn't missed the things he used to do. In fact, he couldn't wait to take Darian dancing and include him in all the fun he used to have.

He sat at the bar looking around and realized he shouldn't be there. Not alone. He should wait until Darian was out of rehab and bring him. He needed to leave. He set his drink down.

"Going so soon? You just walked in."

Matt turned his attention to the cute blond next to him. "Yeah, I shouldn't be here. I have a boyfriend." Oooh, a zing rippled his nerves. Matt *liked* saying he had a boyfriend.

"Oh, honey, too bad. I was just going to ask for a dance?"

Matt shook his head. "No thanks."

He turned away and decided to hit the head before driving an hour back home. The toilets were disgusting, but nothing worse than he'd seen before. As he zipped up, he turned and bumped right into the cute blond from the bar. He hadn't even heard him come in.

"Oh, sorry." Matt tried stepping out of his way but the young man followed each step.

"Come on, just a taste."

Matt froze. He knew exactly what the guy wanted. Matt felt the man's hands glide over his hips. The blond stepped closer and Matt felt a rush of anticipation. It wasn't until the guy's lips touched a particular spot on Matt's neck that the alarms went off. *This is wrong!* Matt jerked back and pushed the precocious youth away. "I *said*, I have a boyfriend!" Matt fled the men's room without another look back.

January 2011

20

January 7, 2011

MATT spent the entire week in bed. He had given up. Nothing he had done went right, so what was the point? He didn't believe in getting sloppy drunk unless he was at a party—and that was mainly in high school—but after losing his plowing job, he had just given up. Logically, he knew Mr. Walsh hadn't fired him. As soon as those little old ladies came to their senses, he would have his job back. It was just the principle of it all.

He was depressed, so he got drunk.

He opened his eyes when he heard his phone vibrating on his nightstand. It was 8:00 a.m. *Who the heck calls at 8:00 a.m.?* His head was pounding. By the time he grabbed it, the call was lost. He checked caller ID, and it was Dan Miller's home number. *Dan.* Matt was angry with him. He was probably calling to yell at Matt or blame him for Darian's injuries. Matt quickly sat up. "Or calling to tell me how Dare is." Matt shook the fogginess from his brain and dialed Dan back. No answer. "Fuck."

Matt crawled out of bed and hobbled down the stairs to find some Tylenol. No one was home. He was surprised his mother hadn't even left a note. The house was like a graveyard. He poured some coffee and sat at the kitchen table. He opened his phone and looked at the pictures on it.

"I miss Darian."

He felt this monster-sized fist squeezing his heart. He flipped to the next picture, and it was Jamie. *Jamie.* "You had so much pressure on you," he said to Jamie's picture. "Dare doing drugs, your mom's abuse, an obsession with your best friend.... You balanced school, family, and a boyfriend. You were there for me, there for your mom and dad, and you helped Darian through his drug addiction. I feel the same pressure now—I do. I've had to withstand more now than ever in my life."

His phone rang again and it was Jason. "Hey man, how's it going?"

"I'm bored out of my mind, but besides that everything is fine. How are you? The guys talking to you yet?"

"No. But I haven't exactly called them either," Matt said.

"I wouldn't. Just chill. I think the chief is right—they'll come around. Are you looking for another job?" Matt appreciated the concern in Jason's voice.

"No," he replied. "My heart's not in it. Besides, I'm at my parents' house. I don't do anything but lie around, and I have no truck. I can wait them out and live on savings for, like, two years."

Jason laughed. "Okay, fair enough. But I talked to Scott, and he's bummed already. They all like you Matt; you won't be out of work long. Just sit tight."

"I am."

THE conversation with Jason alleviated some of his stress, but not all of it. Matt didn't really care about the job as much as he wanted to know about Darian. He'd sit around for months if he had to. The doorbell rang and brought Matt out of his thoughts. He rose and answered the door.

"Dan?" Matt said, shocked to see him.

"I don't know what's wrong with Darian," Mr. Miller said, jumping into a conversation before he entered the house.

Matt pushed open the screen door and gestured for Dan to enter. "What happened? Is Dare okay?" He shut the door and followed Dan into the living room.

It had been some time since Dan Miller was at his parents' house: years, in fact. After the Millers' divorce, Jamie's dad had been phased out of their lives by default. Matt's mom spent a great deal of time with Joan—now Smithers—Miller, so Dan was forced to stay away. Dan and Matt's dad didn't have a great deal in common, and gradually Dan's absence in neighborhood cookouts became normal. Matt thought the whole situation between families was stupid, but it was comforting on some level to know parents could be just as childish as their children.

But despite not visiting in years, Dan made himself comfortable on the couch without an invitation. "Is Darian okay?" Dan asked. "I don't think Darian has ever been okay."

Lori said the same thing, Matt thought. Matt sat in the recliner adjacent to Dan and said, "But something must have happened to make you come here. I mean, you threatened me with a restraining order the last time."

Dan hung his head in shame. "I'm sorry. I knew as soon as I said it, it was an empty threat. I don't even think it is legal, since Darian isn't a minor."

Matt took a deep breath to calm his nerves. He was anxious to know what prompted Dan's visit, but he was scared to provoke him. Dan had acted volatile of late, and Matt didn't want that to happen before he got some answers. Matt asked hesitantly, "Then, tell me, why are you here?"

Dan looked up. His face was drained of the joy Matt always remembered it containing. "I think I need your help."

Matt was shocked. "Help to do what?"

Dan sighed, "To understand." He was on the verge of tears; his cheek muscle quivered. "I want to understand why my son took his own life. I don't know who else to go to. I want to understand why Darian won't talk anymore. I want to understand why God hates me so much he would destroy the lives of the two boys I loved more than anything."

Matt didn't realize he was crying until the phone rang and made them both jump. He hastily wiped his eyes and looked around the room as if to make sure no one was watching. The phone rang again.

"Are you going to answer that?"

"No," Matt said. "The answering machine can get it. It's probably a telemarketer anyway."

Silence settled over them. Dan slumped forward and stared at the floor. The fun-loving guy who used to play catch in the front yard with Matt and Jamie was replaced by a somber shell. No hope shone in his eyes, no joy lifted his speech; Dan sounded as empty as the words Jamie wrote in his journal when the end was near.

I can't do this anymore. I'm so pathetic. Everything I do, everything I attempt only crashes around me. All my efforts are in vain. I can't take the pressure....

DAN had lost hope to the point of desperation. He came here, to Matt, for help. Matt didn't know where to start.

"Why?" Dan asked again as he broke down and cried into his hands.

Why? Matt knew why—part of why. Matt knew about the abuse Jamie took from his mother. He knew Jamie longed for her approval. But what of Darian? Lori said he longed for family. Dan was family. Wasn't he? Lori said Darian hung on to Jamie because he loved Dan just as much. Didn't Dan know that? "Mr. Miller—Dan—surely you know that Darian loves you."

Dan looked up. "Then why won't he talk to me?" he asked desperately. "He's been in the rehab clinic for two weeks, and he hasn't uttered a word. Not one word. He doesn't talk to Dr. Loundas, not even to rehash old information. Kiddo and I used to talk about everything. He told me how he wanted to go back to school someday and take art classes. We made a five-year plan together to save enough to enroll. He used to fantasize about having a house just down the street from Cheryl and me, where he and Jimbo would live. He said they'd have a dog and a vegetable garden, and Jimbo would finally own a red, 1965 Mustang Fastback."

Matt chuckled. "Jamie always did want that model."

"Kiddo had so many plans for the two of them." Dan's eyes seeped tears. "Jimbo was always busy: school, then work, everything piled up around him to consume his time. I never understood why he dashed away so often to visit his mother. I thought he was happy, but he never sat still long enough to ask Darian about his dreams."

It pained Matt to hear it. His tears threatened again. Jamie made him so mad sometimes, but hearing how he neglected Darian just made him angrier. If Jamie was here, Matt would punch him out. "I get so angry at Jamie sometimes," Matt confessed. "I find myself yelling at his picture on my nightstand. I don't understand either."

And it was true; even if Matt had his journals, he still didn't understand why Jamie cracked. Matt had felt plenty of pressure lately, and obviously Dan had too, but what made one person persevere and another succumb was a mystery. Everyone had his or her own breaking point.

Dan lamented, "Jimbo's gone. His absence is profound, but I don't want to lose Kiddo too. Every day he seems further from me."

"Does his doctor say anything? Does she understand the reason he won't talk to you?"

Dan shook his head. "No. She's still trying to figure it out."

"I hate to ask this, but isn't there a patient/doctor confidentiality clause or something? When does that make it okay to tell you stuff?" Matt asked, because he really wanted to know.

"Darian isn't a child, but he has had a history of self-harm and addiction. Dr. Loundas has included me in many of his sessions, and with his permission. It helped me for years to understand what to look for, but he used to be easier to read. Until Jimbo's death, he and I had an open relationship. He'd come to me and tell me his fears and we'd talk them through." Dan looked directly at him. "How much do you know about Darian's past?"

Matt shrugged. "Not loads. Lori filled me in on his family dysfunction and how he started cutting in middle school. She also mentioned a history of drug addiction."

Dan's tears had stopped and his expression grew harder. "Has he confided in you like he used to confide in me?"

"Maybe a little." Matt was feeling uncomfortable.

"And you're sticking to the story of only meeting him recently?"

"Yes, Mr. Miller. I swear, we just met in September." Matt could not explain why every time the situation grew tense, he felt the need to revert to a more formal address. "I don't know why you don't believe me."

"Did you know he was back on painkillers?"

Matt didn't like his accusatory tone. "No!"

"Did you know he has a bazillion pictures of you in his room?"

Matt felt defensive. "Dare said they were Jamie's."

"I find that hard to believe."

"Why not? Darian can't lie worth shit."

Dan's eyebrows went up. He let out an eerie chuckle. "Oh, I assure you, he knows how to lie, and he does it very well."

Matt was shocked. "What? No."

Dan shook his head. "Matt, Darian has shaped his world through years of practice. That's why Dr. Loundas has filled me in on his progress. He reshapes reality in order to avoid the pain of it."

Matt understood. "He sees what he wants to see."

Dan nodded. "Basically. Dr. Loundas said it may have started as a defense mechanism to protect him from the abuse he endured for years. Mental, physical, emotional… you name it. She's worried if he feels he's out of options, he might…." Dan stopped as if the words were horrifying to admit.

Matt filled in that blank. "Do what Jamie did."

Dan nodded. "I couldn't bear losing him too. That's why I need your help. Darian has moved from one coping mechanism to another, for years. Pain from cutting, numbness from drugs, and ecstasy from sex."

"You want me to have sex with him?"

Dan's face got instantly red. "No! Far from it! I think you're what fed his latest addiction. You lured him in when he was most vulnerable and gave him exactly what he needed to escape."

"Mr. Miller, I didn't. I swear. I mean, I did, but it wasn't like that. Darian and I just sort of… happened."

"Just sort of happened? Matt! As soon as I left him alone the two of you were fucking like rabbits!" Dan was seething. "I hear him in the shower; I know what he's doing. He never acted like this until you came along! I've read books. I know sexual addiction has to do with a constant need for physical gratification. Darian fits the profile. Dr. Loundas is working with him, but so far he won't admit his obsession with sex, or his obsession with you. You can help him best by cutting him loose and never bothering him again. I want you to write a letter telling him you're done."

Dan's anger scared Matt, but it wasn't the same as when that anger came from his own father. Matt didn't shrink away this time, because he knew he was right and Mr. Miller was confused. "Mr. Miller, with all due respect, I love Darian with all my heart. I'm not writing him a letter like that. And our relationship isn't just about sex, no matter what you think. What we have together wasn't planned, but I assure you it's real." Matt leaned forward on his chair. He had to set Dan straight. He was tired of being accused of taking advantage of Darian when it was a mutual attraction. "Jamie knew we'd fall for each other, which is why he never introduced us. He was afraid of losing Darian to *me*. That's why it's been so explosive. Dare and I have so much in common it isn't even funny. And as far as sex goes, Jamie was a prude!" A pang of guilt struck him, but Matt pushed past it and continued, "His freaky mother ingrained in him this abnormal withdrawal from exploring pleasure. That's why Darian can't get enough of me. He's finally able to explore his desire, but he's so scared of betraying Jamie, he won't let go!"

Dan denied it. "You're just spouting off, Matt. Defending Darian's behavior. If you didn't know Darian before Jim died, then how do you even know what Jimbo thought? Darian was in love with Jim. End of story," Dan yelled, standing up and leaning over Matt. "You have no fucking clue what you're talking about!"

Matt jumped up in defense and yelled back, "I do too! I have his journals!" As soon as he said it, he knew he shouldn't have. He quieted instantly.

Dan's expression changed. "What?"

Matt closed his eyes and reiterated, "I have his journals. I know Jamie feared losing Darian to me, because I read his journals."

"Why didn't you tell me? All this time I've wondered why he killed himself, yet you have all the answers."

Matt shook his head. "No, I don't. I don't have the answers you want."

"I think you need to let me be the judge of that. I want to read those journals."

"No, you don't."

Dan's voice grew louder. "Yes, I do."

"No, you don't."

"Matt! So help me…." Dan was livid. He lifted his clenched fist in front of Matt's face, but did not strike him.

Matt hadn't seen Dan this irrational since the night he caught Matt in Darian's bed. He didn't think Dan would hit him, but if he did, Matt would take it like a man. Dan wasn't angry with him, not really; Matt knew his anger was from his unanswered questions. Dan wanted answers, just like Matt. Matt tried defusing him with rational thought. "Mr. Miller, knowing what Jamie wrote will not bring him back," he said calmly. "Right now, Darian is the one we need to think about. Darian is the one who is scared, and alone, and hurting in ways we can only dare to imagine. If you want me to help you, then you have to let me see him."

"No," Dan answered indignantly, pulling his shoulders back.

"He'll talk to me, I know he will. He started opening up that day we were in his room."

"Fine. Let me have the journals, and I'll let you talk to Darian."

"No! Look, Dan, you know I'm right. Dare trusts me. Did you know his mother up and left in October?"

Dan turned on his heel and headed toward the door. "I don't have to hear this."

Matt hurried after him. "Did you know he feels like Jamie is haunting him? Mr. Miller, please," he begged as Dan opened the front door. "I'm dying to see Darian! I'll help. I promise. Darian relaxes around me. He'll open up. Just give me the chance to—"

Dan turned sharply and pointed his finger at Matt. "I said, no! I used to be close to him before *you* came along. I used to be the one he talked to, and confided in. Me! I'm not letting you weasel your way into his heart and steal the last remnant of trust he has for me."

Dan's insecurity astounded Matt, but he still pleaded with him as he stormed down the walkway toward his car. "Fine. Shut me out. But you have to stop trying to change Darian if you want him to trust you. Forcing him to cut his hair and do home improvement projects with you won't draw him closer. If you want to know Dare, take a look at what he's drawing." Matt shouted after Dan. "He expresses his feelings on paper. Dan, listen to me!" Dan Miller slammed his car door and sped off.

Matt trudged back to the house and closed the door behind him. What could he do when Dan held all the cards? He took his phone out of his pocket and texted him. *Please, Dan. You have to listen to me. I know Darian.*

Ten minutes later he got the reply: *Stop harassing me.*

Matt flopped on the couch and screamed, "Fuck!"

He felt trapped, but there was nothing to be done about it. He looked around the room. It felt so odd sitting in silence; it was so out of place. His house was normally full of noise and commotion. His eyes lit upon a Bible sitting on the coffee table. He reached forward and pulled it into his lap. "I don't know what to do, Lord. Please, tell me what to do."

Matt wasn't a fan of the "open and point" method of referencing scripture. His dad taught him everything should be read in context. But in the moment, he was desperate.

Matt read Titus 3:9. "But avoid foolish controversies and genealogies and arguments and quarrels about the law, because these are unprofitable and useless."

He sighed and flipped the pages again. James 1:2-3 caught his eye. "Consider it pure joy, my brothers, whenever you face trials of many kinds, because you know the testing of your faith develops perseverance."

His eyes went to the ceiling. "After all this, Lord, I should have the perseverance of a saint." Matt tried one more time and read out loud, "God is love. Whoever lives in love lives in God, and God in him. In this way, love is made complete among us so that we will have confidence on the day of judgment, because in this world we are like him. There is no fear in love. But perfect love drives out fear, because fear has to do with punishment. The one who fears is not made perfect in love."

Matt closed the Bible and closed his eyes. First John 4:16-18 filled his thoughts, and reminded him of everything he'd been through for years. He's been living in fear for so long it was hard to imagine letting it go. "But God said that perfect love drives out fear," he mused. "So, how do I love like that?"

January 19, 2011

MATT got a call from his Aunt Peg, telling him she'd found a few things under the couch. He headed over to give him something to do. Thinking about Darian, missing him, and wishing Dan would answer any one of his thousand text messages was more than enough to deal with. His mind was shot. He longed for something physical to occupy his time. "Too bad Aunt Peggy's car didn't throw a timing belt." Matt chuckled to himself. Of course, if she called in the next ten minutes to tell Matt she was stranded somewhere because the timing belt broke, he'd feel awful.

Matt unlocked the door and went inside. He hadn't been back to the apartment for a while now. He liked living with his parents nowadays, knowing he had another place to stay at any given moment. Aunt Peg was in Philly on business, and he thought he'd sleep in a quiet bedroom for a change. He liked home, but sometimes having his mom poke her head in his room to check on him was a bit excessive. He was fine. She didn't need to worry about him.

At least, he thought he was fine until he walked into the apartment and old memories flooded back in. "I need time," Darian said to him. Only this time he heard it as a drawn-out echo full of static and distortion, like a movie played in slow motion. He shook the sound away. Matt walked over to the couch. "Stop, I can't think when you touch me," Darian said again. The sound was far away and distorted much like the first dream vision. Matt didn't like how these memories decided to crop up unexpectedly. He was doing just fine getting through each day—one day at a time—each one without Darian. Weeks went by. Why now?

He spied a pad and a T-shirt on the breakfast bar and wandered over to them. Aunt Peg had left him a note. He read it out loud. "I found the sketchpad between the couch and the end table when I was vacuuming and the shirt under the bed. Someone is a very fine artist! And that someone seems to enjoy drawing you. I hope you introduce me one day." He smiled. Aunt Peg had drawn a smiley face and some Xs at the bottom. Matt laid the note aside, picked up the T-shirt, and sniffed it. Darian's scent lingered in the fabric. He breathed in deeply before setting it down and picking up the sketchpad. He knew it was Darian's, but he hadn't seen this particular one before. He opened it randomly to the middle. It was a pencil drawing of his kitchen. He smirked. "Darian." He shook his head and flipped the page.

This was a pencil drawing, too, but of Matt. Darian had drawn him sleeping. He'd never seen himself sleeping except for the chalk drawing Darian did of his upper body. This one was less lusty. He lay on his side clutching a pillow to his chest. Most of him was under the bedspread. Only his bare arm and shoulder were exposed. Darian drew each cord of muscle in his arm and each stray hair on his face. Matt's parted lips were so well drawn he was sure if he stared long enough he'd see drool slowly leaking out of them.

Matt flipped the page again.

Intense blue eyes stared back.

This was another drawing in pencil of him, except Darian had colored in his eyes with chalk. They popped from the page. Meridian blue like the deep ocean pulled the looker's eyes to the center of the drawing. These eyes were wide, intent, and hungry. As Matt studied his reflection on the page, he slowly allowed his eyes to take in the rest of the depiction. His lips were stretched around the tip of Darian's rigid penis, and his fist was curled around the base, holding it in position. Darian included enough of his own thighs and knees to complete the faded border of the seductive portrait; however, it was clear by the extensive detail of Matt's face, arms, and shoulders that Matt's actions were the subject. Matt felt his balls shift. This was definitely the most seductive picture he'd ever been in, and he hadn't even posed for it.

Darian simply drew it from memory. Matt adjusted his swelling crotch and flipped the pad again.

Darian certainly had a future in nude portraits, if he wanted one. Matt could see these sketches being bought by a specialty gallery in New York. He just knew someone somewhere would pay thousands to hang a framed picture of two beautiful bodies entwined as he and Darian were in the pages that continued through his art pad. If they were done in oil, it would be even more lucrative. Darian drew everything from that blue-eyed blowjob, to joining doggy style.

Doggy style. Yeah, Matt liked that one! Darian's head hung down, allowing his hair to obscure his face, but Matt would know that body anywhere. Matt was behind him, gripping his hips and leaning over his back, kissing his skin as he pushed in as far as humanly possible. Matt especially liked the way Darian blurred the lines where Matt's pelvis ended and Darian's buttocks began. It was like they were one, joined as one. He could not pull his eyes away.

Matt's visual memories of his experiences with Darian came back in full force. He could clearly see, and hear, the night they met....

MATT fully intended to allow this beautiful young man to cry about whatever he needed to. He was upset and hurting. Perhaps it was an ex-lover? Perhaps it was a dead relative? Whatever the reason—Darian, his name was Darian—was crying, Matt knew he needed to comfort him. Everyone needed comfort. But when that sobbing young man lifted his tear-stained cheeks and looked into Matt's eyes with his deep dark-brown ones, Matt was compelled to cross the line again. He'd promised himself he'd be all comfort and no lust, but the beast within took over. He leaned in and kissed him, again and again. Kissing swiftly turned into groping and shedding of clothes. Before he knew it, they were naked on the couch.

Matt pinned Darian's lithe body to the cushions. He devoured his mouth and thrust himself against Darian's hip. Darian moaned and writhed like nothing Matt ever experienced before. It drove him wild to hear Darian plead, and to feel Darian's fingernails digging marks into his ribs.

"I want to fuck you, Darian. Can I fuck you?" Matt asked breathily between fiery kisses.

"Yes. Please, yes." Darian spoke no more words but opened his legs, allowing one to fall off the couch and support his exposed position.

Matt untangled himself and explained, "I need to get some condoms." He rushed to the other room and returned, only to dump the contents of a box of condoms on the coffee table. He hurriedly tore one open and had it in place in seconds. He fucked Darian on his back the first time, on his knees the second, and seated in his lap for the third.

Darian had quickly and enigmatically replaced every lover Matt had ever pleasured. It was not that those in the past weren't good—some of them were exceptionally talented in the art of seduction and had Matt coming over and over again. What made Darian surpass them all was the way he complemented Matt. From the very first kiss to the last pounding on his ass, Darian moved with Matt in synchronous unity. Darian anticipated Matt's needs, his moves, and his expectations. The two of them wordlessly explored sensations Matt never knew before, and it was astounding. Matt had never had a lover like that, and each time he came, he knew he'd never want different one.

He didn't remember walking to the bed but distinctly remembered fucking Darian over the side of it. He had Darian's legs over each shoulder and each of his hands cupped one of Darian's ass cheeks. After he finished, and Darian successfully milked his own cock, Matt pulled out and aggressively flipped Darian over. He got down on his knees beside the bed where Darian hung over the edge and proceeded to spread his ass cheeks again. Compulsion took over conscious thought, and before Matt could conceive what he was about to do, he had his tongue fully extended and engaged in licking Darian's pulsing orifice.

He was like a hungry lion gorging himself on dead zebra for the first time. There was no holding back. He bit, he licked, he sucked that tender, exposed skin until his attentions provoked a sharp cry of release from his hostage. Only then did his brain catch up and remind him what he'd done. He'd just made Darian come from eating his ass, and that was after he'd just made him come from fucking! And oh my God—he, Matt Dixon, ate a guy's ass! He panted as he watched Darian relax into the bed. Darian wasn't moving. He made delightful sounds like the cooing of a dove or purring of a cat, but he didn't move. And Matt did that. He did it with his tongue.

Matt swirled his tongue around in his mouth. Salt. Salt and a hint of latex. Nothing really yucky. Nothing a little mouthwash would not get rid of. He decided if this was what rimming would do to his very delicious new lover, he'd gladly do it again. He grinned in satisfaction and tongued Darian's hole one more time for good measure before assisting him up to the pillows. Once there, he climbed over his thin frame and gazed into his glassy, sated eyes.

"You are amazing," he whispered.

"No. You." Darian barely responded. "Name? What's your name?"

"Matthias," he whispered back. Why he gave him his proper name and not his nickname, Matt wasn't sure. It just slipped out. He attempted to open his mouth and explain that people normally called him Matt, but Darian's tongue slipped between his open lips, and before he knew it, they were at it again….

MATT'D had the most amazing night, and Darian had become for him the embodiment of fairy-tale love that Matt had sworn off for years. Darian was the one his inner champion fought for. Matt spoke to the open sketchpad. "It was the beginning. Our beginning. And I can't let it end like this." He closed the pad and swiftly snatched it up. "I'm going to visit you whether they like it or not. I can't live another second without you, Darian Weston!"

All he had left to figure out was how he was going to make it happen. First, he texted Lori. *Tell me where Darian is, please.*

Why should I?

Because I need to see him.

That didn't turn out so well the last time.

Come on, pleeease. If you don't, I'm going to visit every rehab center in Pennsylvania, Maryland, and Virginia until I find him!

Oh fine! But you better text me when you know something.

Matt smiled. *Deal.*

21

DARIAN sat at the window looking out at the rain. It reminded him of the dark raining gloom his life had become. He was caged. He was alone. And had no one to talk to but a ghostly hallucination of his dead lover.

"You could join me, you know," Jamie said.

Darian shook his head. "I don't want to."

"Sure you do. Why do you think you went back to drugs? You secretly want it all to end." Jamie spoke quietly, but the words thudded like thunder on Darian's chest.

Darian answered, "No I don't. Not the way you want me to believe. I want to let go of you."

"But you can't."

"You won't let me."

"You won't let yourself."

Darian talked out loud but never turned to face the ghost he didn't believe was there in the first place. Jamie was dead, but for some reason his mind kept conjuring up an image to talk to. He knew he needed to talk to Dr. Loundas about it, but he was afraid she'd think he was crazy and send him off to some other hospital for loonies. For now, he'd take one week at a time and hope to make it through until he could see Matt. He could tell Matt. Matt would believe him. Matt wouldn't think he was crazy.

"Matt," he whispered to the rain. Darian didn't understand why he yearned for Matt so completely, but he did. With each passing day, the need for Matt felt stronger. Dan told him the feeling would fade. Dr. Loundas said his obsession would wane. They were wrong. They didn't understand. Matt was like air, and without him Darian was suffocating.

“It’s been weeks,” Jamie said. “Weeks and he hasn’t rescued you. Your shining knight, the brave fireman, is out fucking someone else. And here you sit. He’ll never treat you as good as I did.”

The more Jamie spoke, the more Darian closed himself off. He had so little of his true self left, he didn’t know if he could last much longer. If Matt didn’t show up soon, he would have to finish it. Jamie would win.

“Where are you?” he asked the rain. Darian was certain, no matter where Matt was, he was thinking about him. He wondered if Matt recalled with pinpoint clarity their first night together, just as he could. Darian relived those moments over and over when the sadness of Jamie’s death was too strong. He couldn’t forget it no matter how hard he tried….

“HARDER…. Oh my God!” Darian exclaimed as Matthias thrust. Darian lost count of how many times they’d done it. All he knew was this was the first time in his life he felt as though he didn’t have to hold anything back. He gave himself over completely to every whim and every desire. Matthias even anticipated what he wanted and manipulated his body in just the right ways. He’d never felt so uninhibited. He’d always wondered what it felt like to rim or be rimmed, and the outcome far exceeded expectations. Jamie would have never considered tonguing his ass!

Guilt pinched at the same moment Matthias bit his neck. *I shouldn’t be thinking such things about Jamie.*

Matthias grabbed his knee and pulled his leg wide, giving his body new sensations and whisking away any and all inappropriate thoughts about Jamie. He was in this bed, with this guy, being fucked in more ways than any m/m romance novel had ever described. And he thrived on it!

SEX with Matt made him feel completely free to explore every fantasy and indulge in every desire. No holds barred. *Jamie was so predictable and mechanical.*

Guilt pinched the muscles of his neck and twisted in his gut. Darian turned to Jamie's apparition. "I'm sorry. I know I shouldn't have compared you."

"But you do all the time. And now you'll have to live with that."

Darian returned to his curled-up position, staring out the window, tears streaming down his cheeks. The rain was comforting. To him, it looked like the entire world was experiencing the gloom he'd felt for the past four months.

January 24, 2011

DARIAN sat in a padded chair by the window, knees pulled to his chest, staring out at the rain. *The world was utterly dismal.* It had been raining for days; he'd lost track of how many days he had been sitting there. It wasn't like he had anything to do. His room was very sparse. Darian had a bed, two chairs by the window, a dresser, presumably for clothes, but he only had a few things, and a television attached to the wall on a metal arm. They made this place look exactly like a hospital. Darian hated hospitals. No wonder he felt so dismal. The environment alone would do it. He had paper and a pencil, but after drawing for hours, he even needed a break from the thing he loved most.

Someone rapped softly on the door.

He gradually turned his face in that direction, not understanding why the person bothered knocking this time when no one had paid that courtesy before. He turned his tired eyes toward the door. It took a few seconds to figure out he wasn't dreaming, but as soon as reality hit him, Darian leapt from his chair. "Matt!" he cried.

Matt grinned and met him halfway across the floor. Darian crashed into him, all arms and legs, trying to embrace him with his entire body. (He was a wild beast besieging his knight.) Darian practically crawled up Matt's body, wrapping his legs around his waist and kissing him passionately. Matt returned his passion and supported Darian's weight by cupping his posterior with one hand and tightening his grip across Darian's back.

“Oh… Matt… so happy… to see… you.” Darian spoke through the barrage of kisses he peppered on Matt’s face. “I didn’t think… I’d get to… see you.”

Matt sucked on Darian’s tongue one last time and pulled back. He tried to talk between Darian’s kisses. “Sorry. I can’t kiss… and talk… same time. I’m not supposed to be here.” Darian held him around the back of his neck and pulled their faces together, touching forehead to forehead, nose to nose. Matt was breathing hard, and so was he. “I snuck in,” Matt explained.

“How?”

Matt turned, still holding Darian wrapped around his waist, and tilted his head toward the door. “Missy.”

“Hi.” She smiled.

Missy. Darian liked Missy. She’d had a crush on him when she was younger, before she found out he was gay. She was a friend of Lori’s girlfriend Sara Montgomery.

Darian smiled back. “Hi, Missy. Thanks. I owe you one for this.”

“Don’t sweat it.” She waved it off.

“But you could get into a lot of trouble.”

She shrugged. “What are they going to do, fire me? I can go somewhere else. Seeing you happy is all that matters.” She smiled warmly and Darian smiled back. “I never want to see that sadness in your eyes again, so breaking your boyfriend in to see you is totally worth it.” She waved again and slowly shut the door. Then popped her head back in to add, “Plus, watching two boys kiss is so hot!” She giggled and shut the door again.

“Are all your friends teenagers?” Matt asked.

“No. Only some. Lori’s my age.”

“How’s the cheek?” Matt asked before kissing it.

“Good. Healed.”

“And the wrist?”

Darian brought his arm around to show Matt the brace. “Last X-ray looked good, so they put me in a brace for another couple weeks. It feels fine, I guess.”

Matt’s expression grew serious. “And withdrawal symptoms?”

Darian was losing his enthusiasm for talking. He didn't want to talk about it. "They hurt like a bitch. The doctors tried to give me something, I think. I don't know. Nothing helped. I hurt all over and nobody cared." He turned his face away and tried to push himself out of Matt's embrace, but Matt wouldn't let go. "Let me go."

"No. I've waited forever to hold you."

Darian pushed at his arms, but with only one good hand, and half the amount of muscle Matt possessed, Darian's efforts were useless. "Matt, let me go!"

"I said no."

Darian squirmed, but Matt held him tight. As always, he couldn't hold himself together in Matt's presence. Darian broke down. He laid his head on Matt's shoulder and cried. "I wanted escape so bad, Matt. Drugs. Pain. Sex. I didn't care. They tied me to the bed so I wouldn't hurt myself. Until the tremors stopped, I was trapped there. I screamed, but nobody cared. And when I went to pee, a nurse went with me to make sure I didn't jerk off. I wasn't even allowed to do that. I hurt so bad, Matt. I hurt so bad."

And Jamie kept watching me the whole time, he thought but couldn't say.

Matt kissed Darian one more time and walked over to the bed. Darian was very light, and Matt maneuvered across the mattress on all fours while Darian clung to his torso. Once up to the pillows, Matt stopped and rested his weight on top of Darian's body. It felt so wonderful. Darian looked into the blue eyes of hope and asked, "Make love to me?" He unwrapped his legs and fully spread open beneath him.

Matt chuckled. He ran his hands all over Darian. He kissed him with slow licks and teasing nibbles. "One-track mind?"

Tension gripped him. "No, I don't. Just because I want sex now doesn't mean it's *all* I think about." Dan may have thought that, and Dr. Loundas may have agreed, but Darian didn't want Matt to know what they postulated about him. It wasn't true. It couldn't be true.

"Dare, why are you averting your eyes? Look at me." When Darian did, Matt explained, "I only meant we were thinking the same thing. It's risky, and I don't relish the thought of getting caught again if someone walks in, but it's what I think about all the time." He kissed

Darian's jaw and his neck, trying to make him relax. "There isn't a moment in the day I don't think about being inside of you. Unless you'd… like to be inside of me?" Matt gave Darian a sly smile.

Darian heard him. Topping was a subject they hadn't talked about. Darian had thought about it before, but something inside kept him silent now. He was scared. Jamie was watching. And Jamie was hardly ever in the room at the same time as Matt.

"Darian? You okay?" Matt tried to shift to the side but Darian's legs were flared out on both sides of Matt's hips, so he remained where he was—between Darian's open thighs. Matt smoothed his hair out of his face and stroked his collarbone. "Dare, are you in there? Why are you looking out the window? Your eyes are miles away. Come back to me." Matt kissed his jaw, and down his neck. He was offering tenderness and waiting for Darian to speak. *Should he?* Was now the time to tell him all his fears?

Jamie narrowed his eyes at him from across the room, and Darian turned his face in the other direction.

"Dare, what's wrong?" Matt's voice was full of concern. "You know you don't have to stay here if you don't want to. You're an adult; they can't hold you against your will."

Darian knew that was true, but where would he go? He needed someone to fix him. "Is thinking about sex wrong?" he asked.

Matt sounded alarmed. "What? No. Why would you ask that? I know Jamie was a prude when it came to sex but—"

"It's not about Jamie!" he snapped.

"Ohhkaaay. Then why do you ask? I'm a guy, I think about sex. Aren't men supposed to think about sex every seven seconds of the day or something? It's normal."

Darian paused, but gradually turned to face Matt. He was nervous because Jamie was watching. "Kinsey Report says that statistic is hyperbolic. It's more like several times a day. But that's only about 54 percent of men. Some don't think about sex at all."

Matt gave him a half smile and joked, "I'd hate to be that guy. I'd rather be the freak one-in-a-million that thinks of sex every seven seconds."

"So… you don't think it's wrong?"

Jamie sneered. "Stop asking him that question. You know it's wrong. You do it to block me out of your life."

Matt said, "No. But you have me concerned why you're asking me. Who's filling your head with nonsense about it being wrong?" Matt waited, but Darian wasn't answering. "Dare, before I met you, I used to think about sex a lot. Maybe not every seven seconds, but at least once a day. Now—it's more like every seven seconds. I think about tasting your skin and brushing my fingers over your sweet spot." He winked down at Darian. "Heck, I can't even take a piss without picturing your hole in front of my cock. I want you all the time. But… I love you. I don't think it's wrong to think about making love to you."

Darian was satisfied with that answer. He titled up his chin and kissed Matt. "So, it's about caring for the person?"

"Um, yeah, I guess. If I went around thinking about sex with everyone I walked past, I'd probably be labeled a pervert, or a sex addict." Matt laughed.

Darian did not. "That isn't funny!"

"What the fuck did I say?" Matt backed off at Darian's scowl. "What's gotten into you? Why are you so defensive? And what has you against sex all of a sudden? I know you have problems, but don't bite my head off. I came here because I missed you." Matt got off of Darian's body. "But if you'd rather I leave, then fine. Whatever…."

His heart screamed, *No!* Darian snagged Matt's arm before he could move far. "No. Don't go. Please? I missed you too. A whole lot." Darian rubbed Matt's chest. "Please don't leave. I think about sex with you too. All the time." He slid his hand under Matt's shirt and up to his nipples. Matt liked when he pinched them. "Being here confuses me. They show me weird pictures. I don't understand." He stretched up and kissed Matt's neck. "Don't leave. I want to make love with you. I want to feel you all over."

"All right, I'll stay." Matt kissed his lips. "Would you like to… *top* this time? We haven't…."

Darian let go of Matt's nipples and lay back down on the bed. He lifted his butt and slipped his sweat pants off. "I do, but not here. When I have you, I want it to be without all these stupid fears in my head." *And without Jamie watching.* He stripped out of his shirt and assisted

Matt in doing the same. "I want it to be special, like when you lit the candles for me."

"Yeah, I liked that. It was Jason's idea." Matt moved his hands over Darian's torso as he lay down. He kissed Darian's stomach, and moved his hand over his thigh.

"I like Jason," Darian said. He wanted to say more, but he got lost in the tingling sensations Matt's lips on his skin produced. Matt's hands moved over his body, and his lips sipped Darian's skin, draining his worry and anxiety. Darian glanced behind Matt and noticed Jamie was gone. Darian took a deep, cleansing breath and allowed Matt to kiss away his fear. He would feel more relaxed if the door locked from the inside, but Darian couldn't be bothered to worry about that right now. He was lost in Matt's kisses.

Darian savored the feel of his hands stroking him and preparing him. He heard Matt tear open a condom packet, and he waited as Matt rolled it down his length. He slid inside Darian as they kissed. He started pumping slowly and built momentum with each deep stroke. Darian pulled one leg wide and held it behind his knee, allowing Matt to go deeper. He held Matt behind his neck with his bad arm and was careful not to clunk Matt in the head with the brace. Being joined like this was what he'd craved for weeks.

They clung, rocked together, released, and relaxed.

NO MATTER how pitiful he felt when Matt asked him to get dressed, Darian knew better than to lie naked on the bed with Matt. They'd risked getting caught once, but he'd be damned if he was going to ask Matt to make love over and over until someone walked in on them. Once would have to be enough.

"Don't give me that look, Dare. You know I want more. I always want more. My body can never have enough of you." Matt zipped his zipper and crawled back onto the bed. He got comfortable on the pillows next to Darian and pulled him close. "Right now, I want to hold you."

Darian looped his leg over Matt's and rested his head on Matt's upper chest. Matt rubbed his cheek on Darian's hair and Darian hugged him tight.

"Darian? Will you talk to me?" Matt questioned softly.

"What about?" Darian tried to act vague, but deep down he knew Matt could see through his casualness.

"Dare, Dan came to my house to talk to me. He's concerned. And I remember what you said that day at your house—about Jamie haunting you, and about your mother moving. You have to be hurting. I want to be here for you. I wish I was with you when you went through withdrawal; I know it was awful. But I'm here now."

Darian remained quiet for the longest time. He didn't know where to start. Just hearing Matt had paid attention to the things he said meant a great deal. "Have you ever been hurt by someone?" he asked. Hearing his question out loud, Darian realized he needed to be more specific. "Like… abused?"

"Yes," Matt said plainly.

"What happened?" Darian asked quietly.

Darian genuinely wanted to know, but also, shifting the topic from Darian's pain onto Matt's made things easier. The lights were dimmed in the room, which helped him loosen up. The one table lamp was bright enough for them to see each other, but it was far enough in the corner not to shine in his eyes. Darian tightened his hold around Matt's middle.

Matt spoke softly. "I was date-raped when I was nineteen. I met a guy in a club, he took me to his place, and he asked if I wanted to 'play'; I said sure. I'd been tied up before, but it was never masochistic. I never wanted to be hurt for pleasure as much as gaining pleasure from relinquishing control. The other few guys enjoyed playing 'the master' with me as their little mouse to flog. It was fun. But this guy…." Matt's voice trailed away.

Darian moved his arm soothingly across Matt's chest and asked, "What did he do?"

"Lots of things," Matt continued. He rubbed Darian's arm as he spoke. "Once I was bound, he had all the power. He blindfolded me. Even now I can't stand having my eyes covered." Matt spoke slowly and deliberately as he filled in the details. "I know there were several men in the room. I couldn't see them, but there were too many hands on me to only be the one. Someone yanked my hair as he jerked my head back. He pulled so hard I know a hunk of it came out. Then I had a dick shoved so far down my throat it was painful."

"Did you choke?"

"No. It tasted like cinnamon. I think he had on a numbing lubricant or something. I came across a few things online over the years that suppress the gag reflex; a couple of them were cinnamon flavored. Whatever it was, he fucked my mouth without caring if he choked me to death."

"Weren't you scared?" Because Darian was scared for him.

"Yeah. More than ever in my life. Thankfully, he pulled out when he came, because I'm not sure I could have swallowed it. He spurted all over my face. Then I felt someone put a ball gag in my mouth. Hands grabbed each leg and each arm. I was freed from the leather restraints only to be flipped over and bound differently. I was chained to a spreader bar with my ass in the air and my weight solely on my shoulder and neck. Someone slapped my ass, which I'm normally fond of, but then two other people grabbed my ass on either side and pulled it apart." Matt hesitated. Darian could feel him shaking. "I guess I should be thankful he pumped my ass with a dildo first, but that fucking thing was huge!" Matt suppressed a maniacal laugh. "It hurt, but it was nothing compared to being treated like a sex toy by at least four other guys. They fucked me so hard." Matt wiped his eyes and breathed hard. "I thought they were going to kill me. I seriously thought they would fuck me until my colon split wide open and toxins streamed from my bowels."

Darian tilted his head up and tenderly kissed Matt's chin.

Matt addressed Darian so sternly it made him jump. "Never do that. Okay? Never, ever, go anywhere with someone you don't know. And never, ever let anyone tie you up." Matt turned on his side and twisted his body to look Darian in the eyes. "I don't want you hurt like that." He stroked the side of Darian's face. "I need you safe."

"I won't. I promise. No strange guys. Only you. I'm safe with you." Darian meant it sincerely.

"I know you shouldn't have come home with me. I took advantage of you in so many ways, and I'm sorry, but I would have never hurt you like that. You know that, right? I would never do anything to you that you didn't like or want. I enjoy kinky sex, but it has to be a mutual thing."

"I know." Darian could see his deep concern and feel Matt's strong affection. It made his heart yearn to tell Matt things he kept bottled up inside. He wanted to speak his feelings, but the words wouldn't come.

"We explore things together, okay? You'll tell me when it's too much?"

Darian gave Matt an impish smile. "Or not enough?" He thought Matt was right when he said they were perfect for one another. He meant to tell him, but he felt guilty admitting it. Jamie wouldn't like it.

"You're such a flirt." Matt grinned and pulled Darian closer.

"No," Darian disagreed. "It's only flirting if I don't make good on my promises. There're plenty of things I want to try with you." Darian tilted his chin closer and claimed a kiss. He touched Matt's lips gently and flicked his tongue out, giving little licks in between kisses.

Matt's kisses were sweet; he let Darian set the pace. Darian didn't want this to escalate into sex again because the risk was too high they'd get caught; but then again… his urges were strong. Darian pushed Matt back and leaned over him on one elbow, being careful of his brace. With his free hand, he palmed Matt's groin. "Can I blow you? Please?" he begged between kissing and groping and squeezing Matt's penis. "I'll do whatever you want. I'm just dying to get my mouth around you. Please, Matt?"

Matt frowned. "No. I told you that first night it's not safe. I've been with too many men."

"And we agreed we'd use condoms until you were tested again. Well, you were tested. And found clean. Let me suck you? Please?"

Matt's expression grew long and Darian knew he was going to say something bad. "Dare," he began as he reached down and stilled Darian's hand, "I need to tell you something."

"What?" He was afraid to ask. He recognized Matt's regretful look as if they'd been intimate for years.

"The wait's going to be longer."

"What? Why? I read online the wait should be two to eight weeks and again at about six months. You should know soon if you're clean unless… you've… been…." His voice trailed off. He didn't want to finish the sentence. He heard Jamie snickering, but he refused to look at him.

"I'm sorry," Matt lamented. "I didn't mean to lie to you even if it was indirectly. It just happened."

"When?" he asked coldly.

"October."

"Before our date?" Darian stopped touching Matt and folded his arms under his chin across Matt's chest. The fun fizzled.

Jamie taunted, "I told you so."

Darian ignored Jamie, but his words went straight to his gut. Darian felt sick. He rationalized with Matt, "We never discussed monogamy. I can't expect you to change overnight. Jamie said you had lots of guys, I guess I should be surprised it was only the one."

"Well, here's the thing…. He wasn't the only guy." Matt fingered Darian's hair and Darian resisted pulling away from his touch. He was angry, and hurt, but he would not listen to Jamie's heckling.

"How many were there?" Darian asked.

"Thirty!" Jamie yelled.

"Two. One I had sex with, and one who gave me a hand job."

"A hand job isn't sex." Darian said it too fast to be believable. He was trying to be cool, but Matt would see through his façade if he wasn't careful.

"Dare, you and I both know it is. But, then there was another night too. Three weeks ago I went clubbing after I got suspended from my job and some guy followed me to the toilet."

"You lost your job?" Darian raised his head up, concerned. Matt's job was a simpler subject.

"Yeah, seems my being gay is an issue. But that's not the point. I cheated on you, Darian, and I feel awful about it." He seriously sounded sorry. "I'm so sorry."

Darian shrugged it off casually, even though inside he wanted to cry. "Sex with someone else isn't cheating unless we're a couple—

which we weren't at the time. And a hand job isn't sex, so I can get past that. Why tell me anyway? You didn't have to."

"I want to be honest with you." Matt caressed his cheek with the back of his knuckles. "No more secrets. I want to give myself only to you. I want to be vulnerable only with you. I want every orgasm to be because of you."

Darian liked his reasons and he smiled. "What happened with the toilet guy?"

"Nothing. He followed me in and tried to kiss me. I knew the moment his lips touched my neck you were the only person in the world I wanted to kiss me like that."

Darian's eyes narrowed and his heart quickened. "He kissed your neck?" Somehow it was worse than sex.

"Yeah. In that spot you like. You know? The indentation next to my Adam's apple, right over my pulse? As soon as his lips touched that spot, I knew it was wrong. I felt so guilty. I shoved him back and ran out of there, straight home. I've been a wreck ever since, trying to figure out how to get in here and see you."

Darian gazed into Matt's eyes quietly before a mischievous thought crept into his mind. "He kissed you. Right there?" He reached out and touched the spot on Matt's neck.

"Yes."

Darian scooted up Matt's chest and kissed that spot. "Right here?" He kissed him again.

Matt shuddered. "Uh-huh." Darian crawled completely on top of Matt and continued to kiss his neck. Darian nipped him right before sucking hard on that spot. Matt slid his hands down to cup Darian's ass as he gave him a hickey. "Oh, Dare, I love it when you're jealous!"

Darian moaned and wiggled on top of Matt. When he was done sucking a huge purple mark on Matt's neck, he leaned back to admire it. "Nobody's gonna touch that spot again."

"Nope. What else is going on in that pretty little head of yours?"

"Nothing. Just… you mentioned… earlier, you mentioned *me* being inside of *you*. Did you mean that?" Something primal made

Darian want to stake claim to his territory. Matt was his, and no one else should touch him.

"Yeah. I'm not going to lie to you. I've thought about it."

"Really? Even after those guys…."

"Yeah, even after. I haven't bottomed since then, so you'll have to take it slow, but I want you to. I want to share everything with you."

Darian grinned wickedly again. He was feeling very possessive. "Would you… let me tie you up?" Darian kissed Matt's neck again waiting for an answer. He liked games. Voicing his fantasies was refreshing.

"Yes," Matt answered. "I trust you." Darian was wiggling again, and he could feel Matt's bulge pressing against his own needy package. Matt made him feel so good sometimes he wanted to scream, and it was great knowing the feeling was mutual.

"Could I… use my dildo on you? Maybe a vibrator?" Darian giggled. He was loving this. He slid his fingers into Matt's short hair behind his ears.

"Ohhhh," Matt groaned again as Darian's mouth assaulted the other side of his neck. "Y-yes. Anything."

Darian giggled some more. "Could I pull—"

With just the slightest tug of Matt's hair, Matt jerked back and shoved Darian away as hard and fast as he could. Matt's head slammed into the headboard, and he winced. He grabbed his neck and groaned, "Ow."

Darian observed calmly. "I'll take that as a *noooo*," he commented as he climbed back on the bed. He sat cross-legged and waited for Matt to calm down. He looked quite freaked.

Matt took a few deep breaths before opening his eyes. "I'm… I'm sorry. I didn't expect…." Matt was panting.

Darian tried soothing him the same way Matt always did for him. "It's okay. I'm here. I'm not going anywhere. Take whatever time you need." Matt reached out and Darian took his hand. He curled his fingers around Matt's.

“Thanks. I’m feeling a little better. I always knew I had a thing about hair pulling. It’s part of the reason I keep my hair short. No one’s tugged on it for years.”

“I understand. I won’t do it again.”

“But I want you to. Not today, obviously, but sometime. I want to get used to you tugging on my hair. I like threading my fingers through yours. And besides, I used to like it… before that guy…. I want to like it again. With you. I trust you.”

“I trust you too.”

Darian leaned forward, and just as their lips touched, the door abruptly opened and Dr. Loundas burst in. “Arrest him!” She pointed angrily at Matt.

The policeman behind her pushed past and grabbed Matt’s arm from his side of the bed. He retrieved his handcuffs from off his belt and slapped them over Matt’s wrist. “You’re coming with me,” he said.

Darian panicked.

As soon as Matt half moved and was half yanked from his position on the bed, Darian leapt to his feet on the other side of the bed. “No!” he shrieked. “Get your hands off him! What are you doing? Stop!” He jumped in front of Matt and the police officer and blocked their exit with his body.

“Restrain him,” Dr. Loundas said, pointing at Darian.

Jamie laughed heartily. “You can’t have him. You lost. Now he’ll be taken away forever.”

Another man, presumably clinic security or a nurse of some sort, took hold of Darian from behind and pried him off of Matt.

Instantly, Darian’s shrieking from seconds ago escalated into high-pitched screeching as he thrashed about like a wild animal. “No!”

Jamie taunted him some more. “Or maybe I’ll follow him and do Matt in myself. Then you won’t be torn between us. There will only be me.” He curled his fingers like claws and advanced on Matt as he was being dragged from the room.

Darian flailed and bashed the startled male nurse in the face with his arm brace. It hurt, but Darian didn’t care. His thin frame slipped through the man's arms and he escaped capture by jumping across the bed.

"Get Mr. Dixon out of here!" Dr. Loundas continued to command as she tried to control the situation. "And restrain this patient!"

Matt was struggling, and Jamie was close to grabbing him around the neck.

"No! Let him go!" Darian was desperate. Matt was yanked backward as Darian jumped on the policeman's back. "Leave Matt alone!"

"Dare, no!" Matt tried to warn him, but it was too late. Darian bit the man on the ear.

The policeman let go of Matt and brutally yanked his wild attacker off his back. Darian fell but quickly recovered and slipped from the policeman's grabbing hands. The nurse was closing in from the other side and someone else pulled Matt's arm.

As Matt slipped through the entrance of the room, Darian snatched the pencil from the table and swung it at Jamie. He heard someone howl as Jamie laughed. Darian's defeated screams echoed all the way down the hall.

22

January 25, 2011

MATT sat in the jail cell all night, wondering if he would ever get his "one phone call" and if he did—whom would he call?

When morning came, he chose to call Hannah. She was the safest one. Hopefully, she'd keep quiet until he could think of an explanation for his mom and dad.

Matt looked up when an officer turned the key in the lock with an audible *clink.*

"Come with me," he instructed.

Matt rose off the hard mattress and did as told. He followed quietly to another dingy, gray room and sat where the officer pointed. He felt like he was in the middle of a CSI investigation. The room was empty except for the table and three chairs. Bars were affixed over the hatch-style window on the door and a large—presumably two-way—mirror extended over half of one wall.

"At least I'm not handcuffed to the table," he mumbled as the door opened again.

Matt expected to see Hannah since he was waiting for her to bail him out, but instead a woman with short, curly hair walked in. He recognized her from the clinic, and for some reason, he felt a twinge of fear. *What was she going to do?*

"I'm Dr. Loundas," she said, standing beside the table next to Matt.

This was going to be bad; he could see it in her eyes. He bowed his head and stared at her practical, black pumps.

"Tell me why I shouldn't press charges?" she asked gruffly.

Matt could not think of a valid reason. He'd broken the law; he knew that. He shrugged without looking up.

Dr. Loundas walked to the other side of the table and sat down. "I'm very angry with you right now. We haven't even met properly, yet I feel so angry toward you for thwarting my efforts to help Darian."

"I wasn't!" Matt sat up and replied honestly. He whined a bit in his response but couldn't help it. "I went there to help him. Dan wouldn't cooperate, so I—"

"Broke into a secured facility by coercing an employee?"

Coming from her, it made everything sound worse.

He nodded. "I guess. I'm sorry."

"In ten minutes, you undid all the therapy we tried to shape Darian with."

"No! We talked. I had him talking to me. He was opening up to me; at least he started to, I think. I told Dan Dare trusts me."

"Oh really? You talked?" She was stern, and apparently not convinced. She held her finger in the air and signaled over her shoulder. A picture appeared on a television screen, which was either behind the two-way mirror or was cleverly disguised as a part of the wall. Either way, it was very clear this was a video tape recording of Matt *in* Darian's room.

Oh my God, they have cameras in the rooms!

Matt was naked, on top of Darian and undulating in such a way no one in their right mind could mistake what was happening. Embarrassed, Matt looked away.

"Mr. Dixon, do I need to explain the serious nature of his addictions? I don't tend to divulge confidential information; however, as you have no idea what you are up against, I feel I need to fill you in, or risk your interference again."

The doctor was so direct. Matt was ashamed. She was right. He may have just met her, but he knew she was right. Everything his mom said, everything Dan said, poured over his guilt. He pushed his pride aside and admitted, "I'm sorry. I was only thinking of myself." He sniffled and felt the tears fighting their way to the surface. "I've had such an awful few months and this last week… I couldn't stand being away from Darian any longer. I need him so much. I tried to tell Dan, but he wouldn't listen. He thinks it's all about sex, but it's not!" Matt begged her forgiveness with his eyes. "You don't know what it's been like. I've lost so much: first Jamie, then my job, my truck, my friends, my father's respect. I couldn't lose Darian too. I had to know my hope was in something real. Being with Darian makes all the pain worth enduring. Even if it is a lie, even if it won't last," he admitted, hanging his head with a sigh. "Even if he doesn't feel the same, and what we have fades when he gets beyond his grief. I needed him now, and I broke the law to have ten minutes of sheer bliss to help me go on. I'm a horribly selfish person. I admit it. I'm sorry. I thought I could help Darian, but I was only thinking of myself. I'm so sorry."

Dr. Loundas sighed. She didn't respond right away. Matt waited, and when she said nothing for the longest time, he had to look up and know what she was doing. She simply stared at him with no readable expression. Then, after a few minutes, she stood up and exited the room.

Matt waited. He had no choice. He wiped his eyes and sat in the uncomfortable silence wondering what would happen next. When he thought he'd never leave the room again, the door opened, and Dr. Loundas reentered with some items in hand and Dan Miller behind her.

Oh fuck!

Dan would not look at him. He sat and stared at the table. Dr. Loundas sat down and looked at Matt, but with a different expression. "Do you know we had to sedate him last night? Darian is now wearing a straightjacket, unconscious, and lying on the floor of a padded room."

And Matt had thought his anguish over last night could not get any worse. "No. I'm so sorry. Dare…." Matt started crying, head in hands.

Dr. Loundas seemed unsympathetic to Matt's grief and kept talking. "I have never seen a patient act out like that before. He turned practically… feral." She shoved a photograph across the table and Matt looked up. It was of a man's arm with a pencil imbedded in the muscle of his forearm. "Evidence of what Darian did right before they sedated him. He snatched the pencil off the table and lashed out as the nurse was trying to restrain him. Last night set free rage in Darian I have never seen. I have always thought of him as a quiet threat, and a threat mainly to himself. This was very unexpected. This is your fault."

"I said I'm sorry." He truly was, but he did not know how to convince her any other way.

Dr. Loundas took a deep breath and said, "I believe you."

"I…." Dan opened his mouth and shut it when the doctor glared at him.

She took back the picture and placed it in a manila folder. "My dilemma is what I should do now. Legally, I feel obligated to let you sit in jail a few days and press charges. The damage in that young man is extremely visual, and no court—given the video footage I have—would doubt you compromised his recovery. Most likely, a jury would side with my conclusion that your involvement pushed him over the edge."

"I didn't mean to." He didn't know what more he could say. "Please don't send me to jail. I'll do anything. Please."

Dr. Loundas fingered her chin and stared at Matt long enough to cause a chill to race down his back. What was she thinking? And why did she build this up like a threat? Matt was terrified of what she would say next. After agonizing minutes, she blinked and proceeded to open another folder before her. "At your suggestion, I allowed Darian to have that pencil, the one he used as a weapon. But before he lashed out, he sketched some very interesting images." She took another paper out and slid it over to Matt.

"My suggestion? I told Dan…." He looked at Mr. Miller, but Mr. Miller looked away.

Matt looked down at the collage of small portraits that littered the eight-by-eleven sheet of paper. One was of Darian lying alone on a bed. He looked so sad. Darkness surrounded his body as he curled into a fetal position. Another sketch showed a body lying in a pool of blood. Matt could only imagine it was Jamie; there was no real way to tell, but it was very gruesome. There was a coffin depicted two inches from it.

Matt needed to observe something else and moved his attention to a picture at the top left—a sketch of a hand holding a photograph. The photo looked like Matt but with curly hair, not his buzz cut. The hand must have been Jamie's. Every time Darian drew his own hand, that Matt had seen, he included the leather wrist cuff he was fond of wearing. This picture didn't have one.

Then Matt's eyes wandered over to a sketch of Darian sitting in a chair with his knees pulled up to his chest and his arms clutching the sides of his head. The area around Darian was shaded in dark with jagged lines, presumably lightning, striking all around. Matt felt the need to hold him bubbling up. Seeing how Darian pictured himself, especially when in conjunction with the one of him lying in bed, was disturbing.

Farther to the right was another sketch of Darian leaning into someone's chest. Strong arms—cords of muscles on the biceps and forearms—held him there. His face looked serene. Eyes closed. The person holding him was not fully drawn, only partial chest and arms. Right where Darian's nose nestled into the shirt of his "comforter" there was a curious symbol. As was true of most of Darian's depictions, this was very realistic, and the symbol on the shirt was over the left breast where most logos would be found. It was mostly buried under Darian's face but Matt though it looked very familiar. Then he looked down to his own shirt. The fire department symbol had the same few lines on the edge. He looked up.

"That's you," Dr. Loundas confirmed matter-of-factly. "I am… not normally hesitant in my decisions. I see what needs to be done, and I follow through. I have never questioned my methods before because there was no need. I have been very successful in helping hundreds of patients. But this… Darian confounds me. He doesn't react in a way I have studied before. His erratic behavior is just that—erratic. I want you to help me, Matt. I believe you can help me."

"What? How? I thought you said I pushed him over the edge?"

"No, I said a jury would side with *my conclusion* that your involvement pushed him over the edge. In truth, I think I pushed him over the edge. I think I pulled him away from the one person he felt safest with, protected by, because I didn't explore his feelings deeply enough and I listened to his guardian's opinions. I was the one who didn't look close enough to see this coming."

Matt relaxed for the first time. "So you don't think Darian's a sex addict?" He wanted to gloat, but Dan wasn't looking.

"I didn't say that. I believe Darian was clinging to you for sexual favors in order to bury his pain… in the beginning. But now, after time, and with what I already know about Darian, I think he's clinging to feelings he doesn't understand."

Dr. Loundas reached over and exchanged that sheet for another. Matt studied the next few pictures. Darian looking at his reflection in a mirror, only the reflection showed horribly jagged cut lines all over his arms and ribs. Jamie holding Darian, yet looking over his shoulder at Matt while he was working on a car—unawares. And finally, one of Matt and Darian lying stretched out on Matt's bed. The thing Matt noticed right away in this one was the picture on the nightstand, which was turned over. *That must have meant something to him.*

"And this one." She passed him another sheet. "Notice the wisplike images hovering over his head. What do you think they are?"

Matt wasn't completely sure but something Darian mentioned before popped into his mind. "Well, I remember Darian saying a few weeks ago that Jamie was haunting him. Perhaps this is his rendition of it. Look," he said, pointing to one sketch of Darian, wide-eyed and scared. "He drew himself, but his eyes are watching this image on the side that looks like a zombie version of Jamie. See?"

"Dan also informed me you mentioned that." She took the paper and studied it. "I do see. Wow, I can't believe I hadn't noticed the resemblance." She put it down and sighed. "This explains even more."

"You really think Jamie is haunting him?"

She smirked. "Mr. Dixon, professionally, I don't ascribe to a belief in ghosts. I'm also not religious. What I do believe in is science, and the unfathomable depths of the human subconscious. The human brain is capable of many things, some of which are beyond our comprehension. If Darian's subconscious is manifesting itself as apparitions of his dead lover, it would explain his fear of opening up. And if he hears his own uncertainties as judgments or mockery from Jimmy, then Darian is extremely close to a psychotic break. I think this outburst could be a turning point."

"A turning point for what?" Dan asked.

Dr. Loundas looked at Dan, and then Matt. "For us to help him."

"Us? You mean I can see him?" Matt couldn't contain his excitement.

She smiled and said, "Yes. But I have to warn you; I have some unorthodox ideas of what we can try. Are you willing to give it your all?"

Matt was scared of the wily look in her eyes, but he agreed. He looked at Dan. "And you're okay with this?"

"No," he grumbled.

"Mr. Miller, please, let it go," Dr. Loundas beseeched him.

"Fine. But I'm still jealous of Darian's attachment to you." He glared at Matt and quickly looked away.

"Seriously?" He couldn't believe his ears.

Dan crossed his arms and huffed loudly. "And for the record, I never asked him to cut his hair, and I wasn't trying to change him. I only intended to do whatever he asked so he'd trust me, yet Darian still chose *you*." Dan pouted, "And I want to read those journals!"

Matt gawked. "Oh my God!"

The doctor reached over and touched his hand. "Matt, Dan and I have been working on Darian's trust issues for a very long time. You must be patient with Mr. Miller. Losing Jimmy hasn't been easy on any of you, I'm sure. But those journals…." She let her thoughts be implied.

"You don't know what you're asking."

"Consider it. For Dan. He needs closure."

Matt looked over and Dan was no longer pouting, he was quietly crying.

"I'll think about it. For now, they're staying where they are. When can I see Darian?" he asked the doctor.

"Soon, but I'm giving it another week. I want the drugs from last night to wear off, and I want to see if he'll behave without restraints. I also want you involved with some group sessions. You, me, and Dan Miller; I think we need to bring Darian's fears to the surface."

"Okay," Matt agreed. Although he was unsure he wanted to push Darian like that.

The door opened and an officer popped his head in. "Doctor, Mr. Dixon's sister is here for him."

"Thank you." She looked at Matt. "Go home. I'll call you in a few days."

Matt nodded and followed the officer out of the room.

On his way down the hall, he passed someone familiar. Mr. Bixler—Officer Bixler, if he was to be respectful of the man's position. This was the man who outed him to the pastor. He didn't think Mr. Bixler noticed him, and he could have kept walking, but that wouldn't solve anything. Matt stopped and walked over to him. "Excuse me, Officer Bixler?"

The man turned Matt's way, and his face blanched. "Matt."

"Yeah. I have to say, what you did to my dad was pretty shitty. I don't care that you hate me, or that you think I'm going to burn in hell, but you were my dad's friend. You betrayed him, and I hope that haunts you the rest of your life."

"Matt, I… I'm sorry."

"No, don't apologize to me. Be a man, suck it up, and go apologize to my dad."

Officer Bixler was stunned. He slowly lowered his eyes and turned away.

Matt felt warm inside. Like his pride could show its face again. He'd been afraid for so long. Pushing beyond his fear and standing up for what was right took more courage than he'd ever used before—including the gumption needed to walk into a burning building, or to come out in front of the church congregation. His dad deserved respect, and Matt wasn't going to let this man get away with stabbing him in the back.

Matt puffed out his chest, and left the police station feeling good.

HANNAH only held her tongue for ten minutes before she let him have it. "You got arrested? I don't believe it! What were you doing there anyway?"

Matt hated having to reveal his stupidity. "I broke in to see Darian. He's a patient."

"Oh my God, that is so romantic." She kept looking at him alternately with watching the road.

"Yeah, not as romantic as seeing the video tape of us having sex in his room."

"Holy shit! Whoa," she exclaimed as she swerved over the double yellow line and back again.

Matt gripped the handle on the door. "Fuck! Hannah. You want me to drive?" Once the car stopped teetering, Matt let go of his anchor.

Hannah ignored him. "They got you on tape? You're such a dumbass. Why on earth would you have sex in a rehab clinic?"

"He's hard to resist. What can I say?"

"What's he there for?"

"Cutting and drugs, among other things. He's not handling Jamie's death very well."

"Oh," she said. "I'm sorry. Is he okay?"

"No. But I think he will be."

The rest of the ride home was quiet.

February 2011

23

February 14, 2011

MATT hummed while washing the dishes. This had been the best couple of weeks of his life. True, it was Valentine's Day, and his valentine was still locked up in a clinic; and also true, he didn't have a job, and his brother was treating him like the plague; but he'd been with Darian for two hours every day and that was fantastic! They talked, really talked.

After an initial group session where everything Darian had been holding onto came tumbling out, Matt was able to sit and talk with him about his dreams and his fears, and Darian wasn't cryptic anymore. He was honest. Doctor Loundas had been correct about Darian's guilt conjuring images of Jamie as a form of self-torture. Watching Darian battle an invisible adversary was painful, but in the end, Darian admitted his love for Matt and how long he had struggled with the shame of moving on so easily. In truth, it hadn't been easy at all, only poorly timed.

Darian also moved past his need to attack Matt every chance he got. Sure, there were a few days filled with hunger and longing where the two of them spent their time making love nonstop, but that fervor faded into the comfortable contentment of simply being together. Darian was no longer clinging to the disembodied sensations. He said it wasn't about the sex; he wanted to be with Matt out of love, and refraining from sex actually felt more normal.

Darian apologized to Dan and confessed he was initially using Matt to forget his pain, but over time the feeling changed. He didn't want to forget Jamie, and with help he was learning how to remember him fondly. Dr. Loundas helped Darian realize the depth of emotion he was avoiding because he felt guilty moving on.

"WOW, you're sure happy!" Matt's mother said as she entered the kitchen with grocery bags in hand.

"Hey, Mom. Yeah, I am." He finished wiping the plate and placed it in the cabinet. He dried his hands and put the towel down. He hugged her harder than normal.

"Matt, I can't breathe."

"Oh, sorry," he said, letting go.

"Here," she said, handing him a piece of mail. "I think it's your settlement."

Matt grabbed it and ripped it open. "Fifteen thousand dollars!" He held up a check from the insurance company.

"That's not enough to buy a new truck," his mother pointed out.

"No, but it's a decent down payment. Now my dilemma is over choosing Ford or Chevy."

His mom laughed. "Wow, you do have a hard life, don't you?" She went to the cabinet and got a glass. After pouring some juice, she walked over to the snack shelf. "I'm glad for the change in you. For weeks, you've been moping around and watching way too much television. What changed? Did you find a job? Is that where you've been running off to every day?"

"No. I've been with Darian." Matt saw that look in her eye. She stopped halfway across the floor and dropped a box of Triscuits. "Mom, before you go all Oprah on me, listen…. It's different. He's been seeing a therapist. And Dr. Loundas has included me and Dan Miller in his sessions. He's working through his problems, and Dr. Loundas thinks our relationship is very healthy."

"She said that?" His mom seemed surprised.

"Yes! In fact, she's encouraging it. Sometimes it feels like couples therapy and shit."

"Matt! Language."

"Sorry. I'm just happy, Mom. When he gets out of the clinic, I want to bring him over. I want you to meet him." Matt hoped she would be as excited as he was. Matt needed the family to accept Darian as a part of his life.

"I can tell. So… what kind of clinic is it?" Why did she have to sound so skeptical? Why couldn't she sound happy and tell him it was all right to bring Darian over?

"It's for drug rehabilitation and self-harm. Darian's had a history of addiction."

"Who's got a history of addiction?" his father asked as he entered the room.

Shit! Matt wasn't ready to bring it up with his dad! They were still on shaky ground.

"Darian," his mom answered.

"Who's Darian?" he asked, taking a beer out of the fridge.

"He's my—" Matt started.

"Boyfriend," Hannah finished, entering from the dining room and placing her cup in the sink.

Matt's shoulders sagged in defeat. "Can't I speak for myself once in a while? What is it with this family?"

"Apparently not," his dad griped. "It took you how many years to admit being a fairy? Twenty-two?"

Matt glared. "I'm twenty-three, and I'd prefer if you didn't call me a fairy. It's not very nice."

"How about queer?" his father responded with an edge of sarcasm, sipping his beer.

Right on the mark, Steven entered the kitchen to further add to Matt's mortification. "Ooh, are we insulting Matt? Did you call him a faggot yet? And don't forget poof or fudge-packer. They hate that."

Matt's mother ended it. "Enough!" she screamed with her hands held high. "We are not insulting our son." She glared at Steven. "Or brother! The term is 'homosexual.' Get over it!"

Everyone stopped what they were doing and stared. His mom rarely raised her voice to such levels, especially when directed at her husband. Even she was shocked at her own behavior. Her next words were quieter, almost embarrassed. "Please. We're a family. I am tired of everyone jabbing at one another with insults and hateful words. Matt is gay, and he has a boyfriend. I for one would like to get to know Darian and have to chance to welcome him into our home. None of you have the right to hurt his feelings or degrade him just because you disagree with his lifestyle. Plenty of people disagree with things we all do, but imagine what the world would be like if every time someone got a divorce there was a protest on the street? Or every time a pastor joined in marriage two people of different races, do you think they would appreciate hate banners and Ku Klux Klan-style demonstrations? I think not! We're Christians. The least we could do is act like it!"

"Like the Christians during the Crusades?" Steven asked. "Instead of killing Muslims, we could kill fags in the name of—"

"Steven!" His mother glared. She pointed her finger at him as if to challenge him to speak another word. Then she looked over at Matt and asked, "What was that quote from Gandhi you used?"

"'Be the change you want to see in the world.' It's actually a paraphrase of something he wrote."

"Steven," she said sternly, "and John"—she looked at them respectively—"putting all your hate into the universe doesn't help anyone. Christ loved people. He met people where they were and showed them his loving kindness. Mother Teresa loved; she met people where they were and cared for the sick and dying. Don't pretend you are so high and mighty that you can't love Matthias for who he is."

Matt was in awe. He'd never in his life heard his mother speak like this. She was the timid one—always following, never asserting control. Even his dad was silent. The air in the room hung still until Hannah started clapping. She stood there looking foolish, but Matt felt compelled to join in. They two of them applauded their mother for her conviction and presentation.

"Mom, that was awesome! I never knew you could be so feisty," Hannah said, walking over to hug her.

"Well, I guess I've listened to your brother and your dad for so many years, it was bound to slip out."

"Well done, Linda. I think this new church is having positive effects on you." Matt's father grinned and stepped over to caress her cheek.

Matt's ears perked up. "You found a new church?"

"Yeah. In Hanover. Amazing place. I've never heard grace preached so poignantly. I think I've wept the last three weeks in a row."

"Dad, why didn't you tell me?"

"I wanted to make sure you'd be comfortable there. It was enough for you to go through such rejection before. I didn't want it to happen again." He put his arm around Matt and squeezed his shoulders. "Matt, I have to say, I think I've learned more about God's love in the last couple months by having a gay son than when I thought you were straight."

Matt never in a million years thought he'd hear his father say that. Relief and joy flooded his heart, and he said, "Thanks, Dad. And the new church?"

His father patted Matt's back and shrugged. "The verdict is still under consideration." He moved away from Matt to casually continue the conversation as he leaned against the kitchen counter. "From what I glean, this pastor's more about telling people who Jesus is, and not so much about telling you what not to do. He's about love and God's grace. He's the most dramatic and passionate preacher I've ever listened to. I really like him. Plus, they even have session meetings at a local pub—craziest thing I ever heard! I like it."

"Wow, I'm glad, Dad. I really am. I'd like to go next time, okay?" asked Matt.

"Okay, Son."

Steven piped in crossly, "Well, I'm not going. Everybody else might be fine with Matt's gayness, but I'm not!" He turned and stormed out of the room.

Hannah answered Matt's hurt expression. "Give him time, Matt. He'll come around."

"So Darian's in a clinic?" his mom asked.

"Yeah, he'll be out in a few weeks. Can I bring him over to meet everyone?" He tried to plead with his eyes. The "puppy-dog" look always worked for Steven.

His dad looked at him and sipped his beer. Matt hated the long pause. Even his mom was watching his dad, waiting for the response to find its way out.

Matt's father tossed his empty bottle into the recycling. "What?" he gruffly asked all the eyes that were glued to his every move.

"Can Matt bring Darian over?" Matt's mom asked.

"Sure," his father answered with a shake of his head. Then he pointed to Matt. "But don't expect me to like him."

Matt grinned. "No, sir! No liking Dare at all, sir." He saluted his father as he walked out of the room.

As soon as the door closed, Matt, Hannah, and their mom burst out laughing.

"He's going to like Darian, isn't he?" Hannah asked.

Matt nodded. "Of course! Darian's too nice not to like, even for Dad."

His mom put her arm around Matt's waist and squeezed. "I'm happy for you, honey. I really am." She pecked him on the cheek. "Ever since we watched *Bareback Mountain*—"

"What?" Hannah shrieked. "What did you watch?" She hopped over to where Matt and their mother stood by the kitchen counter.

Matt rolled his eyes. "It's called *Brokeback Mountain*, Mom. *Brokeback*. What about it?" Matt looked down at her as he hugged her around the shoulders.

"Well, I keep thinking about the ending. It was so touching. I never thought of two men in that context before. Ennis really loved Jack." She sniffled and wiped her nose.

"Wait… Mom watched a gay romance movie? When did that happen? And why wasn't I invited?" Hannah looked hurt.

"Oh brother!" Matt heaved a sigh. These two women were about all he could take. He was glad to be in a relationship with a man.

The phone rang and his mom answered it. "Hello? Yes, one second." She put her hand over the speaker and asked Matt, "Can you tell your father Bob Bixler's on the phone?"

Matt stomach flipped. "Uh, yeah, sure. Did he say what he wanted?" It had been a while since Matt confronted him, and Matt was nervous what the man would say. He took the mobile phone from his mom and walked it into the other room. "Dad, Mom said Bob Bixler is on the phone for you."

His dad looked up and took the phone. He appeared concerned but didn't say anything to Matt. "Hello?" he said, into the receiver. He shooed Matt away with a flick of his wrist. "Uh-huh.... Okay...."

Matt walked back into the kitchen and waited. Both he and his mom sat at the table expectantly. What were they talking about? Matt drummed his fingers on the table.

Matt's father walked into the room ten minutes later. "You'll never believe it, Linda. Bob apologized. Apologized! He said he never intended things to get this far out of hand. Seems Kurt McKinley's wife witnessed Matt and... Darian...," he paused saying Darian's name, but Matt was still chuffed his dad used it at all, "in DC. She flipped out to her husband, and he didn't know how to handle it. He called Bob, and Bob went to Pastor Dennis. Bob said that Dennis assured him it would not be a hate-filled confrontation. He said it was supposed to be a leisurely inquiry." Matt's dad laughed, although not in a funny way. "Leisurely, my ass! Anyway, Bob said he inquired of the elders a couple weeks ago, and they were all in agreement of the way things were handled. He said he pressed the matter, yet was told he had no right to challenge the authority of the ruling members of the church. He was disgusted and left three weeks ago and has been looking for a place to worship that is less... legalistic. So, I invited him along with us on Sunday."

"You did?" Matt asked in shock.

"People make mistakes, Matt. Who am I not to give him a second chance?"

Matt was skeptical but understood his father's generosity. He'd given Matt a chance. Instead of acting out of irrational confusion and fear, his father was slowly working through his personal issues with his son's lifestyle. His dad was a fair man, and Matt strived to be no less than that.

"Okay. I'll give Mr. Bob another chance. But if you invite Pastor Dennis to our new church, I might be sick that day."

His father lifted his eyebrows. "You and me both." He and Matt laughed.

February 28, 2011

MATT was waiting for Darian in the main office of the clinic. As soon as their eyes met, Darian's face lit up. "Hey, I thought Dad was coming to get me?"

After weeks of working through Darian's inability to think of Dan as his father figure, Matt was encouraged to hear him use the term so easily. Matt played it cool. No need to make Darian nervous and second-guess himself. Matt said, "He had some last minute vacuuming to do or something. You know, to get the house perfect for you." Matt hugged him and kissed his cheek.

Dr. Loundas placed her hand on Darian's shoulder. "So, you ready to leave this time?"

Darian nodded.

Matt was relieved. They had gone through the same scenario over a week ago. Dan and Matt both came to pick him up, and Darian had an anxiety attack in the parking lot.

Dr. Loundas continued, "Dan signed everything, so you are good to go. Remember, talk to Matt. Don't be afraid to trust him. If you have any visions that cause concern, then give me a call. We can meet in my office next Thursday to discuss how everything is going for you. Okay?"

Matt appreciated her patience and kindness toward Darian. She had walked Darian through a very difficult part of his life, and never once did she refer to the darkness that lurked in his subconscious as irrelevant or ineffectual. Once he opened up, she took him very seriously. She allowed him to discover through questions that he created his own disturbing images of Jamie. She was extremely intuitive and seemed to understand Darian better than he knew himself. She'd been right about his reluctance to accept Matt's affection and move on, and she saw him through every step to admit his feelings and forgive himself for comparing Jamie with Matt.

After Matt shook Dr. Loundas's hand, he led Darian arm in arm to his new truck. As the clinic doors shut behind them, he felt Darian shiver. *What if he can't do it?* he thought.

Darian pointed. "I like your new truck. Red is the perfect color."

Matt swept his hand toward the truck. "In honor of Jamie. I think he'd like that."

"Me too. Except he'd have preferred a Ford."

Matt led him to the passenger side and leaned into him. Matt's weight pressed him into the truck door as he kissed his neck and up to his ear. Darian shivered, but Matt knew it wasn't from his kisses.

"I feel you shakin', baby. What's wrong?" Matt leaned back and looked him in the eyes. He caressed his jaw and asked, "You nervous about going home?"

Darian nodded. "Yes," he quietly admitted. "It feels odd to walk out that door, with you, knowing I'm free to go where I please. I've been locked up for so long, it was beginning to feel safe in there. What if I go home and it doesn't feel like home?"

Matt smiled softly and kissed Darian's nose, making him grin at the sweet gesture. "Then you come home with me," he replied. "I'll take you anywhere and everywhere until you feel comfortable."

Darian looked into his eyes. "Are you sure?"

"I'm sure," Matt confirmed with a nod as he threaded his fingers through Darian's hair. Darian appeared so timid and vulnerable. Matt knew so much of him had been laid bare in that building behind them, it had to be difficult for Darian not to feel exposed.

Darian licked his lips nervously and whispered, "I love you, Matt."

Matt could never hear that enough. He wished the first time he heard those words had been more romantic than Darian shouting them at the therapist. He could still hear Darian saying them in her office….

"WHAT do you want, Darian?" Dr. Loundas asked.

"I…." Darian couldn't talk. He was rocking his upper body in the chair. Abruptly, he stood and paced the room. He looked at Matt, and then at Dan. He covered his face with his hands and seemed to be struggling to voice his thoughts. He kept shaking his head side to side and mumbling to himself. It took every bit of Matt's strength to stay seated. He needed to hold Darian so badly.

"What do you want, Darian?" the doctor asked again, sternly.

"I… I want…."

"What is it you want?" she asked a third time.

Darian flung his arms down and shouted, "I want Matt! I want to live with Matt! I want to love Matt!" He took a few breaths and turned to look at Matt. More softly he said, "I love you."

Matt stood up and smiled as he took Darian into his arms….

MATT smiled hugely, his face lighting up like never before. "And can I tell you one more time how awesome it is to hear it? Feel free to remind me at least twenty times a day."

Darian had kept it bottled up and hidden from the light of day because he figured if his love for Matt was a deep, dark secret, then he couldn't be judged. Now his heart was laid bare and open to the pain of rejection. Matt knew he was afraid, so he planned to cherish Darian's heart and tenderly accept him—even with all his faults.

Darian laughed. "I'll try."

Matt fingered strands of Darian's hair behind his ear. "I love you, too, more than anything. So why are you still shaking?"

Darian looked away. "Matt… I want to be able to carry on with my life like any sane person. I want to be with you, make love with you, and I don't want to feel guilty about having you in my life."

"But…," Matt coaxed.

"But… now that I'm out of that place… I'm afraid. I feel the fear crawling up my neck like a bug ready to bite me when I'm not expecting it." He looked back at Matt, his gaze darting from Matt's left eye, to his right, and back again. "Just when I started to feel safe, the eight weeks were done. And then it was over nine. What if I'm not ready? What if I'm not okay? What if I'm not strong enough to be on my own?"

Matt understood without hearing the words. "Scared you'll see Jamie?"

Darian nodded.

"How many days has it been?"

“Five,” Darian answered, sinking into Matt’s chest and holding him around the waist. “I know he’s not real, but when he’s looking at me, I can feel him in the room.” Matt wrapped his arms around Darian, and Darian tightened his hold. He tucked his face against Matt’s neck and whispered, “I know I said I wanted to be brave and spend the first night home alone with Dan, but if I chicken out, will you stay the night with me?”

Matt rubbed his back. “Of course I will. But I think you’ll be fine.” Matt patted him, squeezed, and let go, then tilted Darian’s chin up with his finger so Darian would look him in the eyes. “Why don’t we try one of the exercises Dr. Loundas came up with while we drive?” Matt suggested as he opened the passenger’s door to his shiny Silverado and motioned for Darian to get in. “I’ll go first.” He pecked Darian’s lips as he helped him into the cab. “I remember… oooh.” He snapped his fingers. “I remember how Jamie never forgot my birthday. Even if I was working, he’d come by the station and leave something for me inside my cubby—like chocolate or a box of condoms. I always thought that was great.”

Darian laughed. “That’s funny.”

Matt knew this was a nice tool to help Darian focus on positive events from each of their lives with Jamie, but he had to admit he enjoyed it, too, because it allowed him to see what it was like knowing Jamie from a completely different perspective. “Now your turn,” Matt said before he closed the door and ran around to the other side. He got in and started the engine.

“Thank you,” Darian said.

Of course, Matt hadn’t done much, but he knew what Darian meant without the words—he was grateful for the shift in topics. He’d told Matt yesterday how much he appreciated that Matt never discounted his feelings and knew just when to change topics to spare them—reflecting on the positives just like Dr. Loundas instructed. Matt watched Darian stare out the window at the clinic where he had spent the past three months before he pulled out of the parking space. Finally, Darian said, “Um, I remember how Jamie would write little notes on the mirror when I took a shower, like ‘I love you,’ or ‘hey sexy man.’ We saw it on an old episode of *Friends*. It used to make me smile.”

"Good, good," Matt encouraged, opening his hand across the seat for Darian to clasp.

Darian scooted over and reached for Matt's offered hand. "What's this?" he asked, pointing to a package on the seat.

"A present." Matt knew how much Darian loved presents.

"For me?" he asked, snatching it up. "It feels like a book. Is it a book?"

"Duh, of course. I know you love reading. I was going to make you wait until I got you home, but you can open it now if you want." Matt watched the road and stopped at the stop sign.

Darian immediately tore the paper. It was a book, *Conquest* by S. J. Frost. He gasped, "How did you know? I've been wanting to read this forever but never made the time." He turned the paperback over in his hands and read the blurb on the back.

Matt reached over and touched his leg. "Well, it seems we're friends on Goodreads. Lori told me, and I couldn't believe it."

"What? No way!"

"Oh yeah. Eighty-seven books in common, and we practically rate them the same. It's freaky. I noticed you had this on your to-be-read list. A friend recommended it, and I read it last year. It's really good. I thought you'd be surprised."

He put the book on his lap. "I am!" He leaned closer and kissed Matt's cheek. "You are the best boyfriend ever!" After he said it, he fell silent.

Matt slid his arm over Darian's shoulders and pulled him to his side. "I know," he said solemnly. He wasn't trying to be arrogant, and he was sure Darian would get his meaning. He knew letting go of Jamie was the most difficult thing Darian ever had to do. Dr. Loundas told Darian it was natural to feel guilty for moving on.

She speculated that, under normal circumstances, the two of them might have felt the chemistry between them, dated a few times, and known almost right away they were destined to be together. But when that chemistry mixed with bad timing on top of a painful death, Dr. Loundas admitted even she was surprised to see their bond had lasted this long, let alone shown promise of becoming something beautiful.

Matt held Darian all the way back to Dan's house.

Matt parked. "You ready?"

Darian nodded.

Matt undid the seatbelt and turned to face Darian. He continued talking as he took his hand and stroked his fingers. "I love you. Very much. Whatever you got going on, we'll get through it together. Okay? I know I've said that for months, and it's hard for you to believe, but I *will* stand by my words."

When Darian nodded, he continued. "I'll wager I have just as many fears as you. A hell of a lot of what Dr. Loundas said in that place applies to me. I don't act out on it the same, but the fear is still there." Matt kissed him softly for a few seconds. Matt was trying hard to be supportive, but kissing always accompanied his words of wisdom because it broke the tension and gave him time to think about what to say next. Like if he couldn't think of the next sentence fast enough, he filled the void with his lips. It was not a bad tactic at all—Darian was surely not complaining. Matt rubbed his nose over Darian's and continued commenting on Dr. Loundas's observations. "I won't pretend to understand the depth of your pain or experiences, and I won't try to tell you mine are worse or better; what I do want to say is that I'm here for you. I'll listen to anything. No judgment." Matt kissed him soundly one last time.

Darian nodded again. "Okay."

The trust in Darian's eyes melted Matt's heart. Matt added, "Therapist's orders. If there's a problem, we talk about it."

Darian sighed and teased, "You're seriously going to make me regret sharing all those things in front of you."

Matt snickered. "No. I'm just not letting you get away again. You had your space. Now I need closeness."

Looking into Matt's eyes, Darian quietly admitted, "I thought burying him would be the hardest thing I've ever done. It's not. Living every moment afterward is the hardest. Everything I do, I feel guilty."

Matt cupped his jaw. "Don't," he insisted. "No guilt. You can't hold onto it forever. Jamie's gone. You can't feel guilty for living."

"Logically, I know that. And it's not just that, it's everything. I feel guilty for loving you. I feel guilty for not loving him enough. I feel guilty that I compare everything we do together with what Jamie and I did. I feel guilty that I think you're a better lover. I feel guilty—"

"Stop." Matt smoothed Darian's hair away from his face, stroked his forehead, and leaned in to kiss him. "It's normal to go through this. It is. Trust me. I compare everyone I've ever been with to you, and they don't measure up. I know I haven't been in a relationship before, but that was because I didn't see the point. No one made me feel like you do. With you, I'm like a hand grenade, and one little touch on my pin will set off an explosion! And that is *not* meant as a sexual metaphor."

Darian giggled.

"Besides, if there's one thing I learned these many weeks, it's that we can be together and not have sex. We already know we're amazing in bed. But I like the other parts, too, like talking."

"I thought jocks merely grunted," Darian jibed.

Matt chuckled. "Not this jock! I talk... sometimes." Darian smiled and Matt continued, "I go around all day feeling like everything inside of me is on the edge of some ultimate, unrestrained, orgasmic rapture, and all it would take is one touch of your hand, or one whiff of your hair, and I'd explode. You're all I think about. And it's not just the sex; I love every bit of you. I love your eyes, your hands, the way you look at me, the sound of your voice, and the sway in your step. I like how you draw, and you bite your lips when you concentrate. So yeah, I compare you to everyone I meet and everyone I ever knew before, and I still come up with the same answer: you're the one. The only one I ever want."

Darian's face flushed. He had an expression that normally led to buckets of tears.

Matt shook his head, sensing Darian's impending flood. "Dare, don't do it. Don't feel guilty."

He didn't cry, not yet, but his voice cracked and his hands shook. "Every time I think I can go another minute without feeling the guilt, it slams into me again. I can't help it. You say things like that, and my mind compares the two of you. I think, 'Jamie never said things like that.' All those things you do for me, like taking me to the art museum and buying me this book, and kissing me in front of all the guys from your work—which cost you your job—and breaking into rehab to visit me, everything; you treat me like gold, Matt. You even make love more attentively. And then I wonder if Jamie ever really loved me?"

Matt put both arms around Darian and pulled him as close as they could get inside a truck cab. He spoke softly but firmly into Darian's ear. "Jamie did love you, Darian. Please don't doubt that. He had a lot going on. I know that in time he would have said all the things I say to you. He would have taken you to the art museum and made love to you in all the ways you wanted. Trust me. Don't doubt his love. Please." He needed Darian to feel his love, and trust that Jamie loved him. Darian didn't need the real truth; he needed hopeful truth—white lies.

"I don't think I could picture Jamie with a leather flogger." Darian sniffled, stifling a snicker.

Matt laughed. "What?" He pulled back and looked at Darian.

"Jamie—with a flogger. I doubt he'd even know what to do with it. And he would've freaked if I came at him with my dildo."

Matt laughed out loud. "Oh God! You're probably right! Jamie and a dildo. Oh man!"

Darian reached over, rubbed Matt's thigh, and said, "No guilt."

Matt shook his head. "No guilt." He kissed Darian. "Come on," Matt urged. "I'm sure Dan is wondering what is taking so long for us to come inside."

"Oh yeah," Darian agreed.

They got out of the truck, and Darian looked at his hair in the side mirror. "Do I look okay?"

"Loaded question. You know I always think you look beautiful. But yeah, your hair looks awesome, especially now that it's getting longer."

Darian stepped in beside him as they walked to the door. "Yours too."

Matt rubbed his head. "Yeah, I haven't buzzed it for weeks. Too busy. It feels weird because it's touching my neck."

"Let it grow for me? Not real long, but more than the usual half inch?"

Matt grinned. "Yeah. Anything for you, baby." Matt hugged him around his shoulders.

As Matt reached for the door handle, Darian asked, "So… you still think this is all part of God's plan?"

Matt hesitated on the landing. He sighed and nodded. "Yeah, I do. The Bible says 'to everything there is a season, and a time for every purpose under heaven.' I didn't mean to make you mad when I brought it up in group therapy. It just fit the discussion, and it was how I felt."

"I know. And I told you I'm fine with you being religious. I know it's important to you, even if I don't agree with your viewpoints. I appreciate your honesty more than anything else. I like your consistency." Darian put his hands on Matt's chest. "And you're not angry with me for not wanting to go to church with you?"

Matt couldn't blame him for being skeptical. How many Christians did Matt know who said one thing and did another? He never wanted to be like that! "Nope. I don't think anyone should be pressured into going to church. If you want to go, you go. If you don't, you don't. It doesn't change how I feel about you."

"Thank you."

"So, we still good for Sunday after next? After church I'll pick you up, and you can have dinner with my parents and me? That gives you about two weeks to adjust to being home."

"You're serious? Your parents want to meet me?"

"Yup." Matt grinned. "I thought about introducing you tomorrow, but then I reconsidered. I don't want to overwhelm you too fast. My family can be a bit much."

Darian disagreed. "Your family could never be too much. I always wanted a close-knit group like yours. The prospect of your family wanting to meet me is exciting." A gentle smile curved his lips. "Whenever is fine. I'll be ready."

Matt kissed him one more time and then opened the door of the house for Darian. A cacophony of cries echoed through the opening. "Surprise!" Darian gasped at the sight and sound of all his friends gathered in the living room of the house.

Matt watched as tears found their familiar place on Darian's cheeks. He looked around the room and spied Lori and Sara, and Ian, and Missy from the clinic. He saw Jamie's cousin Maggie and her partner. And finally he made eye contact with Dan and Cheryl. Dan was smiling and opening his arms, welcoming Darian into a hug.

Darian fell into his arms.

Matt felt good that he and Dan could be in the same room without angry glares. It took a while, but working together to help Darian strengthened their relationship. It wasn't perfect, but it was better, and he was thankful. After Darian moved on to the next person who wanted a hug, Dan walked over to Matt.

"Thank you for picking him up."

"No worries."

Dan nodded. Awkward silence lingered. "So, any light reading you recommend?"

"Dan."

"What?" he asked innocently. "I'm not referring to the journals."

Matt had to change the subject. "I asked my mom if you guys could come over for dinner soon. She said yes. Dad seemed excited, at least excited for him. He said it would be nice to reconnect."

"Good. Good. I'll have Cheryl call Linda and coordinate a date." More nodding on Dan's part. "You staying tonight?"

"Maybe. Whatever Darian wants."

"Okay."

"I'm going to…." Matt pointed to Darian, who was waving him over, and politely exited his conversation with Dan.

"Yeah, sure, go."

Matt was thankful he was needed elsewhere. Dan may have been trying to talk peaceably, but Matt still felt the strain sometimes. Eventually, it would get easier.

March/ April 2011

24

March 13, 2011

THE first couple of days having Darian home was fun. They spent time together, but Matt also gave him time to spend with Dan and Cheryl. So far, Darian hadn't had any episodes of terror and no hallucinations of any kind. He seemed well on his way to a full recovery.

Dan also seemed more tolerant of Matt's presence. He hadn't made any snide remarks, even though Matt knew he must have been thinking something from the way he stared at every touch and caress and kiss he and Darian shared. Of course, Matt also suspected Dan knew they hadn't had sex in a while either. Maybe he was biding his time and would go off again if Matt put his hands anywhere Dan deemed inappropriate. For this reason, Matt behaved like a good little boy. He held Darian's hand, but never once did he make a move to grab his butt, even when he thought no one was looking. They had learned self-control at the clinic, and Matt patiently waited until he could put to use all the toys they'd discussed purchasing together.

Matt was at peace for the first time in his life. He and Darian were like a real couple. The last step was introducing him to his parents.

"DO THEY know why I was in the clinic?" Darian asked as Matt pulled up to his house Sunday afternoon. Church service had ended at 12:15 p.m., and Matt drove over to Dan's house to pick him up as he'd promised. Darian could have driven separately and met him here, but the two of them enjoyed riding together.

"Yes. It came up last month when my mom asked me why I was humming in the kitchen. We talked about you. Then my sister overheard us and told my dad, and my brother just wanted to insult me throughout the entire conversation. It was actually pretty funny in retrospect." Darian grinned, and Matt caught his expression. "What?" Matt asked.

"You said 'retrospect,'" he answered shyly. "I like using big words. I think it helps the mind expand."

"Me too."

Matt parked by the curb and Darian got out. "It looks the same," Darian observed.

"You've been here?" Matt asked.

"Yeah, duh, after the funeral." He rolled his eyes and Matt punched his arm. Darian let out a playful "Ouch!" He exaggeratedly rubbed the spot Matt had slugged. Darian went on talking as they walked up the sidewalk. "But it was dark when we left, and I was really out of it. I guess I'm thinking of your house years ago. Jamie brought me here once to meet you, but you were working. One of the trees is missing."

Matt led him to the front door. "Bradford Pear. Wind split it down the middle last year. Dad and I had to cut it down." Matt took Darian's hand as he opened the front door. He could smell the mouth-watering aroma of a home-cooked meal.

Darian took a deep breath. "Smells good."

Matt led the way inside. "It should. My mom's a five-star chef when it comes to dinnertime. Mom? Dad?" he called but no one answered. They walked into the kitchen. The Crock-pot was on, but no one was around. Matt found a note on the table.

Matt,

Had to run back to church. Hannah's car won't start and Katie couldn't give her a ride. Dinner is ready. Your dad should be home by 2 o'clock. Steven may or may not come home from Joey's. Sorry. He's being indignant.

Brb,

Mom

A WEIRD feeling crept over Matt as he read about his brother's whereabouts, but it dissolved when Darian slid his arms around his waist. He looked at his watch. 1:15 p.m. "Forty-five minutes," he said with a grin. "Want to see my room?" He wagged his brows.

"Maybe later," Darian said nonchalantly. He glanced around the kitchen as if avoiding Matt's stunned expression. Then he burst out laughing and squeezed his torso. "You are so easy. I'm joking. Yes, I want to see your room."

Matt bounced. "Cool!" He felt giddy as he snatched Darian's hand and pulled him out of the kitchen and up the steps. "Mine's the last door on the right." He led him in and closed the door. Hastily, Matt pointed out the objects in the room. "Desk, TV, dresser, closet, bed. Any questions?"

When he was done with his "tour" Matt turned and watched the softness in Darian's eyes transform into lust. Matt had been trying to show him their relationship was not all about sex, but apparently the wait had been long enough. Darian's licentious gaze revved up Matt's engine, and before he knew it, he was shoving Darian up against the back of the door. "I'll show you the rest later. Right now I want to take of tour of *you*." He kissed him fiercely and brought Darian's arms up above his head. Pressing his body tight against Darian he started grinding his hips. "I want you, Dare."

Darian whimpered, thrusting back. "I want you too. It's been so long." When Matt removed his hands from his wrists, Darian relaxed his arms.

"I know. Keep your arms above your head," Matt instructed, biting Darian's neck and slipping his hands under the hem of Darian's long-sleeved shirt. He explored his soft skin and got down on his knees in order to kiss and lick Darian's stomach. He skillfully undid Darian's belt and slipped his hands inside his jeans to grab his ass. He heard Darian chuckle and looked up. "What?"

"Nothing."

"That's not a *nothing* face. You're up to something." Darian snickered. Matt glowered. He watched Darian's expression as he slid his jeans down. "No underwear. Niiice."

Darian's simple "yup" told Matt something else was up.

"What are you up… to…," he stammered and stared. It was right there, in front of his eyes, but he couldn't believe it. A clear silicone ring rested around the base of Darian's scrotum, forcing his testicles to hang lower. Matt's adrenaline surged. He grabbed Darian's hips and shoved his face into Darian's groin. He nuzzled and licked Darian's inner thighs and ball sac hungrily. He wanted to feel Darian's balls shifting in their constrained space. He had Darian moaning instantly.

"Matt, oh, Matt, yes. Like that. Oh yeah."

Matt heard a door slam and pulled away. "Shit! How the hell is my family home so fast?" He jumped up and helped Darian pull up his jeans. He heard thumping down the hallway and another door slam. "Correction. My mom's home, and that was my sister slamming her door." He watched Darian zip up and fasten his belt. "You gonna be okay like that?" He pointed and grimaced, thinking of his boyfriend's semierection and the cuff around his balls.

"Yeah, I think so. I wore loose jeans on purpose and I got the most flexible cuff they sell. First time wearing one. Feels weird." Darian wiggled his pelvis.

Matt pressed his body against Darian one last time. "And it's totally fuckin' hot!" He licked Darian's lips and stroked his tongue. "You are so hot. If my mom wasn't home, I'd be balls-deep in that ass of yours right now. Wearing a cockring… *oh fuck!*"

Darian batted his lashes. Flirting. "I thought you'd like it."

"Oh yeah." One more kiss and he pulled away. "Come on. Let's go meet my mom." Matt took his hand and opened the door.

"Matt?" Darian pulled him back a step.

Darian looked worried. "What?"

"Are you sure they'll like me?" Darian stammered. "Maybe I shouldn't have worn eyeliner? Is the silver on the corners of my eyes too much? You said to be myself, but what if *myself* isn't what your dad will accept? Is the nail polish too much? Maybe I should have used black instead of purple. What if—"

Matt silenced him with a quick kiss. "They'll love you."

"Jamie didn't like the makeup."

A flashback clip in Matt's mind reminded him of the time Jamie told *Matt* to keep the makeup on. *Why would Jamie contradict himself? All the time. What was okay for me wasn't okay for Darian.* Matt would never understand Jamie. And he would strive every day never to treat Darian like Jamie had.

Matt caressed his cheek. "As we've already discussed, I'm not Jamie." Matt gazed adoringly into Darian's eyes. It amused him how flustered Darian could get but at the same time he didn't want him to work himself up into a frazzled mess over it. "They'll love you," he assured him. Matt kissed Darian's forehead. "And if my dad has a problem with you wearing eye makeup, screw him. You're my boyfriend, not his." Matt winked and continued walking down the hallway. "Besides, it's not that noticeable. More like an accent for the tiny diamond stud in your nose."

Darian's eyes widened. "That's what I was going for."

Matt patted himself on the back for getting it right. Darian always relaxed with compliments. Right before entering the kitchen, Matt leaned in close to Darian's ear and whispered, "Want to know a little secret? I used to wear my mom's makeup when no one was around. I even put on a dress a time or two."

Darian looked shocked. He whispered back, "You did? When?"

"I'll tell you all about it later. Suffice it to say, whatever you do isn't going to bother me in the least."

Darian smiled and kissed Matt's cheek. "I love you."

Matt winked back. "I know."

The two of them quietly entered the kitchen. Matt saw his mom flitting between the dining room and the kitchen, making sure everything was ready to go. Matt put his finger to his lips and winked at Darian. They stood against the kitchen wall and watched her rushing about. After three more trips, she finally noticed them and jumped.

"Oh, Matt, you scared me. I…." She stopped midsentence and smiled at Darian. "Hello, Darian. It's nice to finally meet you. I hope you can forgive my rushing. Dinner was ready and then Hannah called, said her car wouldn't start, which meant I had to get her since John is running late and had to pick up Steven on his way home. And of course when I got to church, the pastor's son had already gotten her car to start. It would have been a waste of time except I needed dinner rolls. It's always something around here!" She wiped off her hands on a towel by the sink.

Matt sauntered over, hand in hand with Darian. He let go, since he was holding his left hand, allowing Darian to extend it to his mom. She blew it off and hugged Darian instead. Matt laughed. Darian had panic in his eyes at first and then sank into her arms, hugging back. Matt'd had a feeling Darian would thrive on her affection; he was right.

Once Matt's mother let Darian go, she smoothed his bangs to the side and said, "I like your hair. It was longer the last time I saw you."

Darian shrugged. "Yeah. I might let it grow again. I don't know. I like change."

"I can tell by the blond highlights." She touched it and patted his cheek. "He's cute, Matt." His mother wiggled her eyebrows and turned to the oven.

Matt groaned. "Mooom. You promised not to embarrass me."

"This isn't embarrassing you. Embarrassing you would be me taking out baby pictures or asking when you plan to get married." She stuck out her tongue and grabbed the rolls she'd finished taking out of the oven.

Matt turned to Darian. "She's kidding. Mom, tell him you're kidding."

She paused on her way to the dining room door and touched Darian's arm. "I'm kidding. I'll let you date for a year, and then I'll start asking him about the wedding." And off she went with her rolls.

Matt was on the verge of panic. He grabbed Darian's hands. "I don't know why she's acting like this. I haven't talked about marriage. And you… well… you and Jamie… I…."

"Matt!" Darian asserted, snapping Matt out of his virtual hysteria. "Chill. It's okay. She's your mom. I think it cool she's messing with you about marriage. It means she's happy for you. It means she likes me." He beamed.

Matt quieted. "I told you. She's great. I knew she'd like you. The one you have to worry about is my brother. And possibly my dad; I'm not sure how he's going to react. My sister will love you. She'll probably stare at you all through dinner." Matt heard the front door open, close, and then squealing ensued. Matt could picture the scene: his sister thumping down the steps and leaping into their dad's arms. Even though his sister was nineteen now, she greeted their father as if she were still six. He smiled internally, glad for his loving family. One he could share with Darian! "That would indicate my dad's home. Just don't take everything he says too seriously. He's still adjusting to my 'coming out.' Sometimes he's okay, but there are lots of times when he's really rude to me. Just give him a chance."

"I will. It'll be fine. Trust me." Darian winked this time. And Matt wondered what else was up his sleeve. The testicle cuff was shock enough; he wasn't sure what else he could handle.

Matt's father walked into the kitchen and placed his briefcase on the floor. "Oh, I hate having to work Sunday mornings. I'll be glad when this merger is over." After placing his coat on the back of a chair, he turned around. His weak smile faded as his gaze shifted from Matt to Darian.

Matt felt sick. He wasn't sure what his father would say.

He walked slowly over to the two of them.

Matt caught a glimpse of his mom entering the room, but she stood in the doorway. Silent.

Matt's dad looked from Matt, to Darian, and back again. When he spoke, his tone was more sarcastic than Matt was hoping for. He hoped for casual, not cynical.

"This is the guy? The *girlfriend*? Must be, he's wearing makeup."

Matt did not like his dad's mockery. He puffed out his chest and was about to set his discourteous father straight when Darian took a step forward and extended his hand.

"Hi. I'm Darian—the *girlfriend*." Darian used the same mocking tone right back.

Matt watched as his dad took Darian's hand and shook. "Huh," he grunted in surprise. "Strong grip. You like football?"

Matt cringed. He knew his dad was not overly happy to meet Darian but went along with it for his mom. For him to "test" Darian was just painful. Since Darian took the initiative to step forward, Matt allowed him to stand his ground now. It was hard reining in his "protector" tendencies, but he managed it.

Darian spoke up confidently. "The Ravens gave away the last game of the playoffs, if you ask me. They played sloppy and lost. I'm glad the Steelers won that game as much as I'm glad they lost in the Super Bowl. The Packers played better. It was tight—a good game. Can't wait to see what happens in the fall. They'll be the team to watch in the next couple years."

Matt's dad nodded. He looked pleased with Darian's answers. "Linda, make sure Darian sits next to me at dinner. I'd like a chance to talk to the lad. Darian, if you'll excuse me, I need to do a few things before dinner. I'll see you in a bit."

Matt watched his dad slip from the room before saying anything to Darian. "Since when do you have a strong grip?"

"I don't," Darian whined, clutching his hand. "I squeezed with all my might and now my hand hurts."

"Oh, baby. Here, let me." Matt took Darian's sore hand and began massaging it. "And the football comments?"

"Google. I read some commentaries before you picked me up."

"You're amazing." He leaned forward to claim a kiss. Even the unexpected gasp from his mother did not make him pull away. Matt eased back, still looking in Darian's luminous eyes. "Sorry, Mom. Didn't mean to cause heart palpitations." He continued rubbing Darian's hand.

His mother strolled up to the two of them. "You didn't. I was merely not expecting *kissing* when I walked into my kitchen, that's all. You caught me by surprise. Feel free… to do your… kissing." She gestured and moved over to the counter. She picked up the bowl of mashed potatoes and wandered back out of the room, glancing a few times in Matt's direction.

As soon as the swinging door to the dining room shut, Matt burst out laughing. "My mom's a trip!"

"What's so funny?"

"You didn't hear her?" he questioned Darian. Then he repeated his mom's words in a silly voice. *"Feel free… to do your… kissing."* He laughed some more.

"I heard that!" his mom bellowed from the other room.

Matt kissed Darian one more time as his sister finally entered the kitchen. "So where's Matt's… wow!"

Matt glanced over and saw her gawking at them.

"Matt! I never guessed you'd pick an artsy guy."

"How can you tell in one second he's an artist?"

Hannah made a face at him. "I said 'artsy' not 'artist,' Sherlock. And I know because he's wearing paisley chucks. What macho guy does that? I figured you'd go for a biker dude." She gave Darian the once-over. "Your guy's got style. I like it."

Darian blushed. "Thank you."

Hannah was embarrassingly bold with her ogling. "Holy shit, Matt, you've got yourself a *hottie*!"

"Mooom," Matt bellowed. "Hannah's being a pain!"

His mother came back in on cue. "Hannah, don't be rude. Or vulgar. Either behave or sit in the living room during dinner. I'll not have you two arguing over Darian. He'll be under enough pressure sitting next to your father. Where's Steven? Your father said he was picking him up."

They all heard Steven as he hollered from the dining room. "Why are we eating in here? What's the big"—he strolled into the kitchen and quieted immediately—"deal? Oh."

"Hey bro," Matt smiled. "This is Dar—"

"I know who it is." Steven's hard stare could cut glass. "Mom, I think I'll pass on dinner."

He turned to leave and his mom stopped him. "Stevie, can you just give your brother a chance?"

"I'm not eating with a bunch of faggots."

"Steven!"

"It's okay, Mom," Matt interjected. "Don't make him stay if he doesn't want to."

She let go of Matt's younger brother's arm and watched him walk out. "Matt. I'm so sorry."

Matt laced his fingers through Darian's. "I knew there would be people who wouldn't accept me."

His mom caressed his cheek. "Give him time. Steven will come around. He loves you, just like we all do." Then she touched Darian's cheek. "As I know we'll love you."

Matt saw a tear in Darian's eye as his mom kissed Darian's forehead and suggested they all have a seat. Knowing Darian was that happy made him ever more proud of the family he had.

DINNER went better than Matt expected. His dad wasn't overbearing. He didn't grill Darian on football or any sports whatsoever. He was polite, for a change, and asked Darian about his job and what he'd like to do in the future. As Matt knew he'd say, Darian said he'd like to go to college and study art. Even that answer didn't prompt ridicule. His father was the most hospitable Matt had seen him in ages, and he was thankful.

LATER, in front of Dan Miller's house, Matt's truck windows fogged up from all the hot air on the inside. Dinner went well, but Matt and Darian's need for one another only heated up as the night went on. They'd been with other people far too long. With Dan and Cheryl, they had restrained themselves out of apprehension and a slight amount of fear. At Matt's house, it was the exact opposite. Darian had the nerve to wear a testicle cuff and grope him during dinner. Matt loved his boldness. So by the time they parked, sex was the only option. As soon as Matt undid his seatbelt, Darian pounced. It was hard maneuvering in the truck, but after Matt moved across the seat from behind the wheel, he was able to remove his jeans and go with Darian's passion.

Darian seemed careless of the prospect of a neighbor noticing them in the truck. The possibility of danger made them both hard and horny. Darian stripped and climbed into Matt's lap. They both needed this and Darian let out a groan as Matt entered his body.

Matt rode out Darian's fervor willingly. He was no longer concerned with being used, nor was he unsure of Darian's feelings toward him. They were in love, and at the moment, in lust for one another.

Darian jammed his hips onto Matt's and pistoned his lower body like a steamship's engine. He rose and fell and gripped Matt's cock with the tight muscles of his anus.

Matt moaned and panted, and when they both shot their loads, he held Darian impossibly long against his chest. He didn't want him to move.

Darian sighed. "I love you." He leaned back, still attached bodily to Matt. "I love being able to do whatever we want. I love how you don't hesitate, even though we could get into big trouble if we got caught out here."

Matt rubbed his thighs, up and down, enjoying the sweatiness and the coarse hairs that prickled his fingers. He also reveled in the way Darian's sphincter pulsed around his flaccid penis. Their closeness was the pinnacle of Matt's happiness, and Matt was so glad to be in a relationship where he felt 100 percent complete. "Baby, I went to jail once for you, I'd do it all over again."

Darian giggled and kissed him. "Maybe we should revisit that conversation about moving in together?" he asked.

"Seriously? Okay," Matt agreed wholeheartedly. "I'll start looking for a place soon."

Tight truck cab or not, they managed to make love one more time before Matt urged Darian to go in and get some sleep. They had plenty of time for sex in the future.

April 1, 2011

APRIL FOOL'S DAY was not Matt's favorite day of the year. People tended to do stupid things, or dare other people to do stupid things. And sometimes there were fireworks involved, which would seem fun until someone blew a finger or two off and then it was just another medical emergency. But, seeing how he still didn't have a job, he also wasn't one of the people who would be called upon when things went wrong. His buddies at the station got those joys.

Matt drove down the road after a long day of hunting for just the right gift for Darian. They were finally going to move in together. After weeks of checking out apartments in Westminster, Eldersburg, and Hanover, they'd finally settled on a place and were supposed to go sign the contract tonight. Matt was elated. Even if he didn't have a job, he was confident he'd find one soon. Regardless, he had enough in savings for several months' rent and figured it would all work out somehow.

He felt the need to give Darian something to commemorate the date, so he went jewelry shopping. The two of them talked all the time about taking things slow, but when they were together, everything seemed urgent. Matt wanted to make sure Darian knew he was serious. Darian was the love of his life and he didn't want to lose him. Jamie had dragged his feet for years. Matt was determined not to make the same mistakes. He looked for hours and found just what he wanted in a shop that happened to be next to a tattoo parlor. Before he knew it, he was asking the tattoo artist to give him the same spider tattoo Jamie and Darian had.

He looked down at the inside of his right wrist and inspected the black widow. The skin was tender and raised in spots, but the design was flawless. It looked exactly like the picture he had on his phone of Jamie's. (Which looked exactly like Darian's.) He hoped Darian would appreciate the sentiment of it, because there was a tiny voice inside his head that told him he should have asked first. Tattoos were permanent.

"Oh, Darian," Matt sighed.

So far, Matt's family adored Darian. Steven still rolled his eyes but had stopped insulting them every time he walked into the room. Matt took his behavioral change as a good sign. His next concern was the new church he attended with his folks. Would they condemn him? And would he be able to bring Darian one day? (When Darian felt comfortable, that is.) The last few sermons blew his old pastor's messages out of the water. Matt could surely see why his dad wanted to attend this church and stopped shopping around. This pastor even mentioned homosexuality from the pulpit and *didn't* equate it with sin. He made it sound like he was ashamed of how the church at large treated gay people. Matt was extremely curious to get to know this pastor and possibly engage him in an intellectual discussion about homosexuality and the Bible. From what he'd heard so far, Matt felt like this guy would respect him, maybe even side with him.

"God created me gay; there has to be a reason for it," Matt wondered to himself as he drove down the road. "Maybe I'm here to head up a new kind of revival where gays and lesbians can gather without fear of persecution. No more will it be said 'God hates gays.' Instead the chant will be, 'God loves gays! God loves gays!'" As he pretend chanted, he pumped his fist in the air. "Yeah, I know He does," he commented with all surety. "It's Satan that doesn't want us to know it."

Matt looked down when his phone buzzed.

Darian texted, *I got off early. I'll be to your house soon.*

Matt picked up the phone and hit the speed dial. After Darian picked up, he said, "Hey, baby. I'm talkin' on my hands-free. Can you hear me clearly?"

"Yup."

"Cool. I'll be home in like half an hour. I can't wait to see you. Does Dan know you're planning on spending the night with me tonight?"

"No. I haven't seen him. I texted, but he didn't reply. I left him a note. Are you sure your mom is okay with it? I know she didn't like the idea because of Steven."

"No, it's fine. She said Steven is staying over at a friend's house. She's a little uncomfortable because we're dating, not married. I told her we'd respect her house and not have sex in my room. She just doesn't want to think of me as an adult, that's what it is. It's not you, it's me. But once we sign the contract and move into our own place, my parents won't have a say over what we do or don't do. I promise."

"Okay. Hey, I got another call coming in. I'll talk to you soon."

"Okay. Bye."

"Bye."

Matt turned onto 97 North and headed home, thinking about the last six months of his life. Last September, he wasn't sure he'd even be able to make it to the next day. Jamie's death hit him so hard. He still felt his friend's absence in his life, but with Darian, he was able to salvage Jamie's memory and keep it living and active in both of their lives. He was ever grateful for that.

Matt was also grateful for the persecution his family went through after he came out at church. He never thought being the recipient of such betrayal and malice would bring him closer to God and closer to his family, but that was exactly what happened. It wasn't easy, but it was worth it. His dad had always been proud of him. He was the "golden child" of the family, after all. But after his dad experienced the same hate and judgment that Matt felt, and his dad wasn't even gay, his respect for Matt grew immensely. His father talked to Matt and treated him more like a man than he had ever done before.

Matt even returned to work, cutting grass for the same little old ladies who had refused his services in the winter. His boss was right, and after some time went by, they forgot all about what they'd heard at bingo about Matt and welcomed him into their homes like before.

Life was back to normal.

MATT'S phone rang and he answered, "Hello."

"Hi, Matt," said Chief Burtrum. "Look, I know it has been a while, but I haven't forgotten about you."

"Hey, Chief. I didn't think you had."

"Well, it seems the guys are all bellyaching about the new guy that got hired. He's technically a volunteer on transfer from another station, but I didn't tell them that. I assigned him your cubby and Scott hasn't let him put a single shred of clothing in it."

Matt laughed. "Oh my gosh, Scott."

"Anyway, I was wondering if you could come in on Monday and have a chat about your job?"

Matt turned the corner and felt the exhilaration of his heart beating faster. "Chief, are you asking what I think you're asking?"

"Matt, they all want you back. I'm only sorry it took this long. Even Billy said—"

"Give me the phone," Matt heard Billy squawk. "Matt, it's Billy. Just get your faggoty ass back to the station."

"Gee, Billy, with an invitation like that…."

"Shut up. You know I'm not good with this. It's just… things aren't the same without you. And I've been thinkin' ever since that ambulance crashed and your guy—Darian, is it?"

"Yes. His name is Darian." Matt could not believe how calm his voice was when his insides were jumping and his pulse was racing. He could hardly think as he turned onto the next street.

Billy continued, "Well, when Darian was on the ground, all I kept thinking about was my Susan. What if that was her?" Matt could hear his ragged breath on the other end. *Was Billy crying?* "Anyway, I've been thinking how much you must love that guy to go through all the shit we put you through. And I want to say, I'm sorry."

Matt was all choked up. Billy's apology was nicer than anything he could have written himself. "Thanks, Billy. Tell the chief I'll be in on Monday."

"I will. And if you want to bring Darian by to play poker again, I promise not to make fun of his name."

"Ha, ha, okay. I will. Thanks."

Matt heard him hang up. He smiled. "Things really are working out," he mused.

MATT parked his truck behind Darian's Nissan and jumped out. The neighbor kids were shooting off fireworks in the front yard, just as Matt suspected they would be, but he couldn't be bothered to ream them out this time. Darian was waiting inside. He entered the house and found his mom making dinner. "Hey, you seen Dare?" he asked.

"He went up to your room."

"Okay, thanks. Call me when dinner's ready."

"Okay, but you remember your promise."

Matt stopped on the stairs and peeked over the railing. "I will. No sex in your house—got it."

"Thank you, dear."

Matt shook his head and went to his room. Darian was waiting for him on the bed. Fully clothed, thankfully, with his arms crossed over his chest. Matt sat on the edge of the bed next to him. “Hey, you okay?” Matt asked.

Darian nodded. “It just feels weird.”

“What does?”

“The thought that tomorrow I will officially be your roommate.”

“I would hardly call you a roommate. You’re my partner, right?”

Darian grinned, which relieved Matt’s worry that something was wrong. “Yeah. I guess I am.”

“Which leads me to….” Matt gestured to something hidden behind his back. He held out an open palm, waved his hand over it like a magician, and not-so-magically, a small box appeared in his palm.

Darian sat up and reached for it.

Matt pulled it back. “Uh, uh, uhn,” he teased, wagging a finger. “First say the magic words.”

“Please?”

“Nope. Try again.”

“Please, may I have the present? My most wonderful, sexy, magnificent lover?” Darian kissed Matt and sat back on the bed, hopeful.

“Okay, that is not what I was going for, but I can’t say no now.” He handed him the box. “Here. Open it.”

Darian opened the box and sucked in a quick breath. He pulled out the simple silver ring and examined the engraving that ran around the outside of the band. He read, “*Je t’aime, mon chéri.*”

“That means ‘I love you, my darling.’ It’s French. You like French.” Matt knew he sounded stupid as soon as the words left his mouth, but Darian didn’t seem to care.

Darian flung his body into Matt’s and squeezed the life out of him. “I love you,” he said in a weak little voice.

“Dare, uh, Dare, I can’t breathe.”

“Sorry,” Darian said, sitting back and wiping his eyes.

Immediately, Matt worried he’d gone too far. Maybe the ring was too much and reminded Darian of Jamie and their engagement. He reached out and stroked Darian's cheek. "I'm sorry. I didn't mean to overdo it. I didn't want you to feel guilty or compare us, or…."

"No, I'm not. I mean, I was. Before you got here, I was thinking about everything that has happened between us in the past six months. Being with me cost you everything, and never once did you complain, or blame me, or walk away. You stayed. Even through all the therapy and rehab, you were there."

Matt squeezed Darian's knee. "No worries, baby. Life's a bitch sometimes; but I plodded on through, and now karma's coming back around. I got you, I got a new truck, and I think I even have my job back."

"Really?"

"Yup. Billy was all but begging on the phone. It was funny. I knew I just needed to wait and everything would work out."

"I wish I had strength like that," Darian said, looking down.

"You do," Matt assured him. Matt cupped the side of Darian's neck and stroked his jaw with his thumb. "To go through everything you've been through and still be able to smile that amazingly radiant smile of yours, I'd say you're one of the strongest people I know."

Darian looked at Matt, but retained his somber expression. "Thanks. It means a lot that you're so supportive."

Matt leaned forward and kissed him. "Is there anything else you want to talk about, or is this expression a result of you not liking my gift?"

Darian grinned a little grin. "Don't worry, I love it," he told Matt as he took the ring out of the box and put it on his finger.

"So you aren't feeling guilty anymore?" Matt asked, still unconvinced that Darian was pleased with the ring.

Darian sighed, "I was. But when you gave me this ring it hit me."

"You don't like it."

"No, I do," Darian assured him, taking Matt's hands in his and squeezing them tight. "The ring made me think, is all. Call it an epiphany or a click of a light bulb shining in the dark spaces of whatever is left of my bizarre-o mind, but I suddenly saw all the guilt that's been festering inside of me as another form of addiction. And what's more, I think guilt can be like this invisible jailor freely moving from person to person, convicting without trial and condemning with no conscience. But I know one thing guilt doesn't: I'm free. You did that for me. You loved me through everything, and I can never feel guilty for that."

"Oh, Darian," Matt sighed. "I love you so much." Matt's motivating element to walk through fire if need be was Darian. "I'd do anything for you," he said. "No cost is too high, no road is too long." Matt pulled him close and held him until he heard his mom calling for them to join the family for dinner.

LATER that evening, when Darian was nestled in his embrace and the house was very still and quiet, Matt thought about his family. His mom, his dad, his sister, and even his brother to some degree, had all accepted Darian into their lives. Darian was his. This beautiful brown-eyed lover—no, partner—made life worth living, and family worth having.

Matt closed his eyes and sighed. Jamie had been the best friend who gave him strength enough to stand, but it was Matt's deep love for Darian that gave him the power to do the impossible. With Darian, he could leap over mountains… and fly!

Epilogue

I LIE here in the darkness and feel his arms around me. I can hear a song playing in the distance. What is it? I hum the tune until the words become loud enough for me to make them out. I sing along. "I've been waiting for a hero, who's brave and strong…."

The words are so true. I feel like I've been waiting all my life for someone to make me feel whole, and show me where I belong.

In Matt's arms, I feel so light it's as if I'm floating.

I'm floating because nothing bad can touch me. I'm free.

The same song continues and Ginny Owens sings what I feel in my heart. Matt's love has made me stronger and braver and I feel like I can do anything.

I was so scared when Jamie died because I couldn't imagine life without him. I reached out, and a shadowy person in the mirror took my hand and led me into the depths of my darkest fears. He was me. I feared myself all along.

I've learned to love again. I've learned to trust Matt's strong embrace. My only question lies in my ability to let go of Jamie's death, and live.

The song fades in the distance, but its words resonate within me. Matt is the one who holds the keys to unlock my soul. He is the one who will cherish me until his last dying breath. In Matt's arms, I'm beautiful, and I'll never be alone again.

WADE KELLY lives and writes in conservative, small-town America where it is not easy to live free and open in one's beliefs. Wade writes passionately about the controversial issues witnessed in real life and strives to make a difference by making people think. Wade does not have a background in writing or philosophy but still draws from personal experience to ponder contentious subjects on paper. When not writing, Wade is thinking about writing and more than likely scribbling notes on old napkins in the car while playing "taxi driver" for her three children. She likes snakes and has a turtle in the bathtub.

Visit Wade Kelly at http://www.writerwadekelly.com,

http://writerwadekelly.blogspot.com/, or

https://twitter.com/WriterWadeKelly.

Contact Wade at writerwadekelly@gmail.com.

Also by WADE KELLY

http://www.dreamspinnerpress.com

Don't miss from WADE KELLY

http://www.dreamspinnerpress.com